Unholy Bonds

A Novel of Suspense and Healing

Leslie Lynch

Copyright

Dedication

To all who suffer the effects of violence in their lives:
May peace be yours, both within and in your relationships.

A portion of the proceeds of this book will be donated to
promote Restorative Justice and to Puppies for Parole.

Note to Readers

Although written as much as possible as a standalone, this book
is a continuation of events that occurred in my previous book,
Hijacked. I'd highly recommend you read it first, to better understand
the dynamics of Ben and Lannis's relationship, as well as the events
that led them to each other.

Chapter One

April

His. She'd been his.

Robert Davis tapped his index finger in a precise, angry tattoo against the clipboard holding his flight planning charts. He still couldn't believe it. Not only had she deprived him of his rightful prey, she'd gotten away.

They never got away. Unless he let them. He told himself he'd let them both slip through his fingers tonight, but he knew it was a lie, and the lie infuriated him.

Too bad he didn't know where she lived. It would be a brash and impulsive move on his part to find her, but he would enjoy exacting some satisfaction for her interference. He discarded the idea as soon as it formed, though. Too risky. He prided himself on his discipline, swiftly decisive once he'd explored problems from all sides, but never hasty.

Distracted, he gave up on planning tomorrow's flight and conjured the image of her leaping up from the booth at the bar a few hours ago. Her clothing was designed to conceal, but it wasn't difficult to imagine the flesh beneath. Supple, toned, and slender in the right places. Lush in the others. A little taller than average, maybe five feet six or seven inches, and lean. But for all that promise, she lacked in spirit.

The sleeves of her T-shirt had quivered, telegraphing her distress. Ripples of her fear had lapped against his skin, sparking his stalking instinct in spite of her pathetic attempt to stand up to him, to speak her piece. He snorted. He liked a woman with some fight, not a mousy librarian type. Even so, his blood had thundered hot and eager from his heart into his fingertips and into his loins. The echo of it pulsed even now, a pale shadow of what might have been.

What should have been.

A sharp rap at the door jarred him from his thoughts. He frowned and hit the mute button on the remote bolted to the bedside table. The table, in turn, was bolted to the floor. He'd found the bolts amusing at first, but now everything about this cheap motel irritated him. He should have treated himself to the Galt House, or the Brown Hotel, places he'd receive the treatment he deserved. The ancient television flickered as naked bodies writhed across the silent screen, and he paid them little attention. Neither the low-budget porn nor his potent imagination replaced the reality that had been stolen from him.

He unfolded his six-foot-four-inch frame and stretched, in no rush to answer the door. No one in Louisville, Kentucky, knew him, except for the woman who'd ruined his evening. And the last thing she'd do was track him down. Nope. Pure pleasure flickered at the memory of her terror, but a surge of anger extinguished it. She'd derailed his hunt. His jaw tightened at the unfairness of it, and he swung the door open without stooping to look through the peephole.

He didn't know what he'd expected, maybe a misdirected pizza delivery or a redneck at the wrong door, but the man in a suit and tie surprised him. He raised an eyebrow and said, "Can I help you?"

"Robert Davis?"

There was something familiar in his manner, and Robert straightened. "Yes." Curiosity edged out the disgruntled frustration of a moment ago. "Why?"

"Step outside, please."

Now he recognized the mannerism. Quiet authority that brooked no opposition. The guy was a cop. A frisson of alarm raised the hairs on his forearms. "I don't think so."

"Suit yourself." The man slipped a badge out of his pocket with practiced ease and displayed it. LOUISVILLE METRO POLICE ran in fancy script around the top of the shield, DUTCH BENNETT, DETECTIVE in block letters across the center. TO SERVE AND PROTECT completed the oval in script at the bottom. "We can do this the easy way or the hard way. Your choice."

Only then did Robert notice the uniformed policeman standing in the shadows, positioned at an angle designed to optimize control of a suspect. Himself, apparently. A glance verified the standard tools of the trade: web belt loaded with a Taser, extra ammo for the Glock holstered at his hip, a baton easily accessible, metal handcuffs glinting in the dim light. He tightened his grip on the door, then shrugged and dropped his hand to his side. "What's this about?"

"I have a warrant for your arrest." Bennett leaned into Robert's space, not a lot, not enough to be overt, but enough to raise his hackles, enough to interject a sense of *come on, make my day.*

Robert frowned and shot him a look that said, *Back off, asshole.*

But the asshole kept talking, his bland tone in stark contrast to a hum of tension beneath the words. "Two counts of felony sexual assault, elevated to Class A by threat of deadly force, criminal confinement resulting in bodily injury—"

He felt his mouth drop open in a stupid *O* of disbelief as the guy continued with a laundry list of charges. His mind churned into overdrive.

"Who?" he asked, interrupting the dry litany.

Bennett narrowed his eyes, rounded out his list with a couple of misdemeanors, then waited a beat. "What? No protestation of innocence?" He bared his teeth in what might pass for a smile, but didn't come close to camouflaging the steel behind it or the quick intelligence in his face.

Too late, Robert realized his error. He'd done all those things, so hadn't questioned the validity of the charges—just which bitch had the backbone to try to nail him for it. Which meant he'd made another error. Someone hadn't been cowed into silence. No way could it have been what's-her-name from the airport earlier this afternoon, and then the bar later. She was too timid by half.

"You have the right to remain silent."

Well, hell, he knew that. He made a sound that might have been a laugh in other circumstances. Now it was a harsh, humorless waste of air, air that suddenly seemed in short supply. He was a lawyer, had studied and written papers and argued the finer points of the Miranda rights the cop was reciting. He'd trampled and exploited and exalted—whichever suited his purposes—those rights. He'd profited from his skillful parsing and finding holes in cases built by cops like this one. He was a defense attorney. One of the best back home in New Jersey.

The uniformed cop pulled handcuffs from his web belt, and Robert shot the man a quelling glare. The detective continued, "Anything you say can and will be used against you in a court of law."

Robert heard the quiet emphasis of the word *will,* saw a flash of triumph that went a step beyond satisfaction at a job well done or business as usual. Why? Confusion clouded his thinking, and the lone important—and *missing*—detail clamored for an answer.

"Who?"

"Lannis Parker." The detective named a date from several years ago, then cocked his head to the side, gauging Robert's reaction.

"I don't know a Lannis Parker." Robert made the statement with utter confidence in its truthfulness. He'd never heard of Lannis Parker.

"We'll discuss this at the station." The detective stowed his badge and motioned him forward, out into the muggy air of the exposed walkway.

Robert turned and dismissed the men with a flick of his wrist. Warrant and Miranda rights notwithstanding, it would take only a phone call or two to straighten this out. "I'll meet you there." He reached for the keys to his borrowed car, tossed casually hours before on the butt-ugly orange molded plastic chair.

"Freeze." The command cracked through the air, tension shimmering behind it.

Too late, he realized he'd stepped out of their line of sight. Adrenaline flooded the backs of his arms, flowed into his palms, his fingertips, and readied him for a brawl. *Not a good idea…* He drew on the discipline of years of martial arts training and froze, then slanted a glance toward the doorway.

The detective had a gun trained on Robert's torso, and the uniform had pulled his Taser. In that instant Robert discovered he didn't like being on the business end of their weapons. These guys were serious, acting like he was dangerous, maybe even armed. His imitation of a marble statue didn't seem to appease them; the weapons remained drawn and ready. Sweat dampened his brow and the palms of his hands. Restraint combined with the adrenaline rush, and translated into a faint trembling of his fingers.

"On the floor, hands behind your head." Detective Bennett stepped back to allow the uniformed officer access. "Do not resist."

Left without a choice, Robert clasped his hands at the back of his skull, sank to his knees, then awkwardly twisted to get an elbow to the floor for balance. The cops swarmed him before he got there, grabbing and yanking his arms behind his back, holding him down with a knee and their bodies, sliding the metal of the cuffs around his wrists, ratcheting them tight, then tighter.

Instinct overrode training.

He jerked, too late for his fists, but maybe not too late for his lethal kicks. He bucked the weight of the uniformed cop, dislodged him, and felt a fleeting moment of exultation. He lashed out with a foot, but met only air. Someone's knee landed on his head, grinding his face into the rough carpet. Their shouts registered over the coarse rasp of his breath, but blood thundered in his ears and he couldn't make out the words. The knee lifted away, then pain blossomed in his side.

It exploded through his body, making him arch and cry out, legs spasming in uncontrollable jerks, arms wrenching nearly out of their sockets, the metal bracelets biting into his skin. He heard his own voice as if it were someone else's, pleading, begging. The words were incoherent, but the meaning clear.

Humiliation flooded him.

They hauled him upright, and Robert scrambled to find his footing—God, he hoped he hadn't peed his pants. Spittle had collected at one side of his mouth and dripped down his chin. He could barely think, and all he could come up with was…he needed to look for chinks in procedure, mistakes he could capitalize on, anything he could use to throw the whole thing back into this guy's face, and he couldn't do that if he lost his focus.

Why did this somehow feel personal? More personal than a simple arrest should. The thought slipped into his mind, then faded. They had him halfway down the stairs before he found his voice again.

"The warrant…what…who?" he gasped.

"Your own words on tape," Detective Bennett ground out.

And he knew.

Lannis Parker. It finally clicked into place. The chick from the airport. He hadn't bothered to remember her name. Only her screams.

She'd set him up.

The conniving, backstabbing, lying, double-crossing bitch had come into the bar tonight, run off the woman he'd picked up, and engaged him in a conversation about their sexual encounter a few years ago. She called it rape. Robert called it a good time. Consensual, of course. A little rough, maybe, but hey, that was the way she'd wanted it. She'd said the conversation was between them, just the two of them. But it had been a setup. *A wire.* They must have wired her. His heart dropped to the soles of his Guccis, and his mind tripped into warp speed, trying to remember exactly what he'd said. Had he said anything incriminating?

"You have the right to an attorney; if you cannot afford one"—Bennett's voice held heavy sarcasm, and Robert caught a faint sneer in his face, quickly smoothed over and replaced with bland professionalism—"one will be appointed for you."

The detective had apparently done his homework, knew Robert owned his own plane, and assumed he could afford a lawyer. Worse, he knew what was on the tape.

Which was…? Just before she'd shoved out of the booth across from him and fled, Miss Lannis Parker had said something that hadn't made sense then and made less sense now.

A second chance, she'd said. A fresh start for her, and for him. An opportunity to make better decisions, make amends, whatever all that meant. A chance to make peace with God. He gave a mental snort. He didn't need God. He just needed a good defense attorney, and since he was one of the best, he didn't need anybody. No matter what, though, it looked like his immediate future included a night in jail.

Some second chance.

~

Lannis Parker held her breath as she watched Detective Bennett and a uniformed cop hustle Robert Davis down the steps of the tired-looking motel, the rusted metal stairs clattering and groaning under their combined weight. Davis wasn't fighting, which surprised her. The police had somehow achieved a level of cooperation Lannis hadn't expected of the man.

The man she knew relished the opportunity to use his fists, derived pleasure from administering a beating. A wave of dizziness washed over her at the memory of Davis's precisely placed blows. She tried not to think of the naive young woman she'd been five years ago, or how irrevocably he'd changed the course of her life in the space of a few hours. An invisible fist of grief for the innocence he'd stolen from her mingled with anger and squeezed her heart.

The anger flashed and eclipsed the grief, a white-hot flash that shocked her with its intensity. She shrank at Davis's proximity even as her fingers itched with the urge to pummel the man.

A spurt of disappointment shot through her. *No.* Too short a step to bitterness, and an even shorter step to the seductive lure of revenge. Lannis had worked too hard at cobbling together a safety net to protect her newly healed psyche. She would not let him steal her peace again.

He wouldn't rape again, either.

She should feel vindicated. Yet Lannis couldn't deny the terror the mere sight of him roused in her, the trembling that began in the deepest parts of her body, the tremors rippling unchecked through her muscles.

She inhaled, but there wasn't enough oxygen, and she inhaled again as a flicker of panic flared. Lannis turned, burying her face in Ben's shoulder. His arms came around her, blanketing her with comfort and protection.

The reality of Ben's presence anchored her, and freed her lungs to accept air. She took a deep breath of his warm scent, and the intensity of her emotions blurred.

Davis couldn't get to her; he was handcuffed and in the custody of two armed officers. He didn't know she stood in the shadows half a block away, witnessing his arrest. He didn't know her fiancé was a DEA agent, and that Ben had spent countless hours equipping her with a much better than rudimentary level of self-defense.

Even so, she felt exposed, almost naked—at least where Ben wasn't touching her. She squeezed her thighs together, then realized the futility of the action. The damage could never be undone, and she forced herself to relax her muscles.

Ben muttered a curse under his breath and said, "I told you this was a bad idea." He hitched a hip onto the front fender of his restored Mustang, which he'd parked close enough to see, but far enough from the motel to be safe.

She shook her head. "I needed to see it happen." She lifted her head and observed the uniformed cop guide Davis's head into the cruiser, then slam the door with a finality that punctuated the moment. And, she hoped, marked the end of a torturous era of her life.

Her breath whooshed out. Closure. A fancy word that covered the events of the day, a day she never wanted to repeat.

"We did it, Ben!" With his help, she'd taken a rapist off the streets. And no other woman would endure the hell he'd visited upon her. As the reality finally sank in, elation rose from her toes, bubbled up through her midsection, and coaxed her lips into a smile.

Lannis hugged her fiancé closer, burrowing into his heat, borrowing his strength. He had championed her tonight, and had taken care of her in a thousand ways since Davis plowed back into her life today. A wordless hum wound its way to her lips, and she decided she needed more than a hug. She lifted her face to Ben for a kiss. His cell phone rang before he could respond, but he gave her a one-armed squeeze and jostled her while unclipping it from his belt.

"Martin." He listened for a moment, then said, "Keep it clean." Another pause. "Thanks, man." He flipped the phone closed, stowed it, then leaned back to peer at Lannis. "Dutch says it was a righteous arrest. No mistakes, nothing for Davis to use to weasel out of the charges." His pale blue eyes were shuttered, his expression frightening for its controlled intensity. It was a good thing she knew him, or he would have intimidated the starch right out of her backbone.

Lannis swallowed. "Good." Relief made her knees weak, and the adrenaline rush of the previous three hours began to ebb. She had a moment of gratitude that Ben was holding her up, so she wouldn't collapse when the inevitable post-adrenaline crash came.

His expression softened. "Dutch must have called in some favors tonight, to get the warrant this fast."

He would know. Ben was the one trained for undercover work. He had dug his equipment out of the trunk of his car, then set her up with his wire and transmitter. He'd given her some pointers, and promised he'd be close.

In the end, he had been relegated to wait in the shadows, forced to listen as Davis gloated over his vile deeds. Lannis had caught a glimpse of the remains of the napkin he'd shredded, sitting twelve feet and a universe apart from her in the bar. A hundred tiny pieces, some of them disintegrating in the condensation from the untouched soda in front of him.

She let go of him to rub her rib cage. She'd only had to wear the wire for about an hour, but remnant sensations kept ghosting up her side. The microphone, clipped to the front of her sports bra, hadn't bothered her, but the wire snaked under the elastic band and managed to irritate one spot until it felt abraded. Now it itched. The transmitter had been the worst. Nestled beneath the waistband of her cargo pants, the sharp-cornered box had cut into her back. *How does Ben stand to wear his gun back there?*

He pulled her close, and Lannis wrapped her arm around him again. "So, what happens now?"

He used a finger to lift her face to his, and gave her the kiss she craved. His familiar taste, along with the heat and resilience of his lips distracted her, and her eyes drifted closed. Emotions tumbled over one another within her, as fear and euphoria gave way to exhaustion. She shivered and sank into his embrace. Without warning, tears seeped from beneath her eyelids.

Ben broke the kiss and used the pad of his thumb to wipe the salty tracks from her cheeks. "Hush," he murmured. "What happens next is we take you home."

"What about Davis—"

"No." The single word was harsh in the darkness. "You're done thinking about him for the day. He's not going to hurt you." His voice softened. "Do you want to stay at my place tonight? In case of nightmares?"

Lannis swiped at her tears. The idea tempted her. Ben knew, better than anyone, how vulnerable she was to the demon dreams, especially on bad days. And today qualified. Bad in capital letters, bold, italicized, and underlined. His solid, reassuring presence and his familiar, mismatched house with its state-of-the-art security system would go a long way toward keeping the terrifying images of her subconscious at bay.

Going to Ben's wouldn't undo everything she'd accomplished, but she wouldn't put today's evil to rest until she faced it alone. It was a hard fact, and there was no way around it. She'd labored to put her past where it belonged, squarely in the category of history. Just because part of her history had reared its ugly head didn't mean she had to get dragged back into it. She shook her head. "I'll be okay." Her voice wavered, betraying her.

He gripped her shoulder and dropped a kiss on her forehead. "You sure?" He gently held her far enough away to see her face.

"Of course." Lannis's eyes were gritty and felt swollen, but she met his gaze without faltering. Hiding nothing, she let him plumb the depths of her eyes for the truth—and hoped her version of the truth would triumph tonight. Shooting for confidence in her voice, she repeated, "I'll be fine." She sounded solid this time, enough that she even believed herself.

Ben assessed her for a moment longer, and apparently satisfied with what he saw, released her. He opened the door, handed her in, then rounded the car and slid into the driver's seat. He fired up the engine, and the growl of the Mustang's dual exhaust system rumbled through her body, infusing her with the illusion of strength. The energy that had sustained her over the past few hours deserted her, and Lannis melted into her bucket seat. Her arms suddenly felt like lead weights, her fingers thick and clumsy. *There it is, the adrenaline crash, right on schedule.* A jaw-cracking yawn surprised her.

Ben chuckled.

Lannis dropped her head back on the headrest, her neck too tired to hold it upright anymore. Yep. Surviving was good, and laughter made survival that much sweeter.

"I love you, Ben," she whispered.

~

Ben Martin shoved the gearshift into reverse and glanced at Lannis. "I love you, too, darlin'," he said. A thread of his tension eased.

Thank God she'd pulled herself together after encountering Davis this afternoon. He'd had serious doubts about her ability to do that when he'd first seen her. Hunkered down in the bathroom at work, fending off her coworkers, her boss…

Of course, if his worst nightmare came to life and he bumped into it unawares, he would probably come unglued, but only for a nanosecond, he thought—then wondered if he was arrogant in his self-assessment. He gave it a moment's consideration. *Nah.* Confident, not arrogant.

Whatever term he used, though, he knew he would avoid the curious amalgam of threat response Lannis had exhibited. She'd combined "fight, flight, or freeze" with either rousing success or dismal failure, depending on how he looked at it. He'd never seen anyone do all three at once. *She got through it. That's all that matters.* She deserved full credit for standing up to the man who'd nearly destroyed her, even though her methods elicited a mental head shake. Lannis had forged a convoluted path toward healing that defied his understanding, too, so it followed that today would be no different.

He scrubbed a hand over his face, the scrape of his whiskers raspy against his palm. It was a good thing he wasn't the arresting officer. He might find a reason to enhance Robert Davis's compliance before they arrived at Metro Corrections. Discomfiture and a bit of surprise sifted through him at his battle to contain his desire for retribution. He'd always viewed cops who dispensed their own brand of justice as unethical at best, weak and narrow-minded at worst. *Guess I'm not immune.* He sighed, resigned to an inevitable, soul-baring conversation with the Almighty later.

Ben caught a whiff of the fragrant stuff Lannis spritzed on after her shower, and dragged in a lungful. Its soft, clean scent went straight to his head, then his heart, and then farther south. She said it was ginger and tropical flowers, but it smelled like grapefruit to him. Fresh and light and tart and a little sweet. Like Lannis. His heart swelled, thinking of the way she'd turned to him, laid her head on his chest, and purred. That was the only description he could come up with that did justice to her contented hum. The low sound that had vibrated through his shirt warmed his chest, and delighted him still.

"Watching you face Davis, listening to what he said…" His stomach clenched. He reached for her hand, his grip more forceful than he'd intended. He consciously relaxed it and stroked her thumb with his. "You are quite a woman."

Ben had waited a long time for her to drop her last wall and turn to him without reservation. It had taken excruciating patience on his part. Coaxing her to trust him was both the most challenging and rewarding endeavor he had ever attempted, and he loved every aspect of it.

The blow she'd taken most to heart, however, was trust in her own judgment. Perhaps for that reason, it was the last to heal. The look on her face a few minutes ago told Ben that maybe, just maybe, she'd taken a big step in repairing that tonight.

Fatigue apparently forgotten, she turned to Ben, her fathomless brown eyes sparkling. Lights and shadows played across her features as they passed beneath streetlamps. "I feel free! It's over!" She smiled, and her dimple appeared. "I didn't realize I was afraid of seeing him again, but as long as he wasn't in jail, it was a possibility."

Ben didn't want to squelch her joy, but the trial wasn't going to be a walk in the park for her. If some quirk of the judicial system ended up spitting Davis back out onto the street, she'd be devastated. One problem at a time. He squeezed her hand again, and let the tension of the past few hours trickle away.

His earlier delight settled into a satisfied glow that spread through his body and radiated to include the woman at his side.

If anyone deserved a second chance in life, Lannis did—and he'd do everything in his power to make sure she got it.

Chapter Two

THE CRUISER COASTED to a stop in front of a blue and yellow garage door set into a nondescript brick building in downtown Louisville. Robert Davis swiveled his head, a half-formed notion of escape in mind. The handcuffs presented the biggest problem, inhibiting his ability to even sit properly, much less run or fight. And where would he run? A flutter of panic tried to break free deep in his gut, and he squelched it. No time for that. *Stay focused.*

The garage door retracted upward abruptly, impressive in its speed, then thunked closed as soon as the car entered a massive garage. It took a moment for his eyes to adjust to the light inside. The guy who'd arrested him came around the car, unlatched his door, and grabbed his arm. Robert shot him a murderous look and, off-balance, managed to scoot far enough to get his feet under him. He stood and caught a breath of exhaust-fume-laden air. The sound of powerful engines at idle echoed and mingled with slurred epithets shouted at the cops by a couple of men, drunk or maybe high, and handcuffed to a bench set in the concrete of the interior driveway.

He could identify. Robert had a long list of curses for the idiot dragging him toward a glassed, brightly lit room. Two cops watched from the other side of the glass, and a blue mat, like the ones at his kickboxing gym, hung along one wall. The word LOOK had been penned on the mat at roughly eye level, with arrows pointing to the word. The incongruity of that flashed through his mind as the glass slid open, smooth and silent on well-oiled tracks. He leaned back in surprise. He hadn't realized it was a door.

The officer gripped his arm and shoved him into the room. Everything happened too fast. He pushed against the officer's grasp, but the two men inside each grabbed an arm and slammed him into the blue mat. The cuffs came off, and the door slid home with a thump.

"Robert Victor Davis?"

He nodded his head and his cheek ground against the cool, rough vinyl.

They barraged him with a rapid-fire stream of questions and instructions, their tag-team approach crowding and distracting him.

They probably intended to intimidate, as well, but Robert wasn't about to allow that to happen.

"Put all your personal effects on the counter," the first one said, wiry and strong despite his deceptively slight build. Guy Number Two, a husky Hardy to the other guy's Laurel, spoke at the same time. "Last chance. Surrender contraband now. If we find it after you've gone through that door"—he inclined his head toward another half-glassed door on the other side of a metal detector—"it's an additional felony charge."

Robert stripped the Rolex off his wrist, worked his wallet out of his back pocket, and tossed them both on the counter. A pang of alarm flared at letting his credit cards, licenses, and hundreds of dollars in cash leave his possession. He fingered the keys to his plane, but the cops had no patience.

"Cooperate, or it's a strip search."

He pulled the keys out and ignored the spasm in his gut as he dropped them next to his wallet, then did the same with his cell phone. He dug in his pocket for the bit of change he'd accumulated over the last few days to use in airport vending machines. He rarely carried coins, as he found them trivial and annoying. Now they bit into his palm, aggravating him even more, and made sharp pinging noises as they hit the counter. One quarter bounced, then fell to the floor and spun for a moment before wobbling to a stop.

His nerves, jangled already, now scraped raw against awareness that his life was spiraling out of control. His hands clenched. He closed his eyes and forced his fists to uncurl, finger by finger.

The officers didn't relent. "Your belt." Laurel tapped at his feet, made motions indicating for him to remove his shoes. Robert toed his Gucci loafers off as he fumbled his belt buckle loose. A female officer slipped in and clipped a wristband on, then disappeared before he realized what she'd done.

"Face the mat, hands up there, feet here." Hardy pointed, and Robert complied, looking over his shoulder as the second guy dumped everything into a plastic bag. The panic he'd squelched earlier flared to life again, and he began to tremble. Laurel searched him, his touch impersonal but intimate. The man's latex-gloved finger slipped beneath his waistband and pulled his slacks away from his body, then slipped beneath the elastic of his silk boxers and pull them away, too. Anger surged at the sense of intrusion, and replaced the panic.

"Good," murmured Hardy. "You've got enough cash to pay the booking fee."

"What?" Robert lifted his gaze and stared into the guy's eyes, half twisting as he did. It was a mistake. Both officers stopped what they'd been doing and body slammed him into the mat.

"Do not move unless I give you permission." Laurel's harsh voice growled the words in his ear.

"Louisville charges twenty-five dollars per booking." Amusement laced Hardy's voice.

Robert bit back his outrage. Twenty-five bucks, unfair as the fee was, didn't matter. He began to sweat, and his face slid on the vinyl. He nodded his head the best he could.

"'Yes, sir,' is the appropriate response."

Okay, so they were on a power trip. He'd show them, once he got out of here. Louisville Metro Corrections could expect a lawsuit. Even so, it took every bit of resolve he had to force the words out. His tone was heavy on the sarcasm, but tone didn't matter. Bending to their will did.

Abruptly they released him, shoved him through the metal detector, and on through another automated Plexiglas door. In a transaction that went as smoothly as the well-oiled doors opening and closing, they transferred him to a room that looked like a bus depot. A dozen or more men, most of them young, sat or paced the area.

Hardy inspected his shoes and handed them back to him. "Don't talk to the women."

A half wall separated the room, and he noticed a few women on the far side of the barrier. Robert snorted. He harbored no interest in striking up a conversation with penny-ante losers, male or female.

The woman who'd banded him had already printed out an adhesive identification tag and slapped it haphazardly on the front of his clear plastic bag. She finished compiling a list of his belongings and slid a form toward him, along with a pen. "Sign here."

Robert glanced at the ID, a detached section of his brain noting that the information was correct, the list complete—minus twenty-five dollars—and scrawled his name. *Twelve hours. I'll have it all back in twelve hours.* She handed the bag and form through a window where a bored-looking clerk impassively locked everything that defined him as an individual in a drawer. He had the sudden, unsettling image of a mausoleum. He shuddered, and shook off the morbid thought.

He slipped his feet into his loafers and looked around. Individual cells lined the outer walls of the room. Several of them were occupied with sullen-looking men. One of them beat on the

Plexiglas with his fists, and shouted muffled vulgarities. No one paid the guy any attention. Robert's name rang out, and he turned.

A young woman, a technician, with riotous red curls that defied their severe styling, beckoned him. She grasped one of his fingers, guided it to the glowing surface of an ultrasonic fingerprint machine. A moment later, his print appeared on the computer screen above.

"Relax your hand." She repeated the exercise until she'd obtained every combination of palm and fingerprints possible.

He endured it in silence, but bit back his response. How was he supposed to relax when he was being arrested? Booked on felony charges.

Felony.

Charges.

Trumped up, no doubt, but there was no getting around the fact that he'd be spending tonight behind bars. It was unconscionable. Incomprehensible. Didn't they know who he was? This should have been resolved with a quick conversation in someone's office. The whole situation reeked of conspiracy. The talk with Detective Bennett hadn't materialized. The guy had said they would meet in the morning, after the arraignment, which meant he expected Robert wouldn't be released on bail.

"Toes on the line, facing me, please." The tech directed him to the photo area.

He ran a hand through his sandy hair and knew the quality of the cut made it look good, even in these circumstances. He put his feet on the painted shoeprints on the floor and looked up. Before he had a chance to decide whether to smile or adopt a suitably unaffected expression, she snapped the picture and told him to face to the right. Robert ground his teeth. Again. The simple fact that the photo was a mug shot was damning enough. A jury would associate it with guilt, warranted or not.

It wouldn't come to that, but he had to consider how any of this could be portrayed or perceived, and proceed accordingly. Nothing else mattered right now. He would save his revenge for later.

"When am I allowed to make my phone call?" he asked, gratified that his voice held steady.

"You can do that now, Mr. Davis." She pointed to boxy blue units attached to the half wall. "Local calls only."

His teeth felt like they would shatter from the sudden added pressure. With effort, he unclenched his jaw and said, "I don't know anyone local." His voice cracked on the last word, and he silently cursed. Furious that he'd been reduced to asking permission, he swallowed hard and said, "May I use my cell phone?"

She leveled a cool glance at him. "No. Nothing comes out of the property room."

Helpless rage roiled in his belly, and he had to clench his fists to curb his nearly uncontrollable need to punch someone.

His vision went red around the edges, and he conjured the face of the woman who'd put him here. Dark hair cut like a pixie, translucent skin hinting of vulnerability, huge dark eyes lending an expression of innocence that was misleading in the extreme. How in hell had she tricked him? Shame at his own gullibility fueled his rage.

Oh, yes, Lannis Parker deserved everything she'd gotten from him.

And more.

He'd heat his blood tonight on fantasies of exactly how he would pay her back.

~

Lannis fumbled her key, missing the slot of the dead bolt in the dark. When she left for the airport this morning, she'd expected to be home well before sunset and hadn't left the porch light on. Darkness usually didn't bother her, but everything about this afternoon and evening was different, and tonight the empty black eyes of the windows spooked her.

Ben shouldered in, took the key from her bloodless fingers, shot the key unerringly into place, turned it, and swung the door open. He reached past her, flicked on the lights, then held the door for her. His hair, dark and in need of a trim, glinted in the light, and a hint of five o'clock shadow lent a roguish air to his appearance. Broad-shouldered and a bit over six feet in height, he didn't have to work at being intimidating when necessary, but Lannis knew, far more intimately, the opposite side of that coin. Restraint, respect, and an overdeveloped sense of responsibility.

She sent him a wobbly smile and he smiled back, although she could see a muscle tick in his jaw. He didn't want her to be alone tonight any more than she did. Maybe she was being stubborn about it—Ben would say "bull-headed"—but she wanted to prove to him and to everyone who cared for her that she would be okay.

Lannis sighed. *Be honest.* She needed to prove it to herself more than anyone.

Ben moved through the house, turning on lights, opening doors. Checking closets.

For monsters. A bubble of laughter surprised her, but Lannis recognized its hysterical roots and clamped her lips over it. She heard him test the security of the window locks and the back door.

He reappeared. "All clear."

"Thank you, Ben." Lannis snagged his jacket and pulled him to her. "Hold me."

His face smoothed. "Always." He gathered her into his arms and settled his chin on her head.

She leaned into his embrace. They stood in silence for several minutes while Lannis replayed the events of the evening in her mind, cringing internally at the intensity of her emotions. The anger, bordering on rage, shocked and frightened her. All this time she'd considered Davis her nemesis, but her own fury was a more insidious threat. Lannis thought she'd gotten past wishing the man ill. It had been necessary, in order to heal. She was beginning to suspect she hadn't healed nearly enough.

Ben released her and went to the door. "Don't forget to lock it."

Lannis rolled her eyes. "For crying out loud, it was only once, and that was before—"

"I know. I'm sorry." He had the grace to look embarrassed, although he didn't blush. "Before you quit drinking."

"It's been almost a year." A defensive tone laced her words. Recognition of its origins stopped her. Lannis groaned and buried her pride. "See you tomorrow." She reached for his hand, lifted it, and kissed the callused tips of his fingers.

He stroked her face, the feather-light brush of his touch warming her skin. "Call me?"

"I will."

He dropped his hand and let himself out. The wooden slats of the steps reverberated with his footsteps. Lannis pushed the door closed with both hands and turned the dead bolt, its click loud in the silence. Suddenly exhausted, she leaned her forehead against the cool wood.

After a moment, she dragged herself upright and set about turning off the lights Ben had turned on.

And checked the closets herself.

~

Evil surrounds her, consuming her. Black, oily, strangling, pure evil, oozing into her pores, into her nose, her mouth, into her soul. Lannis makes an abortive attempt to fight it off, fight free of it, but paralysis grips her. She gathers energy for a scream, but the evil chokes her.

Trapped in her unresponsive body, her breath comes faster and faster, shorter, shallower, gasping, harsh. Her fingers move, and she scrabbles at the dark cloud, an amorphous mist intent on her annihilation, but she can gain no hold on it, can do no battle with the murky, formless being. She feels herself dragged down, down, down, and the evil swells with triumph.

No. NOOOO…

Lannis strains for breath, struggling to escape. *Weakening… Can't let him win. Can't!*

She still has her mind. A blessing? Or a curse?

Something very, very important hovers at the edge of her thoughts. Desperation erupts as she feels herself balanced on the precipice of an abyss, in danger of slipping, falling over the edge, her weight inexorably drawing her to the seething blackness that is Robert Davis. She twists, screams. Or tries to. *Oh God, oh God, oh God, help me.*

~

"Je…sus…" The plea ripped from her throat with the force of a banshee shriek, but emerged as a croak.

The evil vanished.

Just vanished.

Disappeared.

Blessedly clear air bathed Lannis's face and she gulped a lungful, the panic of suffocation making her greedy for breath even as she realized she'd been dreaming. Her eyes popped open and the sight of her room filled her vision, reassuring in its normalcy. Familiar shadows of trees backlit by a streetlight decorated her wall. Softened by sheer curtains, the shapes of the limbs were still tonight.

Her logical, rational pilot's mind took over, and dispassionately processed the weather revealed through the window. *That's right,* she thought, *the stationary front is stalled over the Ohio River Valley and there's no wind, no precip, and I saw the man who raped me today, and he's in jail.*

Of course the nightmare would come tonight. But it didn't mean she was broken. God, she hoped that was true. She didn't know if she had the stamina to heal all over again.

She hiccupped on a sob, swallowed it, and wondered what it would be like to be normal. To go to bed and just sleep. Tears stung the back of her eyelids, and she blinked them away. Everybody had a cross to bear; she wasn't exempt. Lannis deliberately changed the direction of her thoughts and unclenched her hands, proving she truly was not paralyzed.

She'd promised Ben she'd call him, and she knew he meant no matter the time.

Without overthinking it, she rolled and grabbed her bedside phone. Hit speed dial. Ran a trembling hand through her hair. Remembered what saved her from the nightmare. Or rather, who. "Thank you," she whispered. A gentle cloak of peace surrounded her and siphoned away the worst of the tension. She flopped back on her bed and drew a shaky breath.

"Lannis." Ben answered on the first ring, his voice alert, warm, strong. "You okay?"

"You were right." Relieved that she didn't sound too unsteady, Lannis grimaced, though she knew Ben couldn't see. "It was bad." Her heart had slowed, but still thumped so hard it hurt.

"You want to go to the diner, have a cup of coffee? Or tea, for you."

"What time is it?" Still trying to swim free of the dream's thrall, Lannis rubbed her cheek with her free hand.

"Almost four thirty."

She winced. Might as well get up for the day. Past experience told her she would not sleep again, so in that regard she was glad it wasn't two a.m. "Sure. I'll be ready by the time you get here." Ben's state of wakefulness finally registered. He didn't sound like she'd woken him. "Uh, where are you?"

"At the office. I had some research to do, and I was too jazzed to sleep."

She did a mental calculation and decided she could grab a quick shower before he arrived, and swung out of bed as she spoke. "See you in fifteen." Her tone firmed. "But you have to promise you'll take some time off today, get some sleep yourself."

He chuckled. "Bossy." The effect of his gentle taunt was lost when he yawned. "You win," he said sheepishly.

She had reached the bathroom and turned the shower on, stuck a hand in to test the temperature. "Hey, Ben—" The water began to warm, and did its own miracle of anchoring her to reality, washing the remnants of the dream away. "I didn't want a drink this time."

"Good." His voice rumbled through the receiver. "I'm glad you called."

Lannis smiled and disconnected. *I am, too.* Her smile faded.

Damaged goods. Ben had said it wasn't so, and most of the time she believed him. But nights like this revived her doubt that she'd ever triumph over Davis's legacy.

Chapter Three

"My client pleads not guilty, Your Honor, and requests release on his own recognizance."

The lawyer provided by the Commonwealth of Kentucky was a soft-looking man in his late fifties, and he wore a bow tie. A bow tie, for pity's sake. Robert shook his head mentally and barely restrained himself from rolling his eyes. Jordan P. Kline, Esquire, ran a finger between his collar and his neck in what looked like an anxious gesture to Robert. Irritation tripped along his nerve endings. Never, *never* let them see you sweat. You should know better than that, he chided silently. Robert schooled his features into the benign, innocuous expression he'd practiced many times, the one he used right before he tore a prosecution witness to pieces on the stand.

He stared into the camera set up for the video hearing with the self-assurance he wished Kline exhibited, and listened as the DA, or more likely, an assistant DA, shuffled papers. The kid—he sounded just out of law school—said, "Your Honor, the Commonwealth requests Mr. Davis be held without bond."

The judge on the TV screen frowned, his untrimmed eyebrows creating a *V* above reading glasses. "Give me a good reason I shouldn't do as the defense requests."

A smile twitched at the corners of Robert's lips. A sympathetic judge, or maybe one discriminating enough to recognize one of his own.

The young lawyer didn't back down. "Mr. Davis resides in another state, owns a private airplane, and has extensive financial holdings in both the United States and in foreign countries. His passport is current. He presents a flight risk."

Robert blinked. Somebody had done a lot of homework. And fast. The question, *Why?* flickered through his brain.

Kline spoke. "Mr. Davis's financial holdings are excellent reasons for him to cooperate with the court. Failure to return for trial will forfeit his reputation, means of income, and wealth. Of course, he will surrender his passport as a condition of bail."

Davis knew it was a standard concession, but its inclusion raised his hackles. Yet, if it bought his freedom, he would have to consider it.

Paper rustled again, out of the camera's view. The judge tapped a pen on the sheaf of documents in front of him. Why was he dallying? The decision should be a no-brainer. There was no reason to hold him.

The kid spoke again. "Details of the attack fit the profile of a serial rapist. The prosecution requests he be held until trial. If convicted, DNA will be collected for analysis and comparison with unsolved sexual assaults."

Robert felt blood drain from his face, and he turned to his state-appointed attorney. Kline shot him a quick glance, looked away, and cleared his throat, opened his mouth, then closed it.

Incompetent idiot! What was the guy thinking?

"You're fired," Robert said to Kline. He turned to the television screen above him and addressed the man who held his future at his fingertips. "May it please the court, Your Honor, I will represent myself. To take the charges against me in this court, extrapolate them out and draw a conclusion regarding potential for other crimes is…ludicrous. Speculation at best, double jeopardy at worst. There is no evidence to support this inference." He took a shaky breath and ignored his wrinkled, smelly clothing, tried to project the confidence his favorite crisp Armani suit conferred. *Do* not *let them see your fear.*

"Not the wisest course of action, Mr. Davis, but I can't stop you." The judge looked offscreen at the prosecutor and lifted his eyebrows. "Do you have more than a theory, Counselor?"

"Your Honor, evidence includes an audio tape of the defendant in which he says, 'I never did anyone more than once,' in direct reference to the crime for which he is arraigned today."

"Commonwealth prevails. Bail denied. Mr. Davis is to be remanded to custody until trial, which will be set for…" The judge consulted a calendar, named a date in June, and banged the gavel. "Next."

Horror cascaded through Robert. "No. Your Honor, no!" The bailiff grasped his arm, and Robert twisted out of his grip, stepped forward without thinking. "You can't do that!" Belatedly he realized the judge would see his move as aggressive, not to mention stupid, since he was safely ensconced in a courtroom far from the bland concrete-walled arraignment room. The bailiff already had his Taser out and looked pissed, like he'd be delighted for an opportunity to use it.

Robert froze. One experience at the wrong end of a Taser was more than enough. A cold sweat formed on his upper lip and he resisted the urge to swipe a hand over it. He raised his hands, palms open, in a gesture of surrender.

"Order, Mr. Davis." The judge peered at him over his glasses. "Unless you'd like contempt of court added?"

Mutely he shook his head. *No, no more charges, but no jail, please! God help me.* But he didn't believe in God, didn't need God, so where had that come from? If he'd thought first, he would have laughed. A figure of speech, that was all.

A figure of speech that would never have occurred to him yesterday.

Just one more transgression to lay at Lannis Parker's feet.

His breathing hitched on a harsh sound that he meant as a grim snort but sounded suspiciously like a half sob. The bailiff grabbed his arm again, his grip so tight Robert knew he could expect bruises by tomorrow. This time he submitted. And seethed.

When he got out of this mess, Lannis Parker was going to suffer. And she was going to disappear, and no one—no one—would ever be able to tie him to her.

He didn't have time to flesh out his fantasy. With dizzying efficiency, he was marched to the jail for a strip search. It was executed with dispassionate touch, but the clinical thoroughness left him feeling both violated and dehumanized. He surrendered his clothes, pulled on the scratchy oversized orange jail scrubs, then followed the corrections officer to an elevator. It led to an unnumbered floor, through a maze of corridors, and up another elevator until he was hopelessly lost. He'd tried to keep a sense of direction, but it was impossible, which was obviously the point.

A sense of hopelessness compounded the powerlessness that already accompanied him. Even though only one guard herded him, cameras chronicled their movements, with an invisible control center opening doors as they approached and closing them as they passed.

They finally stopped in an old-fashioned cell block, complete with bars instead of Plexiglas, windowless, with cells constructed for two occupants instead of twenty-four. The door to one of the cells clicked open.

Two men stared out at them with unveiled hostility, and the guard shoved Robert in the five-by-ten-foot cage. He stifled his instinct to shove back. He had more important business to tend to.

Which one is the alpha? The burly guy with a Fu Manchu and tattoos beneath the hair on his forearms? Or the scruffy, wiry one whose eyes held the hooded intensity of a predator? He glanced at Fu

Manchu and made his decision. Looked back at the coyote. He curled his lip, met the guy's gaze.

"Home sweet home." The guard's caustic tone belied the words, and Robert ignored him.

But he barely controlled his flinch when the door slid closed behind him. The tension in the cell rose with every fading footstep that carried the guard away. Robert watched as the coyote's eyes narrowed, took his measure, then relaxed into arrogance.

"This one's mine"—Coyote nodded at the upper concrete slab that passed as a bunk—"and that one's Rosie's. You get the floor."

Robert's eyebrows rose. *Rosie?* Then he realized the tattoos were roses, with tangled stems and saber-pointed thorns, vining their way up Fu Manchu's forearms. His eye traced the tattoos as they caressed the guy's biceps and disappeared under the short sleeves of his orange shirt, rolled up to better display said tattoos. On anyone else they'd look wimpy, but the blooms were strategically placed so they expanded when he flexed his muscles, which he did with indolent malice in response to Robert's disbelieving stare. The thorns stretched, lengthened, sharpened, looking for all the world like talons.

Maybe he'd picked wrong.

The wiry guy bared his teeth in a smile that mocked and threatened at the same time. He reached down, unzipped his pants…and urinated on the floor, splashing loudly in the only spot large enough for a man to sleep.

Nope. He'd picked right.

A flush of anger and humiliation heated his face. His temper erupted and carried him two strides through the cell before the guy could put it away.

"Stupid, stupid move, buddy," he muttered, as he shot one foot out and smashed Coyote's balls. The guy's face went pasty white and he dropped like a brick to his knees, both hands clutching his crotch. Robert sliced his forearm down in a blow to Coyote's now-exposed neck and the man collapsed to the floor, writhing and moaning in the puddle of urine. He'd pulled his punch enough that the guy wouldn't be going to the hospital tonight, but he had to establish his position in this prison, beginning with this cell.

He whirled. Just as he'd thought, Rosie was a hair too slow to comprehend and too muscle-bound to react swiftly.

"Back off," Robert snarled. "Unless you want the same."

Rosie hesitated, his bulk balanced on the knife edge of attack versus self-preservation, and the hesitation was enough to tip him into a slide away from confrontation.

"Good." Robert straightened and dropped his fighting stance, but didn't drop his guard. "I'm not going to be here long enough to bother with king-of-the-cell games, so let's dispense with them." He glanced at Coyote, who had regained a bit of color and was staggering to his feet. "I'll stay out of your way, and you stay out of mine. Deal?"

Both men nodded. He nodded back, the motion jerky. Tossed his blanket to the floor, in a corner away from the urine. Slid down the wall to sit with it at his back, watching the two inmates. Took a breath and smelled the reek of his fear. A bead of sweat rolled down his face. He clenched his fists to hide the tremors of his hands.

Their promises notwithstanding, he'd not sleep when night fell.

Chapter Four

May

BEN ROLLED HIS CHAIR back from his desk and stared at his boss. "You've got to be kidding." The words erupted before he thought, and Ben cringed at his rudeness as they hung in the air. Displeasure creased Herm's face, and Ben snapped his own sagging jaw closed. "Can't someone else go?"

Creases deepened into crevasses, and Herm's lips thinned. "No." He held up a hand and forestalled Ben's protest. "I know you've got the wedding coming up, and you'll be back for that, plus the approved vacation after, but I need you, your expertise and skills for this. We're stretched thin as it is." His voice carried a decidedly reproachful tone. "You know that."

Ben knew. As he knew that he was next up for an undercover assignment. He'd played ostrich, though, hoping he could slide beneath Herm's radar, slide a while longer before he got tapped.

And this one would take him out of town. Away from Lannis, when she needed him most. For the first time, he questioned his choice of work. He shook his head.

"Martin, you don't have the luxury of refusing." Herm's voice bristled with censure.

Ben looked up, surprised. "Oh, I'm not refusing, Herm. It's just going to be harder this time. It's the first time I have to factor in someone else." Which was not quite true. However, it had been years, and his ex-wife's needs had come in a distant second to his ambition back then. Ben winced inwardly, and resolved to do better for Lannis.

He sat back. "How soon?" He drummed his fingers on the desk, his brain kicking into overdrive. The wedding was in a few weeks. A simple nuptial Mass with family and close friends. No frills. Informal reception at Ben's house. A barbeque, laughter, celebration. Honeymoon at the lakeside lodge at Rough River State Park. His pulse picked up, thinking about the wedding night, and one corner of his mouth lifted. Then he corralled his thoughts, redirected them.

He'd already arranged for Mike, his best friend and partner, and his wife, Maggie, to oversee closing up Lannis's rental house, transferring her meager possessions to his place. The logistics were covered. Nothing left to tend to on that front.

That left Lannis. Ben had good reason to be concerned for her. She didn't mention sleepless nights unless he asked, but soft shadows beneath her eyes had become the norm rather than the exception since Davis's arrest several weeks ago.

She was in the midst of changing jobs, with training for a new airplane coming up, not to mention moving and getting married. Toss into the mix constant undercurrents of tension regarding Davis and the upcoming trial, and it was enough to stagger anyone. Ben had fully intended to be at her side, to support her through all of it.

Apparently, he'd failed to inform fate of his plans. *The best-laid plans of mice and men…*

He half listened to Herm's briefing, and pigeonholed his emotions. It didn't take long to understand why Herm had picked him for this one. Ben had been building the case for months, and he was the most knowledgeable. It had to be him, and recent developments ratcheted the timetable from "soon" to "right now." He sifted through options quickly, but knew they were untenable before he'd gotten past the first one.

Ben grabbed a pen and began to scratch lists as Herm talked. He and his boss thought alike, so he anticipated most of what he was saying and kept ahead of him, adding a quick note here or there as needed. He slashed a line down the center of the paper and started a list of things he needed to talk over with Lannis this evening.

He glanced at his watch. He'd told her he'd pick her up after her meeting at the assistant DA's office, which should be winding up soon. He'd take a long lunch and give her a few more hours of heads-up time than she would have had otherwise.

It was the best he could do.

And unfortunately, all he could do.

A couple of hours later, a basket of the best tortilla chips in Louisville sat between them, no buffer to the news Ben had just delivered. His gut clenched at the expression on Lannis's face, and the normally mouthwatering aromas of the Mexican restaurant caused his stomach to churn. He felt like a heel laying it out in brutal terms, but the last thing she needed was to be babied.

"Tomorrow?" She blanched and went from looking merely thunderstruck to haunted.

Ben reached across the table and covered her hand. "You'll be okay." He hoped his voice conveyed assurance, rather than the hollow apprehension he felt. If she suspected the depth of his concern, she'd be hurt. He silently wrestled with the distinction between concern and lack of trust. Semantics, or a matter of degree?

Lannis grabbed his hand and gave it a convulsive squeeze, then took a deep breath. "This is what I've been working toward for months, isn't it?" Color returned to her face in the form of two ruddy spots on her ashen cheeks. "Don't worry. I'll deal with it."

She didn't look all that sure of herself, though. Ben muttered a mild curse under his breath, and briefly considered calling in sick for the next several weeks. But that was a nonstarter, and he knew it. Besides, they both had to learn to deal with the separations his job entailed. He steeled himself, and told himself he had to trust her. It rang hollow, though, and disappointment rolled through him. He couldn't untangle the emotion enough to tell if it was aimed more at her or at himself.

"I can't call you. I'll have a different cell phone, and can't risk someone getting hold of your phone number on it." Ben rotated his shoulders, trying to dislodge the guilt that pressed heavy on them. Lannis knew far better than anyone the risks of his work, to both of them. She'd barely survived an attack triggered by nothing more than association with him.

Last fall, Terrance "King" LeMasters, unable to track Ben far enough to exact revenge for destroying his two-bit drug business, had used Lannis as a punching bag and left a message with her for him. Ben had gotten it, loud and clear. It had taken only a few hours for him to put together a case that got LeMasters sent to prison after the fact, but he'd failed her. He'd done penance by taking care of her after surgery to repair the damage incurred at LeMasters's hands.

The silver lining to that disaster, which Ben could not regret, was that their cautious friendship had slipped into the uncharted territory of love. Hopefully marriage would confer more protection, not more exposure.

"I'll be fine." She flashed a smile that wobbled at the edges. "You know I have a list of resources. And I'll use it if anything comes up." Left unsaid was Ben's placement on that list. Number one.

"Mike can get a message to me if necessary." Ben nudged the basket of tortilla chips closer to Lannis with his free hand. "Eat. And tell me how this morning went." As usual, stress robbed her of appetite. Another pang of remorse at his imminent departure rolled through him.

She wrinkled her nose but took a chip and bypassed salsa for the guacamole. "Pete Delaney's a nice guy, but the subject matter was tough." She grimaced. "He told me I can't talk to you about the details, so I won't. But I can tell you it was a lot harder to talk to him than Detective Bennett." Their food came, and she let go of his hand to spoon leftover salsa onto her taco salad. "Oh. He let slip that it was a lucky break that the judge denied bail back at the arraignment. Which is fine with me"—she flashed another smile, this one a lot more solid—"but I don't understand much about the legal wrangling. Do you?"

Ben forced himself to take a bite of his burrito. His stomach finally settled down as he chewed and swallowed. "First, thanks to your wire, they've got enough to hold him till trial. Plus, he's got financial holdings out of the country and a valid passport, so Pete made the case for him being a flight risk."

Her eyes widened and she snickered. "I'm sorry. It's not funny, but he's a pilot, and calling him a flight risk is an oxymoron." Her color warmed as her expression lightened.

One corner of Ben's mouth kicked up. It was nice to see her sense of humor had revived.

"How did Pete know about his financial holdings? That wasn't in the tapes."

"Uh…" Ben ducked his head. "That's the research I was working on that night. When you called." He cleared his throat. "That's what I was doing so late at the office."

Comprehension flickered across her features. "Ah." A faint flush tinted her skin. "Thank you." She put her fork down and gave him a penetrating look. "Don't worry about me while you're gone. Do your job the way it needs to be done, and be safe about it."

She squared her shoulders, and he could almost hear her telling herself to be strong. If repeating the sentiment enough times was sufficient to make it reality, she'd be fine.

Trouble was, positive thinking didn't always translate to positive outcomes. He wanted to kick himself for the thought, but there was too much truth in it, and he hated that he couldn't be here to protect her.

Her voice dropped to a husky whisper. "Come back to me in a few weeks and we'll get married."

Surprise stole his breath, and he covered it with a cough. Ben knew he shouldn't—and he'd do his level best to make this the last comparison he ever made between the two women—but he couldn't help comparing Lannis's reaction to his ex-wife, Deb's. Granted, he and Deb had both been too young and self-centered to marry, and the marriage had lasted longer than it deserved to. Deb would have pitched a fit, complete with tears and recriminations, and a pout lasting twice as long as he would be gone. He hadn't realized he'd expected the same from Lannis.

Heat rose up his neck, and he winked at her. "You got a deal, darlin'."

A second chance. He guessed he got one, too, whether he thought he needed it or not.

Chapter Five

LANNIS SURVEYED the ground school classroom, which had undergone a brief transformation for the going-away party Louisville Air had thrown for her. Streamers still dangled from the dispatch desk, and Mylar balloons proclaiming GOOD LUCK and CONGRATULATIONS bobbed gently above it. A good chunk of the sheet cake sat abandoned amidst remnants of used paper plates, plastic forks, and disposable cups. Nancy, the receptionist, had encouraged Lannis to take the leftover cake home. But if she did, most of it would wind up in the trash.

"Nancy," she called, "why don't you give the rest of the cake to the morning crew?" They'd missed out, since the parties always happened in the afternoons. She'd heard enough grousing over the years to know they'd appreciate getting in on the goodies from at least one celebration. Between the mechanics and the line guys, the cake would be gone before most of the flight instructors trickled in tomorrow. Heck, if Maurice got to it first, there wouldn't be any left for the rest of them. She grinned, picturing the rotund mechanic whose sweet tooth rivaled his uncanny ability to diagnose and repair planes.

A moment passed, followed by quick footsteps from the lobby, and Nancy poked her head around the door frame. "Good idea, Lannis. If you're sure you don't want it." She added, "You could freeze it, save it for Ben."

Lannis shook her head. "No. But thanks." She smiled at Nancy, orchestrator of all celebrations at Louisville Air. "I doubt the guys will complain."

"Better than doughnuts," Nancy pronounced cheerily, and stepped into the room to give Lannis a spontaneous hug. "I'm gonna miss you, sweetie. You've been a fixture around here for a long time." The phone trilled from the other room, and the receptionist dashed to answer it, saving Lannis from a mushy good-bye.

Nancy was right. Lannis had been here in one capacity or another for eight years. First as a student and working the line, then as a flight instructor, adding ratings and certifications as fast as her money would allow. She'd flown traffic reporters and aerial photographers and sightseers along with instructional flights. This building had been the center of her life and her focus—most of it in a good way.

She'd never forget the day her dad saw the sign advertising free airplane rides for kids and impulsively veered into the parking lot. She'd protested. After all, she'd been fourteen and no kid, at least in *her* mind. But his enthusiasm had been contagious, and she forgot to act cool as the pilot put her in the front seat and let her handle the yoke for the takeoff. The thrill as the wheels left the ground eclipsed anything she'd ever experienced, and fifteen minutes of seeing her world from the wondrous new vantage point sealed the deal. She knew what she wanted to be when she grew up. A pilot.

And now she was one. She sent a silent prayer of gratitude heavenward for the gift her dad had given her that day. Sadness flashed through her at the memory of his death just months after she'd begun flying lessons. *If he could see me now…* But if she believed in an afterlife, which she did, then he likely knew all about her accomplishments. Her spirits rose as she went into the deserted ground school room.

Lannis was glad of the solitude as she cleaned out her cubicle. She swept a hand into the corner of the bookshelf above her desk. Not expecting to find anything, she raised her eyebrows when her fingertips encountered a flat square of cardboard. She tugged, and it came loose from where it had wedged between slats. *Huh.* So that's where her crosswind component wheel had gone. She'd given it up as lost or appropriated by a less-than-honest student months ago. She smiled and dropped it into the sack half-filled with odds and ends left from her teaching space. There had been days she'd dragged herself in to sit at this desk with all the enthusiasm of a soda left out overnight, but nostalgia lent a rosy glow to even those memories.

She was going to miss the planes. Lannis visualized them, tied down on the ramp for the night. They were good friends, quirky and loyal and predictably unpredictable. There was 44 Lima, with its persnickety starter; the Katana's Plexiglas half-moon canopy that provided the most awesome flight visibility outside of free fall, but required a ball cap to prevent sunburn; the Maule's surprisingly underpowered heater and leaky door seals that made winter flying miserable.

She wouldn't miss the hand-operated pump for de-ice fluid, though, or the bulky propane preheater for cold-soaked engines. The Children's Hospital's planes were hangared—a heated hangar, no less—so the pilots, ergo Lannis, didn't have to deal with quite so many cold weather issues. She pumped a mental fist in the air. *Yes!*

She went to the custodial closet and grabbed dust rags and polish, and scrubbed out her shelf, polished her desktop, then stepped back.

It was time to go home.

Time to move on.

Time to let go of people who'd become more important to her than she ever would have thought. She realized she'd miss them more than the planes, more than the work, more than the familiarity she'd clung to for far too long.

Orvis Larson had been her first chief pilot, her boss, and now, her friend. And he was kicking her out of the nest, which they both knew should have happened a couple of years ago. She would miss him. But she could stop in to ask his advice or plumb the depths of his experience anytime.

This afternoon she realized he'd turned into a surrogate father figure somewhere along the line, and the revelation had shaken her. It wasn't a bad one, just a surprise, and once she thought about it, a bit predictable. He'd provided guidance, mentorship, and opportunities as she'd advanced through her ratings. Nobody could ever replace her father, but Orvis filled a small corner of the dad-shaped hole in her heart.

A pang of loss brought tears to Lannis's eyes, and she blinked them away. She'd avoided public weepiness so far, and wanted to keep it that way. She'd save the good cry for the privacy of home.

Why had she been so bull-headed and not told Ben how badly she wanted a drink that day, when he told her he had to leave? Worse, the urge had never quite left her. The meeting with the assistant DA had rattled her more than she'd let on, and thoughts of Davis were never far beneath the surface. The vision of a shot of tequila complemented by a twist of lime and a sprinkle of salt on her wrist stimulated her salivary glands. Swallowing, she mentally backed away from the edge of the slippery slope. No matter how tempting, she had to blot the image from her mind. One misstep was capable of tipping her into a cycle of bad decisions followed by worse consequences. She'd already gone down that road.

Choices.

It all came down to choices. She squared her shoulders and made one, the only one that mattered for this moment.

Lannis would call Althea now, before she left work, so she'd be accountable for not stopping at the liquor store on the way home. She would be tempted, all right, even after calling Althea. No question about it. But temptation itself didn't matter; her response did. Tonight she would walk straight home.

And take one day, one hour at a time.

One breath at a time.

Until Ben came home.

~

Robert Davis detested the Louisville judicial system.

It had taken days, but he'd finally gotten a letter to his lawyer buddy, Stan, back in New Jersey. *Get me out of here,* he'd scrawled. *Now!* Stan had taken his sweet time, but finally showed up and tried to talk him into accepting counsel, someone other than Jordan P. Kline—stupid prick—but he'd flatly refused. Stan then suggested angling for a plea bargain, but even if the DA's office was receptive, Robert would be left with a criminal record. He nailed Stan with a murderous look, his hands itching to do violence to the man he considered a friend. Stan had thrown up his hands and gone back to his own far more successful practice.

The only thing he'd accomplished was getting Robert's plane moved to a less expensive tie-down at a quieter airport. And sticking Robert with charges for an expensive airline ticket and several nights at the Galt House, one of the most exclusive hotels in town, while Robert rotted in a cell at Metro Corrections, a few blocks away.

He ground his teeth. Whoever had done all the research was right; he did have extensive holdings. But what they didn't know was that he was heavily mortgaged, and every day without income meant a day closer to foreclosure. He'd done the math in his head and figured he had about another month before the banks came calling. Stan had gone home with instructions to begin liquidating his rental properties, but sales of commercial real estate took time to accomplish. With the downturn in the economy, he'd be lucky to net enough to pay off the liens.

Even the sale of his plane wouldn't bring enough to keep him above water.

He yearned for the freedom that flying gave him. The power, the knowledge that he was one of a select few who had the skills to command an aircraft. The challenge. To be unfettered and above the ordinary. Oh, how he missed it. He couldn't even see the sky, couldn't read the clouds, couldn't test his understanding of meteorology against the professional forecasters.

The prospect of losing his plane infuriated him—but that bluster camouflaged his fear of losing everything. Especially the freedom already ripped from him.

He hated being cooped up, trapped. He hated feeling impotent and helpless. He hated the terminology of jail: incarceration, corrections officer, cell block, lockdown. He was beginning to hate pushups.

He hated the food. Everything was orange, brown, or white. Gravy or cheese sauce on everything, even the vegetables, which had to come out of industrial-sized cans and gave "overprocessed" new shades of meaning—primarily anemic, putrid shades of green. The meat was mostly unidentifiable, in which case he allowed that the gravy was perhaps fortuitous.

His body craved the freedom of a four-mile run on the beach and, contrarily, became more sluggish each day. Because he was a good inmate—oh, did *that* grate—he'd earned the right to leave his cell for an hour a day. What a treat. A chance to mingle with Jefferson County's biggest losers.

Coyote had been moved. Robert didn't know if it was within the jail or out to a prison or if he'd been released. It didn't matter. He still shared with Rosie, and had staked his claim to the upper bunk before the cell door clanged shut behind Coyote. Rosie hadn't been inclined to see it his way, but Robert had been only too pleased to let his body have its first really good workout in weeks. Rosie hadn't been so pleased.

However, Robert had to admit he would have preferred Coyote as a cell mate. The guy had a certain sharpness of mind that appealed to him. They had their obvious differences, the first being that Coyote was a scum-sucking failure of humanity and a felon. But Robert could overlook that in favor of playing mind games with someone clever enough to make it worthwhile, enough of a match to break the abysmal monotony of imprisonment.

But none of that mattered. He needed to focus on his defense. Maybe do more discovery. He'd already obtained a transcript of the tape, a copy of Lannis Parker's statement, a very short list of evidence, and the names of all the cops involved. He dismissed her statement out of hand. Her word against his, and he knew how to discredit her on the stand. And take the stand she would. That was the other reason he'd rejected a plea bargain. He relished the opportunity to drag her through her own mud, slash her testimony to bloody ribbons. Destroy her, legally, in open court.

He frowned. His own words were a bit more of a problem, but not insurmountable. His subconscious worked in strange ways. One of these days he'd wake up and the solution would glitter with glorious clarity like a neon sign in front of him, and he'd wonder why it hadn't come to him before. Or, if it was so obvious, why he hadn't seen it.

But his biggest question simmered in the back of his mind. Why had the Commonwealth of Kentucky bothered with prosecuting such an old case? One based on *he said, she said?* They were wasting money and time. The sense that there was more to this still hovered over the whole business. Not a conspiracy. He wasn't that paranoid. Damned if he could figure out why, but he'd keep looking, see if he could figure out what he was missing.

He sure as hell didn't have anything else to do.

And any prospect of having the opportunity to do anything else depended on his defense.

He pondered his options and smiled.

He knew his next step.

~

Lannis hauled the last box into the kitchen, slapped a piece of tape on it, and grabbed the felt-tip marker. She visualized Ben's place, and printed BEDROOM in big letters on the top. A trill of anticipation shimmered down her spine and settled low in her belly. Excitement was a welcome change from the draining anxiety she'd battled for seven days. And nights.

She'd made it, though, one step at a time.

But she could relax for a moment, enjoy a daydream about Ben, and she flopped into a chair. Her face warmed at the direction the daydream went, and other parts of her body heated up as well. Flustered, she started to get up and brew a cup of tea to distract herself, but sank back down. They were getting married in three weeks, and if a bride couldn't fantasize about her husband-to-be, who could?

They'd chosen to wait until marriage to have sex—*no, make love*—because Ben held to his Catholic beliefs as naturally as he breathed. She'd initially felt rejected, and not a little confused. After all, that was what men wanted, wasn't it?

And if they couldn't seduce, they took.

Lannis had learned differently with Ben. He understood, better than Lannis had at first, her bone-deep need to be valued as a person, as a woman, as herself.

A smile teased her lips. Oh, he had made his intent quite clear, staking his claim to her heart and her affections with unrelenting, almost ruthless, devotion. He would not be denied and yet, she felt safe with him.

Safe enough to let her guard down and expose her embarrassing, quirky secrets to his scrutiny.

Safe enough to explore the fascinating territory of attraction, and discover that her reaction to Ben was normal, not warped by the trauma of her past. Lannis suspected Ben was even more relieved at that revelation than she was, although she'd been surprised to find relief was only the first step for her. She thought it was the goal, but no. Exploring her sexuality without pressure had created tantalizing possibilities and a lifetime of mysteries to unravel.

In an unexpected bonus, she'd learned deeper lessons he could never fathom. She would never view herself as disposable or shameful again. Lannis glanced down at her body. No longer a traitor inviting abuse, it was a gift, ready to be given freely to Ben.

Her pulse quickened as she imagined that moment.

The phone rang and she stood, answering the kitchen extension. It was Pete Delaney.

"Davis wants you to do a deposition."

Dread cooled the warmth of pleasure from her fast-fading daydream. "What's that?"

"He has the right to interview you before the trial. It's called discovery."

Lannis sank crookedly into the chair, and it slid an inch or so across the tile, squealing until it found purchase and stopped. "What else does he want? Everything I have to say is in the statement."

"I know." Pete sighed. "Legally I can't block him. If he can come up with questions, he has a right to ask them. That's a keystone of our legal system, to allow the accused full opportunity to defend themselves."

Lannis's mind went blank. She licked her lips, but even her tongue was dry and it didn't do much good.

Pete continued, obviously unaware of her response. "Can you be downtown next Tuesday? Two o'clock?"

She managed to squeak a marginally affirmative, wordless sound, and wished she could say no. Could she?

The room seemed to close in on her. She stood, went to the door, and opened it. A wall of humid air rushed in, and for once, she didn't care about the electricity the underpowered air conditioner would use. Her throat worked as she tried to swallow past the lump in her throat. Damn Robert Davis! Not content to invade her dreams, now he had the audacity to insinuate his way into her waking day. Her hand shook as she gripped the door frame for support.

But if she allowed him to intimidate her, some other woman would go through hell at his hands. She knew to the marrow of her bones that he would strike again if freed. Did she have the strength to withstand him? Lannis straightened her spine. It wasn't solely her battle any longer. She'd give it her all, and if she failed? She'd go down fighting. She swiped at sweat that had formed on her upper lip.

Pete finally caught on to her silence and, correctly recognizing it as distress, said, "I'll be with you. We'll meet with Davis in the jail's conference area. My job is to run interference, keep his questions relevant, protect you from his badgering." He hesitated, then added, "Unfortunately, I think his only reason for doing this is to devil you." Regret tinged his voice. "Sometimes the justice system is less a matter of justice and more of a chess game. I can only say the bulk of outcomes favor the side of fairness."

Surely there was another option. "Do I have to do it in person? Can't he submit a list of questions, and I can answer them in writing, like I did for the statement?" The image of a jewel-toned wine cooler shimmered in her mind, right behind the pain at her temples. Lannis slammed a door on the picture, but the memory of liquor's bite and numbing qualities lingered. She squeezed her eyes shut, then opened them. *Nope.* Not going there. At all. She focused on her goal. Put a lid on Davis's freedom. Keep other women out of his hands.

"Uh, that's not the normal course in criminal law, but they do it all the time in civil actions."

"But usually it's with the defendant's lawyer, not the defendant, right?" Lannis hoped her limited television-watching experience reasonably approximated reality. Probably not, though, given the inaccuracy of reporting that surrounded airplane crashes. She knew *that* firsthand.

Pete blew his breath out in a tight sound of irritation, or perhaps frustration. "Yes. I can play cat and mouse with Davis, try to put him off." His words were clipped. "As long as you understand it may end up being no more than simple delaying tactics."

Lannis couldn't read Pete's voice. She detected an undercurrent of something. Fatigue? Overwork? Was she too demanding? Her ease with him eroded a bit. "You're on my side, aren't you?" The words popped out, and she heard an edge of hostility in them. She gripped the phone tighter, and wondered if she was overreacting.

"Of course I am. It's more work for me, but I'll do it." The words rolled downhill, slowing at the end.

The hostility of a moment ago erupted into full-fledged anger. Anger at Davis for coming into her life, then making a repeat appearance. Anger at his attempts to keep her entrenched in victimhood. Anger at herself for—for—

Shit. For being human.

Lannis knew she was taking it out on the wrong person, but even so, her words took on a life of their own. "I didn't want any of this to happen, Pete. I never wanted to see Robert Davis, not ever, ever again." She shoved a hand through her hair. "But it did, and you know what? I'm worth the effort to prosecute him, and worth the effort to protect."

"Whoa, Lannis." He sounded surprised, and a little pissed off. "Yours isn't the only case I'm working. I have an intern from the University of Louisville School of Law, and I'll put her on it for you. It'll be a good exercise for her."

Lannis knew the DA's office was overworked and understaffed, but a sense of abandonment shot through her anyway. "You *will* supervise her?" She managed bare courtesy, but only by the thinnest of margins.

"Yes." Pete's tone was frosty. "I'll have her keep you up-to-date."

"Super." Lannis tried to sound grateful, and failed. "Thanks." She hung up and dropped her face in her hands. Had he passed her case to the intern because he didn't think it was a good one? Or should she take him at his word? The answer to that question pricked at her conscience. She had a tendency to read more into what people said than what they really meant.

And her deepest fear. What if her attempt to hold Robert Davis accountable failed? What if he walked, free to rape again?

She groaned and blinked back tears. It would be a matter of time—seconds, or minutes, or maybe if she was lucky, an hour or two—before a devastating, potentially irresistible craving for alcohol ambushed her.

But alcohol wasn't the answer. No matter how much she yearned to hide inside a bottle, doing so would give Davis another victory.

Lannis stood, anger fizzing in her veins. She needed an antidote. Long strides carried her into her bedroom, and she yanked the closet door open, then settled her gaze on the dress she'd chosen for the wedding. The edge of her temper blurred.

She touched the soft, rose-tinted cream satin. The fabric rippled over her hand, cool and smooth like a gentle waterfall. The sensation anchored and calmed her. Her emotion ebbed, and one corner of her mouth quirked up. Ben refused to see the dress before the wedding, and since she'd never worn anything so girly in her life… Well, the look in his eyes would be priceless.

Lannis closed the door and sighed. Back to square one. Call Althea, now. Find a noon meeting if she didn't think she could make it until evening. Pull out her well-worn list of things to do when life got rough and pick one, then do it.

Most of all, remember she wasn't alone, even though she felt like it. She would not—*would not*—let Davis's machinations or Pete's attitude drag her down.

She had too much to lose.

And far too much to gain.

Chapter Six

Ben RAPPED TWICE, quick and sharp, the second tap louder than the first—his signature knock for Lannis—then stepped back so she could see him through the peephole he'd helped her install a few months ago. Footsteps crossed the floor inside, then hesitated. He imagined her on the other side of the door, peering with one-eyed caution through the fish-eye lens. A flurry of thumps and rattles vibrated the door as she threw dead bolts and secondary locks. She flung it open and he caught a glimpse of pure joy on her face.

It sent a bolt of life to the still-numb depths where he'd hidden his feelings. A long-simmering dispute between the principal targets of his investigation had sparked, and they had killed each other. Hell of a reason for coming home early.

"Ben!" Lannis launched herself into his arms and he caught her, staggered once, then found his balance and inhaled the fresh grapefruit scent of her hair.

The tension of the last few weeks ebbed, leaving him with a far different sort of tension. Anticipation and self-denial sparred in his gut, and he clutched her, clinging to the solid sturdiness of her body, her heat, her *aliveness*. Suddenly he was desperate to be one with her. Five more days…

"You're home early!"

"Yep." He angled for a kiss. She gave it to him, bumping the bill of his ball cap in her eagerness. He sank into her embrace, closed his eyes against the ruthless world he'd left behind, and reveled in the solace she offered. But it quickly grew far too heated. Ben dragged himself from the seduction of her mouth, from the softness of her body pressed so close to his.

He bit back a groan, the force of his desire nearly overwhelming. Reluctantly, he set her a scant inch away, but couldn't find it in himself to let go.

She beamed at him. "Orientation was great, 'cept for one guy, but—"

The haze of desire cleared a bit. *Oh, yeah.* She'd done her first week of ground training for her new job. Wait a minute. What about one guy? Protective instincts, never dormant and especially vigilant in reference to Lannis, poked their heads up.

"—he's no big deal, and Pete, I don't know what's up with him, but I have to go downtown for—"

Ben's head began to spin with the rapid subject changes.

"—a deposition, and I just realized—" She sucked in a breath, then closed her mouth.

He gave her a gentle nudge, needing space in order to stay in control of the temptation she posed. "Realized what?" She turned, led the way to her kitchen. He kicked the door closed and followed, enjoying the view.

"Nothing." She flashed a smile over her shoulder. "Iced tea or hot?"

Nothing? He doubted it, but he didn't feel like calling her on it. He wanted to bask in the glow of the kiss. "Iced."

Lannis busied herself preparing a glass for him, then sat across the gingham-covered table. Her gaze dropped to the tablecloth, her lashes resting over fragile, bruised-looking shadows beneath her eyes. Ben hadn't noticed the shadows until now.

He gave a mental sigh. Whether he felt like calling her on it or not didn't matter. "What did you realize, Lannis?" He leaned back in his chair, crossed one ankle over the opposite knee, and took a long swallow of the sun tea she'd poured.

"Uh…" She glanced up at him, then shifted her gaze.

There it was, her tell, clear as a neon sign. "Spit it out," he said, and snagged one of her hands with his.

A delicate flush turned her cheeks pink. "It's a good thing I don't play poker, isn't it?" Her dimple flashed, then smoothed, and her eyes clouded. "Davis." She shrugged, as if the one word encompassed every tribulation in her life—and maybe it did.

Ben made a nondescript sound of encouragement.

"He's playing legal games. I guess I should have anticipated that, but…" Her brow furrowed. "I should have known better." Her voice wobbled. "And Pete…well, I just expected more from him."

He tipped his head in acknowledgment and kept his voice neutral. "It's never as straightforward as you think it'll be."

Lannis attempted a smile, but it faded. "Mom's coming Friday."

He released her hand, took his hat off, and scratched his head. "Uh, yeah. Along with Lynette and Rich, and my family." He bit the inside of his cheek to keep from blurting out something he'd regret. Like, *Stop talking in riddles.*

Ben stood. Two steps took him to the window, and two more would carry him back to the table. He needed to do something to expend his unfocused energy. Lannis hadn't poured herself anything to drink. Maybe a cup of that herbal tea she liked so much… He filled the teakettle, set it on the stove and lit the burner, then turned, only to see she'd begun drawing circles on the table with her forefinger. She was withdrawing from him, her shoulders hunched and her lips pressed in a tight, silent line.

Well, hell. He liked that even less than her code-talking. In fact, it pissed him off. He could handle most anything except Lannis shutting him out.

Ben grabbed a chair and sat, scooted close to her, then ducked to get his face in line with her downcast eyes. "Darlin'," he said, stopping half a tone short of using his cop voice. He covered her hand, stilling it. "What's bugging you?"

She studied him through her lashes, and the moment stretched. Finally she gave a little sigh and said, "It didn't occur to me that pressing charges means I'm pushed into disclosing the rape to the world. I was so focused on catching Davis, holding him accountable—well, *that* part escaped me. It's been my secret for almost five years. Betsy—"

Lannis had recently graduated from sessions with her counselor. Most of what she had discussed with Betsy remained private. That suited him fine and, truth be told, he hoped she hadn't decided this was the moment to unburden herself to *him*. Details, anyway. He never wanted to know the details.

"Betsy and I talked about disclosure, and when I'd know I was ready, but I had a choice at that point. Now I don't." Her lower lip trembled. "I…I can't keep it from Mom or Lynette anymore. I don't really care about anyone else knowing, but I feel so…so *naked*."

"Don't you think they'd want to support you?" He had always found it odd that Lannis hadn't confided in her mom.

She flashed him a look that said *you know better.* "You know how ashamed I felt."

Somehow, the past tense of her last word seemed more present, like it was shimmering in the air between them. He sighed. "You were the victim of a crime, Lannis. There's nothing shameful in that."

Her eyes sparked. "Well, if that's so true, how come the one in four women in this country who've been raped don't ever talk about it?" She scowled. "Nobody hesitates to talk about being burglarized, or mugged."

She had him there. But she was wrong. He set his jaw. "That's not the point. You cut Millie and Lynnie out of your life for four years after it happened—"

"And now I've lost control of what and when I want to disclose." She snapped her mouth closed, her lips set in a mulish line.

Ben rubbed the bridge of his nose. "I hate to break it to you, but you've never had as much control as you thought." He deliberately gentled his tone. "Nobody does. Getting it out in the open could be good for all of you."

She started to tug her hand free, but Ben tightened his grip. "Don't. We're in this together."

"But how or when do I—" Her face crumpled. "And it's our wedding—"

"Not this weekend." Ben got up and pulled her into his arms and settled back into his chair. "Save it until after our honeymoon. It'll keep."

"What if Mike, or Maggie, or Orvis—"

"I'll mention it to them and they'll respect your wishes. This is a time of celebration. Let it be." He rocked her in his embrace, stroked her back, and after a few moments felt her muscles loosen. The teakettle gave a preliminary squeal, then settled into a shriek. Ben reached past Lannis to turn the burner off and slid the kettle to the side. It quieted immediately, and Lannis snuggled into him, letting her head fall on his shoulder.

"Tea?" Ben turned her a bit so she could see her tea caddy. She nodded but made no move to choose from her mind-numbing stash of tea bags, with distinctions ranging from fully leaded or decaf, flavored or unflavored, from flower petals to just about every color of the rainbow he'd never associated with edible foods. He rifled through them and found one labeled CHAMOMILE, and thought he remembered her saying that was her favorite for bedtime. Close enough. He managed to rip open the foil pack and drop the bag into the mug sitting on the counter, then one-handedly poured hot water without spilling too much.

"Besides, secrets have a way of tying a person up in knots, end up hurting you worse than the people you're trying to protect." He tried to keep a faint chiding tone out of the words.

"Yeah, I know." Her voice trailed off. Tears tickled the sensitive skin of his neck, and she spoke so softly he almost missed the words. "And then Pete… Between the two of them, I just…" She took a deep breath and gathered her composure. Her words floated out on the exhale. "He r-robbed me."

Ben had the unsettled sensation of having fallen down Alice's rabbit hole. Amend that: Lannis's rabbit hole. But at least she was talking to him, and that made her rabbit hole tolerable, even worthwhile. Even so, and especially because he was bone-deep tired, he had to dig for patience. He propped his chin on her head. "Do you mean Davis robbed you? Or Pete?"

Her voice muffled in his chest, she said, "Davis, although Pete was real abrupt with me when he called. He acted like my case wasn't important." She rubbed her nose, then worked her arm from between the chair and his body and finally got it where she wanted it, around his waist. "Everything's getting all mixed together. There are so many changes right now, and sometimes a drink sounds too good." She lifted her head and looked Ben in the eyes. "But yes, Davis robbed me of my choice to disclose at my pace."

Ben's heart clenched, and he ignored Davis and the trial for the moment. "Have you been going to AA?"

She nodded and gave him a tight smile. "It hasn't been easy, but one day at a time…"

He let his breath out slowly. "Good for you." *Trust.* As difficult as it was for him to keep his mitts out of it, he had to trust her to do this part on her own. "If you understood Pete's workload, you'd give him a bit of leeway to be abrupt."

"I've seen his desk. But I wonder if my case isn't strong enough to take to trial." Lannis's voice trailed off, turning the statement into an unasked question.

Ben made a sound that was a cross between a snort and a humorless laugh. "Pete wouldn't have gone forward if it was weak, and he would've offered a plea bargain if he thought that was the best he could get."

Her expression sharpened and her eyes narrowed.

"Don't get riled. He doesn't need your permission or approval to do that, so just the fact he hasn't speaks volumes." Ben gave her a squeeze and released her. "D'you want honey?"

Lannis accepted the change of subject, or at least didn't argue. She disentangled herself from Ben, stood, and reached for her ancient honey bear. She dosed her tea with a generous spoonful, discarded the bag, and returned to her own chair.

"The guy at work?" Ben dumped the leftover ice from his glass in the sink, leaned against the counter, and tamped down his urge to play proverbial rescuing knight to her damsel in distress.

Lannis waved a hand, dismissing Ben's question. "Aviation is a male-dominated field. There's one like him in every workplace." She sipped her tea. "He's a jerk, but nothing more. I can handle him." Her eyes lit up and she smiled, her dimple showing at last. "I can hardly wait, Ben! I get to fly the King Air, and they're talking about getting a Learjet in a couple of months…"

So much for the damsel in distress concept. Relief, along with a twinge of guilt for feeling it, flowed through Ben as he settled in to listen, and he purposely closed his mind against the reason he'd come home early. Time enough—later—to deal with pointless vendettas and bullets and wasted lives. He'd take his own advice, and leave that till after their honeymoon at Rough River.

Chapter Seven

"IT LOOKS GREAT, MOM." Lannis started to fidget, but stopped herself before she messed up Millie Parker's handiwork. Her mother fluttered around Lannis in a haze of pride and unshed tears, patting the hairdo she'd spent the better part of an hour creating.

Lannis would have shown up with her hair clean, air-dried, and finger-fluffed the way she did it every day, but she'd deprived her mother and sister of the chance to fuss over her at her first wedding, such as it was. She winced inwardly. That marriage had been the mistake of a lifetime. On second thought, maybe she'd done Millie and Lynette a service by not even telling them about the impulsive justice-of-the-peace ceremony until after the divorce six months later.

It was a wonder they still spoke to her.

Lannis blinked away sudden tears. She'd missed them, and hadn't even realized it. They seemed to have forgiven her for the estrangement, even if her motives were inscrutable to them. Too much time had slipped away, and Lannis resolved to make the most of the renewed relationships.

Starting right now. She smiled at Lynette, who beamed in return and took her own dress off its hanger.

Millie spritzed hair spray on Lannis's curls, and the mist drifted into her face. An ominous tickle suddenly took hold in the back of her sinuses. *Uh-oh.* No way was she going to wreck her mom's contribution to her wedding day. Lannis grabbed a tissue with one hand and squeezed her nose with the other.

Millie froze. Lannis froze. Lynette, trapped in place with one foot in and one foot out of her dress, looked comically distressed on the other side of the small dressing room.

Lannis scrunched her face and the urge to sneeze passed. She burst out laughing. Lynette joined her, then Millie, and Lannis looked at them, love expanding her heart. Their whoops were loud enough to compete with the sedate organ music in the sanctuary. She opened her arms, and they fell together in a three-way embrace, gales of laughter giving way to giggles.

"No sappy stuff." Lannis tried for a stern tone but another giggle ruined the effect. "I'm glad you're here. Let's get on with it before my eyeballs start leaking." She stepped back. Millie had beaten her to the leaking part, and Lannis gently dabbed the tissue to her mom's eyes, careful to tidy up the mascara smears without creating more.

Millie touched the flowers in Lannis's hair, then cupped her cheek and smiled. "You look lovely." She straightened, replacing the nostalgia in her eyes with backbone steel, then grabbed a handful of tissues on her way out.

Lannis zipped Lynette's dress and looked for hanging threads, missed tags, or errant lace from undergarments. "You're set, sis." Lannis held her arms out and twirled. "Did I remember everything?"

Luxurious fabric flowed and swirled and settled into graceful folds. An asymmetrical hemline played peek-a-boo with her knees and calves, slender and shapely from daily running. The neckline revealed a hint of cleavage, but remained far more modest than most of the dresses she'd tried on, and the bodice hugged her torso. Wide straps created a sleeveless look, and the back was cut low, complementing her shoulders and arms, toned and strong from a combination of the demands of her work and time spent at Ben's gym. The pearlescent ivory satin with shimmering, barely-there rose overtones lit up her skin and eyes. She'd added a touch of eye shadow and lip gloss, but sunlight had provided the blush in her cheeks.

She looked beautiful, felt beautiful. And could hardly wait to see Ben's response.

Lynette grinned. "Absolutely." She frowned, managing to look pretty even with furrows in her forehead. "I still think you should wear high heels. I have these—" She rummaged in her bag and pulled out a pair that would match. They dangled from her hand, classy and sleek and sexy.

Lannis shook her head, and hung on to her smile as it tried to slide away. She felt abruptly fragile. *I don't need to explain. Especially today.* No need to give voice to her refusal to wear high heels because she couldn't run in them, couldn't escape the Robert Davises of the world while wearing stilettos. Irritation tinged with bitterness nipped her nerve endings. She would not—*would not*—let Davis have any room, not even a toehold, in her life today, of all days.

She took a breath, blew hot resentment out with the exhale, and strove to keep her tone light. "No. But thank you." She touched Lynette gently on the arm and pointed toward the door. "It's time."

Lynette dropped the shoes back in her bag with a motion that said *I tried.* She picked up her bouquet and, as the strains of the opening hymn began, gathered Lannis in a fierce hug. Letting go,

Lynette regarded her older sister, expressive eyes filled with both wisdom and wistfulness. With a slight shock, Lannis realized Lynette had grown up and turned into a woman, complete with maturity and strength that matched her own. Before the awareness had time to register, Lynette gave her a small, poignant smile and turned, beginning her dignified walk down the aisle.

You with me, God? The thought followed a jig of nervousness that tripped up her spine. Wedding day jitters, that was all. She hoped. She was surer of this decision, this step, than any she'd made, any she'd taken, for years. Did she want to back out? *No.* The answer came before the question could fully form. Could she imagine life without Ben? No, again. *He's a gift—my gift—from God...*

A sense of calm settled over her like a gossamer shawl, and the dance on her back changed its tempo, morphing into a quiet, joyful waltz of certainty, with a counterpoint trill of anticipation.

Thank you. Lannis Parker smiled, lifted her head, squared her shoulders, and stepped into her new life as Mrs. Benjamin Jackson Martin. The trill crescendoed into a symphony of eagerness as she entered the sanctuary. She craned her neck for a glimpse of her groom, peering past her family on the left, and his on the right. Millie had regained her composure and beamed. Rich, Carly in his arms, had eyes only for Lynette. Helen, Ben's mom, blinked back unshed tears, and Dave, his dad, scratched his nose in a poorly camouflaged bid to hide his emotion. Mindy, his younger sister, didn't hold back; she swiped at her tears, her expression simultaneously proud, envious, and tinged with a little sadness. Maggie's welcoming smile encouraged Lannis from the second row.

As precious as all these people had become to her, none provided the sense of completion she longed for. Then suddenly, he was there, Mike at his side, and Father Paul beyond them. Her heart gave a little skip of happiness. She picked up her pace as she walked toward Ben and sought his gaze.

When she found it, the look in his eyes was all she needed. And it had nothing to do with her dress.

~

ECHOES OF THE CELEBRATION shimmered in the evening air. Taillights of departing cars winked between tree trunks on their way down Ben's winding driveway, and the aroma of barbecued ribs drifted behind his house, mingling with the light, sweet scent of honeysuckle from the hedgerow. *My driveway, my house...* A neighbor's dog barked a warning as the cars passed, then fell silent.

No one could see her waving anymore, and Lannis dropped her arm. The hum of anticipation, subdued but never silent during the party, returned with a flourish. And brought with it unexpected shyness.

Ben. She should feel absolutely comfortable with him, and after all they'd been through together, she did…and didn't.

Husband. A shiver raced up her vertebrae, and she disguised it by picking up a stray napkin and dropping it in the trash can near the door.

All the women had bulldozed their way from the patio to the kitchen, cleaning up after the party with cheerful efficiency. Which was quite nice of them, but left Lannis without a task to do, nothing to focus on—except Ben, and the rest of the evening.

Another shiver tripped across her shoulders and she glanced up, looking for him.

He was lounging against the maple tree, watching her. Heat and desire and pure male possessiveness blazed in his eyes. Answering heat, answering desire pooled deep in her belly, and in her hidden feminine places. Her breathing hitched.

After all the waiting, the preparation, and the purposeful restraint, their final step of intimacy awaited. In spite of her past experience, she felt like a blushing schoolgirl. An aroused blushing schoolgirl. She caught her lower lip between her teeth and willed her embarrassment to subside, but her neck and face warmed, revealing her riotous emotions anyway.

He pushed himself away from the tree. "Mrs. Martin, it is my pleasure and honor to present our home to you." The deep timbre of his voice, almost a rumble, countered the formality of his speech.

Feeling not unlike a deer paralyzed by headlights, Lannis stood rooted in place as he strode across the patio and swept her off her feet. She squeaked and grabbed him, arms slipping around his neck.

"You're going to carry me across the threshold?" Surprise chased the shivers away and made her voice breathy. She'd spent nearly a month living here last fall, recuperating from surgery while Ben cared for her, so she'd not expected this particular tradition.

He dropped a kiss on her forehead. "Of course." He paused, slowing his steps, and treated her to another smoldering look from scant inches away. She felt her pulse ratchet higher, and her breathing went shallow. Of their own volition, her lips parted. He took that as an invitation and covered her mouth with his, tasting her and sending his tongue to tangle with hers in leisurely, arrogant confidence.

She met him with a hunger that ignited them both. Her awareness diminished until she knew only the alternate bunching and release of his muscles as he carried her. The heat of his arms surrounded her, and his strength imbued her with a sense of safety. Vague changes in light and shadow flickered past.

Then darkness.

He broke the kiss and released her legs to allow them to slide down his body. Lannis felt his arousal against her abdomen, inhaled the warm scent of his skin and the charcoal smoke trapped in the fibers of his dress shirt. His shoulders blocked the thin ray of silver light—from the hallway?—and softly limned his silhouette. *The bedroom.* He'd carried her to the bedroom. She tipped her head back to look at him.

Lannis couldn't see his eyes.

He unzipped her dress, slid his hands up her back, across her shoulder blades, and traced her collarbones with his thumbs. With deliberate, gentle movements, he teased the wide straps of the bodice to the top of her arms, then smoothed the fabric down to her elbows in a caress. Her skin rippled into goose bumps where he touched it, and she shivered.

She still couldn't see his eyes.

Couldn't. See. His eyes.

She couldn't see his face, could only see the bulk of broad shoulders between her and the door, and suddenly wasn't sure it *was* him, didn't know this man except that he was big, bigger than her, and her brain screamed, *Danger! Get away! Run, run, RUN!* and her clothes were partly off, and *Where am I—*

Panic sucked the air from her lungs, and Lannis knocked hands away from her arms with a convulsive, instinctual movement, then clutched at her breasts. She stumbled back a step and bumped into something solid and her breath returned in a gasp.

"Lannis!"

A shadow reached for her and she twisted, tried to force her quivering muscles to rouse, to respond, to run, and tripped instead, falling on softness that could only be a bed.

Light flooded the room and the man darted in front of her and she scrambled away, hampered by bands of fabric trapping her elbows, skirts hobbling her legs. Terror rasped in and out of her chest in painful gulps.

"Lannis." The man crouched so his face was even with her eyes. "It's me. Ben."

Recognition roared into her awareness, snapped her into the present, into reality. "Oh, no…" Stricken, she could only stare at him, shame racing through her veins along with abruptly unfocused adrenaline. Her cheeks burned and she wished the earth would open and swallow her.

"Can I touch you now?" His tone was matter-of-fact and neutral.

"Y-yes." Her hands ached, and she looked at them, saw her knuckles were white, the rich burgundy of the duvet twisted in her fists. Ben covered her hands with his, and she let go of the comforter, fingers tingling. He ran his hands up her arms and engulfed her in a bear hug, lifting her off the bed. Twisting, he rearranged the pillows, then sat, settling her on his lap.

"I'm sorr—" she began.

He gave a quick shake of his head, murmured, "Hush," and stroked her back. "No need."

She was suddenly very cold, and welcomed the heat of his palm on her skin.

"Flashback?"

She nodded and buried her face in his neck. *I thought I was over this.* Would the damn memories ambush her at random moments for the rest of her life?

"What triggered it?"

Lannis blew her frustration out in a short breath. "I—I couldn't see your eyes."

Ben was silent for a moment. "How about if we leave the light on?"

Hope kindled deep in her heart, and started to edge humiliation to the side. "Um, okay." She lifted her face and sought his eyes. He smiled and studied her as if she were the most important thing in his life. *But I feel like a failure.* Lannis slammed her mind on the thought and dropped her gaze while she struggled to corral her emotions.

"Anything else?"

Lannis cleared her throat and spoke into his shirt. "I guess the opposite of flashbacks is to be in the here and now, so…"

Ben put a finger under her chin and lifted it. "Lannis."

He waited while she dredged up the courage to let him see her vulnerability. Her flaws. *Again.* She sighed and opened her eyes. His, only inches away, were dark with desire, the pale blue of his irises pushed into thin rims by dilated pupils.

"Then when we make love, you will look at me. See *me.*"

It was a command, and arousal reawakened, flickering along Lannis's nerve endings. Her lips parted with a tiny involuntary gasp.

Satisfaction, quintessentially male, sparked the desire simmering in his eyes into a smoky flame. One corner of his mouth quirked up. "Don't worry, darlin'. You'll never wonder who you're with."

He lowered his head oh-so-slowly, a volcano erupting at a glacier's pace, giving her every opportunity to stop him. Giving her the freedom to say yes.

"Oh, Ben…" She breathed his name and acceptance tangled with anticipation, fanning the embers of her arousal into riots of sensation.

His lips brushed hers, and she answered him with the language of her body, hungry and unreserved, eyes open.

He pulled away and whispered, "Say it, Lannis. Out loud. Say it for me."

Eyes wide, her gaze locked with his, she answered, "Yes." Then, because she needed to say the words as much as he wanted to hear them, "Yes, yes… Make love to me, Ben. Let me make love to you."

A shudder rolled through him and he sighed, bending his head to offer a deeper kiss.

Secure again, Lannis surrendered to his touch, then returned it twofold…and called forth his surrender, as well. Ben capitulated with a groan and passion, his kisses covering her face, following the sensitive lines of her neck. Suddenly the layers of clothing between them were too much. She fumbled the buttons of his shirt undone and pushed it aside, greedy to fill her palms with the texture of coarse hair scattered across the heated skin of his chest, to caress the strong, smooth curve of his shoulder, to press every inch of her skin to his.

To open her arms, her body, her heart.

He captured her hands, slowing her. "Don't rush," he murmured. "We'll get there." He continued at a lazy pace, his touches creating pleasure so exquisite it bordered on pain, his lovemaking both tender and selfless.

Lannis's greed faded, then underwent a quiet transformation. For the first time, her own pleasure wasn't the goal. His was.

She'd never done this. Not this way.

Lannis had never made love, because she'd never loved.

The flash of understanding tilted her universe. Her focus, the reason for her existence, shifted. She needed to show him. In this, action eclipsed words.

She showed him by slipping the bodice of her dress down to her hips, and letting the straps of her barely-there bra slide down her arms. His gaze sharpened, and he gently touched her through the fabric, then unhooked the front clasp and rid her of it with a caress that somehow took the rest of her clothing with it.

She showed him by kissing his scars in silent honor of the strength of his character, and spent extra time on the ragged one on his arm that had brought them together.

She showed him by accepting the atonement of his lips on *her* scar, the one she refused to look at. The one Ben carried unnecessary guilt over. She ran her fingers through his hair and murmured, "It wasn't your fault," granting him absolution. With a start, she realized *he* had someone to exorcise from their bedroom, too. King LeMasters, the low-level drug dealer who'd retaliated against Ben last year by beating her within an inch of her life.

He buried his face between her breasts for a moment, tense, seeking her hand with his. She caught his hand, squeezed it, and he gripped her with an intensity that threatened to crush her fingers. After a moment, he nodded and relaxed his grasp.

Then he lifted his head and trapped her with an expression that said *now*. Lannis's heart fluttered, and her breath caught in exquisite anticipation. Ben shifted and silently demanded her gaze as he joined their bodies. The intimacy of it staggered her, even after the sea change of the last few minutes. She wanted to look away…but she couldn't have blinked or turned if her life depended on it. His eyes probed the secret depths she hid from everyone except him, and she finally understood.

Her life *did* depend on maintaining the visual link. Strength, courage, vulnerability, and love—especially love—flowed from Ben's eyes, and Lannis recognized he'd bared his heart to her as much as he'd asked her to open herself to him.

Her last barrier fell.

She didn't need to protect her most secret places anymore, because Ben knew and cherished what she concealed from everyone else. Ben saw her brokenness, but didn't see her as broken. Ben would protect her vulnerabilities, even as he championed her strength. Shaken at the depth of her emotions, she pulled him closer and clung to him, needing his warmth, his strength as her anchor. *They shall become one* floated through her mind before she lost all sense of self in waves of sensation. Time slowed, then stopped. He shattered from giving himself to her, and she shattered in giving herself to him.

Time shifted, reawakened. Moments gathered themselves from where they'd collapsed, and staggered into a shuffling march, trying to keep up with the slow rhythm of Ben's heart as it thudded against her breast.

Ben…husband…making love. Home. Concepts—rich, complex concepts—to add to her spartan emotional vocabulary of the last several years. Joy burbled beneath her ribs and filled her lungs until she exhaled a burst of half sob, half laugh, and tears surprised her.

Ben lifted his head, framed her face between his hands, and kissed her eyelids, then kissed her tears. Then he tucked her next to him, pulled the covers over them both, and held her in silence until she stilled. Until she melted against him.

So many blessings…

And she slept in peace.

Chapter Eight

June

"DAVIS."

The shout roused Robert from a fitful doze and preceded a jailer's appearance at the door of his cell. He shook the sleep, if he could call it that, from his muzzy-headed brain, and rubbed his eyes. True rest had eluded him since his arrest weeks ago. No, the weeks had dragged into two months, and sleeping with an eye toward survival meant no sleep at all. He regarded his fellow prisoners as beneath him, and they knew it. His domination of Rosie had its desired effect; no one bothered Robert. But every man in the cell block was rooting for his comeuppance, and secretly—or perhaps not so secretly—plotted to be the one to provide it.

He'd begun to wonder which he'd die from first—sleep deprivation or a shiv to the kidneys.

The jailer—*oops, corrections officer*—consulted a clipboard, frowned, and flipped a piece of paper up. "Davis. Robert V."

"Yeah." Robert cleared his throat and slid down from his bunk.

"Bring everything." The guy made an impatient *hurry-up* motion and flipped the pages on his clipboard again.

Robert's pulse picked up, but only managed to go from dull, why-bother thuds to stuck-in-molasses thumps. His mind struggled to keep up, but subsided. He'd seen enough guys get moved or released to recognize the procedure. Where would they move him? And why? He began to ask, but the jailer tapped his foot and looked with barely restrained impatience at the door to the cell block. He shrugged and gathered his toiletries, blanket, and file of legal papers. It was amazing how little one needed to exist.

Yup. Survival and existence. That was what he'd been reduced to. Bitterness crawled like bile in his throat, and he hefted his ridiculously small pile of belongings, then followed the guy down the corridor.

Then down an elevator, backward through the maze—he thought, anyway—and into the area where they'd processed him into the jail. Fully awake now, he cataloged small details of the trek. They wouldn't bring him here for a simple move within the facility, and his attention piqued at the prospect of transfer. Which was odd. The trial was only a month away, and it didn't make sense to move him. Maybe the jail was overcrowded. Or, more to the point, *too* overcrowded. Robert could attest to that. His cell, designed for two inmates, had housed three most of the time he'd been here.

"Where's Meacham?" The guard threw the clipboard down on a desk littered with papers and empty coffee cups, then said, "Wait here," and stalked into the next room. Robert raised his eyebrows. It was his first solitary moment since the fateful evening at the motel. A murmured conversation punctuated with a heartfelt curse floated in from the other room, and the corrections officer stormed back.

"Meacham's on break and I don't have time to babysit you." He grabbed a pair of scissors, snipped the plastic ID bracelet from Robert's wrist, and glanced at it. He dug through the files on the desk, found what he was looking for, and flipped the folder open. A moment passed while he tapped a finger on the page, then straightened and went out.

He returned in less than a minute with Robert's belongings, everything that had been tallied and tucked into a drawer. "Get dressed. The issued clothing goes there." He indicated a large rolling laundry cart, and laid out the small plastic bag filled with Robert's money, credit cards, and cell phone. His watch. His ring.

Robert's heart skittered into triple-pace rhythm. Questions slammed through his mind like storms in a squall line, but he closed his mouth over them, afraid to jinx what appeared to be his release. Instead, he shed the despised jail wear, donned his wrinkled slacks and shirt, then slid his feet into dirty socks and soft Gucci shoes in silence. The fetid stench of incarceration clung to his skin and he desperately wanted a shower, but he shoved the yearning aside. He fastened his eyes on the jailer while he slipped his belt into its loops and buckled it.

"Verify that your belongings are all accounted for, and sign here." The guy's voice dripped with irritation.

Robert complied. Quickly. Efficiently. His fingers shook as he scrawled his name. The court had confiscated his pilot licenses, but he wasn't going to mention that. He could replace those later.

The guy escorted him to an electronically locked door, entered a code, waited for the click, opened it, and pointed. "That way."

He held his breath as he stepped with feigned composure into a small, glassed-in lobby that opened onto the street, waiting for the ax to fall, for a shout, a clatter of feet, some attempt to chase and rearrest him. His stomach clenched and nausea churned. All the hairs on his back stood up and prickles of fear danced across his buttocks and the tops of his shoulders. For a moment he thought he might pass out, but he took a gulp of air and balled his hands into fists, achieving enough steel to remain upright.

The door swished closed behind him and gave a soft snick as it locked.

His breath whooshed out. *Hurry.*

Robert quickened his steps, pushing past a clot of people in front of the door, and slipped past a guy using the phone, like he had every right in the world to walk out to the street. Maybe he did, and maybe he didn't. He understood nothing of what had just happened.

Questions swirled through his mind. Why? Why had he been freed? Had the DA dropped charges? Had someone talked the judge into allowing bail? If so, who'd posted it for him? If it was bail, there should have been paperwork indicating he had to return for trial…but the jailer had given him nothing. The unanswered questions rolled in on themselves and gave him no guidance. *Later. From home.* He'd get out of Louisville, then get answers.

He was free! Free—and determined to stay that way. Heat and humidity and a sea of bodies assailed him. For the first time in this vile city, he didn't care. He took the two steps down to the sidewalk in one stride, then hesitated. Where to go? He had money, credit cards, his plane.

But it was late afternoon and he was tired…no, more than tired. Exhaustion, bone deep and unremitting, sapped what little stamina still lingered in his muscles. And he had enough experience with adrenaline to know the impending crash would leave him drunk with fatigue, unable to think clearly. He glanced up, and the weather made his decision for him. The sky was dark, lightning slashing through roiling clouds to the west. Storms would hit before he could even get to his plane. He needed a good night's sleep. A hot shower to scrub his pores clean. A chance to regroup.

He gave a moment's thought to catching a commercial flight, but abruptly couldn't tolerate the idea of being confined in a jet, or going through airport security. A shudder rippled under his skin. He'd had more than enough confinement and more than enough cops to last him a lifetime. The muscles in his jaw tightened. One more thing to lay at Lannis Parker's feet.

And with that he knew.

He'd pay a visit to Ms. Parker. Nothing illegal, mind you. He needed more time to plan for a real payback, but in the meantime he could make her life miserable. Legally.

Robert smiled and knew it wasn't a nice one. He stretched his legs and walked—free!—a few blocks before hailing a taxi. Went to the regional airport and took another taxi across the river to the general aviation airport where his plane sat waiting. Got keys to the courtesy car. Dug through his file and found Lannis Parker's address from her statement to the DA. Pored over a borrowed map of Louisville, and in less than seven minutes knew how to get to her house.

Whistling, he picked up the car and rolled out of the airport lot, giddy with freedom and a heady throb of power returning, expanding beat by beat, filling his veins.

~

"Megan Marie Ross! Get down this instant!" Maggie brushed a hand across her forehead and wondered what had possessed her to think she could bring the kids to Lannis's house. Sure, it was childproofed. There was nothing left but boxes, but they were stacked on each other and Megan had turned into a mountain goat the minute she'd seen them. Luckily Marty was too young to climb, but as closely as he followed his adored older sister, he could be injured if—no, make that *when* she lost her grip. *I should've gotten a sitter.*

Megan stiffened at her mother's voice and lost her balance, scrabbling at the smooth cardboard with pudgy toddler fingers. Cursing under her breath, Maggie leaped across the hardwood floor and caught the three-year-old in mid-fall, bumping Marty onto his diapered butt in the process. Yowls of outrage erupted from both children, and Maggie squatted, grabbing one kid in each arm. "Hush, hush, you're not hurt—"

A loud knock at the front door startled the children into silence, and both heads swiveled toward the sound. Maggie stood, surprise lifting her eyebrows. The guys had been gone for a half hour, and she didn't expect them back soon. Nor had any neighbors had shown interest in the move. "Wait here." She borrowed Mike's "cop voice" and Megan responded to the command, grabbing her brother around his waist. He twisted, trying to escape her grip, but gave up without much of a fight. He plopped to the floor and stuck his thumb in his mouth.

Maggie peered through the peephole and didn't recognize the man standing outside. Glad Mike had made sure she locked the door before he left, she called out, "What do you want?"

The guy cocked his head. A puzzled expression crossed his face, and he stepped back to glance at the number over the porch. He looked back at Maggie and said, "I'm looking for Lannis Parker."

Well, he was in the right place, but obviously didn't know she'd married or moved. Maggie undid the chain, threw the dead bolt, and opened the door. "She doesn't live here anymore." Some instinct stopped her from saying more.

He loomed over her—Maggie had to tilt her head back, he was so tall—and peered over her shoulder at the boxes. The kids. "Yours?" His eyes flicked toward them. Muscles in his jaw worked, like he was grinding his teeth.

Is he irritated? Angry? Why? A frisson of unease slid up Maggie's back, and she casually changed her stance, closing the door until it was only open a few inches, bracing her shoulder and hip behind it. She lifted her chin. She didn't know if the guy meant her kids or the boxes, but it didn't matter. Neither was his business. "Yes." Let him think she was moving in.

He hesitated for a moment and frowned, then shoved his hands into pockets…of very expensive clothing. Expensive but rumpled, like he'd slept in them. *Odd.* His hair was straw-colored, so his beard stubble was pale and hard to see, but up close it was obvious he was a day late for a shave, maybe more. A faint odor hovered about him and drifted to her nostrils, stale but pungent and unpleasant. He didn't outright stink, but she wrinkled her nose.

"I…owe her something." His eyes narrowed, and lines bracketed the hard slash of his lips. "Do you know her forwarding address?" His expression, shadowed by the porch overhang and the overcast skies, appeared deliberately shuttered, but couldn't camouflage his underlying intensity. The question hung in the still air between them.

Maggie's unease blossomed into full-fledged fear, and she slammed the door, hands already scrabbling for the dead bolt, but he'd stuck his foot in the opening and it wouldn't close. "Get out! Go away!" Her voice was shrill and she kicked at his foot, throwing her full weight against the door. Marty began to wail behind her, and she wished she hadn't set her cell phone down in the kitchen.

The guy didn't try to push his way in, just leaned down until his cold, disconcertingly fierce blue eyes were level with Maggie's. "Somebody knows where she is. Tell them to let her know…Bob…stopped by. I'll catch her another time." He didn't sound courteous, or condescending, or even civil, though the words could have been offered in the spirit of any of those sentiments. Heat simmered behind the icy delivery.

Threatening. That was what it was. *Threatening.* Maggie's breath came in small pants as she cowered behind the suddenly insubstantial panel of wood, holding it like a shield and clinging to the illusion that she was holding him off.

He pushed the door, one-handed, enough to free his foot, then let go and she tumbled into it as it slammed, her fingers clumsy as she fumbled the locks closed. She popped up and peered through the peephole again, to make sure he was leaving. He strolled to a white car parked at the curb, and Maggie frantically memorized details. She was lousy with cars, couldn't tell makes or models anyway, especially through the distorting wide-angle lens of the peephole. She darted to the front window and leaned around the sash, irrationally afraid he'd look back and see her. A glance told her the car was not quite new, not quite clean, and not quite big enough for his frame. He squeezed himself in, and the heavens opened with a blinding flash and crack of thunder, the deluge obscuring any identifying features. Like the license plate. He pulled away at a sedate pace, and she saw brake lights flicker briefly before the rain-distorted shape disappeared.

Only then did she hear her children's cries. She spun and ran to them, snatched them up, as panicked as they. They wrapped their tiny arms around her and buried their faces against her shoulders. Guilt crashed through her, and Maggie sprinted for the kitchen, for her cell phone.

She'd endangered her children. And herself, but she didn't let that thought linger. Sure, she'd started out being cautious, but she'd let her guard down too easily. A shudder rolled through her as her imagination produced picture after picture of what could have happened. *Mike will be so angry that I opened the door to a stranger.* Maggie snatched the phone and set the kids on the counter, all of them huddling together as she hit speed dial. The connection took what felt like forever and it rang four times. Just when she thought it would go to voice mail, finally—*thank you, God*—he answered. "Yo, Maggie. Whassup?"

"Oh, Mike!" Her breath caught, and she began to cry. The kids, calm in her arms a moment ago but frightened by her tears, joined their wails to hers. "Some guy at the door—I was so scared—he seemed *evil.* He just left, and—"

"Maggie, get a grip!"

Mike's sharp order cut through her terror as surely as if he'd slapped her, and Maggie stopped babbling. Gulped a breath and let it shudder out. Found enough composure to organize her thoughts, to start over. She pressed Marty to her chest, and awkwardly patted Megan. "This guy came to the door looking for Lannis…"

~

Mike Ross's fingers tightened on his cell phone, and his gut clenched as he listened to Maggie. "He asked for Lannis by name?"

"Yes, but Parker, not Martin, so he didn't know her very well. Everybody she's close to knows she and Ben got married last week."

True. "He owes her money?" That sounded fishy. Lannis got by, paycheck to paycheck, barely above the poverty level. She didn't have money to loan.

"No." Maggie's voice rang with absolute conviction. "He said he owed her *something,* not money."

"Did he give a last name?"

"No, just 'Bob,' and he hesitated before he said it, almost like he stopped himself from saying something else."

"What did he look like?"

"Early to midthirties. Tall, maybe six three, six four. Athletic build. You know, trim but with muscles? Blond hair around three or four inches long, but it looked shaggy, like it needs to be trimmed. Blue eyes…bright blue like Megan's, not pale like Ben's. Really nice clothes, but once I opened the door I noticed they were wrinkled. And the guy was in serious need of deodorant."

The hairs on Mike's forearms stood at attention. "Describe his clothes."

"Navy blue windbreaker with white trim on the shoulders and a designer logo. White button-down shirt, no tie, medium-gray dress slacks, expensive-looking leather loafers. A fancy watch. It may have been a Rolex."

It can't be. But Maggie's description of Robert Davis was dead-on, including the clothes he'd been wearing the night of the arrest. *How in blazes did he get out of jail?* Mike's heart leaped against his ribs and a string of curses galloped through his mind, along with a jumbled list of phone calls he needed to make. ASAP. "He's gone? You're sure?" He knew his voice was sharp, but Maggie's safety mattered more than her feelings.

"Yes…" A note of uncertainty undercut the usual vibrancy of her voice.

"Is he *gone,* Maggie?"

"I don't see his car anymore, but the rain—"

"Get into the bathroom and lock the door. Now." Mike jumped into the truck, transferring the phone to his other hand, grinding the starter. "Do not open it until the police show up, which should be three to five minutes. I'm going to hang up and call them. You call 911 if Davis shows up before they do."

"Davis?" Maggie's voice climbed an octave and lost its strength. "The guy who raped Lannis?"

"Yeah, Mag. I'm on my way." He ended the call and dialed one-handed as he tore down Ben's driveway, and cursed the gate when it glided open at its usual measured, serene tempo, cursed his cell phone when bars disappeared and it searched for service. And searched, and searched.

He slid onto the main road and gunned the engine, slewing around the corner, hydroplaning on the straightaway, praying he'd make it to Maggie and the kids in time.

~

"Police." Thunderous pounding at the front door accompanied a man's shout. "Open up, Mrs. Ross."

Maggie flung the bathroom door open and dashed through the bare living room. Red and blue lights flashed from outside and created a surreal mosaic on the far wall. She scrabbled the locks undone, threw the door open just as a Louisville police officer grabbed for a battering ram from his partner. "I'm—we're—okay." Her voice was breathless, like she'd just run a hundred-yard sprint, and her hands trembled. She knew what Mike's work entailed, but had never been on the receiving end. Relief flooded her, and her appreciation mingled with a swirl of dark emotions she didn't want to examine. Like how frightened she'd been, how vulnerable. Megan ran to her, and Maggie scooped her up, murmuring reassurances she desperately wanted to believe, too.

The two policemen searched the house quickly, efficiently, their focus intense, reassuring, and at the same time, a bit alarming. Once clear, they relaxed, and one spoke into a shoulder mike while the other pulled out paper and pen. Maggie's tremors graduated into full-body shakes, and one of the men grasped her elbows and urged her to the floor. Which was a good thing, because Maggie's legs gave out and she dropped the last few inches to the hardwood. She sucked air into suddenly starving lungs and knew she was hyperventilating, but couldn't stop.

"Are you injured?" His concern, underlaid with kindness, undid her.

She shook her head, then laughed, surprising herself. "N-n-no." Her laughter spiraled into uncontrolled giggles…and she discovered it was impossible to hyperventilate and laugh at the same time. Then tears blurred her vision and rolled down her cheeks. A small, rational part of Maggie's brain shrank in embarrassment, appalled at her hysteria.

The officer lifted Megan out of her arms and said, "It's the adrenaline. You'll be fine in a few minutes." Marty toddled out, held his arms up in silent demand, and the guy snagged him, too.

Just as quickly as they came on, the giggles stopped. One sob escaped, and Maggie swiped at her face. She closed her mouth over any other sounds of weakness, and—finally—her red-headed temper flared, saving her from any more naked, guilt-ridden emotions. She inhaled, clambered upright, took Marty, and said, "What do you need to know?"

She recounted everything to the police, and one of them went to his cruiser to make some radio calls. He turned off the flashing light bars, and an atmosphere of efficient situation management replaced the initial crisis mode. Maggie ripped the tape off a box, dumped its contents on the kitchen counter, and gave it to the kids. They entertained themselves climbing in and out of it, playing peek-a-boo, or seeing if they could both fit inside at one time.

The rumble of the rental truck announced Mike's return. Maggie heard the door slam and his footsteps thud up the porch. He burst in, hair dripping, his eyes a breath away from wild as he rapidly scanned the room, assessing the situation. Marty saw him and screeched, "Da!" then launched into a mad crawl toward him. Megan jumped out from behind the box. "Daddy!" Not to be outdone, she raced to him, shouting, "Mommy and us played hide-and-seek in the bathroom, and then the *policemans* came!"

Mike crouched, braced himself, and caught them. Sent Maggie a hard look over the top of their heads. She lifted her chin. He'd read her the riot act once they got home and the kids were in bed. She knew she'd earned it, but a good, loud fight was exactly what she needed. Lots of yelling and posturing, and enough resilience in their relationship to be safe and angry at the same time. And the making up afterward… She raised one eyebrow the tiniest bit, and Mike's expression softened, a smile ghosting across his face.

The smile disappeared when he asked the cop, "What did you find out?"

"They're still doing a head count, but right now it looks like he's not there."

Mike's mouth tightened. "Maggie, let's get the kids home. By then we should know more." He looked at the remaining boxes. "It's too rainy to finish today. We can get the rest tomorrow in the van."

Maggie picked up her purse and pulled out the key to Lannis's house. The implications of Mike's statement dribbled past the present moment. Her heart ached for Lannis. *What an awful way to end their honeymoon.* But they wouldn't get home till late tomorrow.

Maybe Davis would be back behind bars by then.

She hoped.

~

Paradoxically, freedom did not translate to comfort or ease for Robert Davis. The edginess of incarceration clung to him even after he'd showered in the privacy of his budget motel room, after he'd scrubbed the stench of fear and desperation from his skin, after he'd shaken out and donned his own clothing again.

He'd paid cash and given a false name to the clerk, unwilling to trust his good fortune or the Louisville justice system quite yet. He'd hung out the do-not-disturb sign, jammed the room's lone chair under the doorknob, and clipped the gap in the drapes closed with a slacks hangar. The specter of cops on his tail haunted him, and he'd ordered a pizza instead of going out to eat. With meats of discernible origins and real vegetables in a rainbow of colors, it beat jail food, but he was just as much a prisoner in this room without bars as he had been in his cell a few hours ago. He gritted his teeth, dropped his head, ran his hands through his hair, and fisted his hands at his temples. A wave of nausea struck him and the pizza took a lazy roll in his gut.

He wanted to drive back to the small airport where his airplane was tied down and check on it. Get his suitcase, clean clothes. Cell phone charger. Charts. He hadn't bothered before his side trip to Lannis Parker's house. He'd been too intent on revenge. Now thunderstorms rolled through, one after another, lethal with lightning and torrential rainfall and dangerous flooding. And in spite of what he wanted to do, he was too exhausted to deal with it.

He couldn't deal with the relative safety of his motel room, either.

He couldn't bring himself to strip off his stale, wrinkled clothes for bed. The habit of semi-wakefulness and unrelenting alertness wouldn't abandon him, even though there was no rational need. He couldn't bring himself to turn off the bathroom light, as unfamiliar shadows and sounds from the corridor or the street jerked him out of his fitful doze, over and over. Solitude and privacy should have calmed and restored him, but instead, the lack of male grunts, snores, moans, and farts sharpened his awareness. He could hear his own breath as it eddied through his sinuses. The whispery movement of air grated on his nerves, but he didn't want to turn on the radio or television because they masked the outside noises.

Robert opened his eyes and stared at the ceiling—for maybe the thirtieth time. The cheap motel didn't have a clock radio, and he refused to pick up his watch to check the time. Dawn had to be hours away. But...for the first time in two months he was alone. And realization crept into his mind, the seed of an urge long denied.

There was one thing he felt safe enough to do. His pulse picked up, his mouth went dry. He bared his teeth. Anticipation sensitized his nerve endings, and his fingertips left a hot trail of electricity as they grazed his torso on their way to his belt. He slipped it off with practiced ease, unbuttoned, unzipped...and unleashed his rage, holding his anger in his heart as he caressed himself, holding Lannis Parker's face in his mind. His power fed on her fear, devouring it, savoring her terror, the memory of her humiliation making him hot, hotter, until pain mingled with pleasure...stroking, stoking, smoldering, smoking, until *ohgodohgodohgahhh*—he exploded in the mother of all orgasms.

It went on and on, making up for the weeks of forced celibacy, making up for his impotent rage, making up for his loss of freedom. He shuddered, taut muscles quivering, and groaned a long, inarticulate sound. The aftermath slammed into him as hard as his release had, and he went limp, sinking mindless, boneless, and sated into the mattress. He gasped air into his lungs and rolled heavily to his stomach. His arm flopped to the side, then slid off the bed, and he didn't have the energy to pull it back up. His eyelids drooped, then closed, and his breath soughed out.

His inner power wasn't up to its normal level, but it was well on its way. The pieces of his world clicked back into a semblance of normal, and he was finally able to surrender to the restorative slumber he'd needed for weeks.

He'd put the rest of his life to rights tomorrow.

Chapter Nine

Rᴏʙᴇʀᴛ Dᴀᴠɪѕ ᴛᴀᴘᴘᴇᴅ a pen against the counter in the cramped pilot lounge and tried to contain his frustration. Sunshine teased him through fleeting breaks in the dreary ground fog. He wished he'd acquired his instrument rating so he could file a flight plan and fly out. Or better yet, that he'd left the plane at Bowman. Only a few miles away, across the Ohio River, the Kentucky airport enjoyed clear weather this morning. In either case, he could have been long gone and far away, but no. He was stuck. Trapped by a localized, misplaced cloud.

If he could convince himself the cloud was only a couple of hundred feet thick, or that no one was making an instrument approach at the same time he took off, he might have risked it, but common sense held him captive. Robert clicked the mouse on the computer's aviation page and checked the automated weather reporting system. A glance at the numbers told him the trend of excruciatingly lethargic improvement in visibility continued, and had *finally* accelerated. At this rate, he'd be able to get off the ground in a half hour, or at worst, forty-five minutes.

Robert was more than ready to take off. He'd checked weather between Kentucky and New Jersey, turned in the loaner car, preflighted the plane, and gotten a much-needed change of clothes from his suitcase.

Then he'd walked behind the small flight office and found a Dumpster filled with empty oil cans, broken parts, and packing materials discarded by the maintenance shop. He pitched all the toiletries from the jail into the bin and wiped his hands on his windbreaker, as though the memory of the place still contaminated his skin.

Now, inactivity fueled the edginess that had been his only companion since his release yesterday. He pushed to his feet and decided to wait in the plane. The receptionist said something cordial to him as he went past, and he gave her a distracted nod. The sound of his footsteps dissipated in directionless, muted thuds as he crossed the ramp. Humidity clung to his face and seeped into his jacket. A fine layer of dew decorated the wings and windshield of his plane. He opened the door and leaned in, rifling through his charts one more time. All were neatly folded to show the individual legs of his journey, all in order—Kentucky, Indiana, and Ohio on top, with his East Coast charts underneath—and en-route radio and navigation frequencies noted in careful, precise handwriting on the tablet clipped to his kneeboard.

If he couldn't get airborne before the top of the hour, he'd call for a weather update on the phone. Otherwise, he'd check the newest forecast by radio from the air, but he didn't expect bad weather this early in the day. He should be home by midafternoon, before the worst of the daily thunderstorm buildup, although every minute of delay pushed him closer to the possibility of deadly confrontations with the powerful clouds and the certainty of course deviations. Which would mean he might not make it all the way home today, after all. Disappointment tightened the muscles in his jaw, and he made a conscious effort to relax it.

"Mr. Davis?" A man's voice, laconic and polite, came from behind him.

Robert jerked and bumped his head on the sharp edge of the doorjamb. *A line guy?* He'd paid up after the kid had topped off the fuel tanks, so… He turned and his stomach took a nosedive. All the way to the asphalt of the ramp beneath the plane's wheels. A law enforcement officer, clad in a brown uniform, stood near the baggage door.

"Louisville Metro Corrections made an error."

Dizziness slammed into Robert, and he tightened his grip on the frame. *A mistake?* The implications drove all thought from his mind.

"Step away from the plane, if you would, sir." The man's tone matched the words. Polite. Courteous. Underlaid with steel and authority.

Robert's heart pounded so hard its pulse roared in his ears. *No!* He squeezed his eyes closed, then forced them open. And stared at the business end of the cop's gun. The small hole was trained with steady assurance on his chest, and as he watched, a red light beneath it came on. He glanced down involuntarily and found a corresponding red dot on his shirt.

"Yes." The word cracked through the air, and the courtesy of the previous moment disappeared.

Yes? What was the guy talking about? His fingers went cold, and sweat trickled down one temple. "Ah…" He had to stop to clear his throat, then swallowed over a dry lump of fear. "You don't need the gun." He moved his hands away from his body cautiously, and noted as he did that they were trembling. "Sir."

The man did not lower the weapon. "Well, now, when a person I'm arresting shouts *no*, I'm inclined to believe they are indicating a propensity to resist."

"I did?" Then he understood. The roaring a moment ago had been more than internal. He gave a little shake of his head. Irritation snaked across his shoulders and covered the panic that unfurled inside him. Curses boiled to his lips, but he bit them back even as he welcomed the rage. It muted the wings of the terrified bird caged within his ribs, beating a frantic, useless tattoo against its prison.

Jail. Robert's blood left him and took his breath with it. *A person I'm arresting.* He thought he might pass out. If only the weather had been clear, if only he'd taken off into the clouds, instrument rated or not, if only...

If only he'd never seen Lannis Parker, never spoken with her, never touched her.

The county sheriff's deputy—for that's what he was, now that Robert could read the insignia on his uniform—kept speaking, and the words flickered in and out between bursts of static like a poorly tuned radio station.

"—not considered an escapee—"

"—if you cooperate—"

"—no charges—"

"Hold it." Robert raised a hand, palm open. "Are you saying I have a choice?"

A slight smile lightened the deputy's face, although the gun remained trained on Robert's chest. "I can't rightly say that's the case, but if you come willingly, you're no worse off than you were. If you make it hard, well, the charges will range from resisting arrest to attempted escape."

Robert stared at the gun, knowing the officer had no qualms about using it, knowing he had no choice, at least not a real one. His heart plummeted, dragging the panicked bird into a mire of bleak misery.

He wanted to fight. He wanted to run, to fly. He wanted to go home. He wanted all of this to be over. But what he wanted was at the bottom of anyone's list, especially anyone with a gun. His shoulders sagged. "Let me make arrangements for my plane, get it locked up."

"We'll take care of that." The officer motioned with the gun. "Hands on the plane."

By now, Robert had intimate knowledge of what was expected. Choking back a primal roar of fury mingled with anguish, he turned.

Put his palms on the cool, smooth aluminum skin of his plane's fuselage. Spread his feet. Endured the pat down. Curled his fingers against the nearly uncontrollable urge to use his martial arts skills.

And knew that no matter what the cop had said, he was worse off than he'd been before.

~

Lannis grabbed the suitcase filled with dirty laundry and headed into Ben's house—*no, my house…my house*—and opened it up to dump muddy hiking clothes in front of the washing machine. She started to sort them, then decided she needed to hit the bathroom before exposing her bladder to the stimulus of running water sounds. She didn't normally drink coffee, but they'd stopped at one of those ubiquitous coffee bars for pastries on the way home. The double mocha latte she'd had, complete with whipped cream and chocolate syrup drizzled on top, was now having a predictable effect. She was accustomed to "holding it" while she flew, but with relief only a few steps away…

She headed through the house, pausing to open the living room drapes on the way, and noticed a piece of paper on the kitchen table, weighted on one corner with the salt shaker. She picked it up, scanned it, and wrinkled her forehead. "Ben." She raised her voice, as he was still in the garage unloading their camping gear.

"Yeah?" His answer was muffled.

"Mike left a note for you, wants you to call him ASAP." Lannis started walking toward the bathroom.

"Okay. I'll get to it in a few minutes."

She stopped. "The ASAP is underlined twice," she yelled.

The door to the garage opened and he appeared, hand outstretched. He already had his cell phone out and hit a button, probably speed dial, while he asked, "Does it say anything else?"

"No." Lannis walked back and handed the note to him, her errand forgotten. She marveled at the change in Ben. Cheerful whistling and relaxed muscles disappeared, replaced in less than a breath with the impassive focus she knew so well. His game face. Contentment curled through her, alongside her curiosity. She, Lannis Renee Parker Martin, was intimately acquainted with Ben's *non*-game face, and currently held the highest-ranking position as the stimulus likely to create it. She leaned on the counter and smiled at him.

"It's me." Ben transferred the phone to his other ear and grabbed a pen out of the squatty, garishly glazed clay cylinder he'd made in junior high.

Lannis shoved the notepad to him, and he raised his gaze, softened it, and winked at her.

"Just walked in the door." He returned his full attention to Mike. "*What?*" He straightened and shot a quick, guarded glance at Lannis. "When?"

Her smile faded, and she pushed away from the counter. Did he have to go back out on the undercover thing? Right now? He still had four days of vacation, and his boss had promised—

"This morning? You're sure?"

He turned slightly away from her, and Lannis's stomach dropped. She crossed her arms and told herself to get a grip. But she didn't usually get vibes like this from Ben. She had no idea what was going on, but his body language screamed that it had to do with her. Somehow.

Mike kept talking, and Ben grew so still Lannis couldn't see him breathe. His profile took on a hard, fierce edge, and even in his stillness, he appeared ready for war. He made an indeterminate sound, part question, part command. Lannis's heart clenched, and she dug her fingernails into the palms of her hands.

"She okay?" At Mike's answer, Ben's ferocity diminished and his unearthly stillness vanished. He listened for another few seconds, and the tension eased from his shoulders. "You would have called me, right?" Ben exhaled, long and quiet, and said, "Thanks, buddy. Appreciate it."

He snapped the phone closed and turned back to Lannis, stuck an arm out, and pulled her to his side. She leaned into him.

"Metro Corrections released Robert Davis yesterday afternoon by mistake."

Panic raced through Lannis, and she stiffened.

"They've got him back in custody." He gave her shoulder a little jiggle. "It's okay, darlin'."

"How?" The strangled sound squeezed its way past paralyzed vocal cords.

He shrugged. "Name mix-up, as far as anyone can tell. The guy was supposed to release a Robert B. Daviess. It's close, real close." He set her away from him and studied her face. "You're safe, Lannis. Mike would've called me at the lake if you were in danger."

Lannis gulped a breath and nodded. Yes. Yes, Mike would have called, even on their honeymoon. A shudder rolled through her and she wrapped her arms around Ben. She fought with her emotions, struggling to rein in the fear. Suddenly anger blossomed in her chest, fury that Davis had intruded on another moment in her life, their lives.

"He did it on purpose, didn't he?" She nearly sputtered the words, and Ben grasped her upper arm.

"No, Lannis. Think about it." Patience laced his voice. "Mike said Davis didn't know why he'd been released, but he didn't ask, either. The guy didn't look the gift horse in the mouth, just took what was presented at face value."

His logic filtered through Lannis's anger, and her ire faded. She sagged against him and sighed. "I guess…yeah, I suppose that makes sense."

"Are you okay?" Ben didn't wait long for an answer. "Because there's another part you need to know."

Dread gathered in Lannis's belly, but she'd found her anchor again. She nodded into his chest and gripped the back of his shirt. Ben never coddled her, never kept truth from her. It was a hard policy, but a necessary one.

"Davis went to your rental house and left a threat with Maggie." Ben tightened his hold on her when she gasped. "Before you get upset, Maggie's okay, and if it hadn't been for that, Davis would have been back in New Jersey by now. No one would've known he was out of jail, no one would've been looking for him. As it was, they caught him at his plane this morning, just before the weather cleared."

Her ears roared, and she flushed hot and, inexplicably, cold at the same time. She opened her mouth, not knowing what she intended to say, then closed it because there was nothing *to* say. Dear God…

"M-Maggie's okay?" Her voice wavered, but she didn't care. She didn't have to impress Ben with a macho act.

"She's fine."

A twinge of guilt teased Lannis, but she rejected it as quickly as she recognized it. Robert Davis bore all the responsibility here, not her. But she would talk to Maggie, make sure she was really "fine," and be a good listener if Maggie needed one.

All's well that ends well. That was about the most positive conclusion she could draw from the situation, and Lannis decided to take Ben's lead. It had happened, it was over, no harm done. Plenty of foul, absolutely, but no harm.

She hoped, for Maggie's sake.

Chapter Ten

"Ben, I can't do this over the phone. I need to go home." Lannis turned from the red pepper she'd just sliced and put the kitchen knife down. He was intent on lighting the grill and didn't answer for a moment. There was something wrong with the igniter, and he leaned down to tinker with it. His athletic shorts did nothing to hide the well-defined muscles beneath them, and his T-shirt, ragged and covered with old paint splotches, did a fine job of showcasing his truly magnificent shoulders, biceps, and triceps. She drank in the sight of him, all tanned and strong and hers. Happiness filled her. Again. Ben's laid-back approach to problems was rubbing off on her. She hadn't been this relaxed in…she didn't know how long.

To be distracted or not be distracted, that was the question.

Lannis sighed. Not yet. But he was a temptation.

The fire caught with a soft whoosh, and Ben faced her. "You can break in your new car, drive up this weekend." He crooked an eyebrow at her.

"Yeah, that's what I was thinking." It was time her mom and sister knew about the rape.

He'd been reassigned from his undercover op, but had to go back to wherever it had taken place to tie up loose ends.

"Are you okay to do that on your own?" He eyed the stack of red pepper slices, then padded across the stone patio in his bare feet and pilfered one.

Lannis knew he didn't mean the drive. He meant the conversation. The disclosure. A sliver of apprehension crept up her spine. "Yes," she answered, trying to convince herself, too.

They'd spent the last four days getting her boxes unpacked, getting her a car and a cell phone. *Getting it on…* A thrill chased the apprehension away and her face warmed at the memories.

They could have put off some of the settling-in chores and gone to visit her mom together, but Lannis had wanted the precious days with Ben. And the nights. She hadn't known she could fall even more deeply love with him, but each night as he laid her bare to his scrutiny, then held her tenderly while he murmured his love and took her over the edge, she did.

"Yes," she said again and smiled at him. "I'll be okay."

"Do you want to call your mom now, or after supper?"

Typical Ben. "Accountability" was his middle name. Lannis tossed him another slice of red pepper. "After. Get those steaks on, big boy. Everything else is about ready." A pang of loss shimmered through her heart. The last evening of their honeymoon, their last evening together for a while. He'd already begun to pack, and the plan was for her to drop him at the airport on her way to work tomorrow. He wouldn't tell her where he was headed, only that Mike would get in touch with him if she needed.

Aw, hell. The steaks could wait. She wanted a distraction.

She walked over to the grill and shut it off. Her smart husband didn't miss a beat, didn't ask questions, just engulfed her hand in his and led her to bed.

~

Lannis stopped three times during the five-hour drive, two stops more than necessary, and yes, she dawdled at the truck stops, gawking at displays of weird stuff that couldn't be found anywhere else, except maybe carnivals. She'd admit it. She'd even admit to using her new car's break-in process as the scapegoat. By taking back roads instead of interstate, she'd managed to stretch the drive out to nearly six hours.

Now, as she turned onto the street and approached the house she'd grown up in, Lannis knew crunch time had come. She breathed a prayer that the next twenty-four hours would go well.

Her relationship with her family, newly restored after more than four years of estrangement, still felt fragile and tenuous. Months of treading with delicate caution around a minefield of unasked questions, unspoken opinions, unresolved misunderstandings—all in the interest of constructing a safe framework for their interactions— had taken its toll. She could have told them about the rape when she'd allowed them back into her life, but she'd had too much to deal with at the time. The beating, the subsequent surgery—and her terror that her success in AA would be washed away by narcotics post-op. Fears for Ben's safety. Ending her self-imposed exile.

Yeah, Lannis could cut herself a break. She just hadn't been ready to disclose to her mom. Or Lynette. Definitely not Rich. She shuddered. Nope. When she had finally gone home, her brother-in-law had barely veiled his hostility out of respect for his wife's wishes, but made it clear to Lannis that she'd already hurt her little sister badly and he wouldn't tolerate another round. Nor would he allow access to either Lynette or Carly, her two-year-old niece, if Lannis fell off the wagon—no matter what Lynette wanted. He'd softened once they got to know each other, but still…

Planning for the wedding smoothed over some of the awkward times in the last few months—and kept things superficial. Everything she'd learned in AA prodded her to face the reality of her life. She needed to stir up the stagnant pond of secrets and let fresh, healing water flow into her relationships. It might hurt—heck, it *would* hurt—but Lannis saw with sudden clarity that maintaining her boundary on this issue, especially now, imprisoned more than protected her.

She parked her car, took a deep breath, and got out. The slam of her door brought Lynette to the front of the house, and she held the drape to the side, waving at Lannis from the front window. Lynette grinned and pointed at the car, then gave her a thumbs-up. Lannis smiled back and stretched, then reached inside for her travel bag. Carly hadn't appeared, and Lannis deduced she must be down for a nap. Usually her toddler's compact body bounced in unrestrained enthusiasm on the couch when Auntie Lannie showed up, her small hands leaving drool-smeared prints on the window. Lannis hadn't visited often, but found she missed the child's zealous greeting.

"How was the honeymoon?" Lynette kept her voice soft as she opened the door.

Lannis set her bag on the wood floor in the entryway and gave Lynette a hug. "It was great, sis. We had a cozy little cabin right on the shoreline. No phones, no schedule." She heard wistfulness in her voice and deliberately changed the subject. "How do you like my new car?"

"I love the color! When do I get a ride?"

Lannis glanced upstairs. "After Carly wakes up?" The house was almost tomb-like in its silence. "Mom's still at work, right? Where's Rich?"

"She'll be home in an hour or so. Rich went to the store. Do you want to put your stuff away, then come help me with dinner before the tornado wakes up?"

Lannis grinned. "Tornado" was right. It amazed her how many adults it took to watch over one miniature person. "Sure." She snagged her bag and took the steps two at a time. She tossed the duffel on the twin bed in her old room and slipped softly down the stairs to the kitchen.

She and Lynette laughed and traded jokes about married life while they got potatoes in the oven and made a salad. Rich came back with a refilled propane tank for the grill and set about hooking it up. Carly woke and called for her mama from her crib with increasing insistence and decreasing patience, so Lynette dried her hands and went to get her. Murmurs of the mother and child reunion floated down the stairs, and Lannis smiled. She looked around. There was nothing left to do for supper, so she wandered outside and inhaled the evening's flower-scented air. A fine, underlying hum of tension wormed its way into her consciousness. She'd been able to ignore it by keeping busy, but she couldn't now that she was still. She shook her hands, trying to rid her skin of the discomfiting crawl of anxiety.

She heard her mom's car pull into the driveway out front, and the slam of the car door. A moment later, Millie poked her head out the sliding door, and Rich gave his mother-in-law a quick hug and a peck on the cheek. He squeezed past Millie and went inside. Millie's face lit up when she spotted Lannis and she gave her a distracted wave, then disappeared, probably to change out of her work clothes. Rich's deep voice mingled with Millie's soft alto, and their laughter drifted on the air.

A pang of longing surprised Lannis. They—her mom, Lynette, and Rich—all shared an easy camaraderie that Lannis envied, falling into rhythms and patterns polished by time and familiarity. She missed this so much, yet still saw herself as an outsider in her own family. Once she'd said what she came here to say, would she feel closer to them, or farther away?

Tension gripped her midsection. She pasted a smile on her face, went in and borrowed Carly from her parents, then took her out to the swing set Millie had bought a couple of months ago. The toddler's uninhibited joy was the perfect therapy. Her giggles were contagious, and Lannis embraced the reprieve gratefully, though she knew it was temporary.

Dinner came and went, and Lannis forced herself to laugh and eat, even though her stomach wanted to revolt. Not long afterward, Lynette put Carly down for the night. Millie poured a glass of wine for herself and sighed as she sank into a lawn chair. Lannis had a moment of intense longing for wine, too, but pushed the thought aside and fixed a glass of ice water, mostly to have something for her hands to do while she talked. She crushed a sprig of mint from the herb garden, dipped it in sugar, and set it atop the ice. It was impossible to slow her galloping heart or still her trembling fingers. Time had run out. She couldn't put off the uncomfortable task any longer.

She took a seat across from Millie and sent her mother a smile that felt pretty anemic and probably looked that way, but Millie didn't pick up on it, just put her feet up on a chunk of log that doubled as a planter. Rich and Lynette appeared, and Lannis caught the quick glance Rich sent at her glass, his assessment of its contents. If she'd had enough energy, she might have felt a spurt of righteous anger, but she didn't. She supposed she deserved it, a simple consequence of bad decisions she'd made long before Rich even met her, but yearning for Ben's acceptance rolled through her, and she tightened her grip on the glass.

"It's a lovely evening," Millie murmured. She turned her head and returned Lannis's smile. "I'm glad you had time to come visit. We didn't get to spend nearly enough time together before the wedding."

A lawn chair squeaked as Lynette sat, and another scraped across the stone patio as Rich dragged it next to Lynette's. He sat down and glanced at his wife, patted his thighs, and grasped her feet when she lifted them to his lap. They shared an intimate look as he began to massage her feet.

"We have something to tell you." Lynette blushed, looking even younger and prettier as she spoke. Rich patted her foot, the gesture proprietary, comforting, and encouraging all at the same time. Lynette beamed. "We're going to have another baby!"

"Wha—! Lynnie! Rich!" Millie's wine sloshed over the edge of the glass as she vaulted up from her chair. "How wonderful! When?" She set the wine down and embraced them both.

Lannis froze. *Oh, no.* How could she ruin their happiness with news of the trial? She grabbed a napkin from the dispenser on the table and sopped up Millie's wine…and had an absurd compulsion to stuff the sodden paper in her mouth and suck the alcohol from it. She closed her hand over the napkin in a convulsive movement, then turned and pitched it across the yard toward the commercial trash bin Millie shared with her next-door neighbor. It landed short, but she didn't make a move to pick it up. She scrubbed her hands on her jeans, and, acutely aware of her hesitation, stepped around the table to join in the group hug. *Please don't notice.* She forced words of congratulation out of her mouth, trying to sound as excited as Millie.

"Middle of February." Lynette's reply was muffled as she spoke into Millie's embrace.

Lannis stepped back, grasped Rich's hand, gave it a quick pump. "Congratulations, guys." Her stomach responded as if she were on a carnival ride, and she swallowed against a wave of nausea. Lynette and Millie launched into a discussion of morning sickness—it hadn't hit yet—and maternity clothes—Lynette still had the ones from her pregnancy with Carly. Rich leaned back, a satisfied expression on his face, and made no effort to join the conversation.

Lannis stuffed her hands into the back pockets of her cargo pants and hoped her silence didn't sound as loud to everyone else as it did to her. She made some more interested noises—she was interested, after all—but felt at a loss about what to say. None of her friends had experienced pregnancy, and Lannis had missed Lynette's first one. She truly had no idea what to talk about, so took the opportunity to go pick up the discarded napkin and dispose of it properly. By the time she sat down, Millie had returned to her lawn chair and a contented silence fell over the group.

Rather, contentment blanketed the trio who lived in Ohio. Jitters spread from Lannis's stomach to her limbs, and she grabbed one knee to keep it from bouncing. "I have some news, too," she blurted. Appalled, she clamped her mouth shut as three heads swiveled to give her the attention she'd just invited.

Millie's eyes lit up. "Are you pregnant, too?"

Lynette squealed. "That'd be so cool! Close cousins!"

Lannis shook her head, and a hysterical bubble of laughter worked its way north. "No! No, I'm not pregnant!" A drop of sweat trickled between her breasts, and she suppressed the urge to giggle. Warmth rushed up her neck and into her cheeks. "It's a little soon for that!"

"Well, you and Ben wouldn't be the first to anticipate your marriage vows," Millie said tartly. She took a sip of her wine. "What's your news?"

Mom, this is hard enough without you drinking in front of me. Lannis slammed her mind on the thought. Alcohol was her problem, not Millie's, and she had no right demand to anyone else's abstinence. She took a deep, shuddering breath and gripped her water glass, her hand slipping on the drops of condensation decorating the outside. "There's a trial coming up, and I'm involved. In fact, I'm the plaintiff."

"You're suing somebody?" Rich straightened, and his eyes darkened.

"Not like a lawsuit. It's a criminal trial." If she hadn't gained their full attention before, she certainly had now.

"I don't understand." Millie wore an expression of bafflement.

Lynette was a bit quicker. "Somebody did something to you?" Her eyes widened, and concern sharpened her features. "A criminal?"

"Yes." The sound of Lannis's voice hung in the air as she scrambled for a way to say it gently. But there was no way to soften the blow. She faced Millie. "Mom, remember when I was hurt and you came to the hospital?"

Millie's eyes brightened. "Of course. Is it his trial?" She frowned. "I thought you said he already went to prison, though."

"No. I mean, yes." Lannis huffed a breath of frustration. King LeMasters had saved Kentucky the cost of a trial after a reality check with the public defender. "Yes, that's all over and done. This is something else. The reason I cut off contact with you years ago. Remember, I told you I didn't want to talk about it?" Her mom had accepted her reticence, content with baby steps toward reconciliation—all Lannis was capable of offering at the time.

Millie nodded, her wine forgotten. "What happened?" she whispered.

Lannis leaned forward and took her mom's hands in hers. "I was raped." Her heart thumped hard, then settled into a gallop even as it twisted in compassion for her mother. Putting herself in her mom's shoes, Lannis would be devastated if her child withheld a crisis of this magnitude from her.

Millie gasped and her face paled. "Oh, baby…"

Lynette's chair clattered on the rocks as she leaped up. She wailed, a primal sound of anguish, and flung herself at Lannis.

"Are you sure?" Millie asked.

Lannis had let one of Millie's hands go so she could catch Lynette, bracing one leg against the planter. She swung her head back to gape at her mom. "Am I *sure*?" She patted Lynette awkwardly and wondered if she'd lost her grip on the English language.

Her mom nodded. "Are you sure it was rape?" She fluttered her free hand. "Sometimes a woman has regrets after—"

"Mom!" Lannis's voice had a wheezy tone, not too different than it had after LeMasters kicked her. Pain, jagged and sharp, sliced through her heart. "How can you say that?" Lannis reeled at the inference. Of all the potential responses she'd imagined, she hadn't expected this. *Does Mom really think I'm capable of ruining someone's life over morning-after angst?* Did Millie see her as that shallow and self-centered?

Lynette turned her face to Millie, scrubbing her tears on Lannis's shirt as she did. "If that's what she says, that's what happened, Mom!" she said hotly. Then, as abruptly as she'd embraced Lannis, she squeaked and the warmth of her arms was plucked away.

Lannis looked up. Rich glowered at her over Lynette's head. He clasped his wife to his side, his gaze shooting daggers at Lannis. "You have done nothing but manipulate and upset Lynette since you came back into her life. I don't buy your story about staying sober, and I don't buy this bullshit. You are a lying, vindictive bitch, and you're on a vendetta to skewer some poor sap."

Lynette looked up at her husband, her mouth an *O* of shock, then burst into tears again and pushed at his chest.

A red haze of fury darkened Lannis's vision, and she stood in a fluid movement, letting go of Millie's other hand. The instinct to strike out, to defend herself, to return pain for pain flooded her. She curled her hands into fists and took a breath, the flower-scented air suddenly cloying—and the memory of Ben's lazy voice cut through the haze of her anger. *The only person you're responsible for is you. You can't choreograph anyone else's feelings. Let 'em be, and take care of yourself.*

She let out her pent-up breath and released her fists, one finger at a time. This wasn't worth a feud, and the last thing she wanted to do was create a rift between Rich and Lynette. She'd always known that not everyone would be sympathetic. Hence, her initial failure to report the assault. And hence her reluctance to risk reactions like this by making the attack known, if only in private and only in general terms.

"Mom, Rich…" The shards of pain in her heart gave way to a great shattering, and she braced to shelter herself from the wave of agony. "The justice system is too overworked to bother with unsubstantiated cases. It happened—it *really* happened"—she shot a glance at Millie—"and there is hard evidence that the guy actually did it." She locked onto Rich's gaze and held it without wavering. "He's not a poor sap. He's a predator who gets his jollies by hurting women." She shrugged. "He may walk. There's no guarantee that the trial will go my way, but that doesn't mean the assault didn't happen."

She shifted her gaze to Lynette. "It's okay, Lynnie. *I'm* okay." Her voice softened. "Honey, don't let this come between you and Rich. He's entitled to his opinion, and the truth is, I've earned a lot of his ill will. I've made mistakes and I've hurt you. I'm sorry. I'm going to keep trying to make it up to you." Lannis stepped forward and opened her arms. She glanced at Rich and lifted an eyebrow. He scowled but loosened his grip on Lynette, who flew into Lannis's embrace. "Hush, sis. I know you just found out, so it's fresh pain for you, but it's over and I've recovered." She leaned back and searched Lynette's eyes. "I'm all right."

Lynette hiccupped and nodded.

"Good. You need to take care of yourself and the baby." Lannis smiled, a tremulous effort, but it was enough to elicit a wobbly one from Lynette. She gave her sister a gentle push toward Rich, dropped her arms to her side, and turned to Millie. "All things considered, I think it's best if I head back home tonight."

Millie made an inarticulate sound that could mean anything. Protest at Lannis's decision to leave? Or relief? Whatever she intended to convey, the significance of her ensuing silence spoke louder than empty words or angry recriminations.

Lannis picked up Lynette's forgotten chair and righted it, touched Millie's shoulder, and walked to the sliding door. She turned and said, "Give Carly a big hug for me," then went to gather her things.

She didn't bother with the trunk, just pitched her bag in the foot well of the front seat. Her hands trembled as she fit the key into the ignition, and it took her two tries to slip it home. No one came to the front of the house to wave good-bye, and Lannis's heart ached with the added rejection. Her car purred to life, and she pulled away from the curb, careful to check several times for traffic through tear-blurred eyes. A few blocks later, the sob she'd been fighting burst forth, and she guided the car blindly to the side of the street. She bent her forehead to the steering wheel and let the tears flow, her body shaking from the force of her weeping. Even grief of that scale couldn't sustain extended tears, and after a time, her distress shuddered to a standstill. She swiped the back of her hand beneath her nose, sniffed, and muttered, "Well, that went well." The sarcasm lent a bit of starch to her spine, and she sat back, getting her bearings.

She'd stopped in front of a strip of small businesses. A dry cleaners, closed for the day. A combination card shop and bookstore, still open. And a liquor store, neon sign glowing bright in the dusk.

Just like that, the bone-deep craving for a drink slapped her in the face, in her gut, and her fingers nearly twitched with the urge to get her hands on a bottle. "Oh God…" She moaned. *Did I do that on purpose?* She clutched the steering wheel and sat paralyzed for several long moments, then sent a jerky look to the street and pulled out.

She clenched her teeth and held her breath, then drove…straight ahead past the strip mall, down the street toward the interstate. Glad her gas tank was full, and that she'd surpassed the engine break-in miles, Lannis put mental blinders on, her only focus to get on the interstate and stay on it until she got home.

Home.

She hiccupped. Ben was busy, but she could call him if she needed. Oh, how she needed… A ringing deep in one of the pockets of her cargo pants startled her, and she jumped. Her cell phone, the one Ben insisted that she carry. She'd already forgotten she had it. She scrabbled one hand past the flap of the pocket and pulled the phone out, flipping it open without looking at the display.

"Hello?" Her heart caught in her throat when she realized it might be her mom, or Lynette, and she regretted not checking caller ID. It was too late now. She wouldn't hang up like a coward.

"Is Clarence there?" It was a woman, her voice old and querulous.

"Who?" Lannis said, heat flooding her face at the stupidity of her answer. "Uh, I mean, you have the wrong number, ma'am."

"Who is this?" the woman demanded. "Where's Clarence?"

Lannis held the phone away from her ear and shot a disbelieving glance at it. She replaced it and said, "You called this number in error, ma'am. Try again."

The woman groused for a moment longer, then hung up. A burst of rusty laughter escaped Lannis, and tension eased from her shoulders. *An unlikely angel?* She wouldn't go quite that far, but the interruption couldn't have come at a more opportune moment.

The crisis had passed, and she'd come through it unscathed instead of undone. Like she often said about a flight student's early landing attempts, it wasn't a thing of beauty, but it was good enough. The sharp edge of pain of thirty minutes ago began to abate.

She took a shuddering breath. Lannis had secretly hoped for so much more from her mom. Even from Rich. Grateful for Lynette's support but distressed at the potential rift in her sister's marriage, Lannis grieved for what could have been.

She had over four hours of driving left. Lannis settled in to let the feelings roll through her. A discomfiting technique, it remained the most effective method for her to get past her distress. Experience had taught her not to avoid it.

The pain would diminish, and she'd always have a hole in her heart from what had just transpired. But she wasn't trapped by her circumstances anymore. Free to choose, she turned her mind toward her heart's desire, and chose the way of peace, not vengeance; of love, not bitterness.

And a tendril of serenity wrapped itself around the gaping chasm in her heart.

Chapter Eleven

July

SHOWTIME. The trial had been delayed twice, but the day had finally arrived.

Lannis smoothed her new blouse and took one last glance in the mirror. The classic lines of her slacks were offset by contemporary details, and she shrugged the matching jacket on, glad for Maggie's eye for fashion. Their foray to the malls the other day had netted the sage-green linen suit, although they'd had a brief battle of wills regarding which section of the store to shop. Maggie had made a beeline for the dresses and skirted suits. Lannis dug in her heels, unable to verbalize her horror at the prospect of baring her legs to Robert Davis's leer in court. It didn't matter how traditional and non-revealing they were; panic had blindsided her as racks of dresses swallowed Maggie's petite frame.

"You look great, darlin'." Ben planted a damp kiss on her cheek as he passed her on his way from the shower. His nearly shoulder-length hair lent him a roguish, dangerous air. Her personal pirate. A smile tugged her lips upward, but disappeared almost as quickly as it came.

The mirror showed an almost too-buttoned-up young woman, somber and pale. Lannis made a noise of disgust and slapped some color into her cheeks. Pete had told her to dress conservatively for court, and she had. But she didn't need to look like a vampire. Ground training for her new job had kept her inside far more than usual, so the meager start she'd gotten on a summertime tan had faded. Combined with anticipation of today's events, a vampire was exactly what she resembled.

She put a hand to the neck of the pale green silk blouse, and wondered if she should undo the top button. It would look fine, not at all risqué or sloppy. Familiar panic began to well in her chest, and she dropped her hand to her side. *Okay, then. Buttoned to the gills, it is.*

Ben reappeared behind her, his hair slicked back into a tidy ponytail and secured with a black elastic hair band. Still prepared to go back undercover if needed, he wouldn't return to his usual hairstyle until cleared. He finished tucking his shirt into dress slacks, the ends of his tie hanging loose on either side of his neck. He caught her gaze in the mirror. "You'll do fine, Lannis. Relax." He stood behind her and put his hands on her shoulders. "Be yourself."

Lannis smiled again, and this one stuck. *Be myself, huh?* Maggie's bewildered response to Lannis's stubborn streak at the mall had highlighted what Lannis privately referred to as her "personal weirdness." That would go over well in court. *Not.*

Ben leaned down to nuzzle and kiss her neck, and a delicate flush heated her skin as she remembered his lovemaking of the night before. He stepped back and began working on his tie, the molten look in his eyes telling her he was thinking the same thing.

The distraction worked. Tension uncoiled in her back, and she turned her attention to the trial and her part in it. Weird or not, she had a job to do, and Lannis focused on her testimony. Pete Delaney had coached her a few days ago, and she felt prepared enough to take the stand, to say in public the words she'd only uttered aloud twice. That wouldn't be easy, but the hard part would be seeing Robert Davis again. No, the hardest part would be claiming her voice while in his presence. He sucked her breath from her lungs with nothing more than a look, and since he was acting as his own attorney, he would question her directly, with only air molecules separating them.

She gave a moment's gratitude for the University of Louisville intern's work, which had netted an impersonal exchange of papers rather than the face-to-face deposition Davis had angled for nearly two months ago.

Lannis straightened her spine and drew her shoulders back. She had done everything she could to prepare. Pete had warned her the jury might free Davis, and she told herself she was ready for that possibility. Whatever happened, after today, or at worst, after tomorrow, she'd never have to think about Robert Davis again. Ever.

"Ben," she said. "I'm ready. Let's go."

~

Robert Davis tugged his tie into place, then leaned over to buff his Guccis one more time with the sleeve of his suit jacket. His jailhouse haircut left a lot to be desired, but the inmate entrusted with barbering had done the best he could. At least it was even, and didn't look like a hatchet job. Robert dismissed his concerns about his hair. Overall, he looked like what he was…or at least what he wanted the jury to see. A successful lawyer. Intelligent, charming, and wrongly accused. *Oh, yeah. Especially the wrongly accused part.* So innocuous no one would believe Lannis Parker, no one could believe him capable of such violence. He smiled, visualizing Ted Bundy.

He had schmoozed the jurors during the selection process this morning, and relished the opportunity to continue playing them while he decimated Ms. Parker on the stand. Robert managed to get four men on the six-person panel. Three out of the four were blue-collar, and the fourth a college student whose posture and attitude screamed his displeasure at being here. One woman was an accountant and kept sneaking glances at her watch. The other, a reticent, middle-aged black woman, was a wild card, but Robert counted on her natural reserve to keep her from being much of an influence.

Sparring with the young DA as they haggled over potential jurors had made his blood sing. It was the first time he'd felt truly alive for three months, and he had to rein in his excitement over how close he was to freedom. It wouldn't sit well with the jury. He smiled into the burnished metal mirror. This acting job had to be Oscar-worthy, or he'd spend the next several years in prison. He'd have to be careful. He craved, with a bone-deep and burning desire, to rip Lannis apart—figuratively, if not physically—to humiliate her, make her doubt her own testimony and tangle her in her own words from the first moment of the trial until the conclusion: His acquittal. A shudder ran up his spine. It *had* to result in acquittal; he couldn't countenance a conviction.

If he let the jury see his rage, he'd lose his freedom. It would mess with her mind if he pretended at the gallant, generous, and forgiving gentleman held at the mercy of an unbalanced, unreliable, conniving woman. Or he could hide his fury from the jury, and let her see it during questioning. That approach had its risks, though. The judge might pick up on it, although if they acquitted him, it didn't matter. But if—and the *if* made his blood run cold—if he were convicted, the judge had some leeway in his sentence. He couldn't afford to alienate the judge.

He made his decision. Raising his eyebrows, he affected an expression of benign bewilderment at his unnecessary incarceration, and let the attitude of benevolence settle into his shoulders.

The bailiff called his name, and Robert turned, ready to try the most important case of his life.

He strode into the courtroom as though he owned it, and couldn't resist searching for his accuser.

His first glimpse of Lannis Parker pleased him. She'd lost weight. Robert would know. He remembered the athletic sturdiness of her body and her strength as she fought him. While not exactly ill, she had a frailty about her that was new. Her skin was wan, her complexion pasty in contrast to the ruddy health she'd radiated the night she'd set him up, the night he'd been arrested. His lips thinned at the memory.

Her pantsuit, in a shade of green that reminded him of what passed as vegetables in jail, conferred a sense of understated elegance…although the thinness of her wrists poking out of the sleeves of the jacket shot her right past elegant to fragile. She looked worse than he did.

Piece of cake. With any luck, he'd be home tomorrow. Robert covered a smirk as he took his place and set his notes on the table. He glanced at her sideways, not lingering, but enough to see Ms. Parker avoiding him with all the intensity of a student who'd failed to do her homework. The judge entered, and the bailiff called court to order. Robert pulled his attention forward, schooling his expression as he did. Time to get to work.

~

Every nerve in Lannis's body screeched to alert when Robert Davis walked into the courtroom, and her breath stalled for a long moment. She glimpsed his suit, his shoes as he passed by, and ducked her head so she wouldn't have to see him. Yet. She knew she had to face him, but if she could at least get her composure first…

She studied the yellow legal pad on the table in front of her, then picked up the pen next to it and began to doodle. Her hand shook, though, and she put the pen down, clasped her hands in her lap. For now, the only defense she could employ was avoidance.

Pete Delaney and Davis quibbled over Dutch Bennett's testimony, and ended up with Dutch's assertion that her allegations, while unsubstantiated with physical evidence, had enough of a ring of truth for him to follow up. Pete entered Louisville Air's record of Davis's fueling and overnight tie-down charges for the date of the attack. Davis countered with the lack of substantive evidence, and Lannis began to worry that it might be enough to provide the reasonable doubt needed for acquittal. She picked up the pen and gripped it tighter. She sent up a silent prayer, although she couldn't articulate her plea. Strength maybe, and courage. She needed both.

Pete brought experts in, and they discussed typical responses to rape, talked about post-traumatic stress disorder. Both the experts deflected Davis's attempts to discredit them, and her hopes rose again.

Then it was Ben's turn as a witness. Lannis raised her head and caught his gaze as he swore his oath. He acknowledged her with the barest flicker of his eyes, then returned his full attention to Pete. He had his cop face on and used his cop voice, and she felt safer with him in the room. His confidence was contagious, and hope buoyed deep within Lannis's heart.

Lannis knew the answers to all the questions Pete posed, and made tiny check marks on the paper as he led Ben through the events leading up to Davis's arrest.

What were his credentials? He listed an impressive array of training events and experience in his quiet, yet authoritative manner.

Yes, he'd called Dutch Bennett.

Why? Lannis Parker was a friend, and he thought he could help.

Yes, he was an agent for the Drug Enforcement Agency, and routinely kept his wire, transmitter, and recorder in his car.

Yes, he'd outfitted Lannis Parker with them.

Yes, he'd coached her regarding what Robert Davis needed to say on tape.

No, he hadn't told her what to say; how could he? He was not a witness to the crime.

Yes, the proper protocols had been followed for the tracking of evidence. A long, boring recitation followed and culminated with the entering of the recording into the court's evidence.

Pete Delaney thanked Ben and sat down next to Lannis.

Davis uncoiled himself from his chair, and this time Lannis could not tear her gaze from him, following him in hypnotized fascination as he approached Ben. His gait was fluid and unhurried, yet Lannis sensed an undercurrent of…threat? Yes, that was it. Davis looked like a panther stalking his prey, and she couldn't repress a shiver.

Ben hadn't looked at her since he took the stand, and Lannis marveled at his focus, his calm. With a small jolt, she realized this was the first time Ben would speak to the man who'd raped her, and she saw his lips thin as he waited for the cross-examination.

When Davis spoke, he didn't waste time on formalities. "Mr. Martin, why did you give credence to Ms. Parker's allegations?"

~

Ben took a slow breath. Why, indeed? "Because she's never given me reason to doubt her. She's never lied or stretched the truth."

"Do you wire everyone who has a story?" Davis's expression was bland, but his eyes flashed with challenge, and Ben sent him a severe look.

"No. Of course not. Only people whose testimony is credible, or who are in a position to provide evidence."

"You felt she could provide evidence about a crime you did not witness and she did not report? That doesn't sound so credible to me. It sounds like someone with a vendetta, at the least misguided, perhaps even unbalanced."

Pete Delaney shot to his feet before Davis finished. "Objection. Conjecture."

"Sustained. Strike Mr. Davis's remark from the record." The judge leveled a warning glare at him. "Stick to the facts, Counselor."

Davis meekly inclined his head to the judge and turned back to Ben with a slight shrug, his palms open and facing up. "Yes, Your Honor," he said, but the canny look in his eyes told Ben the man harbored no remorse. Davis had shifted slightly so the jury could see his posture, but not his eyes. The jab at Lannis's credibility would linger in the jurors' minds no matter what the judge said, and Ben knew it as well as Davis did. "Can you explain why you wired Ms. Parker that day, Mr. Martin?"

Ben's patience frayed, and he reined it in. "Like I already said. Lannis has never lied to me. She didn't want to tell me about it in the first place, and she hates talking about it. That doesn't fit at all with false reporting of rape or sexual assault, and is more in line with typical responses to rape."

"So she fit a profile." Davis glanced at Lannis, whose wide-eyed gaze met his. Davis's eyes sharpened, and his eyes locked with Lannis's for a breath, then another. And another. Lannis broke the contact and dipped her face, a flush surging up her neck. Hectic color settled like roses on the pale canvas of her features. She fumbled the pen she'd been holding and bobbled it before she captured it, then pretended great concentration on the legal pad in front of her. Davis swung his attention to Ben, a question in his eyes, if not on his lips.

Ben tensed, unsure of the ramifications of the byplay between Lannis and Robert Davis. It could be totally innocuous…or not, although he couldn't put a finger on why it felt dangerous. Protective instincts flooded his limbs, and he curled his hands into fists, forced himself to stay seated. "Is that a question?" Ben had been taught to never initiate an exchange while on the stand, but Davis needed distracting.

It worked.

The furrow in Davis's forehead smoothed, and he nodded. "Yes. Tell the court about the profile she fits."

Maybe it had worked too well. Ben straightened his fingers and slid a hand down the crease of his slacks. She was a victim, but he needed to walk a tightrope of not portraying her as weak or vindictive. "Used to. She doesn't fit it anymore. Lannis was socially isolated and hypervigilant when I met her. She exhibited symptoms of post-traumatic stress disorder when pressured into situations that replicated aspects of the attack, or provoked memories of it, so she exerted rigid control over her environment in order to avoid those situations."

"What made you deduce these, uh, traits were anything other than her normal personality?" Davis looked away from Ben and picked a piece of lint from the lapel of his suit, then looked back.

"She tried hard to hide all of that from everyone. And for the most part she was successful." *Very successful.* Ben flashed back to the night he'd stumbled into Lannis's secrets. He'd been stunned to see her crumple, and still felt nothing but gratitude that she'd come through that night with her psyche unscathed. But Lannis was a scrappy survivor. He'd known that then, and she'd proven herself in that regard over and over since.

"What makes you an expert, Mr. Martin? You're a law enforcement officer, not a psychologist."

Davis's voice tugged Ben out of his memories. "True," Ben said, "but I have some training in sexual assault through the law enforcement academies I've completed. My job requires me to be highly observant. I'd seen PTSD in a guy I knew who came back from Iraq, so when I saw Lannis exhibiting some of the same behaviors, I put two and two together."

"And came up with *rape*, Mr. Martin?" Davis's voice dripped with sarcasm. "You equate armed combat with a woman who behaves erratically and you draw the conclusion she was *raped*?"

"I didn't say she behaved erratically." Ben pinned Davis with a stare. "The opposite, in fact. She was disciplined and focused, very conscientious, very thoughtful. She was more cautious in some situations than necessary. I didn't draw the conclusion that she'd been raped. I drew the conclusion she might be experiencing PTSD. She disclosed the rape to me when I pressed her to explain what I saw as unusually intense fear, given the circumstances—the first time she'd disclosed it to anyone, I might add, and nearly four years after the fact."

"So when I landed at Bowman in April, she turned to you for your undercover skills," Davis said dryly, with what Ben could only describe as a slight wink at the jury.

Ben tamped down his irritation. "No. She was terrified of you. The last thing she wanted was to see you or speak to you. The wire was one of several options we discussed, and yes, it was my idea." He paused. "Seeing as how I use them routinely in my work, it wasn't much of a stretch."

"What other…options…did you discuss?" Davis's emphasis on the word lent a snide air to the question.

"Walking away from the situation and letting you fly away without consequences. Confronting you privately so you had the opportunity to see how you had impacted her life with your actions. Or the wire, to see if you'd implicate yourself enough to get a warrant for your arrest." Ben stopped short of Lannis's wish to save any more women from sexual predation by Davis. That would get thrown out by the judge, and might give Davis enough leverage for a successful appeal.

"What did you coach her to say?"

Anger darkened Ben's vision, and he took a deep breath, then let it out slowly. "I did not coach her to say anything. I coached her about what you needed to say in order to substantiate a warrant." He shoved the picture of this man brutalizing Lannis out of his mind. Ben was glad he didn't know the details of what Davis had done to her, but on the other hand, his imagination had filled in the blanks all too well. It wouldn't serve her to lose his composure or get sucked into Davis's manipulations.

Davis abruptly lost interest in Ben's testimony, and said, "No further questions."

Ben stood, sending Davis one last blistering glare. He wanted to tear the man limb from limb, and his palms itched with the desire, but he controlled his rage. The impotence he felt at being denied frontier justice for Lannis's sake shook him to the core. Ben believed in the justice system. How could he not, given his choice of life's work? But Old Testament "eye for an eye" theology had a certain appeal.

The bad part was, Ben didn't feel much remorse for entertaining the thoughts. He'd have a chat with the Almighty about that later, but for now, he had to be content with the equivalent of a dirty look.

Of which, Davis finally took note. In a silent, instinctual response, he met Ben's gaze and returned the sentiment, eyes narrowing and glittering, his posture altering slightly, taking on an offensive stance. His face took on a feral expression. *Bring it on, buddy,* his body language seemed to say, a double-dare answer to Ben's unspoken challenge.

Even though he hadn't planned it, Ben took advantage of the moment. His lips quirked up in a surprised, satisfied smile as he stepped past Davis, making the man rotate toward the jury box, letting the jury see his face for themselves.

He lifted his hand in a subtle salute to Lannis on his way out, and she sent him a tremulous smile. His heart twisted, wishing he could stay by her side.

~

Lannis's gaze followed Ben out of the courtroom, then settled on Pete Delaney, seated at her right. Her heart began to pound heavily against her ribs, and her palms went damp. She wiped them surreptitiously on her slacks, then snagged her water bottle and took a swig. She was up next, and she had the wild thought of asking Pete to request a recess, but the sooner she faced Davis, the sooner all this would be over. Pete's papers rustled as he stood, and called her to the stand as state's witness. *Too late now.*

She stood and walked on unsteady legs to the chair, raised her right hand when told by the bailiff, and swore her oath. *So help me God.* Something deep inside her became calm, and she realized that she could take those words as a promise from God as well as a promise from her to the court. The anxiety of the past hour drained away.

Lannis lifted her head and stared at Robert Davis with a confidence she hadn't felt for weeks, maybe even months, certainly not since that day in April when she'd literally bumped into him at the counter of the flight school. She sat and folded her hands gently in her lap. The worst had been done. The rape. The second worst was over, too. The wire. Robert Davis could not hurt her any more than he already had. A tiny part of her scoffed at her optimism, and she squelched it.

Pete purposely stood between her and Davis, and Lannis brought her attention fully to him. He gave her an encouraging smile. "State your full name for the court, please."

"Lannis Renee Parker Martin." Pete had told her to include her maiden name, as that was how the warrant and subsequent charges had listed her. He went on to ask her about her work and duties, and to explain what the term "transient pilot" meant—all simple, straightforward questions that also served the purpose of relaxing her.

She glanced at the jury as she answered, as Pete had stressed the need to connect with them. Louisville juries tended to acquit on sexual assault cases, and it was paramount that she open herself to their scrutiny, letting them see her as normal, vulnerable yet strong, as a human being. And as much as it galled her, as a victim.

"Tell us about the events of July 14…"

With a jolt, Lannis thought, *the date…that's…that's next week.* Exactly five years after the attack. An anniversary that had crippled her emotionally each of the past four summers. How had she missed its approach this year? Too focused on the trial to notice? The sea changes in her life? A roaring began in her ears, and she gripped her hands together to keep them from trembling. Her vision narrowed, and she gulped a lungful of air. "Uh…I, uh…"

Pete's face loomed in front of her. "Ms. Martin? Are you okay?" A bottle of water appeared—from the bailiff?—and he took it, pressing it into her hands. She gripped it like a lifeline, and it tugged momentarily as Pete unscrewed the lid. The plastic was icy, and Lannis's fingers felt no warmer. Pete put his hand beneath hers and gently urged her to lift the bottle to her lips, and abruptly she broke from her trance. She took a sip, then one more, and set it on the flat railing around the witness stand.

"Mrs. Martin, can you continue?" The judge's voice anchored her, and she looked up at him.

"Yes, Your Honor." She nodded, guessing she looked white as Pete's shirt. "I'm sorry. I'm…okay." She didn't feel entirely fine, but resolve came from somewhere and gave her a bit of starch for her back. She sniffed and rubbed a quick hand across her upper lip, then settled in her chair again. Dear God, she thought, and took a deep breath. It shuddered in, then out. She opened her mouth, and thankfully words came out. "I was at work."

Pete stepped back. A question flickered in his eyes. He probably envisioned the case evaporating in a puff of wasted taxpayer money and his time. She tried to smile in reassurance but it likely looked like a grimace. "This guy came into the office around five. It was Robert Davis, only I didn't know that yet. He was laying over for the night. He got the keys for the courtesy car and asked Nancy, the receptionist, about cheap places to stay. I was finishing my paperwork for the day.

"We both left at the same time. He asked if I wanted to go for a drink, and I thought he seemed nice enough, so I said, sure."

"Did anyone hear that conversation, Ms. Martin?"

"No, we were alone in the parking lot. I found out where he was staying, and said I'd meet him there. It wasn't that far from my house, and I planned to walk."

Pete interrupted again. "Why walk?"

"I didn't have a car, and I figured that would give him time to check in to his motel. Besides, I had to drop some paperwork in one of the hangars on the way. And I didn't want to get in a car with him, didn't feel comfortable with that." Lannis looked at Pete, and he nodded a silent go-ahead. "So I met him at the motel, the Bluebird Inn on Taylorsville Road, and we walked together to the bar. He was from New Jersey, and we talked about the differences in flying on the East Coast versus here."

"What was the name of the bar?"

Lannis went blank for a moment. Pete hadn't told her he'd ask that. When he'd interviewed her in his office months ago he'd asked, but hadn't pressed her beyond the generalities of the name of the strip mall. "I don't remember. It was a little hole-in-the-wall place with a funny name, sort of seedy. The River Rat, or something. It went out of business, or moved a while ago. I think there's a Subway sandwich place there now."

Pete slid a piece of paper out of his file and handed it to the judge. "Enter this into evidence, if the court pleases. Deeds of ownership dating back to the date of the alleged crime, showing the River Rat bar in the location Subway now occupies."

Lannis blinked. That was a subtle way to demonstrate her veracity, but Pete had taken a risk by doing it that way. She sat up a bit straighter, slightly wary of what he might throw at her next. But all he said was, "Go ahead."

"So, uh, he had a beer, and we shared an order of loaded potato skins. I had a glass of wine. We talked about flying. He told me about the corridors for light airplane traffic that went past the Statue of Liberty in New York City. I hadn't known that, found it interesting. He told me he had New York charts in his bag at the motel and invited me to come see them. So I thought, okay, he's nice enough, that'll probably be safe."

"I'm sorry to interrupt, Lannis, but why do you keep using the word 'safe'?" Pete inclined his head toward the jury and lifted his eyebrows slightly.

She'd been so focused on Pete, she'd forgotten to look at the jury. Lannis shifted and glanced at them, and found the six jurors watching her with a mixture of curiosity, horrified fascination, compassion, and disinterest. The alternate regarded her with undisguised disgust, and she hoped he wouldn't be required to substitute for anyone.

She took a breath and plowed on. "I felt a little uncomfortable. He hadn't hit on me, not any more than any other guy, but I had this sense of…unease. Nothing remarkable, nothing I could put my finger on, but enough that I decided I needed to be cautious. So I thought as long as he left the door open at the motel, it would be fine."

Pete nodded at her to continue.

"We walked back to the motel, and I asked him to leave the door open. He didn't seem surprised by my request, just propped it open with a chair. He spread the charts out on the bed, pointed out the Statue of Liberty, other landmarks, and his home airport on Long Island. I asked him why he lived in New Jersey and hangared his plane on Long Island. He laughed and said he'd gotten a cheaper deal. I got absorbed in looking at the light airplane corridors, and barely noticed him get up and go to the back of the room. When he returned, instead of stopping, he went to the door, slid the chair out of the way, and closed it."

Lannis's heart began to thud in her chest and her mouth went dry. "That's when I knew." She paused, glanced at her hands, then back at the jury. "That's when I knew what he was going to do." Her voice stayed steady, and she was glad of it. "The look on his face…it was almost gleeful.

"He stayed between me and the door, and told me not to bother screaming, because no one would hear, and if they did, the place was such a dive nobody would bother coming to see why.

"He told me about the martial arts gym he went to in Manhattan, and started throwing punches at me. By this time, I was up against the wall, and shaking my head no. He hit me a lot of times. I don't remember any pain, just the sound. He was very deliberate and very careful. He used his fists, his feet, and I didn't know which he'd throw next. I'd put my hands up to protect my face, and he'd kick me in the ribs. So I'd put them down to protect my body, and he'd throw a kick or a punch at my face, although he never hit me above my shoulders. None of the punches landed where they might show. I didn't notice that until later. He taunted me the whole time."

Lannis grabbed the water and took a long drink. This time she couldn't look at the jury. She focused on Pete's tie and kept talking, trying to ignore the man sitting mere feet beyond him. She couldn't see Robert Davis—*Thank you, God*—and concentrated on breathing as she spoke.

"I told him I didn't want to do this, I didn't w-want to have s-sex."

Pete's tie was maroon, with subtle waves of deep red woven through.

"So he turned it into a debate, asked me why I didn't want to, and countered it with why I *should* want to, why my wishes and values didn't count. By that time he'd gotten most of my clothes off, and I was crying, probably begging, but to be honest, there are parts of what happened that I don't remember clearly."

Pete's tie tack was pearlescent, set in a square, burnished gold background.

"I told him I'd get pregnant, and h-he s-said he knew how to make sure that didn't happen." Lannis gulped a breath. "He threw me on the bed and…he forced me to, you know…in my mouth, down my throat, and I fought so hard he almost ripped my cheek with his…and I couldn't breathe and I couldn't get him off and I don't know how long that lasted because I was fighting for my life, from one breath to the next." The words rushed out in a flood.

Pete made a move toward her. Lannis stiffened and put a hand up to stop him. She shook her head. "No. I need to finish this now." He halted, and she resumed speaking.

"I prayed that he'd come, so it would be over, but he didn't. He finally rolled off of me, and the look on his face then… He could hardly wait to see my reaction. He had his wh-whole h-hand inside me, twisting it back and forth. It hurt so bad it took my breath away.

"My mind left my body, and I watched him brutalize me from somewhere above us in the room." She gulped. "I watched myself scream and scream, and thrash, and rip at the sheets. He…well, he gloated."

Blood rushed in her ears. Pete's shirt was white, his suit an unassuming gray, and a handkerchief that matched his tie poked cheerily out of the breast pocket. Her hands trembled.

"I don't know how long that lasted. Eventually, he got bored and quit. When he got up to go to the bathroom, I sort of got sucked back into my body. I sat up and puked on the bed. I put my clothes on. He didn't stop me. Then I opened the door and walked out. Went home. Took a hot shower and scrubbed myself raw, brushed my teeth and mouth and throat until my gums bled. Tried to count the bruises, but lost track, and thought I'd faint every time I got to twenty. Went to bed. Got up the next morning and tried to pretend it hadn't happened."

Lannis finally looked up, looked at Pete. His eyes were filled with compassion, but thank God, not pity. "Why didn't you report the assault, Lannis?"

"I…I didn't think anyone would believe me. I was in shock. I wasn't thinking clearly. He'd messed with my head, telling me my *no* didn't matter, and that no one would help. The whole time he kept saying, 'You like it rough, don't you,' and 'I know you want this, you like it this way.'"

She fixed her gaze on the buttons of Pete's suit. "I couldn't wrap my mind around what had happened. He wasn't a stranger in an alley, he would say it was consensual. He didn't ejaculate, so I didn't think there would be any DNA, and it didn't dawn on me for years that the bruises were evidence." She took a deep breath and shrugged. "Besides, the thought of exposing myself to doctors and an exam, and an interview with the police…I just couldn't handle it."

Pete's manner became more brisk, and he said, "You need to tell the court which body parts were involved, Ms. Martin."

Heat flooded her face, and Lannis ducked her head. She mumbled the words, embarrassed to say them aloud, in reference to herself, and in public. Even the interview with Dutch Bennett hadn't been this bad. But she needed to pull herself together.

Robert Davis's cross-examination would be far worse. And it was next.

Dread filled her as Pete Delaney turned her over to her rapist so he could exercise his constitutional rights.

Chapter Twelve

ROBERT DAVIS SCRAWLED a couple more notes and took his time before he moved from his table. He would have loved to see the bitch's face while she recounted the events of five years ago. She sounded rattled. Embarrassed. Shaky. Her attorney had done a good job of shielding her, but there was no chance of that anymore. She was his. And he would rip her testimony to shreds, use her words against her until the jury couldn't help but see how unreliable she was.

He lifted his gaze slowly, relishing the first moment of contact, the first clash of her eyes with his. Would she be as terrified as she'd been in the motel room five years ago? Would her hands tremble? Power coalesced in his belly, expanded upward into his chest and downward into his groin, and he felt himself grow hard. He buttoned his suit coat as he stood, confident that the cut would hide that bit of evidence, and stepped toward the witness box.

His attention lingered on her legs, hidden by those god-awful green slacks, then slid up past her hands, pale and clasped in her lap but not trembling. Disappointment pricked his ego, but he let it go. She'd be trembling by the time he was finished. Then up her torso, a moment longer than necessary on her breasts, long enough to note her soft intake of breath, a breath that lifted those breasts against the soft fabric of her blouse. Her pulse galloped against the pale skin of her neck, and then, ever so slowly, he let his gaze stroke her cheeks in what he knew was an unwanted caress, across her full lips…to her eyes.

Wary. Wary, but unafraid. Another dart stung his ego. She should be afraid. He'd fix that, too, but he reminded himself to be careful. He couldn't be too obvious about it. "No longer Ms. Parker? Congratulations on your nuptials, Mrs. Martin." Her eyes widened, and she looked momentarily nonplussed, as though she didn't know how to respond. She settled on a silent nod of acknowledgment and lifted her chin the slightest bit.

"We had a sexual encounter on the date and in the place already entered as evidence, did we not, Mrs. Martin?" He turned slightly toward the jury, his arousal beginning to abate.

She looked confused again. "Is that a question or a statement?"

He let a drop of sarcasm enter his voice. "It's a question. Did we or did we not have a sexual encounter on the date in question?"

Her confusion disappeared. "A sexual encounter of the *forced* kind." She clipped the words off, her tone acerbic.

"Ah, but that's the rub, isn't it?" He gestured to the jury. "You and your attorney have evidence, proof, even, of our sexual encounter. We all agree on that. But there's absolutely no evidence that force played a part of it. There was no report of a crime, because a crime wasn't committed." He spun and advanced toward her. "Tell the court again why you didn't report anything."

Fight sparked in her eyes. "Because I was too traumatized to think clearly."

"You didn't think anyone would believe you."

"No, I didn't. But that was the trauma talking."

"No one would believe you because there was no evidence."

"There was evidence. I just didn't realize it."

"It's still your word against mine, Mrs. Martin. By the way, if you were so damaged by our sexual intercourse, how did you manage to get past that enough to be capable of marriage?"

"Objection!" Pete leaped to his feet. "Irrelevant."

"Sustained. The jury will ignore the question." The judge peered over his glasses. "You know the rules, Counselor. Follow them."

Lannis Martin scowled like she wanted to take him on, but Robert settled back on his heels and eyed her. "When did you decide you'd been raped, Mrs. Martin?"

Uncertainty flickered across her features. "I knew what had happened was wrong right away. During…" She stopped and swallowed.

Then she lifted her gaze and looked him dead in the eye. Her lips firmed. "I didn't 'decide' I'd been raped. I knew. Whether or not I reported doesn't matter. What matters is what happened, and the recording is pretty clear—"

"I'm not talking about the recording." Robert interrupted her, anxiety spiking in his gut. He couldn't afford for her to take control of the testimony. The damn recording was the only thing holding their case together. He needed to cut her credibility off at the knees, so those words would lose their power.

"You're a fairly athletic person, aren't you, Mrs. Martin? And you work outdoors, in a male-dominated field, correct?"

The wariness reappeared on her face, and Robert relaxed a hair.

"Uh, yes, I'm a runner, and I go to the gym sometimes with—I go to the gym once or twice a week. And yes, women pilots are a minority, about fifteen percent of the workforce." She flicked a glance at the jury.

"So you are accustomed to rigorous physical activity."

She narrowed her eyes. "Yes."

"Describe for the court some of the activities your job requires."

Her chin rose in a feisty gesture, stirring his predatory instincts into the stalking mode.

"Why?" She stared down her nose at him, regal and cautious and untouchable. "I already did, when I first began to testify."

"It's a reasonable question, Mrs. Martin." He swept his hand toward the jury. "You spoke about your credentials, and that you teach both ground and practical aspects of flight. These people are giving generously of their time, and I'm sure they'd like to know all the facts pertinent to the case they're being asked to weigh." He put the slightest emphasis on the word *facts*, and stifled a smile when two of the men of the jury straightened. One of them even sniffed, adopting an air of haughtiness. This was turning into a circus, and Robert silently congratulated himself on his role as ringmaster. He was doing a superb job of it, too. "Mrs. Martin?" he prompted when she continued staring at him, tightlipped.

She sent a look toward the assistant DA, who gave her a quiet nod. She shrugged and returned her attention to the jury. "I don't know what this has to do with anything, but at the time of the attack, I was flight instructing at Louisville Air. There's some time inside working with students at a desk, but most of the work is outside. We generally fly about six times a day, average, year-round. We don't fly in thunderstorms, or in clouds when it's near freezing." She sent him a quizzical look and stopped.

"Do you climb on the planes to preflight them?" Robert kept his tone neutral.

"Yes."

"Check oil? Look in engine compartments?"

"Yes." This time irritation shimmered in her eyes.

"Do you move the planes by hand?"

"Yes, sometimes. We have tow bars for that, if the tug isn't available."

"Are the doors to the hangars automated?"

"They are now, but they weren't then."

"How tall are the hangar doors?"

"I'd guess about thirty feet."

"So they are heavy."

"Yes."

"Athletic as you are, you're not a very large person. Is it—excuse me—was it difficult for you to open and close the doors?"

"Yes. It was hard for everyone, even the guys."

The judge interrupted. "Is there any point to this line of questioning, Mr. Davis?"

"Yes." He pivoted toward the judge and nodded, then swung around to address the jury. "Ms. Parker—I mean, Mrs. Martin, by her own admission is athletic, strong enough to hold her own in a man's profession, and is not bothered by extremes in work conditions. Would it not follow, then, that she might *like* her sex rough, even ask for it that way?"

Pete Delaney shot up from his chair. "Objection!"

The sound of the judge's gavel cracked through the courtroom. "Sustained." His face turned ruddy with anger. "Counselor, keep your conjecture to yourself. If you can't, I would be pleased to add contempt of court to the charges you already face." He addressed the jury. "Ignore that statement."

Robert tipped his head again in faux submission. "My apologies, Your Honor." *Careful.* He'd almost forgotten *he* was on trial. *Remember, don't alienate the judge.* He bit back a curse and schooled his features into a benign, innocuous, faintly injured expression.

"Mrs. Martin, we heard earlier from an expert on post-traumatic stress syndrome." He raised an eyebrow, inviting agreement. She didn't respond. "Tell the court about your symptoms."

Shame, or maybe embarrassment flickered across her features. "Um. Well, at first I partied too much, and drank a lot."

"You *partied?*" Robert didn't have to feign surprise this time.

A blush crept up her neck, then lit her cheeks. "Uh…yeah."

"Wild parties? Booze? Sex? Drugs?"

"No drugs." The words popped out, and her eyes widened as she said, "I've never done any kind of drugs."

It took her a moment to realize what she *hadn't* said. Robert stifled a grin when her expression went from earnest to horrified.

"I…uh, I didn't mean it that way." She tried to control a fidget and grasped her hands together.

"How did you mean it, Mrs. Martin?" He rocked back on his heels, enjoying the sight of the state's star witness squirming in her chair.

She ducked her head. "I was running away from the memories and trying to numb the emotional pain."

"Are you sure you're not just blaming your character faults on our uninspiring sexual encounter?"

That brought her head up. Her eyes sparked with anger. "I have my faults, no doubt about it. But this is cause and effect. You rape, I try to cope. Yes, I screwed up. I'm not blaming you for that. I take full responsibility for my bad choices."

"Whoa." Robert held his hand up. "Stick to the question. Tell the court about the parties."

She shot him a mutinous look and clamped her lips together, then crossed her arms and leaned back in her chair. He noticed she'd curled her hands into fists, and a glimmer of satisfaction took root.

"Mrs. Martin?"

She sent a pleading look at the assistant DA, and he must have signaled her to answer. Her tongue darted out and moistened her lips. "I changed a lot after you raped me."

"Mrs. Martin, I must ask you to refrain from using the word rape in reference to the sex we had. That is prejudicial, and you cannot do that any more than I am allowed to speculate about your sexual proclivities." He stretched out *proclivities,* letting scorn color the word. Robert brushed his jacket back and set his hands on his hips. He leaned in, crowding her, using his size and proximity to intimidate her. "Would you like to try that again?"

Her eyes smoldered with anger. "Sure." She bit the word out. "After the…encounter in your motel room, I tried to erase it from my memory." She gave the word *encounter* the same dry sarcasm as he'd used for *proclivities.* "I drank, too much. I was so ashamed, I cut off all contact with my family and friends. I became very isolated."

"But you said you partied. And you did not deny both alcohol and sex."

Her composure faltered, and she glanced down at her hands. Robert could hardly believe his good fortune. Unless he was reading her all wrong, she'd slept around afterward. This was going to be even easier than he'd hoped. He corralled his excitement. Best not let *that* show. "Need I remind you that you are under oath?"

She stilled, and her hesitation stretched out several moments. When she spoke, her voice carried only as far as the jury box. "Yes. It was a warped attempt to regain control of my body, combined with an irrational belief that I was not allowed to say no." She lifted her head and stared at him, but she didn't appear to see him. Rather, her attention had turned inward, and she looked haunted. "You trained me very well in those two hours."

One of the women on the jury inhaled sharply. Robert didn't dare look over at her. *Damn it!* He had no idea whether the juror was responding to Lannis's admission of promiscuity, or the last words she'd uttered. The bitch kept sliding those little comments in, parrying his stabs at her credibility.

"How many men did you have intercourse with during your—"

"Objection!" Delaney's voice rang out, and he slapped the flat of his hand down on the table. "Irrelevant!"

Robert didn't slow down even though Delaney drowned out some of his words. "—alleged post-traumatic stress interlude?"

"Sustained, Counselor." The judge pounded his gavel again. "Mr. Davis, you will refrain from asking the witness about her sexual history, with the exception of the encounter being tried." He peered over his glasses at Robert. "She is not on trial. You are. You're a lawyer. You know a victim's history is inadmissible."

"With all due respect, Your Honor, the witness opened the door to this line of questioning." Robert kept his tone mild. He didn't expect the judge to let him continue, but hey, it was worth a try.

"She may have opened it, but I won't allow you to step through it. Move on, Counselor, and take care that you don't badger the witness."

Badger the witness? Robert straightened. "The witness is hostile, Your Honor. I am not badgering her, I'm simply trying to get her to answer my questions." He was gratified when the judge looked at Lannis Parker…Martin.

"Young lady, answer the questions put to you. If the DA objects, hold your tongue until I've ruled, and we'll go on from there. Otherwise, this trial will drag on until next week."

She looked properly chastened, but that sense of mutiny still simmered beneath her barely composed demeanor. He glanced at the jury, satisfied to see varying degrees of revulsion on several faces. They looked like they'd be happy to pin a scarlet *A* to her breast.

Robert paused and regrouped. He'd not gone as far as he wanted in assassinating her character, but he'd cast enough of a slur on it to create a chasm between her credibility and her claims. She'd inadvertently helped him, and that might be enough. Most juries did not like to convict on rape charges, maybe because of a general distaste of listening to uncomfortably intimate allegations, followed by the chore of wading through a thicket of truths, half truths, and outright lies to determine whose motives were least impure. *He said* versus *she said* often didn't carry enough credence to swing the burden of proof far enough for a jury to convict. He hoped it was true today, especially given the lack of physical evidence.

Except for the recording. Robert wanted it thrown out. The state's entire case rested on it. The detective, Bennett, and the DEA agent, Ben Martin, had done everything right. There were no holes, no procedural errors he could capitalize on. The transcript was damning enough, although Robert thought he could mitigate its effectiveness, but to hear the words… The audio would convey authenticity and emotion beyond the words themselves. He feared that would sway the jury.

His thoughts took a detour. He'd become so used to reading her surname as Parker that her married name had skated right past him. But his mental review just now included more Martins than seemed normal. Lannis Parker *Martin*. Ben *Martin*. Martin called himself her friend. She'd recently married.

Had she married *him*? The DEA agent?

Like the locking mechanism on an old-fashioned mechanical safe, cylinders began to click into place.

The sense that the arrest had had a personal aspect.

The vulnerable, deer-in-the-headlights look he'd caught on Ms. Parker/Mrs. Martin's face when the DEA agent, Ben Martin— *Martin, damn it!*—had testified.

No wonder it felt like a setup.

He spun, rounding on Lannis Parker/Martin—whoever the hell she was—and slammed his hands on the railing guarding the witness chair. "You're married to that DEA guy, aren't you? Aren't you?" His voice escalated with each word until he was shouting. He shook the rail in his fury. She shrank from him, her face losing all color.

She shot a terrified glance at the judge and edged her way up the chair, bringing her feet to the seat. "Y-yes."

The bailiff reached him and grabbed him by the arm. Robert shook the guy off, dimly aware of shouts and the pounding of approaching footsteps.

"You deserved everything you got from me, you little slut! You should've stayed shut up!"

She gathered herself into a crouch, then vaulted over the back of the chair, one hand on the judge's bench as if she planned to leap behind him next.

The judge shouted, "Order! Order," and banged the gavel in time with his words.

Someone tackled Robert, and he went down hard on the cold marble floor. Bodies landed on top of him, so many he couldn't move, and the familiar icy bite of handcuffs circled his wrists. They hauled him upright, and he knew he should control himself, stop the words from spewing from his lips, but they had a life of their own. "You weren't worth the trouble! Not then, not now. You didn't even make it worth my while! Rape wasn't enough! I should've shut you up forever!"

Deputies dragged him toward the door, and Robert howled his rage. "Why? Why didn't you keep quiet? Why did you do this to me?" The cops bundled him through the door into the long hallway that led back to the jail, and he jerked against them, fighting every step of the way, though his efforts were so ineffectual they didn't bother with Tasers.

He'd lost.

Hung by his own words.

Again.

He didn't realize he was crying until snot diluted by his tears dripped off his nose onto his Armani suit.

Chapter Thirteen

August

AUGUST HEAT PRESSED on Ben's shoulders. He inhaled, dragging sweltering, humid air past his contrarily dry throat. At least he'd finished mowing before the heat built today, and was glad for the refuge of the garage, working out of reach of the brutal sun. Sweat trickled down his nose, then hung suspended from the tip as if afraid to make the long drop to the concrete garage floor. He took an absentminded swipe at it and lost his grip on the wrench holding the Mustang's carburetor.

Both toppled, then thunked onto the worn wood of his workbench, the carburetor rattling as it rolled a few inches. He muttered a mild curse and lifted an elbow so he could do a better job of mopping his face with the sleeve of his T-shirt. His shirt came away wet, but his eyes began to burn. *No choice but to wash the salt away.* He needed a drink, anyway. Lannis had a pitcher of sweetened sun tea in the fridge, and his salivary glands began to anticipate the icy tang. He sighed and turned to go inside, crossing the shadowy area beyond the light above his work area.

He took the two steps in one leap and grabbed the doorknob, twisted it. His hand slid around the cool metal, but the knob didn't rotate, and his momentum carried him to an abrupt stop. He thudded into the door, which shook under his weight, knocked the breath from his lungs, and did not budge. Ben staggered back, using the knob as an anchor now, and did a quick two-step on the stairs to catch his balance.

He gritted his teeth, counted to ten, then dropped his forehead on the cool wood of the door and counted to ten again. *She's done it again.* Did he need to start carrying a house key every time he left the house proper? He dug deep and found enough patience to speak without bellowing.

"Lannis." He congratulated himself for sounding as if nothing was out of the ordinary.

No answer.

"Lannis." What was she doing in there? He couldn't hear the vacuum or any kitchen appliances, so she should be able to hear him. He raised his voice to a near shout. "Lannis!" Belatedly, he added,

"Darlin'," then rapped on the door, restraining himself from beating it with his fist.

Ah. Noises. Footsteps approaching on the kitchen tile. She fumbled the locking mechanism open and the knob turned, a smooth movement against his palm. He loosened his hold on it, and Lannis pulled the door open, peering around it.

"Uh…sorry, Ben." Lannis eyed him warily, with a smile that looked as fake as an underage drinker's ID, her expression both bright and guilty. "Do you want some iced tea? You look like you could use some."

He could, but refused to let her distract him. "This is the third time this week, Lannis." Ben tried to keep the growl out of his voice, but failed. She glanced away and retreated into herself, becoming somehow smaller, more distant, and more fragile, even though she hadn't moved a muscle.

How does she do *that?* It made him feel like a heel, and a spark of anger flared. It wasn't his fault. It was Robert Davis's. Or maybe even Lannis's. Why couldn't she get past this? Was she even trying? He clamped down on his irritation, realizing that assigning blame was pointless at best, and counterproductive no matter how tempting it might be.

"He's in prison. For eight years." After Davis's ignominious exit from the courtroom a month ago, the trial had sputtered to a quick end. Pete Delaney played the recording. The jury deliberated for less than an hour and delivered a conviction. Freed to run his DNA, the lab had produced hits on two cold cases, one in Illinois, the other in Pennsylvania. Davis was battling those from behind bars, but Ben didn't foresee the guy having a chance of accomplishing anything other than postponing the inevitable.

"I know." She lifted her gaze, the wariness replaced by shame. Her expression was troubled, with a haunted quality Ben never wanted to see again.

Guilt smacked him between the eyes, and he felt even worse than he had a moment ago. No, what Robert Davis had done to Lannis wasn't Ben's fault, but she needed the security to work through her own recovery without her jerk of a husband making it harder. He made a note to stash a spare key somewhere that the average burglar wouldn't find it, and so this wouldn't be an issue again. On his part, anyway.

"Come here," he commanded and snagged her around the shoulders, pulling her close. She resisted for a moment, then sighed and rested her head on his chest, pressing the fabric of his T-shirt into the dampness of his chest. The air conditioning kicked on, its faint breeze rippling across his skin, cooling the sweat on his arms and brow. "How are we going to deal with this?" He rocked her, and she finally slipped her arms around his waist.

She shrugged, the motion both tentative and final. "I don't want to talk about it."

"That's part of the problem," Ben said. He shifted so he could see her face. "You can't bury it. It happened. It's part of your history, and you need to come to terms with it."

Lannis compressed her lips and her eyes darkened. Her silence only lasted a few seconds, and when she broke it, the words spewed forth in a torrent of emotion. "I thought I dealt with it! I've stopped all my really bad coping mechanisms. I don't drink anymore, I've got a great job, I'm not isolated like I was when I met you." She tugged loose from his embrace and stepped back. "I've done therapy. I've made my peace with God over it, and I've forgiven Davis, at least the best I can, because I know that's the only way to move on, the only way for me to heal." She turned and paced away from Ben, gesturing with her hands, her movements jerky and abrupt. "I can't help that the nightmares are coming back. I can't help that I need to lock the doors. I can't help that I'm hurting *us*, and I hate that!"

She turned to face him, and Ben read anguish in the lines of her body. The muscles of her neck were taut, her shoulders tight.

"I can see what I'm doing, but I'm powerless to stop it. I'm sorry, Ben." Tears welled in her eyes. Her voice dropped to a whisper. "I'm sorry."

Ben closed the distance she'd put between them and pulled her into an embrace. "We'll work it out together. We're a team now." Although, for the life of him, he didn't know what to suggest. He went with the obvious. "Betsy?"

Lannis tensed in his arms. "No. There's nothing she can do for me, or Althea, for that matter."

"Why not?" Betsy was the counselor Lannis had seen once she'd decided to face the fallout from the rape. Ben had been the first person she'd confided in. He'd listened to her when she needed to talk about it, which, thanks to her natural reticence, wasn't often. He couldn't see any reason to keep hashing it over, but hey. That was what therapists did, and conventional wisdom held that talking about trauma helped with healing. Now Althea, maybe he could understand a bit better. Lannis had moved beyond her need to do more than check in with her AA sponsor periodically. He didn't know if Lannis had even disclosed the rape to Althea, at least up until the trial.

"I can't explain it." She shrugged again. "It's like that part is done. There's nothing new to talk about. I'm doing everything I'm supposed to. Journaling, the little exercises she gave me, taking care of myself. But I sense what needs doing now is more spiritual, like God is asking me to go somewhere else with the experience."

Going somewhere spiritual with a rape? Ben released her and stepped back, scratched his head, and blinked. His eyes still stung from the salt in his sweat. "Uh, you've got me stumped there." *Understatement of the year.*

Lannis took a deep breath and looked away. For a minute, Ben thought she might not finish the conversation. With the weirdness factor she'd just introduced, he didn't particularly want to explore it any further, and he almost hoped she'd back away from it. He'd let her have a pass if she did, letting her standard "Never mind" go without a challenge. This time, anyway.

Then she sighed, and the stiffness in her shoulders deflated. "Forgive us our sins as we forgive those who sin against us."

"You've already gone above and beyond on that count." The words flew out before he thought about them, and she flinched.

"Love your enemies." She held up a hand to stop him from saying anything more. "Love your neighbor as yourself."

Ben stared at her. "What? You think you need to *love* Robert Davis?" He didn't have to manufacture any extra incredulity in his voice.

Lannis's chin came up, and her lips thinned. "No, not like I love you. But yes, I think I need to go a step further than what I've done."

"You're out of your mind, Lannis." Ben scrubbed a hand through his hair, now dry and stiff from perspiration. "You just need to let the whole thing go, let Davis rot in jail. That's what he deserves. In fact, he's such a scum-sucking bottom feeder, he needs to stay locked up until he's too decrepit to wipe his own—" Ben bit back his words. Lannis had heard worse, but he tried to keep it clean at home.

She lifted one shoulder, still looking defensive. "Maybe. That part isn't mine to judge. I'm talking about making peace between him and me, so he can be free to make his own peace with God."

"Aw, for crying out loud!" He slashed a hand through the air. "That's his problem. He's a grown man. Leave him alone to figure it out. He's got plenty of time."

Lannis stilled. "Is it, Ben? Is it his problem? Or is it ours?" She lifted a hand and touched his forearm. "It's like he's a silent partner in our marriage."

Ben shook his head, denying the sting of her words. "No." His throat tightened, and he swallowed against the strangling combination of fear and rage. "No, he's not. It's you and me, no one else."

"Yes, he is, Ben." Her hand softened, and she stroked his arm with a gentleness that nearly undid him. "Until I can let you make love to me in the dark, he's still in our bedroom, in our bed. Until you can sleep knowing that I won't wake you with screams from nightmares, he's still the monster hiding in the closet. Until I'm ready to" —her voice cracked—"have a baby with you…" Tears clogged her voice. "Until then, Ben, he's an invisible intruder, and he drives a wedge between you and me." Her hand trembled on his sleeve.

Ben snagged Lannis and drew her to him, clutching her tight, almost too tight, afraid she'd leave him, afraid her withdrawal of a few minutes ago presaged a step in that direction. He shook his head, more slowly this time. His breath shuddered as he admitted the truth of what she'd said. He settled his chin on the top of her head. "Yeah, I guess he's the one who locks me out of my own house, too, isn't he?" He lightened his tone, trying to make a joke of the situation.

Lannis gave a soft, wavering laugh that tickled his ribs. "I'm sorry, Ben. It doesn't make logical sense, but I can't help it. I'm so frustrated. I've stood up to him twice. He's in prison, and I know in my head he can't hurt me—and he can't hurt anyone else, for the time being. But when he got out of jail, and then at the trial…" Her voice hitched again.

Ben rubbed his hand up her back. "Hush, darlin'. I know. You *are* safe now. We'll get through this." He lifted her chin so he could see her eyes. She met his gaze with both anguish and clarity. "Whatever it takes. We'll face it together."

He had no idea where his promise would take them, or how it would take shape. But by God, he'd do his best to rid them of Robert Davis.

Whatever it takes.

~

Bulky, scarred double doors burst open, slamming against the walls with enough force to make their wire-reinforced glass tremble. The prison SWAT team poured into the dayroom like a horde of angry beetles dispatched with military precision. "Break it up! Break it up, *now!*" Indistinguishable in helmets and Plexiglas face shields, their body armor and shin protectors reinforced the sense of inevitable doom. "Everybody on the floor!"

Robert Davis ignored the orders. Facing the certainty of retribution and oblivious to the pain in his fist, he continued to pummel the face of the guy who'd pissed him off. Harlan. What a stupid name. It fit the moron like the spandex T-shirts his girlfriend sent him. God, it felt good to punch his anger onto flesh, to smash a nose. To let his rage fly. The consequences didn't matter. In fact, he welcomed them. He'd vent more of his fury on the take-down crew, and relish the downtime in solitary.

His vision narrowed, and he only got a couple more satisfying jabs in before the Taser jolted him. *Shit!* He hated that thing. What were they, a bunch of pussies, afraid to take him on? The fight stuttered to a halt, and he grunted as he thudded to the concrete floor. Deprived of his battle with the corrections officers, the only menace he could muster was a rumbled growl as two guards grabbed him under the arms and dragged him away.

Harlan, the sap, whimpered a gurgled, "He started it, man!" as they both got shackled with brutal efficiency. Blood flowed from the guy's nose, which was more crooked than it had been five minutes ago. Harlan would get to stop at the infirmary before his stint in solitary. *Good.* Robert couldn't change much about his life these days, but rearranging someone's face brought a glimmer of pleasure to the mind-numbing monotony. And gave him the power to choose where he'd spend the next few days.

Robert didn't doubt he'd made a new enemy, not to mention the whole cell block had it in for him now. They'd all be on lockdown through visiting hours tomorrow, while Robert milked his isolation for all it was worth. With any luck he'd get a month of quiet, and maybe he could find some peace in his own company. He even welcomed the lack of sunlight. Rather than respite, the sun, free to rise and set, rubbed salt into the wounds that incarceration had burned into his soul.

Hauled upright, he staggered, then twisted and head butted the officer on his left—and bounced off the Plexiglas protecting the guy's face. *Stupid move.* But resisting would gain him even more time in solitary. He yearned to retreat from the unrelenting press of stinking male bodies, the constant assault of varying degrees of Kentucky accents mangling English as he'd learned it, and the prowling undercurrent of gangs and threat of violence. What he really longed for was his house, graceful and refined, presiding on the quiet street of his sterile but affluent neighborhood in Atlantic City.

The house he didn't really like, but whose address garnered invitations to gatherings of the elite. The house that trumpeted his success to the world. The house that had just been sold at auction to pay the debts his arrest had triggered.

As the guards yanked his arms up behind his back, forcing him to bend forward into an awkward duck walk, he spat toward his bunk, where the confetti of today's mail littered the blanket.

In solitary, denial of mail privileges was part of the punishment.

Since his mail only brought bad news these days, it would be a relief—maybe even a blessing—to get a respite from it.

A blessing. His thoughts turned to Lannis Parker Martin. Why did words like that pop up in his thoughts? He cursed her viciously in his mind. He didn't need *blessings.* He didn't need God, but somehow she'd inserted that notion in his mind, and he couldn't seem to shake it. What he really didn't need was to be in prison as his empire crumbled around him. Watching his appeal moving at the speed of frozen molasses enraged him, never mind his powerlessness as Pennsylvania and Illinois slowly prevailed in their battles for his extradition.

His leg shackles clanked as they hustled him through a maze of hallways into the holding cell, and dropped him none too gently on the concrete bunk. Thanks to his attack on the guard, they secured his cuffs to a U-bolt recessed in the wall. Robert bared his teeth at the guards in a farce of a smile, and his distorted reflection in the Plexiglas face masks struck him as funny.

He laughed—an unused, rusty sound—and saw their eyes widen a bit. He'd surprised them. Hell, he'd surprised himself. Then the laughter took on a life of its own, and he toppled to the side, hee-hawing so hard his ribs ached. The guards retreated, eyeing him warily, and slammed the door.

The joke was on them, after all. He'd gotten exactly what he wanted. Robert snorted and guffawed, pulled his legs up as far as the chain would allow him, and let the laughter rip until it threatened to turn into sobs. *No.* He would not give in to a display of helplessness. He sobered, swallowed his weakness, and set his jaw.

Not helpless. Not powerless. Resolve surged through his veins. He'd use his time in solitary to fantasize about taking Lannis whoever-the-hell-she-was down a peg. Or just plain down.

A smile, a real one, crept back to his face.

Who knew? Maybe the fantasy could come to fruition in reality someday.

Chapter Fourteen

September

SOME DAYS ROBERT DAVIS wished he'd chosen the route of good behavior. He'd have a job by now, as if a job in prison was something to be coveted. It might relieve the unending tedium that made him want to bloody his head against the wall of his cell, if for nothing else than a trip to the infirmary. A change of scenery, as if one locked space really differed from another locked space. Or maybe just the spice of variety, personality-wise. Rubbing shoulders with an armed robber versus a murderer, or drug dealers versus career burglars. Didn't make much difference. Street smarts abounded in this hellhole, but almost all the inmates were uneducated, most of them nearly illiterate. The sheer number of drug-dealing idiots was nearly as mind-numbing as solitary confinement, with which he was now intimately acquainted.

And truth be known, he'd become weary of the game involved in attaining the goal of solitude. Its luster had dulled. He'd lost his heart for the necessary conflict, and had finally tired of being beaten and tased. Nor did he know how much more he could tolerate of the monochromatic existence. No glimpse of sun or moon, cloud or stars, leaves green with summer lushness or rich with autumn colors. He didn't consider himself a particularly poetic man, but his longing for even the smallest freedoms had thrust him into an interior landscape where he did, totally unlike himself, wax poetic.

Surely a person could not die from boredom…but he might go slowly insane from it. Maybe he was already on his way. Waxing poetic was probably an early sign.

Voices intruded on his musings. For the most part, he tuned them out, along with the ubiquitous noise of prison life. That nearly *did* drive him crazy, all the boasting, the whining, the incessant talking about appeals. Especially the appeals. Nobody in prison was guilty; just ask them. Every last man in the place was innocent. A smile ghosted across his lips. *Nah.* For the most part, they were just as guilty as he was, just pissed off they'd gotten caught.

King LeMasters led the whining in his current cell block. Robert snickered. The only thing King reigned over was bellyaching. He was always going on about some undercover cop, BJ, who had double-crossed him, and the bitch he'd beaten up, the one who had ID'd him and got him put away. He was going on—and on and on—about it again.

"Yeah, BJ, he tricked me, man. The guy wore a wire and coerced me into incriminating myself. Entrapment, you know. No witnesses, an' he couldn't prove it, but the public defender sold me out, man. Flat-out sold me to the Dee-part-ment of Co-rec-shuns." A chorus of grunts acknowledged this illustration of gross maltreatment, and Robert shut down the part of his brain that focused on details.

He couldn't afford to shut down entirely. His life depended on his ability to read the seething mass of angry men around him. Since he'd made only enemies in this garbage pit, he had no allies to clue him in to the latest plan to assassinate him. Meanwhile, he'd heard King's tirade enough times to know that the guy had no chance whatsoever with his appeal.

"—and then that Lannis Parker bitch nailed me."

Robert went still, every cell of his body instantly alert and focused on stupid King LeMasters. *Lannis Parker!* How many Lannis Parkers were there? Hers was an unusual name, at least her first name. His heart thudded into triple-time. What were the odds?

"—picked me out of a *voice* lineup. Never even saw me, but still ID'd me." King followed his litany of abuse with a string of foul curses that didn't even rise to the level of creative.

Robert shoved to his feet and inserted himself into the group around King. Silence fell, and the men traded uneasy glances. He wasn't surprised. Usually when Robert abandoned his strategy of invisible vigilance, all hell broke loose and everyone suffered. He didn't want to lose that advantage. He relied on his reputation as unpredictable and vicious, but that paled in his haste to hear what King had to say about Lannis Parker. How in blazes had it happened that she'd put *both* of them behind bars?

Two men. Impossible. His mind couldn't accept it, denied it, and yet it had to be true. Robert shoved the denial aside with brutal efficiency. He placed himself in front of King, intentionally looming over the young man, his stance a heartbeat short of aggressive, but belligerent enough to make everyone think twice about jumping him.

"Lannis Parker." He uttered the name with a voice devoid of emotion, pinned the whiny drug dealer with a steady, threatening gaze. "Where? How?"

King's bravado wavered, but he puffed his chest out and said, "What do you care, old man?" The other inmates faded away, in a bid to be judged uninvolved in the inevitable fight.

"Where?" he repeated, his tone soft but deadly. King bared his teeth and tried to shove past him, but Robert blocked him. "Where, you scumbag?" He grabbed King's shirt and hauled him close enough that he could smell the other man's rotten breath. He wrinkled his nose. "You need to see the dentist." When King volunteered nothing more, Robert added, "I can help you with that," and fixed him with a humorless smile.

"You got something you can give me, man, besides dental work?" King punctuated the words by spitting in Robert's face.

Fury rose in Robert's chest, up his throat, and a red mist swam before his eyes. He swiped the spittle from his cheek with an angry motion of his hand. Nobody spat at him and got away with it. He'd had more contact with bodily fluids in his five months in custody than he'd had in his entire life up till then, never mind that he'd contributed his share to the cesspool. The depth of his revulsion was bottomless. An abyss.

He drew back his fist to smash King's face, maybe loosen some of his rotten teeth. Even better, some of the few good ones. A visit to the dentist while incarcerated never resulted in fillings, or caps, or preventive services. It resulted in extractions. Without anesthetic. Robert figured that was exactly what King needed. He'd initiate the process, and KYDOC would finish it up for him. He bared his own teeth in anticipation, his heart pounding under the influence of the gallon or so of adrenaline that had exploded into his system when he heard the name Lannis Parker.

Lannis Parker.

The reason for his encounter with King returned, flooding his mind with clarity and chasing the haze of fury away. He stayed his fist, then dropped it to his side. He loosened his grip on LeMasters's shirt—not much, just a little. King's question echoed, now that his temper had faded.

Why not? A bit of legal counsel as barter for information. Not enough advice to do any real good, but hell, King wouldn't know that. Why waste his time in solitary when he could outwit LeMasters, break the monotony, and get what he wanted in the process? Robert's lips quirked up in a hint of a real smile.

He breathed the word, "Okay," into King's face, then paused, hearing for the first time the loudspeaker commanding all prisoners to cease physical contact. For the first time it was not in his interest to trigger a riot, and he shoved King away, took a step back.

"I'll trade you your next legal move for anything you know about Lannis Parker."

King's expressions flickered from fear to relief, from bluster to cocky wariness. Robert could almost see the wheels turning in the younger guy's head, and he saw the moment that King decided to take him up on his offer.

"Cool, man." King looked him up and down, his assessment far more brazen than was prudent, given Robert's reputation. "They say you're a lawyer. That true?"

Robert gave him a curt nod. "No guarantees, but I know some loopholes, some strategies you might try." He shrugged his shoulders, straightening his shirt.

A smile, a genuine one, wreathed King's face. "Later, then, dude."

Footsteps clattered across the concrete floor, and Robert moved another step away, raising his arms in the classic pose of surrender. Guards surrounded him, shackled his hands behind his back, yanked them up high, and frog-marched him out of the cell block.

He'd get a stint of solitary out of this. Physical contact was strictly prohibited, and even though the situation had not escalated to a brawl, he'd be punished. Since he'd stood down, though, he wouldn't be in the hole for long.

But when he got out… When he got out, he and King LeMasters would have a very interesting conversation.

Robert smiled. A predatory, merciless baring of teeth, but also a lifting of lips that mirrored his mood. Life behind bars suddenly had purpose.

Chapter Fifteen

LANNIS PICKED UP the stack of paper from the dispatch desk. "Thanks, Will." The dispatcher's slight build, combined with apparently bottomless energy, made her think of an elfin dervish. He juggled the planes, their maintenance, and ambulance arrangements with an ease that boggled her mind.

Will gave her a jaunty little salute and leaned back in his chair. "You're with Eric in the King Air today, a transport over to Paducah."

She stifled a groan. "Great." The word emerged sounding weak to her own ears, but not as sarcastic as it could have. She hoped. Sketching a wave in return, she headed for the pilot lounge to prep the flight.

Eric again. She'd managed to keep her distance from the guy around the office, but had been paired to fly with him the last two flights. Like she'd told Ben, Eric was nothing more than a pain, but what a thorn he could be. He took every opportunity to quiz her on aircraft systems, or the finer points of the Federal Air Regulations, aiming to trip her up with his—in his mind—superior knowledge. Her lips quirked up in a tiny smile. She'd held her own in the verbal sparring, even though it irritated her that he obviously felt justified in initiating it. In fact, she'd outmaneuvered him on a few of those fine points, and he'd had to subside in defeat.

Not such a good strategy, now that she thought about it. Every pilot she knew was a perfectionist, and hated any semblance of failure. Add being bested by a woman to the mix, and some men, Eric in particular, took it like a bull taunted by a red flag. She didn't seek the man's approval, or even friendship, but she didn't need him as an enemy. She had enough of those, starting with her own mother. To be fair, *enemy* was a bit harsh in regard to Millie. Silence did not equate to enmity, but Millie's last words had cut deep, and the wound was still raw.

Lannis shoved that thought out of her head before it had time to gel. Well, she tried. At Ben's urging, she'd been sending brief letters and e-mails to both her mom and Lynette every couple of weeks. After more than two months of logging in to her e-mail, or walking to the mailbox with her heart in her throat, hoping for a letter, heck, even a card, or a post-it note stuck to a postcard, and finding nothing, she'd barricaded her feelings against the pain of their rejection.

Lynette would be over halfway through her pregnancy, and probably knew if Lannis would be aunt to a boy or another girl. Pain clogged her throat and pressed on her heart. How she regretted not getting to watch little Carly grow. It seemed history was repeating itself in spite of her efforts. She shook her head, then set the papers down in the lounge and headed for the restroom. *Not the time for this.* A quick rinse of tears from her eyes would help put this behind her for now. She had Eric to deal with today, although the joy of a flight in the King Air would offset both his acerbic personality and the heartache of her personal life.

The cool water soothed and grounded her emotions. Lannis took a deep breath. *Ten minutes to review Will's paperwork and verify the numbers, another five to file the flight plan, and then out to preflight the King Air.* The air left her lungs in a relieved sigh, and her lips curved upward. Eric would show up in a half hour, so she had that much time to herself.

She straightened, patted her face dry, and resolved to maintain a professional, civil, polite, businesslike, and distinctly impersonal tone with her captain today. For the most part, her personal imperative required her to avoid isolation and avoid creating emotional barriers…but in this case, the imperative for survival allowed for at least a picket fence. Her smile ticked a bit higher. *Or six-foot planks ensuring total privacy.* As long as she didn't go for bricks and mortar, or piles of boulders à la the Great Wall of China, she'd be okay.

Energized, she headed back to the pilot lounge.

Only to find Eric rifling through her papers, leaving them in an untidy heap. One sheet slid off the desk and fluttered to the floor. She made a sound, perhaps a squeak of dismay, or more likely, a territorial growl given the startled look on his face when Eric jerked his gaze up to meet hers. Lannis bit back the words that leaped to her tongue.

That's my job, Eric.

Back off, you officious bastard.

Outta my space, big boy.

She began to narrow her eyes but remembered her silent pledge of a moment ago, and consciously widened them instead. "Good morning, Captain Hanson," she said smoothly. It took all her resolve to make her tone pleasant and bland. "I'll have those ready for you in about ten minutes."

His neck flushed a distasteful crimson above the crisp white collar of his uniform, and he straightened, one hand dropping to adjust the drape of his slacks. "Thought you'd be done by now." *His* tone was a shade shy of belligerent.

Lannis stilled, and when she spoke, her voice was quiet, her words precise. "You are a half hour early. The paperwork will be ready on time, the preflight will be done on time, the flight will launch on time." She bared her teeth in what could in no way be mistaken for a smile. "Unless you insist on spending your time underfoot." Her eyes were narrowed now.

"I'll make a run to Joe's Java, Martin." Only a couple of inches taller than Lannis, Eric managed a sneer as he attempted to look down his nose at her. He snagged his leather jacket and tossed it over his shoulder. "Back in thirty." He hesitated, as though he was considering adding an ultimatum, but wheeled and strode out of the room.

Lannis waited a moment, then released a pent-up breath. She doubted Eric would bring a cup of coffee back for her. In spite of her efforts to contain her emotions, her movements were jerky with anger as she picked up and reorganized the flight release papers. With brisk efficiency, she tapped them into the neat stack she'd started with, then sat to run the numbers.

Twenty minutes later, Lannis ducked under the wing of the King Air, glad for the fresh air, the breeze, and the heat of the sun on her back. Mostly she was glad for the physical outlet for her frustration. She forced herself to slow down and concentrate on the preflight. It was too easy to let Eric distract her, and she couldn't afford that on several levels, safety and self-preservation being primary.

She didn't understand his hostility. He'd fostered the attitude since the day she'd been introduced to the rest of the pilots, so it wasn't something she'd done. Maybe she'd beat out a friend of his for the job. *Huh.* That was a possibility, she supposed. She didn't know who else had been in the running, only that her own interview had gone smoothly. Her qualifications weren't stellar, yet were above average by a long shot. An ex-military pilot, or a charter or corporate pilot looking for a change, would have trumped her easily. On the other hand, lots of flight instructors with far less experience than she had salivated at the opportunity to fly for Children's Hospital. Several even applied, but hadn't been offered interviews. She knew she was fortunate. Wouldn't call herself lucky, because hard work played a big part in it, but nonetheless she was grateful.

Lannis sighed. Recognizing Eric's humanity forced her to see him as three-dimensional—and humanity was always messy, even a quagmire at times. Her mind flashed to her mom, then—unbidden—to Robert Davis. Discomfort crawled up her spine. She didn't want to think about Robert Davis's humanity. And while Millie's silence created a relentless dagger of pain, Lannis could at least understand the warped reasoning behind it. She could try harder to understand Eric, even though the guy was like fingernails screeching across a chalkboard to her.

She completed the exterior preflight and climbed the stairs, wending her way into the copilot's seat. The medical transport team would be here shortly, and she glanced at the docks for their equipment as she went by. Looked good to her, but other than the pressure in the oxygen bottle, it wasn't her bailiwick. She dropped the completed paperwork on Eric's seat with a satisfied smile. Like she'd told him, it was ready on time. Early, actually.

Speaking of Eric, she heard him clatter up the stairs. She turned and pasted a pleasant expression on her face. "Flight plan is filed, weight and balance checked, no navigational aid outages. We're good to go."

He nodded, bobbling his coffee as he stowed his flight bag behind his seat. One cup, as she'd expected.

"Do you want me to hold that while you get settled, sir?" She figured she was laying it on pretty thick, but if it kept the peace, or at least avoided outright warfare, it was a fair price. He ignored her olive branch and settled in, balancing his cup next to the magnetic compass as he fastened his seat belt. Lannis gave a mental shrug and peered out the Plexiglas windshield, looking for the transport team.

"The fuel sumped clean?" Eric flipped through the sheets too fast to be reading the computer printout. Nor could he see her careful notations showing she'd double-checked and verified the weather and Will's calculations.

She snapped her head around to stare at him and straightened in her seat. "Are you kidding?" Flight students were taught to sump the fuel tanks for water or debris in their first lesson. Eric knew that as well as Lannis did. He lifted his eyes and met her stunned gaze. The insult was deliberate. His expression was shuttered. She sensed he expected her to lose her confidence, or maybe even her temper.

Well, he had something to learn about Lannis Parker Martin. "Yes, Captain Hanson." She leaned back, relaxing her shoulders, tamping down her competitive urge to give back as much as he shoveled at her. She lifted an eyebrow and listed everything she'd done to prep the flight. To the letter. Without waiting for an answer, she added, "Maintenance released the plane with no squawks"— items that needed fixing before the plane could be declared airworthy—"and Flight Service reports no changes in the forecast…" She droned on, focusing on the *calm* and *professional* aspects of her earlier resolution. "Would you like a blow-by-blow review of my preflight?"

A muscle in his jaw began to jump, and his eyebrows drew together. "That's enough. I don't need your attitude."

"I don't need yours, either, Captain." Lannis regretted her words as soon as they flew out of her mouth. Almost. *Maybe it's time to clear the air.* She leaned forward. "What do you have against me? I've proved my capability to the FAA and to the company, or I wouldn't be here. I've continued to 'prove' myself to you, even though you're not the chief pilot." She made little quotation marks in the air with her forefingers. "I've passed all my check rides with excellent ratings, so it can't be my job performance." Lannis knew she'd exceeded requirements in all areas in her new job…mostly because she studied so much at home that Ben gently distracted and coaxed her to balance work and play, a balance she still found difficult to achieve on her own.

Eric gritted his teeth and leaned forward, coming nose to nose with Lannis. She barely controlled a flinch. He jabbed a finger in the general vicinity of Lannis's chest and let loose. "You're nothing but a troublemaker. Everybody has to walk on eggshells around you. I'm sick of having to monitor my every word for fear of offending you." He put sarcastic emphasis on the word *offending.*

Lannis shrank back. Troublemaker? He'd managed to confound her in spite of her mental walls. She didn't know how anyone could do any more than she had to maintain a low profile. In fact, she had to work hard to temper her propensity for privacy that bordered on invisibility. "What?" She felt her jaw drop. "Have you never worked with a woman before? I appreciate that you don't use four-letter words or tell vulgar jokes in front of me, but…" Her voice trailed off, her confusion leaving her speechless. What in the world was he talking about? She lifted a hand, palm up in question.

Eric leaned back, too, his face flushed with emotion. "Not that. No, I mean…" He paused, as if he were debating whether to continue. He narrowed his eyes and spoke in a deadly quiet voice. "I read the transcripts. You sent a guy to prison. You're a messed-up, manipulative female. How do I know you're not going to turn on me next? How do I know you're not going to manufacture some bullshit harassment charge and cost me my job?"

Lannis felt as if a giant fist had gotten hold of her lungs and choked all the air out. Her muscles took charge and she scrambled out of her seat, shedding her shoulder harness and seat belt on the way. *Air.* She needed air. Her fingernails scrabbled against the fabric that lined the interior of the cabin, and she stumbled down the stairs, jangling the plastic-covered chain handrails. Her feet hit the asphalt, and she took a gulp of steamy air, flinging a hand out to steady herself on the fuselage.

Will it never end? She suppressed an urge to keep running but kept gulping air like she'd just finished a hundred-yard sprint. The ambulance chose that moment to roll through the gate, and it coasted to a stop mere feet in front of her. Lannis pivoted and pasted a smile on her face, as though she'd planned to be out here to greet the transport team. Her heart felt like wood, burnt and crumbling to ashes, but she had no time to succumb to emotion. She scrubbed her palms against the fine twill of her black uniform slacks and swung up the stairs.

Settling the tiny patient—it was an infant—and seeing that the medical team was properly secured gave Lannis a few moments to regain her composure. The door latched smoothly, but she gave it an extra moment of attention, battling a wave of anxiety at the prospect of sitting next to Eric for the next hour and a half. When she couldn't avoid him any longer, she found some starch for her shoulders and wove through the now-crowded cabin before sliding into her seat.

Professional to the nth degree. That was Lannis's plan, and Eric apparently opted for the same. The flight was smooth, managed with quiet efficiency, if not with easy camaraderie. It would have taken a psychic to detect the undercurrents of hostility sparking between them, and Lannis drew satisfaction from that. By mutual, unspoken agreement, they went separate ways for the two-hour wait while the baby was moved to the hospital in Paducah, then repeated the exercise on the way home. By the time they'd disgorged the transport team and cleaned the plane, Lannis was exhausted from the strain, but she couldn't let Eric go without finishing the conversation.

"Captain Hanson." She ran a few steps to catch him on the ramp. She didn't want to have this discussion where anyone could overhear, but she dreaded the idea of closeting herself behind the door of the conference room with him. She might have felt the same about being trapped in a plane with him, but the cockpit had windows, a great view that gave the illusion of room and space, and plenty of tasks to keep her occupied.

He swung around, a mulish expression on his face. "What, Ms. Martin?"

"Listen. It never occurred to me that guys might see it that way." This was true, although it didn't address her knee-jerk reaction to his accusations. He lifted one eyebrow. Waited. "If you really read the transcript—" She had to pause and swallow. Knowing he'd read it made her feel naked. Heat crept up her neck to her cheeks. "—then you know *I* didn't send Robert Davis to prison. His actions, his confession sent him to prison. I didn't go out of my way to accuse him. Getting the recording and testifying were the hardest things I've ever done, outside of surviving the assault in the first place"—her vocal cords still froze at the word *rape*, even after all this time—"but I didn't do any of it out of vengeance. I did it to get a predator off the streets, so no one else would have to go through what I did."

Lannis searched Eric's eyes, but didn't find any softening or compassion. "Don't worry. I'm not out to emasculate the entire male population." She sighed. "Look, I know we'll never be friends, but you don't need to be afraid of me. I've heard all the off-color jokes, I used to spout foul language with the best of sailors. If you offend me, I'll say so. You won't hear from the boss or the Equal Opportunity folks first." She stepped back. Unable to keep a touch of bitterness out of her voice, she added, "And you won't hear from the cops." She lifted an eyebrow. "I'm not a threat to you, as long as you're not a threat to me."

Eric waited a moment longer, then gave her a curt nod and hitched his flight bag higher on his way to the office. Lannis watched him go, then surrendered to her fatigue, shoulders drooping. She hoisted her flight bag and groaned as the strap bit into her shoulder.

She hoped she'd taken the right approach, and that Eric's animosity would diminish.

More than that, she hoped Ben got home early tonight. She longed to rest in his arms, to hide from the world for a little while, to recharge her energy level until she could face Eric again.

Because only time would tell how that relationship would play out.

~

A BLUE CAR parked at the automated security gate startled Lannis out of her fatigue-induced haze. The long driveway had hidden it from view as she drove up; she hadn't even glimpsed a flash of color or reflection from metal or mirror. Between the stress of dealing with Eric earlier in the day and the discussion she hadn't wanted, she felt off-balance. Unprotected.

Her heart thumped hard, and she braked. Then she thought, this is *my* house, and a spurt of courage fueled by anger morphed her fear into what she bemusedly recognized as arrogance. It was a new sensation for her and didn't fit comfortably. But it mushroomed— too quickly—into aggression, which was even more discomfiting. Lannis experienced a belligerent hope that she could get rid of the tension of her day by kicking someone off their property. *Bring it on. Make my day.*

By now she was close enough to see that the driver was a woman. A woman who was leaning forward with her forehead on the steering wheel, as if exhausted. Lannis's anger drained away. Curiosity and a ripple of compassion replaced it.

A niggling sense of recognition began to eat at the edge of Lannis's mind. She glanced at the license plate. *Ohio.* Awareness slammed into her.

"Lynnie…" By now she'd driven up behind the car, and she shoved the gear into park, then leaped out. "Lynnie! Are you okay? What are you doing here?" She ran to the driver's side and tapped on the window.

Lynette jerked her head up, her eyelids fluttering. She hit the button and rolled down her window. Her eyes were red and swollen, and her usually smooth complexion was marred by blotches of pink. "Lannis!"

Her sister burst into tears, answering the question of *crying versus allergies* as to the source of the uncharacteristic state of her features. An answering wail erupted from the backseat, and Lannis glanced past Lynette's shoulder to see the car seat and all that was visible of her niece: chubby clenched hands waving and feet pumping in combined outrage and distress.

"Lynnie!" Lannis filled her voice with steel and grasped her sister's shoulder, which shuddered with her weeping. "What is going on?" Fear flooded her as she shot a quick glance to Lynette's midsection. *Has she lost the baby?* But no, Lynette looked to be quite pregnant. Lannis gave her a not-quite-gentle shake. "Get a grip. So Carly can calm down, too."

That seemed to do it. Lynette held her breath for a moment, then swiped at the tears on her face. She sat back, wilting against the support of the seat. "I…can we just talk once we get into your house? Carly needs to get out of the car, I need to use the bathroom."

"Sure." Lannis stepped back and keyed in the code for the security gate, which slid open silently. "Go on up and park."

Twenty minutes later, with both Lynette and Carly refreshed, Lannis poured lemonade, took one for herself and handed the other to Lynette. She pointed at the couch. "Okay, spill your guts."

The younger woman sighed and tears welled in her eyes again, but she controlled the tremble of her lips. "Rich…he's not himself lately, at least not the man I fell in love with and married. He wouldn't let me come to support you during the trial."

Lannis's heart squeezed. *She wanted to come!* Warmth built in her midsection and flowed outward into her arms.

"And he's gotten so…so possessive and jealous." Lynette brushed a lock of hair off her face and tucked it behind her ear in a move so feminine and vulnerable that Lannis felt all her big-sister protective genes wake up.

"Plus he flies off the handle a lot. I know he's under a lot of pressure at work. They've laid off a couple of guys, and even though he's a manager, I think he's afraid he's next."

The hairs on Lannis's arms stood at attention. She took a sip of lemonade to cover her concern, then asked with studied nonchalance. "So…do you feel isolated from your friends? Even Mom?"

Lynette's eyes widened. "Yes! How did you know? I've been trying so hard to make life at home good for him, but he's so…touchy." She frowned. "And not in a good way. I never know what's going to set him off. One day it'll be Carly's toys out when he walks in the door, the next, I overcooked the chicken." She held her hands out in bafflement. "You know me, sis. I'm a good cook. I don't overcook anything."

Lannis's mouth went dry. Yes, she *did* know Lynette. She'd always loved to cook, even as a little girl with that stupid bake oven that Millie had gotten for both of them. Lannis had been indifferent to the toy set then, and to this day viewed cooking as a necessary chore. Although, watching Ben at the grill brought a new level of enjoyment to the activity. She jerked her thoughts back to Lynette…who'd won ribbons at the county fair with original recipes every year since she'd first entered at age sixteen.

Nope. Lynette didn't screw up with cooking. Her sister kept talking, seemingly unable to stop, now that she'd started.

"But he loves me, I know he does. He's so sorry after he blows up, and makes it up to me by—" She paused and blushed, then glanced at Lannis through lowered eyelashes. "Well, you know. Anyway." She waved her hand in a weak brush-it-off gesture. "He's just under so much stress. Afraid of the bills if he loses his job, with the new baby coming." Lynette looked bewildered. "It's not like last time, though. We already have the crib and furniture, and Carly was ready for a new booster seat anyway, so we don't need an expensive car seat. I'm going to breast-feed again, so there's no extra cost for formula. Just diapers…" Her voice trailed off, and the pain in it broke Lannis's heart.

"Oh, sweetie! Have you talked to anybody about this?" Lannis guessed not, but hoped she was not her sister's only resource.

Lynette's hair swung as she shook her head. "No. I don't want to embarrass him. Plus, I've seen so many of my friends talk about their marriages and it never helps. It just poisons the people who listen. Like if I say this to someone, they'll remember it even after Rich and I work through it, and that's not fair to him."

She looked so earnest that Lannis would have laughed if the subject hadn't been so critical. Carly ran to her mom, clutching Ben's antique watering can and babbling. Lynette oohed and aahed, showed her how to pretend-water the plants, and she toddled off, intent on her task. Lannis, relieved for the interruption, gathered her thoughts. The next question was necessary, but she hated having to ask it. A frisson of hatred for her brother-in-law slid beneath her skin, and she quickly squelched the emotion. She couldn't afford to get tangled in their marriage, but Lynette's safety depended on an honest answer. Putting her lemonade down, she grasped her sister's hand and asked, "Has he hit you?"

Lynette's eyes went wide, and a blush raced up her neck and stained her cheeks. "No! How could you think that?" She tried to tug her hand free and began to stand.

Lannis tightened her grip. "Sit down, sis. Please. This is for your own good, not an attack on Rich." Lynette hesitated, and Lannis gave her a gentle pull. "Please."

She sat reluctantly. "Why do you say that?" Her expression looked bruised, and tears welled in her eyes.

"Lynnie…I, well, when I was seeing the counselor after…" Lannis stopped and swallowed. "After the r-rape, we talked about some of the risks that come after an attack. One of them is being— sometimes, not always—maybe being predisposed to getting into an abusive relationship. She made me learn the signs and usual progression of abuse so I could gauge and judge my relationships in the future." She squeezed Lynette's hand, then let go. "You're describing everything like the textbooks."

Lynette went from looking bruised to angry. "That's not the way it is, Lannis. Rich is good to me," she said hotly.

Lannis sighed. "I know, and I'm not accusing him of being an abuser. I'm just telling you that he is, for whatever reason, leaning that direction. I know he loves you. Heck, he probably thinks he's protecting you, just like he protects you from my potentially damaging influence on you." She couldn't hide the pain that entered her voice with the last sentence. "And God knows, I deserve it. At least some of it, anyway. I made a lot of really bad choices a few years ago, and I hurt you. I may not agree with his approach, but he means well." She shrugged, acknowledging the irony of the situation. "I mean well, too, Lynnie. He needs to examine his motives and behavior, and change what needs changing, for your sake."

Lynette leaned back on the couch, her brows knit in concentration. "He hasn't hit me," she said with a pointed glance at Lannis, "but his jealousy and his outbursts really scare me. I just couldn't face him tonight. I'm so stressed… This is supposed to be the most wonderful time of our lives, but it's turning into a nightmare. I don't know what to do, how to make it better."

Lannis grabbed Lynette's hand again. "It'll be okay. You're safe here, and once Ben gets home, we'll call Rich together. Maybe hearing from Ben will help Rich hear what you need him to hear." She stood and went to the kitchen for the phone. "Meanwhile, let's call the hotline and talk about options for you." She slanted a glance at Lynette, who looked alarmed, and laughed. "Don't worry. We won't give your name, and you make all the decisions about what's best for you. That's what Ben did with me, the first time I called." She didn't say it, but she was glad she'd done it. That call had heralded the beginnings of her healing.

It appeared this was her chance to pay forward the good deed done on her behalf. She'd always felt more than a twinge of guilt that she couldn't find the courage to volunteer as an advocate for other rape victims. Every time she'd tried, the feelings she thought she'd triumphed over would roar back, and her anxiety forced her to quit. Finally she accepted that route was not for her. Betsy, Althea, Ben…they'd all assured her it was okay, but she'd carried the seed of shame nonetheless.

She punched in the hotline number without even looking at the keypad, and when an advocate answered, handed the phone to Lynette.

~

Ben elbowed the door open and stuck his head into the kitchen. Based on the license plate and child seat in the car parked next to Lannis's, he'd already figured out Lynette and Carly were visiting. What he hadn't figured out was why. Or if Rich had come along. He steeled himself for a potentially tense evening, based on the men's limited encounters in the past. The guy meant well, but had devastated Lannis when he shot off his mouth several months ago, before the trial. Ben didn't cotton to that sort of treatment of a woman, even the scumbag women he had to arrest. And it set even more poorly when aimed at his wife.

Salad—dumped out of a bag if Lannis had made it, or leaves adorned with a mouthwatering array of fruit bits and nuts if Lynette had—sat on the counter, and spaghetti sauce bubbled on the stove, filling the room with a pungent, welcoming aroma. As he stepped into the room, he noted mandarin oranges and sliced almonds gracing the salad greens. A slight grin lifted the corners of his mouth. *Lynnie, then.* A murmur of voices rose from the living room.

"Hey, Lannis," he called. "I'm home." He deposited his computer bag on the floor, then reconsidered and put it on top of the side counter. A couple of strides took him into the living room where Lynette reclined, feet propped the arm of the sofa. He caught a glimpse of a blonde topknot bobbing along behind the couch, and his grin spread. Lannis met him midway across the room. Relief, joy, and a haunted expression flickered across her features in the moment before she wrapped her arms around him. She buried her face in his chest. He automatically rubbed a hand up her back, and noted tension in her muscles.

Carly stood on her tiptoes behind the couch, and peered over its back. Her eyes widened. "Unca Ben!" Everything but the topknot disappeared as she toddled around the back, then halted in a sudden attack of shyness as she rounded the armrest. She stuck a thumb in her mouth and regarded him with huge, serious blue eyes.

Ben dropped a kiss on Lannis's head and whispered, "Don't know what's going on, but we're in it together, darlin'." He gave her a reassuring squeeze and released her, then dropped to one knee to get to Carly's level. "Hey, Lynette, good to see you. Is Rich here, too?" Carly took a tentative step forward, and he smiled at her, giving her his best *I'm a harmless dude* look. Even as he coaxed the child to remember and trust him, he caught the tightening of Lynette's lips at the mention of Rich. Lannis was even easier to read. She'd gone pale, and if her shoulders got any stiffer, they'd shatter.

Carly finally allowed him to ruffle her hair, then extended her hands in the universal plea of little kids. "Up," she said with total confidence in his compliance. He grinned, gathered her into his arms, and stood.

Keeping his voice light for Carly's sake, he turned to the two sisters and said, "What's up?" He glanced at the toddler in his arms and tickled her. "Besides Carly." He waited.

"Uh, maybe after dinner, Ben," Lannis said.

"Or not," he said, a hint of steel underlying his congenial tone.

Lynette sat up, swiveled to plant her feet on the floor, and sighed. Dark circles beneath her eyes made her look even more exhausted than a long drive, an active child, and pregnancy should. "I needed some space," she said. "Lannis says Rich is being verbally abusive, maybe spiraling into a cycle that may lead to physical abuse. She made me call the hotline and talk to a counselor."

Carly wriggled, said, "Dow." Ben set her on her feet, steadying her before she tore off to play with a pile of plastic containers and utensils appropriated from the kitchen for that purpose. He raised his eyebrows, both at the impromptu toy supply and Lynette's words. He felt like he'd been sucker punched. He and Rich had their differences, but he'd never expected the guy to go down *that* road.

"And…" He instinctively sensed she'd clam up if he began asking questions. He was good at interrogation, capable of using the full gamut of techniques from intimidation to empathy, and while this was not an interrogation, he definitely needed to know a lot more than he did.

She took the bait and said, "I'm going to stay here overnight and see a counselor tomorrow morning. They already made me put together a simple safety plan"—her voice hitched, and tears welled in eyes that bore evidence that this was not the first time she'd wept today—"and…well, I hoped maybe you could talk to Rich tonight. He's probably frantic by now, and I'm just not up to dealing with him. Yet." Her lips trembled, and a tear escaped. Lynette swiped at it, then lifted her head in a gesture of determination so like her sister's that Ben almost smiled.

Even so, Ben felt a muscle tick in his jaw. "Are you telling the truth about him not hitting you?" He didn't camouflage the steel in his voice this time.

"Ben!" Lannis shot to her feet from the barstool she'd retreated to as he greeted Carly. "That's really rude! Why are you acting like she's a liar?" She curled her hands into fists.

Ben stopped her with a motion of his hand. "I'm not calling her a liar, Lannis. I want to know the truth of how far this has gone." He searched Lynette's eyes. She looked confused, a little frightened, and annoyed all at the same time. *Good. She's not hiding anything.* She'd look guilty or angry if she was. "Because if he has, he'll regret it, in more ways than one."

"No, he hasn't hit me," Lynette said, sounding aggravated, "and I'm not lying." She stood and put her hands on her hips. "I'm actually sick of talking about this now. And I'm hungry. Real hungry. If you know what's important to your health, you won't mess with a hungry pregnant woman." She shot the same pointed look back at Ben that he'd sent her. "So can we just eat—in peace—and talk about the weather for a while?"

Ben strode to her side and enfolded her in a gentle bear hug. "I believe you. And the answer to all the other is yes. Dinner now, accompanied by bland and boring conversation. The rest will all work out."

Her belly, harder than he expected, pressed against his hip, and he felt a sudden, miniature thump from inside it. Shaken, he realized it was the baby. Kicking. Lynette didn't even react, and in a rush of understanding, Ben saw how normal, how natural, how…common this was to her. Stunned, he let go and turned her toward the table, giving her a little push. A pang of longing broadsided him, a yearning to feel his own baby growing inside Lannis. "I'll, uh, go wash up and be back to help." Which was a pretty stupid thing to say, as the table was already set, and not much remained to be done.

He headed for the hall bath before Lannis caught on to his surge of emotion. When, or probably more accurately, *whether* to start a family was a touchy subject between them. One he didn't want to bring up tonight. Not with everything else going on. But he'd seen how good Lannis was with Carly. She might be afraid to bring a child into a world she viewed as unsafe, yet she embraced any opportunity to spend time with Carly. Plus, she had a knack for making the toddler feel at home, and—blast it—*safe,* a knack not possessed by everyone.

How could she not want that joy for herself? And for him? He'd made it clear how badly he wanted children, hopefully without pushing her too hard.

Rather than respite, his home had turned into a balancing act tonight. Two women. No, make that two *upset* women. An angry, unpredictable man. Undercurrents of violence and fear. And an innocent child to shield from all of it.

As he washed his hands, he closed the door to his emotions. He had a phone call to make in about forty-five minutes, and he settled his mind, focusing on planning his approach.

~

BEN PUNCHED THE LAST NUMBER into the handset, waited for the first ring to go through, and pressed the button to activate the speakerphone. He placed it on the recently cleared table, and slanted a comforting look at Lynette. She'd just returned from getting Carly down for the night, and reached up to tuck a stray lock of hair behind her ear. Lannis wiped her hands on a kitchen towel, hung it, and slid into the chair next to Lynette. She grasped her younger sister's hand and gave it a squeeze. Lynette's eyes flickered, and she dredged up a wan smile.

Three rings. Then a click and a wary "Hello?" from Rich.

"Hey, Rich." A sibilant hiss of indrawn breath on the other end of the connection told Ben that Rich recognized his voice. He introduced himself anyway. "Ben Martin. You're on speakerphone. Lynette and Lannis are here. I figured you'd want to know Lynette and Carly are at our place, and had an uneventful drive."

"What are they doing there?" Rich's voice rose, and a note of panic or anger tinged it. Maybe both, Ben thought. Hard to tell. He started to answer, but Rich beat him.

"Lynette, tell me you're okay." This sounded belligerent.

She leaned toward the phone and spoke in soothing tones. "Yes, Rich. I'm here. Carly and I had good trip." She opened her mouth to say something else, but Rich interrupted her.

"Well that's just dandy." His voice dripped with sarcasm now. "Are you having a nice *vacation?*"

Lynette closed her eyes and straightened her spine. "It's not a vacation, Rich. I feel like I'm running away from you, and that totally sucks. But I needed a break from your attitude."

"Yeah? There's no fixing any of it by you taking off. Come home and we'll work it out." Belligerence gave way to wheedling. "I miss you, and Carly needs her daddy."

"You haven't had time to miss me yet." Irritation flashed across Lynette's face. "Carly needs two parents who treat each other with respect, and you need to pony up with some of that for me. No, let me rephrase. A *lot* of that, Rich. Respect. No more of this business of trying to manipulate and blame me so you can feel like a *man*." Her features twisted, and she blinked back tears. "I'm going to talk to a counselor tomorrow, but I already see that we have major problems, and you'll have to do some serious work if our marriage is to survive this."

"You've been talking to Lannis, haven't you?" he shouted. "She's filling your head with all sorts of bullshit."

"That's enough." Ben used his cop voice. "Rich, Lynette is doing what she needs to do to be safe. Leave her alone for now. Sounds like anger management and some counseling are in order for you."

"That's a load of—" Rich began, but Ben talked over him.

"There is nothing to be gained by bulldozing your way through this. Marriage is a partnership, and neither has the right to push the other around, verbally or physically. From what I've heard Lynette describe, you are only a few short steps from a domestic violence situation. You want a restraining order? Keep it up and she'll get one. Then you'll be out on your…uh, butt"—Ben sent an apologetic glance at the two women even as he replaced the cruder word he'd been about to use—"and you may be looking at separation and divorce down the road. Is that what you want?" He gave the guy a chance to get a word in edgewise. Finally.

Rich stayed silent, and the moment stretched out as Lynette chewed her lip in naked anticipation of his answer. Lannis covered her sister's hand with hers. Ben knew she meant to be comforting, but he also remembered how he felt when Deb left him. The divorce, as amicable as they went, had still left him with a gaping hole in his heart. He glanced at Lannis, sent her a crooked smile. She'd healed that for him, but still, he could identify with Rich. His smile faded. *At least Deb and I didn't have kids.*

At last Rich ground out a reluctant, low, "No."

Lannis touched Lynette's shoulder with the tenderness she usually reserved for Ben, and leaned close to her sister's ear. "Let's leave the men to talk, Lynnie." The younger woman swung her chin-length dark hair in firm refusal, but Lannis tightened her grip on her shoulder and answered with the same steel Ben had put in his voice a few moments ago. "Yes. Let Rich save face. This involves you, but it doesn't all have to be said in front of you." She shot her sister a look fraught with meaning, and all the fight drained out of Lynette. She nodded and stood, exhaustion clear in her posture and features.

"Rich…hon, I love you, but I can't go on like this," she said. "This is nobody's idea except mine. Lannis and Ben didn't know anything until I showed up at their place this afternoon." Her voice hitched. "I want us to work out. I want a good marriage, a happy family. Please…please talk to Ben. I'm going to bed. 'Bye." She turned and trudged toward the hallway, reaching to massage her lower back as she did. Lannis followed, shooting an anxious glance back at Ben.

He sighed, sparing a moment's contemplation of Rich's lack of gratitude for the blessings of a wife and children. He hoped it was only an aberration. His thoughts ricocheted to Lannis. Would she ever conquer her fear and agree to kids? His kids. Would she rub her back, let him knead the soreness out at the end of a long day?

Ben shoved a hand through his hair, leaving it standing on end. His heart felt hollow as he turned back to the phone and set himself to the task of diplomatically herding Rich to more appropriate methods of dealing with life's disappointments.

Saving another man's marriage while his own lurched across rocky terrain.

~

The murmur of low male voices lulled Lannis into a restless doze, but thoughts of her confrontation with Eric chased around her mind, combined with worry over Lynette. When they strayed to Robert Davis, she blew out her breath in a huff of frustrated anger and threw the covers back. She sprang out of bed knowing she couldn't escape the confines of her mind nearly as easily as she'd shed the weight of the comforter.

Lannis took two steps, then stopped. Where was she to go? She didn't want to eavesdrop on Ben and Rich's conversation, so the living area—kitchen, dining, great room—was out. Their bedroom felt like as much a prison as the one housing Davis at the moment. Lynette and Carly were bedded down on the convertible futon in the office Lannis shared with Ben, and she didn't dare risk disturbing Carly by stealing in to grab a flight manual to study.

The small bedroom? Uh, nope. They'd designated it for storage, and it was about as appealing as a closet, since that was pretty much what it resembled at the moment. She had a brief flash of regret that she hadn't agreed to Ben's idea of adding a deck to the master bedroom. One evening he'd held her close, waved his arm in a grand arc to show her the wall he wanted to rip out, enticing her with the sunsets they would see. She'd hesitated, saying it was too costly…which was true in a way, but she hadn't meant monetary cost. Lannis had to admit her own brush with poverty colored her judgment, but it embarrassed her to reveal the real reason she'd hung back.

What if...? Could someone break in? She tried to tell herself that the security system was reliable, that she didn't worry about the other doors, so why should she worry about this one? Because it would be glass? No, windows didn't freak her out. What freaked her out was being asleep and vulnerable. It wasn't rational, but a lot of what she felt wasn't rational, and she felt helpless to change that.

But now she wished she'd acquiesced. She needed to get away, and even if she couldn't slip free of her own skin for a while, it would help if she could walk outside. Fresh air moving against her face, the sight of trees, leaves fluttering in the breeze, stars winking between the branches...

Ben's voice rose, and she heard him say good-bye. Lights flicked off, and his footsteps sounded on the tile floor of the kitchen. The fridge seal made a soft whoosh as he opened it, then sighed as he swung it closed. He crossed onto the carpet of the great room and padded down the hall to the bedroom, popping the top to a can of beer as he walked.

A pang of longing struck Lannis. *A glass of wine would be so*— She slammed the door of her mind on the thought. If she had to call her sponsor tonight she would, but she hoped that talking with Ben would be enough.

His bulk filled the doorway for a moment, and then he entered, a darker shadow among the shadows of the room. He moved in near silence toward the bathroom, and Lannis realized he'd missed seeing her, apparently thinking she was asleep.

"Ben," she said softly, and his shadow paused.

"You still up?" Surprise overlaid fatigue in his voice.

"Couldn't sleep," she said and approached him, sliding her arms around his waist, laying her head on his shoulder, sighing in relief at finally—*finally*—being where she'd needed to be since she'd left work. His free arm came around in its familiar embrace, and he shifted as he lifted the beer and took a long swig. He lowered it and completed the circle of arms, the can chilling her shoulder blade where it balanced. He settled his chin on her head.

Lannis's heart went out to him. He was as tired and stressed out as she was. Maybe this wasn't a good time to talk about her problems. She sagged a little and blinked back a sudden wash of tears.

"I think Rich will be okay," Ben said, his voice rumbling under her cheek. "He's going to call a counselor tomorrow. Didn't really want to, but Lynette and Carly mean the world to him, and he recognizes he needs to make some adjustments." He rubbed a hand up and down her back. "He was shocked to see his actions, his attitude from my—our—perspective. It took a little tough love, but I think he gets it."

Her throat clogged at his words, and Lannis realized her worry about Lynette had been deeper than she'd thought. She nodded, squeezing her eyes tight, and tears spilled over in spite of her efforts to stem them. She choked out a strangled laugh. "Yeah, that's your specialty, Ben. Tough love."

He chuckled. "I suppose." His throat worked against Lannis's hair as he took another long drink. He gave her a quick hug and set her away from him. "Let's get to bed." He swung into the bathroom and tossed the can into the sink. It landed upside down and gurgled as the last bit drained away.

She swiped at her tears and firmed her spine. "Thank you, Ben. I love you."

"Love you, too," he called.

Lannis climbed into the bed, pulled the comforter over her, and fluffed Ben's pillow before she lay down. They'd talk in a day or two about the situation with Eric, maybe after Lynette went home. She could hang on that long. Or maybe she could deal with it on her own. She'd dealt with worse by herself.

Robert Davis's face flashed in her mind, and she cringed. She'd made a mess of dealing with that on her own. She flopped back on her pillow and blew her bangs up in frustration. A thought, gentle and kind and not her own, drifted into her awareness. *It's not good for you to isolate yourself.* An invisible but palpable blanket of caring encircled her. Lannis let go of the tension in her muscles, sagging into it. God, or the universe, or whatever she called it, always shot straight to the heart of the issue. No fancy words, no judgment, no ultimatums. Just a zinger that was as accurate as it was unexpected.

She threw an arm over her eyes. *Okay. Fine. I'll talk to him tomorrow.* Fatigue dragged her into the softness of the sheets, and she was already half-asleep when Ben's weight dipped the mattress. But not too asleep to stop her from rolling into his embrace as he joined her under the covers. Lannis felt him sigh, a soft almost-groan, and she snuggled closer, both seeking and offering solace. He answered with his trademark one-armed hug, and sleep claimed her before she drew her next breath.

Chapter Sixteen

"CARLY—" Lannis lunged for the fern in the toddler's grasp. While she didn't save the frond from getting mangled, she did prevent it from making it into Carly's mouth. *I hope it's not poisonous.* She shuddered and stowed the plant on top of the bookcase. She cast about for something nonlethal the child could play with. The television remote caught her eye. "Here, honey, play with this." Carly took it, and Lannis leaned behind the set to unplug it.

Lannis had been up since six with Carly in an effort to grant Lynette the luxury of sleeping in, but the child's energy level and curiosity made it difficult to keep the noise level down. It would be just her luck that the kid would find the correct buttons to turn it on. Full blast.

The shower went on, then off a few minutes later, and Ben appeared, running a hand through still-damp hair. "Hey, Lannis, I have an early meeting, but with everything last night, I forgot to tell you." He crouched. "What'cha got, little bit?" Carly held out her prize, and he oohed over it for a moment, then patted her on the head and stood.

Lannis tamped down her disappointment. She'd planned on discussing Eric with him over breakfast. "You have any time today?"

He finished tucking in his shirt and gave her a distracted kiss on the cheek. "Yeah, I could maybe do lunch, say at twelve thirty." He filled his travel mug with the coffee she'd brewed between toddler interventions. "You're not flying?"

"No, unless something comes up. We don't have a scheduled transport, and the other team is sitting alert for emergencies." Rarely did the backup team get assigned an emergency flight. "I'll give you a call if we get launched."

He glance at his watch. "Okay. Appleby's?"

"Sure." The restaurant was pretty close to midway between his office and Bowman Field. "See you then."

He grabbed his laptop from the counter where he'd left it last night, and headed out. The door had barely closed when he stuck his head back in. "Hey, does Lynette have the codes for the security gate and the alarm system?"

Lannis snagged a pen and notepad from the counter. "I'll get that for her, Ben. Thanks for remembering." She wrote the codes, then printed out directions to Lynette's appointment and put them on the counter.

By that time, she was bordering on late, so she woke Lynette and left her with a reminder to call either her or Ben if she needed anything.

Lannis grabbed her flight bag, tossed it in the backseat of her car, and backed out of the garage. She shifted into drive and huffed out a sigh. So much for a quiet evening at home, and preparing for a calm, balanced day at work. If she counted the subconscious comfort of lying in Ben's arms while asleep—which she did—then she'd had a peaceful, healing night. But not talking about the tension between her and Eric left her with a niggling sense of unease. She didn't feel as unsettled as she had last night, but she almost felt like she was keeping a secret from Ben.

If she'd learned anything over the past year, she'd learned the seductive power of secrets. They robbed her of her voice and isolated her, and narrowed her world to a myopic vision of ever more restrictive options.

No, she wasn't going to let this become a secret. Lannis tried to anticipate how this morning would play out. It was likely that she'd run into Eric. In a pilot pool as small as this, it was inevitable. She hadn't taken the time to look up the master schedule before she left, but she a vague recollection that Eric had today off. She hoped.

Lannis sighed again, then firmed her resolve, put her worry about Lynette out of her mind, said a quick prayer that Eric be otherwise occupied today, and focused on getting through the morning until lunchtime. When she could talk to Ben.

Which didn't happen.

He called a few minutes before noon, sounding harried and frustrated. "Sorry, darlin'. We've got a situation."

Lannis knew he couldn't elaborate. "It's okay, Ben." She stifled a sigh. "Will you be home on time tonight?"

"Should be." She heard voices in the background, staccato and terse. "Gotta go. I'll call if that changes." He hung up before she could say anything more.

Tension snaked through muscles in her neck, and she rotated her head so she could see the sky through the autumn-colored leaves, then consciously pushed her shoulders earthward. Appleby's on her own didn't sound at all inviting, but she needed a break from the office. Especially since Eric didn't have the day off like she'd thought.

He'd greeted her with a brusque nod, and she returned it with what she hoped came off as confident professionalism. Pretending yesterday hadn't happened, or if she had to acknowledge it, that it didn't matter. Lannis cringed inwardly every time she saw him, though, remembering the leer on his face when he told her he'd read the court transcript. The thought made her squirm with embarrassment.

She made an impulsive decision, swung into her shared desk area, and snagged her jacket and car keys. "Hey, Will, I'm going to run home for lunch."

He sent her his trademark salute and said, "You'll have your cell phone on, right?"

"Of course," she said. "Call me if the hot crew launches, and I'll be back in twenty minutes." She paused. "The plane's already preflighted, and the weather's pretty benign."

"Go. In fact, you don't need to come back this afternoon if we don't need the backup crew. Keep your phone handy, but if you don't hear from me, I'll see you tomorrow."

Lynette's car wasn't parked out front when Lannis drove up. *Huh.* The appointment must have lasted longer than expected. Lannis winced at possible reasons. Surely Lynette hadn't lied to her, and to Ben. She couldn't be getting a restraining order, which the facility in Kentucky couldn't directly assist her with anyway. Her heart gave a little squeeze, and Lannis shut down her car.

She let herself into the house, dropped her keys on the counter, headed for the bedroom. And pulled up short.

A note sat propped on the dining room table, anchored by the pepper mill. She leaned over, tugged it loose, and recognized Lynette's handwriting.

Dear Lannie and Ben,

I'm going home to Rich. The counselor was great, but I—we—need to be back in our own place. Besides, Rich already talked to someone, like he promised Ben, and he says he understands, and that this will never happen again. I love him, and Carly needs her daddy. Bottom line, I trust him to get his act together.

Thanks for the hospitality and for your love and support. I'll call when we get home.

Love,

Lynnie

Lannis's heart sank, and she let the paper flutter to the table. Of course this was the outcome she wanted for her little sister, for her niece, for her brother-in-law—but only after they'd done some real work to fix the situation. What if Rich's promises were empty? What if they weren't, but he didn't have the capability of following through? Was this what the "hearts and flowers" stage of abuse was like? She didn't know. She'd never lived it. She only had Betsy's homework to fall back on, and the book she'd made Lannis read. Which said oftentimes a victim would return to an abusive relationship based on teary apologies accompanied by flowers and gifts, and that the whole cycle would start up again. With escalating consequences the next time. And the next.

Her first instinct was to call Lynette, but she lifted her hand from the phone almost as soon as she touched it. *No.* She needed to talk to Ben, and try to sort out her own paranoia versus Lynette's reality. Bits of last night's conversations asserted themselves in her mind. Lynette's outrage at Ben's questions. Ben's belief that Lynette had told the truth about Rich, and his report of the conversation with her brother-in-law. If Ben didn't believe Rich, he would have said so. Her fear began to subside.

Lynette had done the best thing, to start out with, anyway. No secrets. Lannis noted the irony of her own dilemma with a grimace. Nonetheless, Rich was under the microscope now, and the certain knowledge that he'd be held accountable for his actions was Lynette's cloak of protection.

She rubbed her temples with her forefingers, at a loss for what to do next. The afternoon stretched in front of her, hours of time suddenly open, with no compelling tasks to fill it. Returning to work held no appeal. Not today, at least. Between "Eric avoidance" and Will's conditional release, she had perfect reasons to stay home.

Lannis changed gears in her mind, racked her brain for any errands that needed running, and came up empty. So, what could she do around the house? Inside, not much. She and Ben had cleaned over the weekend, and besides, she felt antsy, didn't want to be inside. She'd planned supper earlier, and simple as it was, it required no prep until time to eat. Her mind went to the yard.

It was a gorgeous fall day, chilly but sunny, and winterizing the perennial beds around the house would be a perfect reason to be outside. A smile teased her lips. A chore she could do for Ben, who liked the full-body involvement of mowing and pruning trees, but hated the detail work of mulching and dividing bulbs. *There you go.*

Useful on several levels. And a great way to keep anxiety and worry at bay.

She resumed her trip to the bedroom, shucking out of her uniform as she went. Moments later, cell phone tucked in a pocket of her jean jacket, she headed for the front garden.

As a strategy for avoidance, digging was effective. Not to mention hypnotic and calming. She couldn't remember when she'd had so much time with so little responsibility. Well, yes, she could. It was when she'd been injured and stayed here with Ben, almost a year ago.

And while the physical exertion worked its healing magic, the downtime opened a Pandora's box of disturbing notions for her to consider.

By the time she drew a forearm across her brow several hours later, well aware she'd need a shower if Will called at this point, she also knew she had far more to talk to Ben about when he arrived. Her stomach churned and she headed for the kitchen, bent on the icy soft drinks in the fridge.

Thank God she wasn't craving alcohol. In fact, this might be a first. Lannis acknowledged the small triumph, or maybe it was major one, but it came at a high cost. She dreaded the coming conversation, knowing that Robert Davis remained the pivotal issue in their marriage—and unless she dealt with him, she might lose it all.

Ben. Her marriage. Their future.

Pain sliced through her heart. She veered to the bedroom, bypassing the kitchen, and crumpled onto the bed. She dragged Ben's pillow to her breast and clutched it, inhaling his now-familiar and comforting scent.

Ben deserved nothing less than honesty…and the desires of his heart.

Lannis needed to either move past her fear or let him go, free to find a woman unburdened by an intrusive past, free to find a woman courageous enough to bear his child.

Before it came to that, she planned on fighting—fiercely—using every means available to become the woman he needed. Unburdened. Courageous. The mother of his child.

There was only one way she could see to accomplish that. A path she did not relish, and that Ben would likely view as crazy. But if she'd learned anything over the past year, she'd learned that honoring her instincts was key.

Honoring this particular idea made her head swim, and she closed her eyes against the sensation.

But she didn't need to focus on that right at this moment. Maggie's face flashed in her mind, harried with the demands of her two rambunctious youngsters, but vibrantly happy as a stay-at-home mom, much the same as Lynette. Except Maggie had a stronger, more equal relationship with her husband. Both women loved their children with a ferocity Lannis could only admire, but what they had that she didn't was the courage to embrace the initial choice.

Pregnancy.

Lannis surged to her feet, shoving Ben's pillow haphazardly to the side, picked up the phone, and hit speed dial for Mike and Maggie's house. A glance at the clock told her she had at least two hours before Ben got home, and that Marty was likely waking from his nap. She had time—

"Hey, Ben, what's up?" Maggie's voice surprised her after only a brief ring on the other end.

"Uh, it's me, Lannis," she said, hating the insecurity voiced by her slight stammer.

"Oh, hi, Lannis." Maggie sounded genuinely pleased, and it took Lannis a moment to realize she so rarely made this particular call, no wonder Maggie thought it was Ben.

"Do you mind if I come over for a while? I have the afternoon off, and…" She trailed off, not wanting to go into detail on the phone.

"Sure. You may get stuck changing a diaper or helping me run herd on the crazy redheads around here." Maggie's tone was teasing, but Lannis could hear the questioning quality beneath.

"Be glad to. I'll be there in fifteen minutes." Lannis paused and added, "Thanks."

As advertised, Megan and Marty stormed the front door as Lannis walked in, and Maggie shooed them away with clucking noises. She lifted hands dusted with flour and said, "Make yourself at home. I'll get the rolls in the oven and then have a bit of a break. We'll have tea and chat."

Megan grabbed Lannis's fingers and tugged her toward the toy box, which appeared to have been upended. Marty had already grabbed a pint-sized truck and was making vrooming noises while scooting along next to it on one knee. Lannis allowed herself to be towed, and Megan launched into a breathless monologue extolling the virtues of her newest doll. Lannis knelt, admired, then gave her a quick hug and went to the kitchen where Maggie was rinsing the last of the soap off her hands.

"Hot or cold? I'll get it started if you have a preference." Lannis felt almost comfortable in Maggie's kitchen. She'd been there often enough with Ben, but this was the first time she'd ever been there without him, and a sudden spurt of shyness made her awkward.

"Cold. I've got a pitcher in the fridge." Maggie toweled her hands dry, then squirted lotion on them.

Lannis snagged two glasses from the dish rack, filled them with ice, then tea, and presented one to Maggie.

Maggie sank into her chair and sighed, then took a long drink. "So…what's going on, Lannis?"

Lannis took a nervous sip and set her glass down. She didn't know any way to soften her question, and glanced at Maggie.

"Spill, girlfriend. Are you and Ben having problems?" Maggie cut to the heart of matters on the best of days, and she didn't mince around now.

Lannis tightened her grip on her glass. She knew Maggie well enough to have expected it, but the woman's directness still took her by surprise sometimes, and this was one of them. "Uh, no, not that way. I mean, not like my sister and her husband or anything." She stopped, and felt her face warm with a blush. "Sorry. Lynnie and Rich are going through a rough patch, and he's teetering on the edge of being abusive. Ben talked to him last night, and Lynnie went back to him already." She shook her head. "I'm worried about them, no doubt. But my question for you is totally unrelated, and no, Ben and I aren't having problems." She made little quote marks in the air when she said "problems." She took a deep breath, and blurted it out.

"I'm terrified to get pregnant." Lannis stole a peek at Maggie, who looked surprised at her statement.

"What are you afraid of? Labor?" Maggie laughed. "While it is a major life event, it's manageable, especially with an epidural." She sent Lannis a shrewd look. "But you've been through so much pain and dealt with it that I can't see that as scaring you." A shriek came from the other room, and she leaned back in her chair. "Megan Ross, stop that right now, or you'll have a time-out." Silence reigned at the threat, and Maggie faced Lannis again.

Lannis cleared her throat. "No, actually, I hadn't thought that far ahead." She felt the blush grow hectic on her cheeks.

Maggie laughed, a bawdy guffaw that hinted at X-rated thoughts. "Now, I'm pretty darn sure that you and Ben aren't having any problems with the mechanics of the process." She lifted an eyebrow.

Lannis buried her face in her hands. "Oh God, no." A strangled laugh burbled up, and she regarded Maggie through her fingers. They both burst out laughing, and when she caught her breath, Lannis sobered and said, "I'm afraid to bring a child into this world. I'm afraid I can't protect him or her from predators like Robert Davis." She shrugged, a helpless motion of one shoulder. "I'm just…afraid." She looked Maggie in the eye. "How do you have the courage to do that?"

"Oh, Lannis." Compassion shone in Maggie's face, and she leaned forward. "Honey, there are no guarantees in life. We almost lost Megan at birth. She had the cord around her neck, and they were trying to do a crash C-section to save her life when she decided to come the natural way. It was touch and go for a few minutes after she was born, but she's fine now."

Lannis's breathing hitched. "I'm sorry. I didn't know."

Maggie shrugged. "And you can't control whether they get sick and a routine cold turns into meningitis, or they get away from you and run into the street." The light in her eyes intensified. "You can be the best parent in the world, and something bad can happen." She leaned back. "Or you can be the worst parent in the world, and they can turn out fine. Of course, the chances of that happening are a lot better if you're a good parent, and you would be."

Maggie reached out and covered Lannis's hand with one of hers. "You have to take a leap of faith. That's it. Most people don't even think about it. You, on the other hand, quite understandably given your experience, try to control as much of your environment as possible. Which will contribute to making you a very responsible and devoted mother." She fell silent, and after a moment, squeezed Lannis's hand, then let go and took another sip of tea.

Emotion gripped Lannis's heart, and she took a gulp from her own glass to try to camouflage it. The intensity ebbed after two or three slow heartbeats, and she drew a deep breath.

"Oh, Lannis? Remember, you aren't in it alone. I've got Mike, and he's my rock. You've got Ben and between the two of them, they're among the top one percent of quality men on this planet. You will be fine."

Twin shrieks from the living room, one of outrage and the other of pain, rocketed Maggie to her feet, and Lannis took her leave as Maggie dispensed major age-appropriate discipline and minor first aid.

As she reached the door, Maggie called out. "Lannis, come over anytime. You don't need to tag along with Ben, and you don't need an invitation. I'm glad you called." She shot a brilliant smile at Lannis, who sent a slightly tremulous one in return.

Two firsts today.

Not even a hint of craving for alcohol.

She'd reached out to a friend and confided without losing her sense of privacy.

Then there was number three, a first she hadn't even realized. She'd laughed in the face of her fears—and discovered humor took some of the sting out. A lot of it, in fact.

She slid into her car and started it, feeling lighter than she had for days.

Chapter Seventeen

"Yo, Lawyer-Man." King LeMasters swaggered toward Robert's bolted-down chair in the communal area of the cell block.

Robert glanced up and gave the guy a brief nod. "You hear anything yet?" He didn't really care, but his new and unexpected status as knight in shining armor to the incarcerated masses deserved nurturing. A little courtesy and pretense of interest went a long way. Never mind that King had turned out to be a dud. The guy was all mouth, no substance, and Robert hadn't learned one blasted bit of information that he hadn't already known about Lannis Parker Martin or Ben "BJ" Martin. Well, except the guy's undercover name for that particular op.

"Naw, not yet, man, but I got hope." The guy flashed a smile, confident that the diamond that sparkled from his gold-capped incisor more than made up for the occasional missing tooth elsewhere.

True to his word, Robert had helped him with a legal filing—child's play, or more appropriately, first-year law student's play—and then other inmates had approached him with requests. Hesitantly at first, their self-interest warring with the unwritten codes spurning sex offenders and anyone associated with the justice system. One guy, then another, and then another, until a gaggle of them hung out wherever he decided to park himself during the day. King joined the three inmates already loitering within earshot, adding to the ridiculous sense that fairy dust was going to rub off of him and magically set them all free. The younger men all did some sort of a jive-greeting, half dancing and weaving and bumping fists.

Robert participated. Again, easy to learn, easy to do, and full of benefits.

Without much effort at all, he'd gone from being pariah to savior. Not bad, not bad at all. He didn't have to watch his back nearly as much, and had begun to catch up on sleep.

One of the correction officers wandered over, probably to break up the party, not that any real celebrating was going on. "How's it going, men?"

No one answered him, but unease fluttered through the group.

Robert had a bit of respect for this guard. The guy had never used undue force in subduing him, and seemed to get that Robert's recent explosions were designed to manipulate, not injure. He inclined his head in greeting a second time, searching his mind for potential infractions that might invite discipline. He came up empty, but shifted, alert and ready.

The guard—his name tag proclaimed the ubiquitous surname Smith—grinned, and Robert glanced up to see what the other corrections officers were doing. Nothing. Their body language indicated relaxed vigilance. Business as usual. *Huh.*

"So, Davis, you doing some community service down here?" Smith's tone was conversational, not confrontational, and he didn't project any sense of machismo. Just his normal, confident *I'm in charge* demeanor.

Robert put his arm on the table, confused as hell, but going for a neutral and—most important—equal attitude. "Yes, sir, you might put it that way."

Smith's grin widened. "Good for you. Took you long enough to figure it out." He winked. "If you mind your manners for a few more weeks, I'll recommend you for yard privileges."

Involuntarily, Robert's chest tightened. *Outdoors.* He hadn't taken a breath of fresh air for months. His lungs were coated with the stink of too many men too close together for too long. Fresh air might actually hurt to breathe after all this time, although coming back inside would be worse. Once he had a taste of it, the stale, overprocessed air of the cell block would feel like a death sentence.

His voice deserted him, but he nodded at Smith, beginning to feel bobble-headed, like one of those stupid dolls. Smith turned to the other inmates and spoke, but Robert tuned him out. Once the carrot had been dangled, he couldn't stop thinking about it.

The sky. He longed to see it, to gaze at the clouds and read them. He'd forced himself to feel only numbness at the loss of his plane. Turned out that was the one possession that really meant anything to him, and it had been the easiest to sell. The rest had been for show, for status, for everyone else. The house, the luxury cars, the damn artwork he'd never liked but some interior decorator had said was sophisticated. None of that mattered anymore.

The plane was a different story. *That* he missed with a visceral pain that could undo him. He couldn't afford to be undone, not in this place. So he buried the heartache under a blanket of indifference and pretended it worked.

Smith finished his little discourse and wandered back to his post, tension unwinding in his wake.

Robert cursed and abruptly shoved to his feet. The problem with the carrot was that they, the system and the guards, could control him. He knew it and they knew it; otherwise Smith wouldn't have bothered tempting him.

His initial reaction was to do the opposite. Start a fight, create a bit of havoc, get thrown in solitary again.

Before he could complete the thought, much less act on it, the buzzer rang, announcing lunch. He automatically stepped into line, glancing behind to verify that no one appeared to be in attack mode, as was his custom. His stomach growled, and he thought of what he'd give up if he went to solitary.

Prison food. Colorless, leached of vitamins and nutrition, dumped from giant cans or reconstituted from powdered form. At least it was hot, and salt, pepper, and ketchup could redeem most anything. Lukewarm, watery coffee dosed with an unhealthy spoonful of sugar was a treat, the closest you could get to dessert in this place.

He shuddered at the thought of having to subsist on the "brick" again—another indication of how spoiled he'd already gotten. The supposedly edible block of undeterminable bits of protein, carbohydrates, and fat bore no resemblance to actual food. Depending on how much hell he'd raised to warrant solitary confinement, the brick had often supplemented the punishment. Not to say he hadn't deserved it. As nutritious as they said it was, Robert was mightily glad to not be forced to gnaw on it in order to relieve the god-awful emptiness of his stomach against his spine.

The line inched forward. An idea took root in his mind. Rather than looking at their control of him, maybe he could work the system to his advantage. Hadn't he thought, just before he went to solitary over LeMasters, that he could have gotten a job by now, simply by choosing the good-behavior route? So, why not?

He didn't have anything to lose.

There was a kernel of freedom to be gained, and if he viewed it as a carrot, so be it.

Outside. His pulse began to thud, and then pound. Yeah, he could do this. He could mind his manners and earn some perks.

"Hey, Lawyer-Man." The guy behind him spoke up, calling him by his new nickname.

Robert half turned to take another look at the sixtyish guy with a limp. He was in for manslaughter, if Robert remembered right. Ran over his wife, claimed he'd had a seizure and didn't know what he'd done. "Yeah?"

"Can you help me with my appeal?"

The guy kept glancing around, never lighting on any one thing for more than a few seconds, never making direct eye contact. Robert figured the guy had run over her on purpose, never had a seizure before or since, and knew full well what he'd done.

Well, why not? The appeal wouldn't go anywhere, but his work, if he wanted to call it that, would buy him some yard time. "Sure. What you got to trade for it?"

Robert might have decided to work the system, but he'd extract something useful from the guy, as well. A man could never have too much information or goods for barter in here. The informal system was about as capitalistic as it could get.

The older guy nodded, a spare, jerky movement, and leaned close to confide in Robert.

Who listened with half an ear and let his mind run with the anticipation of fresh air and sunshine.

Even so, Robert sharpened his gaze, aware that a few troublemakers had given up on appeals, had nothing to lose, and would take him down with them. Until five minutes ago, he would have relished the battle, but now *he* had something to lose.

Tension tightened his muscles as he implemented his brand new plan. Staying *out* of trouble. And damn it all anyway, here came Bo "the Hawk" Hawkins, who had a sixth sense for ferreting out weakness.

Robert looked away, hoping Hawk hadn't noticed, but his stomach clenched. Now that he had reason to avoid a fight, Murphy's Law decreed he'd get one shoved down his throat.

He schooled his features to project plenty of attitude—and hoped he didn't have to act on it.

Chapter Eighteen

A POT OF SPLIT PEA SOUP simmered on the stove, herbs lending a rich aroma to the kitchen as Ben let himself in well after dark. Lynette's car hadn't been in the driveway, and smart cop that he was, silence in the house led him to the conclusion that she wasn't here. Although, Lannis didn't usually cook, so maybe Lynette had gone out for something. Which didn't make much sense, unless Lannis was babysitting Carly.

"Lannis?" He waited a moment, then realized the air conditioner had masked the sound of the shower running in the back of the house. He stowed his laptop where Carly couldn't get to it and headed for the bedroom to change. About halfway there, the distinct lack of Carly's paraphernalia struck him, and he stopped. Nothing of Lynette's, either. *Huh.* He detoured and took a quick glance in the office. The futon had been made up, with no extra pillows or blankets rumpled on it, and the room had reverted to its usual use.

He shook his head. *She's gone back to Rich.* His next thought centered on Lannis. Concern for her carried him on down the hallway. "Lannis, I'm home," he called out as he entered the bedroom.

The water shut off, and she answered. "Hi, Ben. I'll be out in a minute and we can eat."

"Sorry, darlin'." He shrugged out of his holster and toed off his shoes. "I didn't think I'd be this late. Thanks for holding supper."

"I wasn't in the mood to eat without you." Her voice was muffled.

"What's up with Lynette? She's gone." Ben groaned with the relief of shedding his suit, and reached for his wear-softened jeans and a ratty T-shirt.

Lannis appeared, wrapped in a towel, and said, "Guess she went home." She was trying to look unaffected, but disappointment tightened her expression.

Ben took her hand and pulled her toward him, inhaling her sweet, clean scent, and relaxing into her amazing softness. Sometimes all he saw was her strength, and forgot how inviting the satin-smooth warmth of her skin could be. How that could slip his mind, he didn't know. He dropped his head to nuzzle her damp hair. "Try not to worry," he said, knowing she'd worry anyway. "Rich seemed genuinely shocked at my assessment of his behavior. I think they'll be okay." He ran his palm over her bare shoulder.

She sniffed, and he wondered if she was crying. He hoped not. He'd had a day from hell, and no respite from high drama for days. All he wanted was a night in the sanctuary of his own home, a reprieve from the world's problems, just overnight; then he'd be recharged, back up for whatever came his direction. He leaned back and tipped her chin so he could see her eyes. No tears. *Thank You, God.*

"I'll go get the soup off the stove," he said and released his grip. She nodded solemnly and went into the closet for her robe. *Why is she so subdued?* He expected Lynette's situation to weigh on her, but maybe she was more deeply affected than he realized. Ben rubbed a hand across his face, almost too tired to bother with eating, but Lannis would likely skip the meal if he didn't. She still hadn't regained the weight she'd lost over Davis's trial, and she needed to eat. Ergo, he would eat.

He'd found salad in the fridge and cornbread in the oven by the time she padded down the hallway in her robe. "This smells really good, Lannis. Did Lynette start it before she left?"

Lannis sent him an affronted look. "Am I that bad, Ben?" she asked mildly. She lifted an eyebrow, softening her affectation of indignation. "I got off work at noon, and she was gone already." A slight smile lifted the corners of her lips as she slid into her chair. "Unbelievable as it seems, I actually cooked."

Oops. Ben's neck heated. "Sorry. I assumed. Mea culpa." He sat and they held hands while he said grace, then dug in. Silence reigned for several minutes. He was hungrier than he'd thought. However, Lannis spent more energy on pushing her cornbread around on the plate than actually eating it.

He put his spoon down. "Let it go, Lannis. You can't fix their relationship."

Lannis looked up, startled. "I know, Ben. I was thinking about something else."

He sighed. "And that would be…?"

She abandoned her halfhearted attempt to eat. "A couple of things. Well, three."

Ben barely restrained an urge to drop his head into his hands. "Tell me." It came out a bit sharper than he intended, and Lannis eyed him with concern buffered with a healthy dose of wariness. He consciously softened his expression and gave her his undivided attention.

"Maybe you're too tired, or not in a good frame of mind," she said. Ben could almost see her retreat within herself. An image of a turtle popped into his mind.

"No." He didn't think it was a lie, but the fact that he had to assess his answer told him it skirted the edges. But he'd dealt with far worse, both at work and with Lannis. He could do this. Dredging up a smile, he put his hand over hers. "Talk to me."

She hesitated a moment, gathered her thoughts, and launched in. "Well, first, Eric, one of the pilots at work—" She shrugged a shoulder and shot a glance at Ben.

Yeah, he remembered. Lannis kept telling him the guy was harmless, and that she could handle him. He'd let the issue go, figuring he had to trust her ability to navigate her job relationships on her own. But maybe Eric wasn't as innocuous as Lannis had let on. Fatigue forgotten, he straightened.

"—he's been a real jerk lately. More so than usual, but nothing that approaches harassment," she added hastily at Ben's piercing look. "I finally confronted him, and he said he'd read the court transcript." A shudder rolled through her, and she tightened her grip on Ben's hand. "I felt dirty. Violated all over again."

Ben cursed under his breath. It had taken a lot of courage for her to face Davis in trial. She knew it was public information, but he hadn't expected anyone to throw it in her face after the fact. Neither had she.

"I think I'm past that already, but something he said really surprised me." Lannis lifted her gaze. "He's afraid of me." She looked—and sounded—baffled. "Like maybe I'm on the prowl to accuse other guys of harassment, or even assault. Of all the things I expected him to say…" Her voice trailed off.

Ben reined in his protective urges. "This happen today?"

"No. Yesterday, but Lynnie and that whole situation took over."

He nodded. "Yeah, it sure did."

"I just needed to run it by you. I think Eric will be okay. I told him I wasn't out to damage anyone's reputation, or job, or life. I think he heard me." She straightened and pulled her hand free. "And now that's not even the big thing we need to talk about."

Ben shoved a hand through his hair. *That wasn't the* big *issue. Uh-oh.* "And that would be?"

She dropped her hand to her lap and went still. A heartbeat passed, then another. Ben didn't know whether to be alarmed, amused, or accommodating. The longer the silence stretched, the more he leaned toward alarmed.

"I spent a lot of time thinking this afternoon." She waved vaguely toward the front of the house. "Worked in the yard, went head-to-head with my fears about getting pregnant, having a baby." She glanced at him, then looked away, and Ben recognized pain, raw and unconcealed. A frisson of unease began to climb his spine. He nodded encouragement, although he wasn't certain he wanted to hear what she was going to say.

She pulled her gaze up and looked him in the eye. "I'm tired of Davis controlling me, making this decision for us. I went over to Maggie's and we talked. She helped me a lot, and…well, I've turned one corner this afternoon. But there's something I need to do before I can give you the baby—babies—you want."

Ben made a neutral noise in his throat, wishing he'd been a fly on the wall for *that* conversation. He'd get the details another time, but he was getting a bad feeling about Lannis's precondition for pregnancy.

She squared her shoulders, and his stomach clenched.

"I'm going to go talk to Davis in prison."

It was Ben's turn to be shocked speechless. A haze of anger erupted, threatening his control. Lannis had a way of getting under his skin and upsetting his entire world some days. He had a moment of empathy for Rich, although he would never put Lannis through what Rich had put Lynette through. He took a deep breath. And then another. On the third, he opened his eyes, unaware that he'd closed them.

"Why?" He was proud of how calm he sounded.

Now that she'd started, her words gushed forth. "I want to break this hold he still has over me. I'm sick to death of him being a"—she opened her hand, palm up, in a small, helpless gesture— "*voyeur* in our bedroom. Whether it's needing a light on so I know it's you I'm in bed with, or my trusting enough to be able to have your babies, he's just *there*. I hate it."

She put one hand over her heart. "More than that, I feel compelled to *live* my part in 'forgive us our trespasses as we forgive those who trespass against us.' I thought I'd gotten past that part when he was arrested, but he keeps coming back to haunt me. There's always another layer of work I need to do. It's not a one-time deal. It's more like peeling an onion. Bottom line, each layer of forgiveness is another layer of freedom for me. That part is bigger than either of us." Her lips twisted in a crooked smile. "And, you never know. Someday he may say he's sorry."

Unable to hold the sound back, Ben snorted. "He's never going to say that, Lannis. Get over it." His words came out harsh and merciless. "He's a loser. He made his choices. He's not worth all your angst, or your empathy, or your compassion." His hands curled into fists, and he had to consciously relax them. He wanted to hit something—the big bag at the gym came to mind as the most appropriate focus, but it took a distant second to Robert Davis. However, the impulse to beat Davis to a pulp served no purpose, and would only make things worse.

"Why can't you get over this? It's been five years. More than that. You faced him, put him behind bars." Ben tried to be supportive, like the booklet for rape victims' family and friends urged, but he felt himself floundering. "Most victims, or survivors— and I hope to God you view yourself as a survivor—never get that closure. That's history now. You have a new life, a life with me—"

His voice broke, and he inhaled deeply, trying to tamp down the fury that roiled within him. He wasn't sure if he was angrier at Davis for what he'd done, Lannis for staying stuck, or himself for being angry. "You don't fool me. You want kids, too. But you're blaming him instead of taking responsibility for your own choices. You're a coward." Ben wanted to bite the words back, but his temper wanted her to hear them.

Lannis shrank back, blood draining from her face as if he'd slapped her. Two spots of color stood out like clown's paint against the pale skin of her cheeks. Her eyes darkened, and the dark chocolate color turned fathomless. If Ben thought she'd retreated before, he had seen nothing at all.

"I've—I *am* taking responsibility for myself." She faltered. A spark of anger flickered in her eyes. "I'll never be 'over' it, Ben. You know that. I can heal, but I can't undo the wound. The scar will be there forever." Lannis folded her arms across her chest, and he could see the whites of her knuckles as she clutched her robe.

Remorse overrode his temper, but he was afraid it was too late. The shuttered expression on her face said she'd built a wall so high he might never scale it.

"I'm sorry." The sentiment was right on, but stress had commandeered his vocal cords, and the words came out in a near growl. Even worse, he might as well have said them to an empty room. He reached for her hand, palm up, not really expecting her to capitulate that quickly, and she didn't.

Lannis opened her mouth, then closed it and glanced away. When she looked back, a sheen of unspilled tears glistened in her eyes. His heart plummeted.

"Do you forbid me?" Her voice shook a little, but her expression was calm and remote.

"Forbid you?" Ben dropped his head into both hands. *Where in the world did she dig up this whacky idea?* "Uh. No." He lifted his head and regarded her. "Other than breaking your marriage vows, I don't have the right to forbid you to do anything. We are a partnership. We don't own each other."

A tendril of dread insinuated its way through his gut. He didn't own her, but letting go of control made him break out in a cold sweat. He'd been in control of most aspects of his admittedly dangerous life since…

Ben's heart sank. *Since Danny died.* He hadn't thought about Danny for a while, yet his brother influenced every day of his life. Ben had adored him with the blind worship young children reserved for older and omnipotent siblings. In the end, his worship proved to be misplaced, and took its own torturous journey to painful annihilation. Danny's trip down a road paved with dirty needles and contaminated street drugs had pointed Ben with laser precision at his life's work. The horror of Danny's death in a rat-infested basement, undiscovered for days, had cultivated Ben's natural tendency toward a meticulous sense of responsibility, had honed it to a razor-edged need to control his world. Which sometimes required controlling the people in it.

But not Lannis, and not now. He gritted his teeth. He needed to sort out what he could control and what he had to let go. Danny's memories raising their ugly visages complicated everything. He shoved them to the side, knowing he had to deal with it sometime. For now, he had to focus on Lannis. Whose struggle to deal with the man who'd raped her influenced every day of her life, too. Ben winced at the obvious similarities.

She gathered her robe around her and stood. "I didn't expect you to understand, but I thought you'd at least hear me out."

A dagger of pain skewered his heart. "I'm sor—"

She interrupted him, her stance regal and untouchable. "I've done everything I know to do, Ben. *I'm* sorry it hasn't been enough, or fast enough." Her lips tightened, and she looked wounded, a little lost. "This is the only thing I can see with the potential to make a difference. For me, for us. Maybe for Davis." She hesitated, then said, "I didn't think I needed to say it, but maybe I do. I'm not doing this for him. I'm doing it for us." A note of bitterness entered her voice. "Don't worry, I won't come close to breaking my vows to you. With luck, and maybe a little faith, I might get past my *cowardice*." She flicked a glance at him, a glance simultaneously remote and filled with raw pain.

She turned and walked away.

He almost ordered her to return, but swallowed the words. A wave of grief disguised as anger rolled through him, and he couldn't distinguish between the threads of pain over Lannis versus the crater of anguish at Danny's choices and their consequences. Ben's head began to throb.

Lannis paused and pivoted. "I'll be in the office on the futon."

Ben dropped his head into his hands again and let loose a string of blistering curses. He stood, shoving the chair back so hard that it screeched on the floor, tipped, and nearly went over backward. He snagged and righted it without looking, and called out, "I'll take the damn futon, Lannis."

Her answer was a shrug and silence.

"And, darlin'? We *will* work this out." It came out sounding like a threat, and he closed his eyes again, scrubbing a hand down his face. He didn't sound any better than Rich. And he didn't have a clue as to how to "work this out." But by God, they would.

The prospect of losing Lannis shot a lightning bolt of icy terror into his soul. He cursed again, aware that the words, inappropriate as they were, doubled as a prayer that exposed the darkest fear, deepest need of his being.

He hoped God could hear beyond the words.

~

A TREMOR STARTED in Lannis's fingers and climbed her arms, escalated and took over the muscles in her back. She hoped her legs wouldn't give out before she got to the bedroom, now that she was committed to it thanks to Ben's gallantry. *Gallantry served up with hemlock.* The office was much closer, and she wished she could stop there. But mundane considerations of logistics couldn't suppress the utter shock of Ben's words.

How *could* he? How could *Ben* say that to her? *A coward.* Betrayal sliced to her core, and her breath caught in her throat. She'd been secure in his love, secure enough that she was working through her own problems with what she'd thought was his support. Stupidly, naively secure.

Maybe she'd totally misread Ben's patience.

Anger tangled with doubt. This, on top of Eric's accusations yesterday, rattled Lannis to the core. *Maybe Ben's right.*

No. Lannis knew her strengths, and her weaknesses. In fact, she probably knew her weaknesses better than most people knew theirs. She'd had to become well versed in their various manifestations so they didn't lead her blindly into her biggest weakness—drinking.

She didn't think he was right, but it wouldn't hurt so much if there weren't a bit of truth to it. So why would the word *coward* trigger such a response? Was she that prideful that she couldn't examine her own motives? Was she stuck in the past like Ben thought? Or was it simply that Ben, the man to whom she'd given her heart, had uttered them?

A maelstrom of emotion took hold of her. Dear Lord, she was afraid. No, more than afraid. Terrified. Furious. Hurt. Confused. She covered her mouth with her hand, then stuffed her fist into it, trying to hold sobs in. If she started crying, she'd never stop. Her legs held long enough for her to flee into the bedroom, where she pushed the door closed, then slid down to sit with her back against it.

The trouble with loving someone was that they could hurt you worse than anyone else on the planet. Which left her alone, and worse, unprepared for it.

The door jiggled behind her, and Ben tapped on it somewhere above her head. "Lannis." He sounded like the familiar Ben, her husband, the man she'd come to know and trust, and, blast it all, *love* over the past year and a half. "Open up."

But she didn't want to open the door. He'd shown her a side of him she'd never seen, and suddenly she felt like their relationship was on unstable ground, maybe even quicksand. Everything was very confusing, and suddenly all she wanted to do was sleep.

So tired. Lannis dragged herself to her feet, no longer caring whether Ben came in or not. She stumbled to the bed, vaguely aware of the door opening, of Ben's solid presence a few steps behind her. She pulled the covers back—they were almost too heavy to lift—and clambered in, robe and all, and collapsed onto her pillow. Her eyes drifted shut.

The mattress dipped as Ben sat, and she flinched when he touched her temple, smoothing back her hair.

He sighed. "Lannis, I'm sorry. I didn't mean it." He fell silent, and she considered his words through the haze of fatigue that had ambushed her. *Maybe he doesn't think he meant it, but when people blurt things out like that, there's often a kernel of truth there.* She shivered.

If she'd had the energy, she would have told him off. She wanted to tell him how badly he'd hurt her. But he already knew that, and what she wanted more than her next breath was to repair this chink in their relationship. Still, a small, angry, and uncomfortably vindictive part of her wanted him to suffer as deeply as she was.

But she didn't have the energy for any of it.

He kept stroking her face. "Your instincts were right-on, earlier. I wasn't in the best frame of mind to have this discussion tonight." His fingers stilled. "The situation at work today… One of our informants got shot, may not survive. It's not an excuse, but it's a factor."

Lannis's heart clenched. Ben so rarely talked about work that she'd gotten into a comfortable little cocoon of visualizing him doing paperwork, or talking on the phone, rather than interacting with the likes of Terrance "King" LeMasters, the drug dealer who'd figured heavily in their meeting. Or the heart-stopping danger he'd been in then, or the breath-stealing peril he'd dragged her into, all in the interest of keeping himself alive and her safe.

His voice rumbled on. "Let me lie down with you."

Her face had warmed to his touch. At some point tears had escaped despite her efforts to the contrary, and the skin on her cheeks began to tingle as they dried. She shrugged, managed a clumsy swipe at her face. A defeated sigh slipped past her lips.

Ben didn't wait, just lifted the bedclothes and slid in behind her, jeans and all, and pulled the covers over both of them. He looped one arm over her midriff and tugged her close, fitting himself to her back, from head to toe.

Lannis fumbled for his hand, found it, and grasped it like a lifeline. He tensed, slid his other arm under her head, and clasped her even more tightly. He bent his head and buried his face in her hair. She melted into his arms, too exhausted to analyze the dichotomy of why she felt so secure even as the emotional storm still reverberated through her bones.

Ben's muscles went slack, and he sagged into the mattress, his breathing deepening and becoming even. He'd fallen asleep.

A thought crept into her consciousness, and it snapped her eyes wide open. If she was so bent on forgiving Robert Davis for a premeditated, brutal crime, she'd better be able to forgive her husband for a human, unintended mistake.

She should forgive him. No question. It was the right thing to do, even noble. But *coward?*

Pain sliced through her again, not so much at the sentiment. She knew now that she could handle that. But *Ben* had uttered it. That hurt the most, knowing she'd fallen short in his eyes. That she hadn't "gotten over" the rape. Anger flared anew at his lack of understanding. She couldn't undo the event, couldn't delete the memories from her brain. It was like an invisible amputation, a constant and unwelcome companion.

Lannis pushed Ben's hand away, feeling suddenly constricted, trapped.

He roused, murmured something unintelligible, and kissed the nape of her neck.

Well conditioned to his lovemaking by now, her body responded. Warming, softening, in spite of her resentment. Caught between desire and distress, Lannis groaned.

If there was no solving of their differences tonight, at least there could be comfort. And Ben's touch promised plenty of that. Lannis didn't overthink it. She needed comfort.

Desire won.

He took care of the problem of the clothing, piece by piece, layer by layer, until there was nothing separating them at all.

Except the words left unsaid.

Some time later, the mechanical trill of the phone jerked Lannis out of an unsettling dream. Not quite a nightmare, but too close for it to contribute to a restful sleep. Ben had already rolled away from her to snag the handset, leaving her bereft of his touch. Coming awake by degrees, Lannis wondered who was getting called out. These middle-of-the-night calls didn't come often, but always resulted in a hasty departure for one of them.

"Martin." Unlike her, he sounded alert, totally ready for anything.

She sat up, resting on one elbow, waiting for him to hand the phone to her…but he didn't. A tinny voice spoke, rapid-fire, and he listened in silence, his muscles tensing subtly. *Him, then.* Lannis sagged in disappointment. His late-night calls never ended well. He'd be gone for hours at least, maybe a day or more.

She didn't want him to go this time. Well, not ever, but especially not this time. Their argument still shimmered like a gossamer veil between them. Too much was left unfinished.

"I'll be there in an hour." Ben hung up and reached for Lannis.

She snuggled into his embrace and sighed. "How long?"

"Don't know." He stroked her hair, the motion both familiar and preoccupied. "Our informant died. I'm the one who cultivated him. Mike's going as backup. Gotta find out how badly we've been compromised." He disengaged and pushed himself out of bed.

"Undercover?" Apprehension filled her. He gave a distracted nod on his way to the bathroom. Lannis threw the covers back. "I'll get your gun out of the safe."

"No." His voice cracked like a whip, and she froze. "I don't want your fingerprints on it."

"Oh." She relaxed and shrugged. "I'll go make some coffee, then."

He stuck his head out of the bathroom. "No time. Stay in bed."

She shot him a disbelieving look. "You think I'm going to go back to sleep while you get ready to leave for who knows how long? Get real."

He didn't answer, just went into the closet and grabbed what she'd mentally labeled as his undercover duffel, filled with grunge clothing and bogus IDs. Ben sorted through it quickly and pulled on the uniform of a drug dealer, his demeanor changing along with his appearance.

Lannis picked up her nightgown and robe from the floor, tossed the robe on the bed, and tugged the oversized cotton tee over her head. As she poked her arms in the short sleeves, she glanced toward Ben.

He'd only turned on the walk-in closet light and now stood limned by it, backlit, his face in shadow. Lannis's heart skipped, and her breath caught. The transformation always stunned her. It wasn't just the clothes. It was something far deeper and more lethal. He looked as dangerous as he had the night she'd first met him. Actually, she had to say it was more of an encounter than a meeting. She hadn't learned his real name for months.

She hesitated for a nanosecond, but silly as it felt, and especially after their fight, she wanted to reassure herself he had not changed fundamentally, that he was *her* Ben, not this frightening stranger. She stepped in front of him, touched his arm. He glanced at her, and his gaze warmed. The distance he'd already created vanished. His lips quirked upward, and he framed her face with his hands.

"I'll call when I can," he said. "You and Maggie stick together. You'll be fine."

"I know, Ben." I'll miss you, she thought, even though his earlier words still stung. She was half-afraid to jinx him by being clingy, afraid she'd cause him to be distracted when he needed all his wits about him. "Be careful."

"Always." He kissed her but didn't linger, then tweaked her nose. "Gotta go."

She dropped her hands to her side. A few moments later the door closed and his Mustang rumbled out of the garage. Lannis walked to the window, slid the curtain aside with one finger, and watched his taillights wink through the trees until they disappeared.

And tried to ignore the fact that he'd said nothing about what they'd argued about earlier, hadn't mentioned the unfinished discussion, and that the meat of the issue remained unresolved.

She didn't know how long he'd be gone, and neither did he. He rarely called when he was undercover, painfully careful to shield her from his work. She suspected Ben would never entirely forgive himself for the incident that put her in the hospital and King LeMasters in prison, no matter that she didn't hold him responsible and never had. So, they wouldn't talk for an unknown length of time.

She let the curtain flutter back into place. Sighed. *On my own again.*

Which meant she would contact the prison one day this week, speak her piece to Robert Davis in the next few weeks, and finally move on.

A thread of doubt wormed its way into her thoughts. Maybe Ben was right. Maybe she was living in a fantasy world. Maybe she should pretend she was unaffected by the man's crime against her.

But she'd gone that route before, and it hadn't worked.

She huffed out a breath. No, she had to face Davis head-on in order to save herself and save her marriage.

She just hoped she wasn't crippling their relationship instead.

~

Ben plugged the cell phone he used for undercover work into the car's cigarette lighter. He'd forgotten to keep it charged at home, and gave himself a mental kick in the ass. The situation with Lynette and Carly had thrown him off. They'd shown up on the night he usually plugged the stupid thing in. Between them, and Rich, and all the stuff swirling around Lannis…

He couldn't afford these sorts of lapses.

Methodically he began to compartmentalize, shoving everyone and everything into boxes at the back of his brain, storing them to be dealt with later. And they all went, quite obediently, except for Lannis.

Lannis, who had looked so vulnerable as he left the house, who'd put on a brave face for him. Hell, he'd seen past it, seen the uncertainty she'd tried to mask. It ripped his heart out, and made him wonder if this translated to a vulnerability on his part. A weakness that left him open to exploitation. He cursed, then picked up his normal cell phone and called Mike. *Not the time to keep things from my partner.* The details of his personal situation weren't Mike's business, but their effect on Ben was.

Mike picked up on the first ring, and Ben heard Maggie in the background telling him to be careful. His lips lifted in a half smile. The guy hadn't gotten out any faster than he had. And their women were apparently reading off the same page.

"Hey, Mike," he said. "We need to talk before we head out. I'll meet you at Lou's diner. Fifteen minutes." That would give the guy time to finish his good-byes, which Ben could not begrudge.

He thought of Lannis, and wondered if she'd gone back to bed yet. He glanced at his watch. Almost five a.m. *Nah. She'll be up for the day, especially after last night.*

His heart squeezed. Leaving her had gotten harder, but the circumstances made it too hard this time. He'd give anything to take back his harsh words. Well, the one word. The rest of them needed to be out there. But *coward*, that one needed to be recalled.

Although, if he allowed himself to see it, that particular word could be applied to him. He didn't want to think about Robert Davis, didn't want to listen to Lannis say she felt "compelled" to visit the asshole in prison, and didn't want to deal with her harebrained idea.

Tonight's assignment, as messy as it was both professionally and personally, was almost a relief. A reprieve. And with any luck at all, Lannis would forget about the whole thing about seeing Davis before he got home.

Ha. He'd served up a load of cow manure with *that* notion. When it came to Robert Davis, she never forgot. He wished to heaven she would.

The lights of the diner came into view and he pulled into the lot, frustration coursing through his veins when he needed to be focused.

For the second time in eight hours he longed for some gym time. An hour to pummel the life out of a punching bag. A time-out from Lannis, from memories of Danny, from his own unruly emotions.

His skin crawled, and he wondered if this was what Lannis meant when she sometimes said she hated being trapped in her own skin. Well, now he could identify with her on that.

He just didn't have an outlet for it at the moment.

Ben got out of the car, slammed the door a bit harder than necessary, but reined in his urge to slam it to kingdom come. *Don't want to search the junkyards for a replacement door.*

He took a deep breath, squared his shoulders, and headed into the diner.

Game time.

Chapter Nineteen

"Hey, Will." Lannis greeted the dispatcher, who glanced up and grinned at her, eyes alight with mischief.

"Hey, yourself, beautiful." He waggled his eyebrows at her.

Beautiful? Where was he going with *that?* His obvious cheer was contagious, though, and charmed her. Derailed from her original purpose, she stopped, put her hands on her hips, and peered at him. "What's up with you, Will?"

He lit up, his grin widening. "Sheila said yes last night."

"No way!" Lannis answered his grin with one of her own. "You're not kidding, are you?"

Will's weekly proposals to his adored Sheila had become an office joke. She turned him down just as frequently, but never broke it off with him. The next day he'd come in and mope around, grousing at pilots and mechanics alike for a few hours until his intrinsic good nature reemerged. There'd even been an occasional betting pool on which day next week the cycle would repeat.

He leaned back in his chair. "Nope. She wants a June wedding, which I think is too far away, but if that's what it takes to get her to marry me, that's what she gets." Will wore a satisfied expression, and Lannis beamed at him.

"Congratulations, and give my best to Sheila," she said. In an office this small, things like this didn't happen often, and she figured someone would get tasked with a bakery run shortly. Maybe her. "You know, you've taken all the fun out of the betting pool."

Will shot her a leer over the top of his glasses. "No, I haven't. Now they'll be betting about how soon Sheila gets pregnant."

Whoops. Don't want to touch that *subject.* "On that note," Lannis said as she backed out of Will's office, "I'll be in the conference room. Gotta make a phone call."

"No problem. You got the plane ready to go?"

"Of course." Lannis sent him a *get real* look. "And you handed me the weather, so you know we're fine there. Just holler at me if we get a launch call."

She was still smiling when she stepped into the small room furnished with chairs and a utilitarian table. The phone occupied a place of honor at the far end, and the anxiety she'd kept at bay all morning crept back. The palms of her hands went damp, and her pulse quickened. She pulled the door closed behind her, and it latched with a loud click that made her jump. Heat flooded her face, and she muttered, "Way to go, bean brain." She took a deep breath and stared at the phone like it was a living thing, and treacherous.

Her mind went back to Will, and all the betting pools. She never participated. Being a pilot meant that she didn't gamble on much, ever. Yet here she was, risking her marriage on the outcome of a phone call.

Overreacting again. Definitely not keeping the peace, but not risking her marriage. Her relationship with Ben was stronger than that, even though they were at odds regarding this subject. She clung to that thought as she rounded the table and sat. She dug the slip of paper with the number from her pocket, and took a deep breath, smoothing her palms on her slacks.

She dialed, wishing she could talk to Ben about this, knowing she was flying solo on this one, and dredged up the courage anyway.

Ten minutes later she wondered why she'd been so nervous. She'd been put on hold, transferred, put on hold again. *Does the Kentucky prison system even know where he is?* Which generated another thought that brought a new flutter of anxiety to her belly.

Davis *was* still in prison, wasn't he? Her grip tightened on the handset. He'd gotten out, albeit by mistake, from jail. And there was that law now, the one that informed victims when their attacker was to be released from custody. She'd signed up for that, and there had been no call.

At that moment, the line came alive. A woman's rich contralto voice replaced the canned music from a moment before. "Hello. This is Ms. Connor. How may I assist you?"

"Ms. Connor…" The speech she'd rehearsed all morning deserted her, and Lannis felt suddenly and foolishly tongue-tied.

"Yes?" Thankfully, the woman took her hesitation in stride, her voice patient and holding a hint of encouragement.

Lannis shored up her nerve and said, "My name is Lannis Martin, and I was raped by Robert Davis. He was convicted in July for it. I would like to"—she stopped to swallow—"to, um, meet with him."

"Oh, I'm sorry to hear that, Mrs. Martin." She paused, then added, "Sorry about your violation, not that you want to see Mr. Davis."

Lannis hadn't expected an expression of sympathy, and she managed a surprised, "Thank you."

"I would say you're welcome, but it seems an odd context, doesn't it?" The woman chuckled, and rather than seem awkward or dismissive, the soft laughter eased Lannis's tension.

A smile lifted her lips. "Yes, it does. But I understand and appreciate your intent." She took a deep breath. "Can you help me, then, with Davis?" Without thinking, she crossed the fingers of her free hand.

"Well, that depends."

Lannis took the handset from her ear and glanced at it. *It depends?* She put it back to her ear. "On what?"

"All inmates create a list of visitors whom they wish to see. Unless you are on Mr. Davis's list, you won't be admitted."

Her eyebrows rose. "Are you serious?"

"Very." Ms. Connor's tone turned businesslike. "The philosophy of the corrections system is that incarceration is punishment. Prisoners have already forfeited their freedom. They retain some rights, and this is one of them."

"Oh." Her heart sank. Robert Davis could deny her this chance at closure if he wanted. And she was pretty sure he'd do whatever he could to thwart *her* growth and healing. "So…is there a way I can get on his list?"

"May I ask, instead, Mrs. Martin, why you want to see him?" Ms. Connor's question was direct, but without judgmental undertones.

Lannis was stymied. She didn't know this woman, and didn't want to disclose her reason for speaking with him. She'd made up her mind to see the man, but wasn't fond of the prospect of having to explain herself to another third party, and risk the same response Ben had thrown at her. An absurd notion occurred to her.

"Are you protecting him?" The concept boggled her mind, but that made as much sense as anything might.

"In a way, yes, Mrs. Martin." The woman's voice remained neutral. "You are his victim. You may wish to cause him harm." She paused. "While he is in our custody, we are responsible for his welfare and cannot allow such a situation."

Lannis shook her head in wonder. The stories she'd heard about prison life didn't include nosy administrators protecting inmates from their victims. "Well, I don't wish him harm." She couldn't hold back a tiny bite of sarcasm. "I got over that before he went to trial. I had to, for my own sake. Otherwise vengeance would've driven me to self-destruction a long time ago."

"I commend you for that, Mrs. Martin. That's an unusual step for a victim to take. But I still need to know why you wish to gain access to Mr. Davis."

It was beginning to grate on Lannis that the woman referred to Davis with the honorific *mister*. Even more was the roadblock Ms. Connor had thrown in her path. She rubbed her head, feeling a dull ache coming on, then sighed. *No help for it.*

"I want to talk to him"—*she* didn't have to call him *Mr. Davis*—"because his crime has intertwined our lives, for better or worse. Mostly worse." Lannis took a deep breath. "I chose to not do a victim impact statement. I didn't think I needed to. I said everything I needed to in court. Plus, my goals had been accomplished. For him to be held accountable and see justice for his crimes, to keep him from raping again."

She hesitated, and Ms. Connor made an encouraging, "Mm-hmm."

"But there's a lot left unfinished. I want him to hear what he has done to me. I also want him to know that I'm doing my best to forgive and let go, move on. That if he wants to recognize it, this is the best opportunity in his life, given his choices so far, to turn things around."

The ache in her head grew sharper, and she put pressure on the most painful spot with the heel of her hand. "I can't explain it without sounding like a do-gooder or a lunatic." She closed her eyes. "I'm neither," she said, and hoped the woman, whatever title she held, would allow her to proceed.

If not, well, her argument with Ben seemed silly. Worse than silly. Pointless. Stupid.

Lannis straightened in her chair. If she didn't stop this train of thought right now, she'd crash it right into her self-esteem, which would derail her from far more than this quest.

Water under the bridge. Let it go, let God take care of things.

"I see." Ms. Connor's voice broke into her thoughts. "We don't have a program for it in Kentucky, but I've heard of some success with a concept called restorative justice. It sounds a lot like what you're searching for."

Lannis's eyes flicked open. She'd never heard of such a thing. That it existed told her she wasn't the first to take this path. Which gave her some comfort. She wasn't as crazy as Ben thought.

"I'll look into it and see what I can find out. We might be able to facilitate that for you, provided Mr. Davis consents."

"So…do I have to ask him for permission to visit him? Is that the next step?" Lannis couldn't help the spurt of bitterness that she might have to *ask* Davis for anything. He'd enjoy that. She winced at the image.

Ms. Connor laughed, a rich wave of goodwill over the phone lines. "Once I get more information, I'll get back with you and discuss it, let you decide if you still want to proceed. Only then will I contact Mr. Davis and forward your request to him."

Lannis didn't know what she'd been thinking, that maybe since she'd made a decision, everything would fall into place and she'd go to the prison on her next day off to talk to Davis, but she hadn't expected much of what had transpired in this conversation. Maybe it was for the best that it all slow down.

"There's nothing for me to do, then." Lannis felt adrift, now that the plan had been taken out of her hands.

"No, I wouldn't say that. You can research restorative justice on the Internet, see for yourself if it's what you're hoping for. I would be remiss in my own job if I didn't suggest that you speak with a therapist or counselor in the meantime." She paused. "You *have* gotten help for the aftereffects of the rape, haven't you?"

Heat and tension climbed Lannis's neck. "Why do you ask? That's a…" She searched for the right word, and finally settled on, "It's personal."

"Why do I ask?" Ms. Connor sounded surprised. "I'm a social worker. Of course, in this job I work almost solely with inmates, and rarely encounter victims. On those occasions, though, I am often surprised at how few of them have taken care of their own needs after the crime. It seems most folks cope by either pretending it didn't happen or by nursing vindictive fantasies."

Ah. "That's why you wanted to know my motives for wanting to see him." The pain in Lannis's head eased. Not much, but enough to notice.

"Exactly." Her tone turned brisk. "Do you have any more questions?"

"No. Well, except when should I expect to hear from you again?" The call had exhausted Lannis, and she wasn't sure how long she could stand for this process to drag out.

"Give me a week or so."

They exchanged information and ended the call. Lannis replaced the handset, then folded her arms on the table and rested her head on them.

She wanted… She didn't know what she wanted. Maybe a soda, or coffee, maybe some aspirin. Maybe another afternoon off, but that wasn't going to happen. A transport was on the schedule for noon, and she needed to go run the weight and balance, which would take a grand total of five minutes.

A different life, now that was a nice fantasy. A life without the past this one had. She snorted and raised her head, rested her chin on her forearms. Well, fantasy would get her exactly nowhere. *Play the hand you're dealt, girlfriend.*

She sighed and stood. A cold soda, a few minutes outside, then get busy. She knew herself well enough to add a stop at the AA meeting on her way home tonight. Her skin wasn't crawling yet, not quite, anyway, and the craving hadn't hit. But the conditions were ripe for it.

A pang of loneliness shimmied through her. What she really wanted she couldn't have, at least not right now.

Ben.

The safety of his arms.

The security of his love.

She set her spine, squared her shoulders. She'd made sure she could survive and thrive without him precisely because of the current situation. Didn't mean it was easy, but she could do this.

But a tiny voice deep inside warned her, *Be careful.*

Lannis wanted to ignore it, wanted to believe she was immune.

She listened to it.

And sat back down, and dialed Althea.

Chapter Twenty

BEN LIT A CIGARETTE, pretended to take a drag, and beneath his hand muttered, "Got you." Mike had just pulled up to a rundown neighborhood park in Louisville's west end. The mike in his ear came to life with Mike's quick "Loud and clear," then went silent.

Ben dropped his hand and discarded his match on the sidewalk, where it immediately blended in with cigarette butts, broken glass, and the occasional needle that littered the ground. *Great place to have to raise your kids.* He glanced around, especially toward the unkempt perimeter of the park, where paths disappeared into a warren that only the homeless or drug dealers dared penetrate. If no one approached him within an hour or so, he'd go in, but it was a dangerous place for an outsider. His race alone was enough to peg him on that point, but if his cover had held, that wouldn't be a problem. Folks around here knew him as a hard-ass, volatile, upper-level drug dealer, and he commanded respect in those circles.

Unless his now-dead informant had blown his cover. *Three years of cultivating this one…* Too bad they'd lost him.

He flicked ashes on the ground, brought the cancer stick to his lips again, and with nothing else to require his attention, took in the park as he approached it. Apparently there was enough money in the city's budget to mow the grass on occasion, but the sun had long since leached all color from the meager playground equipment. A person could sit on the rickety benches scattered haphazardly throughout only at their own peril. A fountain, ornate and lovely in its heyday, languished neglected and chipped in the center of the green space. Patches of black mold gave it a piebald horse look, and moss grew in the shaded areas. The few puddles of water that remained had become brackish mosquito-breeding pools.

He settled in to wait, expecting a long one, and was surprised when a young black woman sauntered down the street. She stopped at Mike's car and leaned in. He hoped Mike had seen this coming— Ben hadn't—and hidden the surveillance equipment.

"What you lookin' for, mister?"

Mike played along smoothly, and Ben couldn't hold back a grin. "How much for the whole thing?"

No matter how much they planned, and how many possible complications they anticipated, something totally off the wall always happened when working undercover. He loved that part of the job—the challenge, the sheer unexpectedness. Kept him on his toes, kept him sharp.

"Depends on how long you want it." The hooker shifted her stance to provide her mark with a better view of the goods. "A quickie is fifty. You pay for the room." She tossed her head in the direction of the undergrowth. "Or we can go in there if all you want is me on my knees. That's twenty."

Too bad they weren't working vice.

Mike hesitated, then asked, "You got a lead on someone younger?"

Ben raised his eyebrows and forgot to avoid inhaling with the cigarette at his lips. Smoke filled his mouth, his throat, and he choked, breaking into a paroxysm of coughing.

By the time he got it under control, the hooker was stalking away, hips swinging, a string of blistering vulgarities spewing at full volume from her mouth. Most of which could be translated as references to Mike's lineage and pedophilic tendencies. Which was funny in an ironic way, given her youth and willingness to sell herself so cheaply.

"Man, you've got to quit smoking. That cough is getting pretty bad." Mike's drawl was laconic.

"She didn't look like she was much over fifteen, Mike. Since when did you start preferring them in their diapers?"

"It was the only thing I could think of to get rid of her." Then sharply, "Traffic on your six."

Ben straightened, senses coming to full alert, and turned under the guise of ditching what was left of his cigarette. As he ground it beneath the toe of his boot, he threw a glance at the young man approaching him from the woods.

Recognition sparked, and adrenaline flooded his system. *Bingo.* The bait had been snapped up by one of the major players. Rolo, now only steps away, took his role as the Enforcer's numero-uno messenger very seriously. He swaggered with the confidence unique to young men whose lives would end either prematurely or in prison.

"Rolo." Ben touched the bill of his ball cap in greeting.

"BJ." His voice dripped with both derision and grudging respect.

"Whassup, dude?" Ben relaxed fractionally. Unless he misread the respect part, he'd retained his street cred.

"Enforcer wants to see you." Rolo never minced words, in keeping with the gravity of his position. "This way." He motioned to the pathway, invisible to anyone who didn't know it was there.

Ben gave him a long look, letting him know that he didn't kowtow to anyone, not even the Enforcer. When Rolo's gaze flickered, then faltered, he said, "After you," knowing the position of strength was behind one's opponent, and that whoever claimed and retained it had the upper hand. That hadn't changed in millennia.

Just as they ducked into the dim coolness of the woods, Ben heard a plane fly over. He glanced up, a new habit since Lannis had come into his life. It was a twin-engine prop plane, smallish from his vantage on the ground, and he catalogued details about it as it passed out of view. It looked a lot like the King Air she flew. She'd taken him on a tour when she first hired on with the hospital, so he was familiar with the fleet. *Wonder if it's her.*

The moment's distraction unnerved him. *Stay focused, or end up dead.* He followed his own advice and ignored the diminishing drone of the plane as it continued westward.

But the damage had been done. After his heart-to-heart with Mike the other morning, he'd done a good job of putting thoughts of Lannis aside. He never had this problem with Deb. But he'd been young, more gung ho than experienced, and never allowed his emotions to get too deep with his first wife. He was unable to do that with Lannis. No matter how hard he tried, she occupied a big chunk of his consciousness even when he needed her out of it.

A branch slapped in his face and he cursed. Not the time to traipse down memory lane or probe his feelings. He had a job to do, and the deeper he followed Rolo into the woods, the more his gut churned.

He had nothing to base his intuition on, but it had begun tugging at him when they entered the trees. Now it was shouting. He'd thought it was just the adrenaline rush of being undercover, of having made contact. Rolo seemed to be his usual self, but something was off.

At the precise moment he processed the abnormal silence, the lack of bird sounds or chattering squirrels, Rolo turned.

Ben stopped.

Four men stepped out from behind trees, and he realized he'd been led into an ambush. His mind kicked into overdrive and his heart followed. Though they all looked menacing, none of the men had drawn weapons. So maybe it was more of a gauntlet than an ambush.

"Dudes." He sent each man a piercing look. "Problem?"

Rolo glared at him, a look full of so much distrust and hatred that Ben wondered where the guy had learned to act, because he'd sure duped Ben with his affectation of respect earlier. He shifted his weight onto his toes, ready to fight.

"We got cockroaches among us."

Ben realized they hadn't identified him as a traitor. Yet. They would have taken him down already, not stopped to talk. He went on the offensive. "Your problem, not mine."

"Well, it's yours, too. In fact, you got two problems." Rolo leaned into Ben's personal space. "First, you got to prove you ain't one." He peered into Ben's eyes, and tipped his head as if that would aid his assessment of Ben. "And if you can do that to Enforcer's satisfaction, you got to figure out who you can't trust, too."

For all his bluster, Rolo only suspected Ben. That was a relief, but Ben didn't relax. He shoved his face into Rolo's, forcing the younger man to back up a step. "I got no problems at all, Rolo. Number one, I don't trust anybody. Not ever. So it doesn't matter what Enforcer thinks. I don't have anything to prove to him. Either he wants to do business with me or he doesn't. Makes no never-mind to me."

Ben turned, taking a huge chance and knowing it. He walked between the men flanking him, and they did nothing to stop him, just stood sullen and angry as he passed, waiting for Rolo's lead.

Rolo remained silent.

Ben retraced his steps up the path, feeling like his back had a big red bull's-eye painted on it. Sweat beaded on his forehead, and his palms went damp. He shifted his hand and placed it on the butt of his gun, the one he wouldn't let Lannis touch the other morning.

He cursed again, this time out loud. *Not now!* She could *not* invade his thoughts like that.

He kept walking, outwardly calm, inwardly expecting the kick of a bullet between his shoulder blades, the concussive crack that would split the air a nanosecond later. Didn't matter that he'd spent a small fortune on a new high-tech bulletproof vest that looked like a T-shirt…and was wearing it. Bottom line, he never wanted to put equipment like that to the test.

The gunshot never came.

Rolo called out, "BJ," and Ben had to repress a flinch. He slowed, turned, not knowing what to expect.

Chapter Twenty-One

November

A WEEK HAD PASSED since Ben's early-morning departure. Lannis had hung around to help with a quick turn for the King Air crew, which was inbound and expected to land any minute. Her cell phone chirped, and her heart leaped. *Maybe…it could be Ben!* She glanced at her watch as she fished the phone out of her uniform cargo pants, not that she really needed to verify the time. Dusk was falling, and she knew that meant it was around six thirty.

Caller ID said MAGGIE ROSS, and her excitement deflated. But maybe Maggie had news. She flipped the phone open. "Hey, Maggie, what's up?"

"Hey, yourself, Lannis. You want to come over for supper? It's only spaghetti and salad, but it beats another lonely evening."

Lannis could hear Megan and Marty playing choo-choo in the background, in relative harmony for a change. She didn't have to think long. "Sure. Thanks. Do you need me to stop at the store for anything?"

"Nope, I've got it covered."

Maggie began to sign off, but Lannis interrupted her. "Have you heard anything from Mike?" She had detoured into the conference room when her phone rang, and now she nudged the door closed with a hip.

"No, I haven't, but no news is good news." Maggie sounded simultaneously regretful and resigned.

Lannis's spark of hope flickered out. "I'll see you in about forty-five minutes, then." She closed and stowed her phone.

A couple of hours at the Rosses' would delay her eventual return home, which relieved her. It would have been dark by the time she got there either way—not that she hadn't gotten home after dark before. She had, but either Ben had beaten her there and the lights twinkled in cheery welcome, or he was so close on her heels as to make the darkness irrelevant.

"Lifeguard Tango Charlie Hotel cleared to land." The radio transmission, amplified from a speaker over the hangar door, galvanized the ground crew into action. The ambulance awaiting the transport flicked on its lights and moved forward a few feet.

Lannis heard the distinctive whine of the King Air's props on final approach, and she glanced up to check the weather. Low, scudding clouds raced across the sky on an uneasy wind, adding to the spooky factor.

She grabbed a set of chocks and went to wait next to Joe, who had the fuel truck idling in position.

Yeah, lights and laughter would carry her through part of the evening, and she'd take that over another AA meeting anytime. She'd been to three since Ben had left, and called Althea twice, and she was sick of thinking about alcohol, specifically, thinking about avoiding it.

A flurry of activity diverted her attention for the next several minutes, as the inbound team transferred preemie twins. The ambulance raced off, with full lights and sirens.

"Hey, Lannis, would you hook up the ground wire?"

"Got it, Joe." She grabbed the clip and unwound it carefully—it had a tendency to kink—and fastened it to the nose gear. "Go," she shouted, and heard the fuel flow briskly into the tanks in response.

She stayed crouched there until the fueling was done, and as soon as Joe backed off with the hose, unhooked the ground wire and retracted it just as carefully.

"Thanks, Lannis."

She sketched him a wave in response, and ducked her head when the pilots fired up the engines. Prop wash blew past, whipping her hair into a frenzy.

A smile lifted her lips. Little kids were so much fun. At least, Megan and Marty were. So was Carly. The thought of her niece wiped the smile from her face. Lynette had returned a few e-mails since her surprise visit, but not with any consistency. Lannis had begun to give up on her mom ever responding. The last time she'd communicated with *her* was the end of June, and it was a bad memory.

Nothing I can do about any of them. Lannis deliberately changed the direction of her thoughts. She had time to stop at the store and pick up a book, or a toy, for the kids. Not that they needed any more stuff, but they would be so excited, and the prospect cheered her. And maybe a bouquet of flowers for Maggie. Lannis had never thought of Maggie as being anything other than strong and capable, but maybe she could use a pick-me-up, too.

Her internal smile livened. With renewed energy, she went inside and attacked the pile of charts that had been delivered after Will had gone home. Wouldn't take but ten minutes or so to sort and file them in the pilots' individual inboxes. Less work for him

tomorrow, not that he would notice, floating on cloud nine as he
was, but it was a nice gesture.

She sorted quickly, efficiently, then stood the resulting packets
in the upright wooden frame. Her fingers slowed over Eric's box.
He'd been exceedingly polite and icily remote since their blowup last
week. She wondered if he'd ever mellow, but then decided it didn't
matter. It was his decision, not hers, and she'd done all she could to
repair that relationship. Her lips tightened as she pushed his set into
the box. Two more, then she was done.

"Good night, Joe." She stuck her head into the hangar. "Call me
if you need anything."

Joe waved at her. "Get outta here. You were done an hour ago."

"Yeah, yeah." But she took his advice and headed out. If she
stopped at the store, she'd be a few minutes late to the Rosses', but
that was okay.

Her stop was not in vain. The kids' eyes lit up—even more than
they had when they'd answered the door with their mom—and
Megan marched off to "read" to her little brother. Lannis felt a bit
foolish handing the flowers to Maggie, but the obligatory "You
shouldn't have!" was for show only. Blinking back tears, Maggie
ushered her in and went in search of a vase.

Supper was a boisterous affair, not good for conversation, and
Lannis cleaned the kitchen while Maggie got the kids ready for bed.
She got upstairs in time to give each child, sweet smelling and
deceptively angelic, a hug and kiss. Planning to slip out quietly, she
said, "Thanks, Maggie. It was a great time."

Maggie turned. "Oh, you're not going home now, are you? I was
hoping for some actual grown-up time today."

At her earnestness, Lannis relented, and felt her back muscles
ease. The later it got, the less she wanted to face her own dark house
at the end of the winding driveway. The night couldn't get any darker
than it already was. In fact, the moon had risen while they ate, a full
moon, bright and huge. But the clouds swept it in and out of shadow,
resulting in a flickering, almost strobe-light effect. She shivered, and
wished she'd gotten home while it was still light. She probably would
have been okay, with lights, music, and the security system armed.

Maggie tiptoed out, leaving the door ajar so the hall light would
illuminate the kids' room enough to banish monsters, and motioned
for Lannis to precede her down the stairs.

Once there, Maggie set a pot of water on the stove and pulled
out tea bags. "Chamomile?"

Lannis smiled. "Yeah, thanks. It's going to be hard enough to sleep tonight without adding caffeine to the mix."

"Don't I know it." Maggie made a wry face. "You'd think I'd be used to it after all these years."

"Really?" Lannis tried to hide her dismay. "It doesn't get easier?"

Maggie set out spoons and a dish for the used tea bags. "You like honey, right?" At Lannis's nod, she grabbed a pot of honey from the cupboard, and then answered the question. "No. Not easier. Although you get more used to it."

Curious, Lannis asked, "What do you do to make it better while Mike's gone?"

"Oh, we have family here, so that helps a lot. We spend more time with them, I keep busy. Of course, the kids drive my life whether Mike's home or not, and that certainly shapes my days." The pretty redhead shrugged. "It's the nights that are hard. And there's nothing to do for that except endure."

The battered teakettle whined, an anemic *peep-peep* that Lannis would have missed had she been in another room. They busied themselves with their respective preparations, then took their mugs to the living room. Maggie tossed a couple of toys to the floor and sank into the overstuffed cushions. She closed her eyes and leaned her head back, and Lannis saw how tired the young mother was.

"Thank you for the flowers, Lannis." Maggie raised her head and smiled. "I don't buy them for myself. It's a real treat—and a reminder that I'm a grown-up and separate from my children."

Lannis felt her face heat. "You're welcome." She took a sip of her tea. "Thanks for inviting me. Going home to an empty house didn't hold any appeal."

Maggie lifted an eyebrow. "Any special reason? Tonight, I mean?"

Lannis laughed. "Not that I can think of. Other than it's just sort of spooky out there, what with the wind and clouds." She glanced at her hands, then lifted her gaze to Maggie. "I know it's stupid, but most of the time I'm fine. I guess—" The real reason for her distress hit her like jet blast. She let out a dismayed sigh.

Maggie sat up. "Are you all right?"

Lannis managed a nod, embarrassed at her emotion. "Yes, yes. I… Oh, shit!" She set her cup on the coffee table, and buried her face in her hands. "I've been waiting on a phone call—" She hesitated, not wanting to burden Maggie with her problems, but remembered that Maggie had helped her get ready for the trial, and had offered friendship a thousand ways since they'd met.

She lifted her head. "I'm in the process of contacting Davis in prison, to talk to him. It's something I need to do, to complete my healing, and I'd hoped the lady would call me back with details by today." Now she'd have to wait until Monday, which had seemed interminable as her cell phone remained silent this afternoon. "Ben's, uh, not happy with it."

Both of Maggie's eyebrows arched. She began to speak, then stopped. But Maggie and discretion were not words that ever occurred in the same sentence. "Girlfriend, you get yourself into more drama than anyone I know." The sting of the words was softened by the compassion in her eyes. "And you added this on top of, what? The first time Ben left for an assignment since you've been married?" She shook her head. "Ben was right. You need a keeper." She extended her hands to Lannis, and still stunned by Maggie's words, Lannis automatically took them.

A strangled sound escaped Lannis, and she couldn't tell if it was a sob or a laugh. But Maggie's face crinkled into an attractive web of well-developed laugh lines, and Lannis's emotions tipped the same direction. In a moment they were both laughing so hard that Maggie had to race for the bathroom. Lannis wrapped her arms around her torso and toppled sideways on the couch.

With surprise, she realized this *was* the first time Ben had gone out undercover since they'd been married. The last time was when she still lived near the airport. Where she had neighbors who would hear her scream if something happened when she was home alone. Which she had been, then. She sobered, wiping laughter's tears from her cheeks.

Maggie was right. Maybe she should have waited until Ben returned before moving forward on the Robert Davis project. But she hoped she didn't *really* need a keeper.

"Hey, Lannis." Maggie's voice floated out from the bathroom. "Do you want to spend the night? I can clear my sewing off the guest bed."

Lannis didn't think much longer about this invitation than she had the one for dinner. She glanced outside. Still spooky.

"Yes. Thank you." She stood, determined to put Davis out of her mind for the night.

Unless he wormed his way in, through the back door of her mind, in a nightmare.

She shuddered. *Not in front of the kids.*

Well, she could either be alone and scared and have a nightmare, or she could be not alone, not scared, and maybe, just maybe, skate past the nightmare.

She gathered the forgotten and now-cool tea, dumped the remnants in the sink, and met Maggie at the stairs.

Nightmares weren't all that predictable, after all. If they were, she'd simply avoid sleep until daytime.

And since she was off tomorrow, she had that option.

At least she wouldn't be alone.

Chapter Twenty-Two

ROBERT DAVIS LIFTED his face to the sun. He tried not to enjoy it
too much, lest he end up losing the privilege, but it was hard to do.
Smith had made good on his promise—after Robert had turned into
quite the diplomat. He'd refereed disputes, smoothed ruffled
feathers, and flat-out avoided the assholes who wanted to fight. It
had paid off.

He even liked coming out on days like this, chilly enough that
the lightweight prison-issue jacket was barely sufficient to keep him
from freezing his balls off. Today's sun couldn't quite outdo the air
temperature, and he rubbed his hands together, then cupped them
over his face to warm his nose.

"Davis." One of the guards beckoned him.

Anxiety curled in his gut, and he—again—searched his mind for
a possible infraction. There were so many rules, it was easy to break
one without realizing it. It hadn't mattered before, but now it did.
Too much.

God, he hated feeling so apprehensive. It was a short step from
there to *weak*.

He approached the guard, careful to keep his body language
neutral, although sometimes he actually strove for subservient, if it
suited his purpose. Today, though, the sun had infused him with such
pleasure that he couldn't contain himself enough to achieve
subservient.

"Yeah?" The word carried too much attitude, and Robert
winced. Way to go, getting the body language right, then screwing up
the verbal.

The guard—Goss—didn't challenge Robert's tone, but instead
handed him a pass. "You're wanted inside. Go with Nadorff," he
said, indicating another officer waiting behind him.

"What for?" Instantly wary, Robert's attitude evaporated,
leaving him feeling vulnerable and exposed. Not quite panicked, but
disgusted at the rush of fear that threatened to swamp him.

Goss shrugged. "Dunno." He jerked a thumb in the direction of
the massive stone building looming over the yard. "Not your place to
ask questions." His gaze raked over Robert's orange jumpsuit, in a
blatant reminder of his status. "Better git."

Robert frowned. Between anxiety at the meaning of the unknown summons, and irritation at being made to look a fool, his good mood of only moments ago fizzled. Other than outright refusal, which would lead to immediate revocation of his coveted yard privileges, he had no choice. Careful to not make physical contact with Goss—a sacred rule—he shouldered past the guard and fell into step with Nadorff.

By the time he'd been escorted through several sliding gates and subjected to an unannounced search, he'd lost any sense of gain from his recent good behavior, not to mention all sense of direction. Nadorff ushered him into a room furnished with a slate table and half a dozen chairs. A dry-erase board covered most of one wall, and there was a heavily barricaded window at the end. Unfortunately, it opened onto a facing wing, and didn't offer a view of anything except bricks. He couldn't even tell what floor he was on.

"I'll let her know you're here." Nadorff stepped out and picked up a phone. The door swung closed before Robert could hear what he said, although he could see him through an eye-level wire-reinforced window in the door.

Her? Robert scratched his head. He hadn't encountered any women since he'd arrived here several months ago. But that ruled out the warden, not that Robert had any illusions that he warranted an audience with *him*.

The door opened and a woman entered. Robert's first impression was an explosion of color, from ebony skin that contrasted with gleaming white teeth, to bold geometric patterns and vibrant hues of her African-themed clothing. His second impression was *Damn, she's a tall woman*. Not to mention quite *womanly*. The surprise of her so overwhelmed him, he almost didn't notice Nadorff slip in behind her and take up a station next to the door.

"Hello, Mr. Davis." She placed a couple of folders on the table. "Have a seat, please," she said, motioning to a chair across from her. She sat, then looked up at him expectantly.

Mr. Davis? He pulled himself from his stupor and sat.

"Thank you for agreeing to see me today, Mr. Davis."

He nearly snorted. *Agreeing?* He'd had no choice in the matter. Now that he was here, his curiosity was piqued.

"My name is Ms. Connor, and I am a social worker for the Department of Corrections. I have several issues to discuss with you today, but first, do you have anything you wish to bring up?"

Robert gaped at her. Words deserted him momentarily, but then he couldn't help himself. What the hell. He didn't think he'd get disciplined for sarcasm. He joined his hands in a steepled position and rested his chin on the point his fingers made. "The accommodations fall short of my usual standards, and the chef can rarely be congratulated on his efforts." He glanced at the ceiling as if in thought, then added, "My cell mates snore like chainsaws, and Martinez showers once a month whether he needs it or not." He met her gaze. Her eyes had widened fractionally. "Other than a disturbing lack of liberty…" He shrugged.

Laugh lines crinkled at the corners of her eyes. "A sense of humor. Refreshing." She tapped the papers into submission and the skin at the edges of her eyes smoothed. "Mr. Davis, I see that you've only named one person on your visitor list, and you've received no visitors since arriving here."

Robert nodded. He'd put Stan down, but for what reason, he didn't know. He'd fired him as defense counsel, but retained his services in overseeing the collapse of his assets. The guy had power of attorney for him, and the only correspondence he ever sent did nothing more than document Robert's fiscal hemorrhage. His jaw tightened.

"Do you have family or friends you'd like to add?"

"You called me here to discuss my visitor list?" Robert didn't believe that for a heartbeat, but for the life of him, he couldn't fathom why she wanted to talk about his list. Before she could speak, he said, "No. No additions." He wasn't going to get suckered into telling her anything about himself. No secrets, no fodder that could be used against him at some point. "Why?"

"Covering the bases before we get down to business, Mr. Davis. Nothing more than that."

Stop playing games, he wanted to say, but he knew that would come across as potentially threatening. "So, what is the business?"

Ms. Connor regarded him as if she were assessing his mood, or maybe his mental health. He forced himself to relax, schooling his features in a purposely bland expression.

Abruptly, she leaned forward. "Have you ever heard of the concept of restorative justice, Mr. Davis?"

He frowned and started to reply in the negative, but then he remembered reading an article. "I'm not sure. Maybe. Something about the juvie system in Florida."

She beamed as if he were a star pupil and had just found his way through a particularly difficult problem. She leaned back and crossed her arms over her generous bosom, which was covered more than modestly by a high-necked, boxy-styled blouse.

Gaze drawn to where soft flesh lay hidden, he stared, then realized what he'd done. That *was* a punishable offense. *But it's been so long.* He jerked his eyes back to her face and felt sweat break out on his brow.

He swallowed, but his throat had gone dry and it felt like sand grating its way past parched tissues.

She'd begun talking, but the distraction had cost him his hearing, and it took all his concentration to focus on her voice again.

"—very effective with curbing recidivism." She stopped and peered at him. "Are you with me, Mr. Davis?"

"I…ah, is it possible for me to get a drink of water, Ms. Connor?" Robert cleared his throat.

"Of course." She rose and left him with Nadorff. Robert kept his gaze fixed on a chip in the paint on the wall opposite him, and waited in silence, hoping like blazes the guard hadn't picked up on the reason for the glass of water. His heart had begun to thud, and he worked on slowing and calming it.

The door swung open, squeaking at the midpoint of its arc, and Ms. Connor reentered with a paper cup full of water. She set it in the middle of the table, and he waited until Nadorff nodded at him before taking it. The liquid soothed his throat, but did nothing to cool his physical response to her, and he wondered how he was going to stand and walk without blatant evidence of his woody when the interview was over.

Robert deliberately left a swallow or two in the cup, in case he needed it again. "I'm sorry, Ms. Connor. I missed part of what you were saying."

"No problem. As I was explaining…" She went on to tell him about some program where juvenile offenders, rather than going through the standard justice system model of punishment—what happened, who did it, what is the prescribed punishment—were screened and selected for an experimental model called restorative justice. He listened, but wondered with increasing bafflement why she'd brought him here to discuss this.

"So instead of viewing the crimes as violations against the state, restorative justice sees the crimes as violations of dignity. In the former, victims are almost peripheral to justice. In fact, if there's enough evidence, a person can be convicted without the victim's testimony."

Okay, that's personal. Robert flashed to his own trial, and his anger surged at the unfairness of it. An emotion too raw for him to name had simmered beneath the anger then, and now, with the benefit of elapsed time, he could identify it. Shame. He'd been impotent in his own defense. He'd known that, of course, but until now, he hadn't seen how ashamed he felt at his inability to protect himself against a mere girl.

He realized Ms. Connor had stopped, apparently waiting for his response. He managed a nod, and she continued.

"The focus of restorative justice is: who has been harmed, how have lives been impacted, and how can healing occur."

Robert made an impatient noise.

She stopped. "Yes, Mr. Davis?"

To hell with discipline. "So what, Ms. Connor?" He leaned toward her, careful to keep his hands flat on the table for Nadorff's benefit. "Is this some namby-pamby attempt to get me to apologize for raping Lannis Parker…Martin?" He skewered her with his gaze. "Because that isn't going to happen, and if that's what this is all about, I'm ready to go back to my cell."

She wasn't the least bit intimidated by his speech—or his body language. Of course, Nadorff, serving as her bodyguard, stood just yards away. "You always have that option, Mr. Davis, but I'd like you to hear me out. After that, it is up to you to choose your next course of action."

My next course of action? Robert had no idea what she meant, and he teetered on whether to listen or return to the cell block. Curiosity warred with self-righteousness, and after a long moment, curiosity won. He let out a frustrated breath, and gave her a brusque nod. "Go ahead."

"I think you missed part of what I was saying, Mr. Davis. The focus of restorative justice is not on the victim. It is on both the victim and the perpetrator. Let me repeat, so you can hear it this time. Who has been harmed? Your victims—*and you*. How have lives been impacted? Yours certainly has; you reside here." She emphasized her point by tapping an elegant forefinger on the table. "I'm sure you recognize your victims' lives have been irreparably altered. Finally, how can healing occur? Your victims must seek their own healing."

Her voice vibrated with intensity. "What about you? Can you even see that you are in need of healing?" Ms. Connor trapped him in her gaze and he was helpless to escape it. "If so, are you willing to work to achieve it?"

For the second time in a half hour, Robert's voice deserted him. Luckily, she didn't expect any answers right now. She didn't slow down, just kept going like a freight train bearing down on him.

"Your victims *and you* have experienced trauma and shame—"

Robert nearly choked. Had she read his mind? He'd only figured that part out a few minutes ago. Of course, maybe she was referring to the shame of incarceration, which was obvious.

"—and your task is to reestablish honor." She finally paused.

He had no idea how to respond. He grabbed the cup and took a gulp of water in a lame attempt to buy time. He set it down, glad that his hand didn't tremble, because he felt pretty damn shaken. He cleared his throat again. "Uh, reestablish honor." Whatever the hell that meant.

She beamed again. "Yes. Are you in, Mr. Davis?"

It began to dawn on him. Victim, visitor list, restorative justice… "How exactly does this work, Ms. Connor?" Dread settled in his belly.

"If you consent, Mrs. Martin will meet with you—and I will facilitate, of course. You two will engage in dialogue, and at the end of the process, both of you will be able to move on through your individual healing processes."

"You expect me to apologize to her." His voice was flat.

She raised her eyebrows. "Yes, of course."

Robert's knee-jerk response was *not only no, but hell, no*, and he opened his mouth to tell her just that. But he stayed the words at the last possible second, and clamped his teeth together.

Wait a minute. This had possibilities. Face-to-face with Lannis Parker Martin? That had some definite possibilities. *Oh, yeah*. The dread deep within receded, and a heated tendril of anticipation replaced it.

He straightened. "Yes. I'm in. What do I need to do?"

Ms. Connor pulled a form from her stack of papers. "Here, sign this, and…"

Robert signed, printed the name Lannis Martin under Stan's, and took the brochure on restorative justice Ms. Connor wanted him to read.

Yeah, he was up for this.

He smiled his most charming smile at her, thanked her for the opportunity, and went back to the cell block in better spirits than even the sunshine had provided.

Chapter Twenty-Three

LANNIS GOT DOWN on her knees to reach a stubborn sterile equipment wrapper that had fallen behind the built-in harness for pint-sized gurneys. Copilot duties included post-flight cabin cleanup, and as soon as she tugged this piece free, it would be a quick job to vacuum.

Eric stuck his head back in. "About done?" Without waiting for a reply, he added, "We've got an emergency run, over to Columbia, Kentucky."

"Ready in three, but I'm behind on the paperwork, then."

"Don't worry about it. I'll get it started. You do the preflight when you're done in here." He disappeared, and Lannis stepped up her efforts in response to his urgency.

The busier they got, the less of an asshole Eric was. Either that, or he was actually beginning to thaw. Didn't matter. Lannis was just relieved to not feel so defensive, on edge. It sapped her.

And she felt drained enough, with no word from Ben or Mike, precious little from Lynette, and no return call from Ms. Connor at the prison. It had been two weeks, and while she had only *hoped* for news from Ben or Lynette, she'd expected to hear from Ms. Connor. Silence on that front fueled a bout of second-guessing her own motives, and questioning how realistic her goals were. Not to mention way too much time to anticipate actually seeing Robert Davis again.

She pitched the vacuum at the service cart and raced through the preflight inspection. Her cell phone bumped against her thigh, reminding her she had no time to turn it on and check for messages. She pushed her disappointment aside.

She heard Eric's voice, raised over the sound of a two-seat trainer taxiing past, as he shouted something back toward the open hangar. The transport team arrived, ambulance wailing all the way onto the ramp. They never used lights and sirens on the way to the plane, only the other direction—on the way to the hospital. The team piled out and sprinted to the plane. She waved them in, and finished the walk around at the same time Eric got to the retractable steps of the plane.

"After you," he said and motioned her to go first.

She raised her eyebrows in surprise and scrambled in. "Thank you."

He followed, then handed her the paperwork. She slid into her seat, buckled up, and reviewed the numbers quickly. They all looked normal, and she began to program the flight computer.

Eric closed and stowed the door, and briefed the flight nurses. Thanks to preferential treatment as a Lifeguard flight, they had the plane airborne within minutes.

Once air traffic control and the radio had settled into the en-route portion, Lannis asked, "Will they be at the airport, or will the transport team need to stabilize when we get there?" If there was a built-in break, maybe she could check her phone before the end of business hours.

"They were in the process of loading the kid into an ambulance before we even took off. A six-year-old, accidental gunshot wound. Columbia's a small town, and they've got a regional hospital, but not the resources for this."

Lannis nodded her understanding. Scoop and run, at least that's what the EMTs and flight nurses called it. In their case, she'd modified it, mentally, to *scoop and fly*. Situations like this one had the potential to turn into tragedies, and if nothing else, put her own problems into perspective.

"You didn't have a chance to get inside, did you?" Eric's statement surprised her.

Lannis glanced at him. "Uh, no."

"When we get back, make sure you check the bulletin board."

She nodded. "Okay." The board was down a hallway not typically used by pilots and mechanics. "A new letter?"

"Yeah." He smiled, his normally granite features softening. "Twins, three months ago. We picked them up in Pikeville. You were on the trip."

Lannis remembered. A night flight, and the weather had been bad. It had been dicey getting in, and it took the nurses a couple of hours to get the babies stable enough to fly out.

Eric added, "The pics are cute. They went home on Halloween, so they dressed them in costumes—a ladybug and a frog. You know, kinda like those goofy calendars with babies dressed up like flowers and stuff."

She'd forgotten they were fraternal twins, a boy and a girl. Lannis laughed. "That's great. Thanks for telling me. I probably wouldn't have made it into the office for another couple of days."

Air traffic control called, and she keyed the mike to reply. After that, they got busy, and she didn't have time to indulge her preoccupation over Ms. Connor's unreturned call.

The next few hours were tense and fast. The boy started out stable, but halfway back to Louisville, a flurry of activity in the back told Lannis he'd taken a turn for the worse. The charge nurse keyed the intercom. "You guys need to expedite as much as possible. And radio ahead, tell the surgeons to be ready when we get there. We'll be going straight to the OR with him."

They taxied on the knife edge of too fast once they landed, and Lannis bailed out of her seat as soon as she was no longer needed. She had the door open almost before Eric got the engine shut down. The ambulance backed into place, transferred the patient, and screamed out of the airport, leaving a silent mess in the aftermath of the efforts expended in trying to save the kid's life.

She heaved out a breath and sent a quiet prayer skyward. This one needed all the help he could get. Even Eric was subdued as he took the paperwork inside to finish. Lannis pulled on latex gloves for the cleanup. It was rarely necessary, but tonight… She shuddered, but dug in. While she didn't like blood, she wasn't squeamish like some of the guys were. Like Eric. His face had gone pale when he turned around to leave the cockpit, and he'd barreled through the cabin like his backside was on fire.

By the time she was done, the only people left were the night line guy and the next aircrew. She hauled in the bag of biohazard trash and disposed of it, then took a quick detour down the hallway.

Aw… The twins were cute as could be. Her lips curled up in a smile. She still volunteered in the neonatal nursery when she had time, but for some reason or another had missed these guys' stay. They must have been transferred to a different unit once they'd survived the critical stage. Their wizened little faces peered out from outfits that had to be handmade. She didn't think anyplace sold infants' clothing that small, and certainly not Halloween costumes. But she could be wrong. There were lots of preemies. Maybe there was a market.

She headed for her car, finally digging her phone out of her pocket and turning it on. As it booted up, Lannis remembered a conversation she'd had with one of the nurses about six months ago, when she first started working here.

"Isn't this really stressful?" she had asked. "I mean, the kids are so sick if they need our services, and there are so many of them." New to the job, and thoroughly stressed by the myriad changes in her own life at the time, Lannis had wondered out loud to one of the most laid-back flight nurses.

The nurse, only slightly older than Lannis, had looked surprised. "Oh, no. I'm an adrenaline junkie. I love working ER, and this is an extension of that. But in terms of the kids—well, the Children's Hospital serves a large region. Kentucky, parts of Indiana, Illinois, Tennessee, West Virginia. Sometimes Ohio, if Cincinnati's hospital is stretched thin. And this is a relatively densely populated region. We see the sickest of the sick, and what you have to remember is that for every kid we see, there are a thousand or more we don't. Because *they're* healthy."

Lannis paused. Maybe, just maybe, her exposure to tragedy involving children exaggerated its potential in her mind. Which, in turn, exacerbated her fears of getting pregnant. And she was honest enough to recognize faulty reasoning when it hit her in the face. "Okay, God," she whispered. "I get it."

Her phone beeped, indicating she had a voice mail. She glanced at it.

Caller ID said RESTRICTED.

Her heart skipped, then hammered into double-time.

A call from Ben's work or the police department would be a restricted number. They would only call if something were wrong. Adrenaline shot up her spine, then down the backs of her arms. Her fingers trembled as she punched the buttons to access voice mail, and she held her breath as she waited for the agonizingly slow computerized voice to tell her how many voice messages she had— one—and what time it had come in—5:47, three hours ago.

Finally—*finally*—it clicked into the actual message itself.

Chapter Twenty-Four

BEN DREW HIS HANDGUN and held it at the ready as he opened the door to his spartan motel room. A sweeping glance cleared it, except for the bathroom. He took the most defensible route to the tiny room with chipped, stained fixtures. Not much room for anyone to hide in there, but after his brush with the near-ambush a week ago, he wasn't taking chances. Rolo and the Enforcer hadn't tried anything like that since, but undercurrents of hostility and distrust eddied around their every encounter, and the stress was beginning to wear on Ben.

He slid smoothly around the doorjamb, gun raised. Nope. Nobody behind the shower curtain. He flicked the safety on and stowed his gun in a fluid, nearly unconscious motion, then tossed his ball cap on the bed. Only then did he relax, shoving a hand through his hair, then cupping it around the back of his neck to rub some of the tension away.

Walking back to the door, he snagged the lone flimsy chair and jammed it up under the knob as a second-line barrier to unauthorized entry. He threw the dead bolt, then crouched by the bed and lifted the spread, a stiff polyester specimen that poked him in the nose when he slept. The box spring shifted when he applied pressure, and he slipped his hand in beneath it, in the space behind the support, and groped for his other cell phone, the one he used to talk with Mike.

Ah. There it was. He withdrew it, and shook dust bunnies off his fingers as he dropped the mattress back into place. Fatigue dragged at him, and he gave a moment's thought to skipping the check-in, but duty won out. He hit speed dial and sat on the bed—perhaps a tactical error, as he longed for nothing more than to lie back and close his eyes. But he knew he'd fall asleep mid-sentence if he did, so he stretched instead, and kicked his shoes off.

"Yo, Ben." Mike sounded like the call had wakened him, which it probably had. Four in the morning was about right for the criminal element to be hitting the sack. Running out of darkness behind which to hide their illegal activities.

He needed to stop thinking in cop language. Something might slip when he was with the gangs. "Hey, Mike. I didn't get much tonight." Unspoken was *again*. "We have an ID on the Enforcer yet?" The guy was so paranoid he wore gloves of some type all the time, and fingerprints were out of the question. So Ben had gone for second best and snagged a marijuana butt that the guy had smoked, turned it over to Mike, who in turn sent it for DNA testing.

"No, and the lab said the backlog is huge. It'll be months."

"I was afraid of that." Ben sighed and rubbed his eyes. "Any other news I need to know?" The bed, hard and uninviting, was looking better by the second.

"Not business." Bedclothes rustled in the background. "I called Maggie from a pay phone, though."

Ben's eyebrows rose, along with his interest. "Tell me." Suddenly awake, he straightened.

"She and the kids are fine. Lannis has come over several times, stayed the night last Friday."

Ben's heart made a small leap at Lannis's name. "She okay?"

"Yeah, Maggie said she's doing great."

"Great, good." He sounded like an idiot, but he couldn't stop the grin that creased his face. "That's good to hear."

"Except for the prison shit."

What? Ben stilled. This didn't sound good. "What prison shit?"

"She apparently tracked Davis down in the prison system and asked to see him. The lady called back this week with details."

I thought— Ben closed his eyes and felt his jaw tense. Hadn't they tabled the idea after their fight that night? Or had she decided she needed to do it no matter what he thought? He couldn't remember the details of the argument—but he did know they had left it hanging. Another tactical error on his part, he now saw with the benefit of hindsight. Of course, he hadn't known he'd get this callout, but still...

"Lannis talked to Maggie about it?" Ben pinched the bridge of his nose. That seemed out of character for Lannis, private as she was.

"Yeah. She stopped in on her way home from work." Mike paused to yawn. "Figured you knew about this."

Ben heard the question in Mike's voice. "Sorta." The bed creaked as he shifted. "Listen," he said, changing the subject. "I'm going without the wire again tomorrow"—which was really today on the calendar, and a risk no matter what day it was—"because the Enforcer is getting really twitchy, unpredictable."

Silence. Then a sigh. "Should we pull you? I'm no good to you as backup if we can't communicate. I don't even know anything other than your general location."

"I know. I've thought about it, too." Ben stood, and holding the phone between cheek and shoulder, unbuttoned, then unzipped his jeans. "But I'm close. One of his gofers, a kid named JaJuan, likes to flap his lips. Makes him feel like a man. I caught a reference to a storage unit tonight, but no ID or address." He slid his jeans down his legs and kicked them off. "Give me one more night, then if I've come up empty, we'll regroup."

"It goes against my better judgment, but…" Another sigh. "Okay. But check in earlier next time, buddy."

Ben agreed, hung up, hid the phone again, and lay down between the scratchy sheets. But sleep, in spite of his bone-deep weariness, proved elusive. A distorted replay of the fight with Lannis looped through his mind. His shouted "We *will* work through this" took center stage, followed closely by the image of her walking away from him, closing the door on him, shutting him out.

And now she'd gone and initiated contact with Robert Davis. His stomach churned, and he wanted—simultaneously—to throttle her and claim her in the most primal means possible. Both goals, when he thought about it, could be accomplished in the same raw act of physical union.

A wave of homesickness rolled through him. He stared at the ceiling, where the reflection of the neon motel sign flickered in hypnotic rhythm. *Homesick?* He hadn't felt homesick since the Christmas he spent in Iraq. Maybe he should listen to Mike's instinct, and abandon this mission. Maybe he wasn't as close as he thought he was. Maybe it didn't matter as much as he thought it did.

He was distracted, no question, and not up to his usual level of performance. Mike had picked up on it, and seemed more concerned about it than Ben was.

He sat up, twisted his torso to relieve the kinks, then repositioned on his stomach. He was too tired to think, much less make smart decisions. He rechecked his gun on the bedside table, and punched his pillow until it resembled its intended purpose. And, in a pattern that was becoming predictable, he shoved everything out of his mind until morning, except for Lannis, who refused to go quietly.

A tap at the door woke him, dragging him from what must have been sleep, although the last thought he'd had seemed to have been only a moment ago. Sunshine streamed through gaps in the drapes. Ben grabbed his gun and thumbed the safety off, scrambling to remember where he was, and why.

"Housekeeping." The voice was light, feminine, and in a singsong dialect of English. Definitely not a native speaker of the language.

"Later." His voice emerged as a croak, and he cleared his throat as he set his gun back on the table. Blinking, he realized he *had* slept. It didn't happen often, but those nights he hadn't thought he'd slept ended up being nights he might as well have not bothered. He got up for a drink of water, washed his eyes out, and squinted at his watch. After eleven. His stomach rumbled, and he sighed. His fractured reflection stared back at him from the cracked mirror. Unshaven, pale—except for bruised-looking circles beneath bloodshot eyes—and listless. For someone who'd never done drugs in his life, he sure didn't look it.

Might as well get something to eat. Ben didn't think food would help his thought processes much more than the decidedly unrestful night of sleep had. A quick shower might, though, and he reached all of a foot and a half to turn the spigot on, shed his underwear, and stepped in. About halfway through, the blessedly steamy water woke him up, but waking didn't improve the direction of his thoughts.

He waffled on whether to abort the mission or continue. JaJuan *was* a viable lead. A loose cannon, as well, but other than a tendency toward hyperbole, the kid had accurate information. And Ben sensed he was close to the piece they wanted. If they could shut down the Enforcer, a good portion of Louisville's crime would fade away, along with a healthy—or rather, unhealthy—chunk of the drug traffic.

Ben used the towel to wipe the fogged-over mirror clean. The biggest reason he should abort the mission looked back at him. The muscles in his jaw tightened. His eyes glittered back at him, piercing and intelligent, and so like Danny's that his heart squeezed.

He'd been thirteen, barely, when Danny had gone missing. Their mother's keening cries, his father's quiet desperation, his own hollow fear, and Mindy's confusion, to be expected for a nine-year-old. These were what he remembered. That Danny had been a victim, as much as murdered by the greed of a drug dealer. Murdered by the drugs themselves that seduced, then destroyed the person Ben had held most dear.

A wave of grief washed over Ben, grief so stark and fresh he might have just learned of Danny's death five minutes ago. He bent over the sink, gut-wrenched by the pain, and a guttural noise ripped from his throat, part sob, part agonized groan. He clenched his fist, and tried to rein in his emotion with force of will.

As an adult, he knew Danny bore some culpability in his death. No one held him down and shoved pills in his mouth or forced him to smoke marijuana, or later, forced him to snort cocaine. He'd made those choices, innocuous as they seemed at first, on his own.

But that knowledge did nothing to ease Ben's pain. It made it worse. A trembling took hold of his soul, then expanded to his limbs. Danny had abandoned him for some stupid high, and white-hot rage had burned deep inside Ben ever since. He'd hidden it from himself and from everyone else, but he had to face it now.

Ben dashed a tear away, angry at his weakness, angry at Danny all over again. The only way to ease the pain, the rage, was to atone for Danny. The time for vengeance was long past. Ben could bear his brother's death now, today, only by atoning for Danny's bad choices. Grant his death some redeeming quality, any redeeming quality. To sow some bit of good in the tangle of sorrow spawned by the tragedy of his making.

Ben's focus narrowed to the sole means of atonement available to him. To do battle with the seething, self-serving, underground industry that *did* prey on the young, the vulnerable. To cripple the cycle of addiction, mental illness, homelessness, and death. To take down men like the Enforcer and his minions.

He looked at his reflection in the mirror again. Danny's face seemed to blur his own features, and he wondered why he'd never seen the resemblance before. He did now, and his resolve firmed.

It's a go. A deep breath shuddered through him, and Ben thinned his lips. He ran a hand through his wet hair in lieu of a comb, pulled his clothes on with brisk efficiency, and armed himself.

Food first, then head out to track down the Enforcer.

Chapter Twenty-Five

LANNIS PICKED UP the mail from the bricked box at the street end of the driveway. She reminded herself to tell Maggie she'd volunteered to fly over Thanksgiving and wouldn't celebrate at the Ross household. The pilots split duty time between one holiday or the other, and she figured there was a better chance that the guys would be home by Christmas. They'd better be. She didn't want to contemplate the possibility that she'd miss both holidays with her new husband. Distracted by her thoughts, she absently sorted through the stack she'd pulled from the box. Bills, flyers, junk mail, a couple of magazines… Her hand stilled at a manila envelope. She glanced at the return address. Davis's prison.

The voice message last week had been from Ms. Connor, telling her she'd been added to Robert Davis's approved visitor list—but Lannis hadn't expected anything in the mail.

Her breath caught. Was it from *him*? Or was it from Ms. Connor? Suppressing an urge to rip it open right there, in the road, she tucked the mail under her arm and climbed back in her car. By the time she'd gotten into the house and rearmed the security system, her pulse had evened out, and she'd achieved a semblance of calm— although it was a higher baseline level of calm than before she'd discovered the envelope.

The thought flitted through her mind that maybe she should wait until morning to open it, maybe even go to Maggie's tonight if she couldn't wait to open it.

Nope. She wanted to know what was in it, whether the timing was smart or not. She sat at the kitchen table, hesitated long enough to take a fortifying breath, then, careful to not tear the return address, slit the envelope open. Peering in she saw a stack of papers, some stapled, some loose, and pulled them out. The staples gave her a sense that it wasn't from Davis, himself, and some of the dread that had gathered in her stomach began to drain away.

She spread the pages out. A cover letter, signed by Ms. Shauna Connor. Her signature was bold and full of little flourishes that stopped just short of being flowery. A set of forms, a questionnaire of some sort, and a couple of brochures about restorative justice. Lannis doubted that she'd learn much that she didn't already know about the concept. She'd taken Ms. Connor's advice and researched it on the Internet.

Relieved that nothing appeared to be in Davis's handwriting, or from him, she picked up the cover letter and skimmed it. Ms. Connor would meet with Mr. Davis to prepare for the process, but he'd already agreed to allow Lannis to visit. Her pulse quickened. *She's spoken with him.* Lannis didn't know why that made it seem suddenly more real, but as long as Davis was in prison somewhere, he was "out of sight, out of mind." He'd reverted to academic, theoretical existence rather than flesh-and-blood reality in her mind.

Which of course, made perfect psychological sense. Denial was a great coping mechanism.

But this was real. She knew she could walk away at any given moment. She wasn't committed to going through with it, at least externally. She could write Ms. Connor back and say she'd changed her mind.

She wouldn't. Lannis picked up the forms and a pen, and began filling in blanks. It didn't take long. The questionnaire wasn't so easy. It asked for an account of the crime, then her responses in the aftermath. What was her motivation in pursuing this avenue? What did she hope to gain from it? Did she recognize any unrealistic expectations on her part?

She sighed. *Not tonight.* All valid questions, she supposed, but it grated on her that she had to explain herself to Ms. Connor. It felt…it felt like *she* was under the microscope, that *she* was being judged. A wave of longing for a drink washed over her.

Yeah, yeah. Lannis shrugged it off. *Get over it.* She stood, needing to leave this alone for a while. *Like maybe a week.* She smiled at her feeble attempt at humor, and stretched. She was tired. Besides, she went on night shift tomorrow, so she might as well go to bed early. The chances that she'd actually be able to sleep in the afternoon would be better, especially if she squeezed in an early-morning run.

~

Robert Davis is free—free!—and he lurks outside her cage, stalking her, his nostrils twitching at her scent. She knows that, in the strange way of dreams, even though she can't see him. She can almost see him, though, a shadowy figure materializing from behind a tree, then disappearing in a puff of black mist. A slight movement catches her eye and she turns, grasping the rough bars of her prison. There! There he is! Her heart pounds, thuds, slams within the bars of her ribs, as unable to escape danger as she is.

She puts her back to the side of the cage farthest from him, but he fades away again, only to form as a vapor outside the bars, next to her. She jerks away from his essence, flings herself at the other corner, panting in terror. Her sleep shirt rides up her thighs as she scrambles away, and she tugs at it one-handed in a vain attempt to cover herself. Little mewls of distress escape her lips.

In utter desperation, she throws herself at the bars, clawing at them, flinging her body at them, even trying to bite through them. Her teeth shatter in her mouth, and she spits pieces out, blood dribbling down her chin, tears mingling with them, dripping onto her hands, making her fingers slip on the metal.

His malevolent laugh snakes through the night, an easy laugh, a patient laugh. Davis is in no hurry. He toys with her terror, poking a finger through the bars into the cage, making her fear spiral higher, higher, tighter, until she thinks she'll die of it.

And wishes she would. Wishes it would be over, done, dead.

She strikes at his hand, but her fist slides through a cloud instead, then connects with the bar, and pain explodes through her knuckles, reverberating through the bones in her wrist, and rocketing up her arm. Cradling her injured arm, she slides down the bars, her back scraping on the jagged bits of grit in the paint, bruises already forming on her shoulders and arms from her earlier attempts to batter her way out of the enclosure.

Dear God, oh dear God… She can't finish the plea, but rage suddenly rises from a place inside her, from a reservoir of strength she didn't know existed.

"You coward!" She screams the words at Davis, feeling them expand and echo in her mind and in the air around her. "Let me see you, so I can fight you! What are you afraid of?"

She feels rather than sees his anger. The air shimmers, and he morphs from shadow into substance next to her, in the cage this time.

In the cage with her.

Her eyes roll back in her head, and she wonders if a nightmare could truly kill her. If she swoons, is it like the saying about falling in a dream? That if you land, you'd die? If she faints, will Davis succeed, will he kill her?

Please, God…deliver me.

~

Lannis woke, gasping, and rolled out of bed, tumbling to the floor, sheets tangling around her legs. She kicked her feet loose and scrambled to a crouch. Her lungs heaved like bellows, and she couldn't hear over the pounding of her pulse in her ears. She scrabbled for the drawer in the bedside table, tried and failed to pull it open, then managed to snag it. Her hand fumbled on the contents, but she found what she sought. The gun—Ben's gun—was cool against her fingers, but she bobbled and almost dropped it.

Now trembling from toes to shoulders, she flicked the safety off and crab-walked into the corner where she could see everything in the room. Gun in position but wobbling in her grip, she blinked furiously and tried to assess her surroundings.

Nothing. No intruder, no threat, nothing out of the ordinary. Her breathing slowed and she held it, listening. Her heart still raced, but the pounding had faded and she could hear now. The house was quiet except for the hum of the furnace and the refrigerator. The security alarm was silent. *Someone could have disabled it.* But she shook that thought off quickly. Ben had rigged a failsafe, one that would trigger if someone tried to do just that.

Her breath whooshed out.

A dream. It was a dream. Just a dream. Her muscles went slack and she sagged, the gun's barrel drooping to the floor. A sob caught in her throat, and she brought a hand up to cover her mouth.

Thank you, God, for not letting me die in my nightmare…but couldn't you have pulled me out of it a little sooner? Lannis felt a twinge of guilt for grousing at him, but decided he was big enough to handle it. She dragged herself to her feet, thumbed the safety back on, but didn't put the weapon away. The trembling had subsided; now chills racked her body. She clicked the light on in the closet and grabbed a sweatshirt, pulled it on over her sleep shirt, and tugged jeans and shoes on, as well.

Gun in hand, she turned on the bedroom light, then the bathroom light, and went down the hallway turning on every light she passed. By the time she got to the kitchen, she'd sorted out what was real and what was nightmare. The papers from Ms. Connor—the obvious trigger for the dream—were still out on the table, and without looking at them, she scooped them all up and shoved them in a drawer.

Lannis put a pot of water on to boil, pulled out the chamomile tea and honey, and flipped on the outdoor floodlights, illuminating everything within thirty feet of the house. Ben preferred to use them judiciously, as they drew a lot of electricity and therefore cost a lot, but Lannis would have gone nose to nose with him on it tonight, if he'd been here. And she would have won.

If he'd been here… A spurt of anger at his absence flared. And just as quickly, she squelched it. *Unfair, not to mention irrational. Get a grip.*

Anxiety still tap-danced through her veins. She finally glanced at the clock, noting it was 1:12 in the morning. She grimaced. *Still time to get to a bar or a liquor store…* No. *No.* Not going there, either literally or figuratively. Period. But she didn't want to call Althea this late. Or Maggie. Her breath shuddered on an inhale. Lannis sensed she needed to connect with someone, or she'd start a downhill slide she might not be able to halt.

The teakettle whistled. Hers was sharp and piercing, as opposed to Maggie's wimpy one, and she jumped. Hurrying to remove it from the stove, she burned a finger and finally let go of the gun, setting it within reach on the counter.

Nursing the small burn, Lannis glanced at the front of the fridge. There were several magnetic stickers on it, and her gaze narrowed on two of them. One, the local number, was the twenty-four-hour rape crisis line. The other was a national number, also twenty-four hour. Her tension eased. Not much, but some.

She picked up the phone and dialed.

She might not get back to sleep tonight—she shuddered at the idea of succumbing to such a vulnerable state again, and so soon—but she'd do at least one thing to help herself.

Good thing she was flipping her schedule, rotating to the night shift for a couple of weeks. She was sick and tired of dealing with nighttime, with Ben gone.

"Crisis hotline," a female voice said.

Lannis brought her attention back to the phone, but not before a wordless, fervent prayer for his return. *Soon.* And hoped God would act a bit more swiftly than he had on her nightmare.

Chapter Twenty-Six

As long as Ms. Connor didn't request his presence during his yard time, Robert was fine with their meetings. Not that there had been many after the first one, just one last week that focused mostly on educating him on the history and process of restorative justice. He was already sick of hearing about it, but he put on a good face for her, bless her voluptuous little heart. The next meeting was scheduled for today, and he whistled tunelessly as he took another lap around the starkly fenced yard.

It had gotten cold last night. His breath puffed out in white clouds, and he had to watch for patches of ice in low-lying depressions worn by countless men like him. He picked up his pace to a jog, and wondered when she'd call for him. Today's meeting would "explore his motivation behind the crime." He grinned. She was so naive, especially for someone who worked with felons.

He raped because he could. Because he was stronger than his victims, because he was smarter than his victims. Because he was smarter than the cops. He glanced at the razor wire topping the twelve-foot fence. *Except for one time.*

The familiar spurt of anger at Lannis Parker Martin warmed him from the inside.

But he was beginning to make the best of his stay here. Once his survival became more certain—it would never be assured, not here—life took on sort of a suspended, dreamy quality. He didn't have to do anything for himself. They fed him, did his laundry. He didn't like the food, and the clothes weren't his, but he did try to look on the bright side, now that he could get out in the fresh air once a day. He saw his "clients" during what he'd mentally designated as his "office hours." The work was minimally interesting, and kept his mind from degenerating into lobotomized sludge. Barely.

But now he had some entertainment to look forward to. Ms. Connor's generous femininity, for one. She wouldn't have caught his eye had he encountered her on the outside, but she was good for plenty of fantasy material. Beggars couldn't be choosers, though, and he rubbed his hands together again, this time in anticipation of today's meeting. He had to pretend he wasn't affected, which took a bit more concentration than he wanted to expend. He'd rather concentrate on her, and the implicit promise of her gender.

He wondered what she would wear. Already he knew she preferred those wild jungle-type prints, and a range of deep colors. The relief from prison gray, prison green, prison puke, made sessions with her worth it, just for the novelty of her clothes.

But the best part was fantasizing about her without her clothes. Especially since policy and common sense required she dress modestly. Gave him more to peel off in his mind's eye.

"Davis." The guard shouted his name, a hint of frustration in his voice making Robert wonder if he'd missed the initial summons.

He changed direction and trotted over to the guy. "Yeah?"

In a transaction that mirrored the one from three weeks ago, the guard issued him a pass and sent him off to see the luscious Ms. Connor.

Who didn't disappoint him, in spite of the fact that she'd so rudely cut his yard time short. She'd only cheated him out of about five minutes, though, so he figured he could be magnanimous and forgive her.

She wore deep purple today, a turtleneck knit blouse topped with a roomy jacket, also purple, but with little gold abstract designs in it, and black slacks. He'd never been much for women's fashions, but he was developing an obsessive interest in hers.

She carried her ubiquitous files, and pulled out a blank legal pad, apparently for notes. Robert dragged himself out of his fixation on her attire enough to remember he needed to be careful with his behavior. Otherwise, he'd screw up his opportunity to see Lannis, never mind the error of giving away information that could be used to control him.

He conveniently pushed aside the reality that his life was pretty much out of his control these days.

He'd stood as Ms. Connor entered, and now that she'd settled in her chair, he sat. A different officer stood bodyguard duty for her today, and Robert hadn't even bothered to look at the guy's nametag. But the thought occurred to him that Ms. Connor would ask him to talk about subjects he didn't care for the guard to hear.

All the more reason to be remote, and control his part of the conversation.

"Mr. Davis, how are you?" She slanted her deep chocolate gaze at him.

"Fine, fine." *Play the game.* He sent her a benign smile.

"Wonderful." Her laugh lines deepened briefly, then smoothed.

Does she really mean that? He couldn't truthfully define anything about his existence at the moment as *wonderful,* but her earnestness told him she believed it, at some level, anyway.

"Let's get to work, then, shall we?" She didn't wait for his acknowledgment, but plowed on. "Tell me why you wish to continue with the restorative justice process." She leaned back in her chair and gave him all her attention.

Robert sat up. He needed to tread carefully here, to project sincerity. His lawyer's mind spun up, clicked into gear. "It's a fascinating concept, Ms. Connor. I'm intrigued by the results—very impressive, by the way—in Florida, and in New Zealand. They seem almost too good to be true, and yet tantalizing, almost irresistible if they are. I'd be honored to be part of this grassroots movement."

Ms. Connor gave him no response, no nod of the head to encourage him, no interested "mm-hmm." In fact, her features underwent a subtle shift, going a bit distant. Not icy, not angry, just…distant.

He kept his expression open, going for guileless, authentic, genuine, whatever it took to sell his line of bullshit to her, but inside he scrambled for understanding. He'd said something wrong, but he didn't know what.

"I see." Ms. Connor picked up her pen and wrote something at the top of the page of her legal pad.

Robert tried to read it, but the angle was awkward. He was getting a bad feeling about this. He lifted his gaze to hers, and this time read disappointment in her eyes. His heart sank. Maybe— No, no *maybe* about it. Obviously he'd laid it on a bit thick. He backpedalled in an attempt to undo the damage.

"Can you help me out here, Ms. Connor? Because it's clear you're not satisfied with my answer." The palms of his hands went damp, like he was some rookie law student in front of his first judge, and he cursed himself silently, feeling his opportunity to bedevil Lannis Martin slide through his fingers.

She tapped her pen on the tablet and remained silent for a few moments, long enough for sweat to form on his upper lip. He removed it with a swipe of his forearm.

"Mr. Davis, this is not a matter to be taken lightly. And I do not care to be buffaloed by your lies."

"Lies?" She'd seen right through him, and Robert scrambled for a defense she'd swallow. "I'm not lying." He wasn't telling the whole truth, either, but that wasn't the issue. "Nothing I said is a lie." The problem with the accusation was he couldn't prove her wrong, not when the outcome teetered on how she interpreted his words.

He went for brutal honesty, or as much as he could comfortably reveal. "Look, Ms. Connor. I have nothing to lose and everything to gain. If I don't do this process, nothing changes for me. If I do, I may stand to gain some level of self-improvement. Either way, nothing gets worse for me than it already is. So, yeah, Ms. Connor, I'm interested if for nothing else than the possibilities."

She regarded him for a long moment. Finally, she sighed. "Mr. Davis, your motives are as slippery as a greased pig in a poke, and entirely self-serving. I do not have time to waste on this endeavor if you are simply playing the system." She picked up her files and made ready to leave.

Stunned, a precious few seconds passed before he gathered his thoughts. "No—please, Ms. Connor." To his horror, he realized her opinion had come to mean more to him than he'd thought—or wanted. "Give me another chance. Don't give up on me." He tried to stem the flow, but now uncorked, words poured out of him like verbal diarrhea. "I'll do whatever you want, just please— please…don't throw me away." *What? Don't throw me away?* Shock stole his breath, along with his voice. He couldn't believe he'd said that.

Don't throw me away like my mother did. His mother… He never thought about her. Never. He clenched his fists, took a shaky breath, willed the thought away.

Like my mother did. The image echoed and reverberated in his mind, gaining power simply by its existence.

He spent no energy thinking about his past, ever. He especially *never* thought about his slut of a mother, selling herself in exchange for drugs from the time he could remember. She hadn't even bothered with the intermediate step of selling herself for money, then buying the drugs. He'd grown up Dumpster diving while she was passed out or high, and had sworn he'd claw his way out of poverty and never look back.

Which he had, no thanks to the woman who'd literally thrown him away, sentencing him to a life of evading the wolves on the streets. All simply because he was inconvenient.

A roar began in his ears that crescendoed until he couldn't hear Ms. Connor or the guard. Robert shook his head, then shook it again. His hands were clenched into fists, and his fists were shaking, his knees jittering up and down. A howl built deep within him.

How many times had she screamed at him that she would have had an abortion if she'd had the money?

...throw me away...like my mother...

He swallowed convulsively, cramming the howl, the pain, the rage back down into the basement of his psyche where it belonged. He clamped his lips over any more words that might spew out, forced himself to glance at the guard, who had pulled his Taser but hadn't deployed it. Yet.

He felt like a rabbit desperately zigging and zagging to outwit, outrun a fox. He scrambled to put a lid on the memories that had erupted, to defuse the situation, to exert some bit of influence on Ms. Connor—without disclosing anything about his mother.

But first, the guard. Robert raised his hands, trembling ever so slightly, and carefully placed them on the back of his head. "Not a threat." The words came out guttural, a near growl.

He shifted his gaze to Ms. Connor. "I'm calm, under control." His voice broke on the last word, betraying him. He clamped his lips together. He was under control, but barely, and far from calm.

She'd drawn away in alarm, dropping her files in an untidy heap, and regarded him with wary eyes. "Are you certain, Mr. Davis?"

Her use of his name, the respectful address of *mister*, shot to his exposed, vulnerable depths, and nearly undid him. He opened his mouth to answer, but had to take a quick breath to steady the raw emotion roiling beneath the surface. He settled on a silent nod instead.

Ms. Connor cautiously sat down again, sending a glance rife with meaning toward the guard. The man lifted his eyebrows in question, and she nodded, a brief motion backed with resolve. He shrugged and stowed his Taser.

"Now, Mr. Davis, perhaps we can get some real work accomplished." She straightened her papers again and leaned forward. "Can you give me a better answer to your motivation for pursuing this process?"

Robert lowered his arms slowly, stalling, buying time. His hands no longer trembled when he placed them on the table, and relief spurted through him. Crisis passed, he caught Ms. Connor's gaze and said what he'd somehow figured out she wanted to hear.

"Peace, Ms. Connor. It's all about peace, Ms. Parker's"—he gritted his teeth, not believing any of it, but knowing it was what he had to say—"I mean, Mrs. Martin's. And mine. Hers depends on me, and somehow mine depends on her." He turned his hands palm up on the table. "I'll be honest. I don't understand it. It sounds like voodoo, or New Age woo-woo stuff, but if it works, fine. Great, even."

Her expression lost a bit of its wariness. "Good, Mr. Davis," she said, her voice conveying approval. "We can work with that." She launched into a mini-lecture on what she'd learned about fucking restorative justice since the last meeting.

Robert listened with half an ear, spending the rest of his energy on reburying every last thought, every feeling he'd ever had about the woman who'd given birth to him. And building a wall around the subject, so she couldn't perturb him—or worse—again.

Try as he might, he couldn't eradicate the plea that had been unleashed in the firestorm of emotion.

Please don't throw me away.

Wasn't it enough that his material empire had collapsed? Wasn't it enough he'd been deprived of freedom? Was emotional annihilation at the hands of Lannis Parker, administered by the no-longer-appealing but ever-so-well-meaning Ms. Connor, next?

Robert kept his face bland, although if she'd looked, Ms. Connor would have seen the muscle in his jaw tick.

Come hell or high water, and he was betting on hell, he would protect himself from both of them.

No one was going to get the best of him.

No one.

Chapter Twenty-Seven

December

LANNIS PULLED HER CAR into a visitor slot and shut down the engine. *Imposing* didn't come close to describing the building. Dark gray stone, maybe half a dozen stories tall, heavily barred windows, towers at the center and each corner. She shivered, her response primal and at odds with the tranquility of the brilliant winter day.

The structure loomed over the miniscule parking lot like a medieval castle. It even gave the impression it would be cold inside, in spite of the plumes of smoke drifting from numerous chimneys scattered throughout the grounds. She was surprised there wasn't a moat, although the lake lapping gently at the far side of the parking lot contributed to the image. Bare shrubs decorated a tiny patch of now-dormant sod at the entrance, the only concession to landscaping.

She'd flown over the prison complexes east of Louisville more times than she could remember, and had expected a modern, sleek campus like those, notable only for the perimeter fence topped by rolls of razor wire. But this…

It scared her spitless. And if it scared her, how had Robert Davis reacted to the specter of incarceration within those unforgiving walls? Rage came immediately to mind, a continuation of the animal-like howl of disbelief he'd emitted as he'd been hauled from the courtroom in July. Her stomach clenched, and she hoped he didn't unleash his fury on her. For a moment she doubted her purpose, and her hand crept toward the ignition in a perfectly reasonable instinct of self-preservation, of flight.

But she dropped her hand to her knee, then wiped both palms on the soft fabric of her cargo pants. She had to do this. Her own peace depended on it, and so did her marriage. A pang of sorrow tangled with the trepidation threatening to paralyze her. *Ben.* She owed it to him, and to them, to end the grip of Davis's power over her memories.

Too much was at stake to quit now. She didn't know how this would play out, but she knew, to the marrow of her bones, that by the end of today she'd know if she would ever have the courage to embrace pregnancy and motherhood. Lannis inhaled a deep breath, then straightened and willed her anxiety to leave along with the exhale. Enough of it did that her muscles responded. She opened the door and stepped into the crisp air.

The glass door opened into a lobby that could have housed an office, or a bank. Quiet, efficient, clean. A receptionist glanced up and said, "Mrs. Martin?"

Surprise made her pause, but she quickly realized the social worker had cleared the way for her visit. The normalcy was disconcerting, compared to the intensity of purpose for the next few hours. "Yes," she said, and approached the desk.

"I'll page Ms. Connor and get you started." The young woman pulled a file from her desktop and handed it to Lannis. "May I make a copy of your driver's license for our records?"

By the time Ms. Connor arrived, Lannis had filled out the ubiquitous paperwork, been cleared through the metal detector, and tagged as a visitor. It was little different than going through airport security. Even so, Lannis's anxiety vacillated from high to low, or at least lower, then back to high. Her palms were damp, and she wiped them on her cargo pants before shaking Ms. Connor's hand.

A tall, strikingly beautiful black woman dressed in a suit made from traditional African kente fabric, Ms. Connor's firm grip and direct manner put Lannis at ease even before she spoke. "Hello, Mrs. Martin. You have a great deal of courage to be here today. If there is anything I can do to facilitate a positive outcome for you, please tell me."

"The anticipation is killing me," Lannis admitted. She'd listened to her favorite CDs on the drive, but music could only go so far in distracting her. And she didn't feel brave at all. Self-doubt eroded the conviction that buoyed her in quiet moments, leaving her questioning her sanity in pursuing a meeting with Robert Davis. "Either we do this now, or I run away." She hazarded a smile, feeling it wobble on her lips.

An answering smile wreathed Ms. Connor's face, and she said, "If you're sure… There's no shame in walking away, and you can terminate the interview at any time."

Lannis nodded her understanding. They'd covered the ground rules in a phone call a few days ago. She lifted her chin, squared her shoulders, and said, "I'm as ready as I'll ever be."

A few minutes later, her confidence dissolved right past doubt into a cold clutch of fear that matched the exterior of the prison. A third door squealed and thunked into place behind them, and a bead of sweat trickled between her shoulder blades.

The sensation of being trapped was one of Lannis's triggers, and all the locked doors were doing nothing to ease her discomfort. The knowledge of armed guards should have made her feel safe, but on the contrary, anxiety spiraled higher in her gut with each step deeper into this…this dungeon.

Ms. Connor stopped at a closed door marked CONFERENCE ROOM and said, "We're here. Mr. Davis is waiting inside." She glanced at Lannis, empathy warming her fathomless eyes. "You up for this?"

A fine tremor began in Lannis's thighs, her fingers. She took a gulp of air. *Not enough oxygen.* Her vision began to narrow, and she buckled at the waist, dropping her head below the level of her heart. The position felt frighteningly familiar as she struggled to gain control over her emotions. She'd known this day, this meeting, would dredge up all sorts of memories, and she'd done her best to prepare. But there was no preparing for some things, some moments, and this was one of them.

Ms. Connor touched her shoulder and Lannis flinched—hard—jerking away and nearly losing her balance. The woman's hand left her shoulder as though scalded, and she heard her murmur, "Oh, dear. I'm sorry. I wasn't thinking." She tried to wave the social worker off, tell her it was okay, take responsibility for her own response, but embarrassment—*No, be honest: shame*—clogged the words in her throat.

Then she remembered why the posture felt so familiar. *Ben.* He'd cared for her several times when she'd been terrified, or weak, or ill, gently pressing her down till her head was between her knees, giving her time, space, and air to recover on her own. Comfort flooded her, with liquid warmth pouring into her cold hands. Air finally flowed into her lungs and she stood, the light-headedness easing as oxygen worked its magic.

Ms. Connor hovered, a worried expression on her face. "Are you sure you want to go through with this?"

Lannis shimmied a little, shaking her arms and legs to rid her skin of the prickly sense adrenaline had left in it. She ran both hands through her hair, and let a frustrated breath whoosh out. If she fled now, she'd never have the courage to face Davis. "I'm fine," she said, and willed it to be true. She found the strength to fix Ms. Connor with a steady gaze.

After a moment's assessment, the woman shrugged. "Your call." She opened the door and stepped to the side to allow Lannis to enter.

Robert Davis sat with his back to the door, at the end of a three-by-ten-foot table, his hands flat on the expanse of no-nonsense slate.

Lannis's breath seized. She would have recognized him anywhere, even with his back to her.

He wore an orange jumpsuit, with KY DOC printed in block letters on the back. There was one window, heavily grated, that looked out on a facing wing of the building. A dry-erase board decorated one wall. Half a dozen chairs occupied the remaining spaces around the table.

Davis had shorn his hair. Lannis could see the bumps of his skull through his blond buzz cut, and she wondered suddenly how he felt about giving up his civilized veneer. The evidence that his life had been turned inside out—like hers—gave rise to a tiny spurt of courage.

She exhaled, looked past him to where she would sit, and the courage evaporated. An invisible vice tightened around her heart, and she balked in the doorway. The prospect of walking past him to get to her chair at the other end, which would leave him between her and the door… Anxiety gripped her, and she fought an urge to hyperventilate.

She couldn't do it, couldn't put herself in that indefensible position.

But she didn't have to settle for someone else's plan. She swallowed over the lump in her throat. "Ms. Connor, could you ask him to sit at the other end of the table, please?" she asked, glad her voice didn't shake, or come out an octave higher than normal.

Davis swiveled in his chair and settled his cold, blue-eyed gaze on her. He lifted an eyebrow, and said, "No problem. I'll move." He rose with lethal grace and ambled to the other end of the table, resuming his outstretched-hands position. The chair protested as he sat, then quieted.

Unfortunately, now she had to face him as she entered. He never blinked, just watched her with a slightly mocking, calculating look. Lannis suppressed a shiver, then squared her shoulders and slid into the seat closest to the door. Davis's lip curled in a lopsided smile.

A fleeting question about his motives raced through her mind, but Lannis dismissed it. *Doesn't matter. Only thing that matters is what I can control.*

Without waiting for Ms. Connor to facilitate, or mediate, or whatever she was supposed to do, Lannis said, "Yeah, I'm afraid of you—" She went blank. Should she call him Mr. Davis? In her mind, she'd always called him by his full name, or his surname, without the courtesy of title. She chickened out. Unable to utter his name, she took a quick breath and let that part slide. "But my fear is well-deserved, rational, and logical. I'd be a fool to not be wary."

Davis went very still, and an image of a mountain lion stalking its prey flashed through Lannis's mind. Her breathing hitched.

"What do you want from me, Lannis?" His voice was low, his accent clean and cultured, the tone innocuous, yet nearly palpable intensity vibrated between them.

What did she want? So simple, so impossible, so essential. The speech she'd labored over all week flew out of her mind, and for a moment she was silent. "I want…" She sighed, glanced at her hands, then back at him. "We are bound by your crime, both of us shackled in one way or another. I don't need to know 'why me.' I was just unlucky enough to get in your crosshairs."

As odd as the timing seemed, a sense of calm infused her, and Lannis relaxed slightly. For the first time, she felt confirmation that the course she'd chosen was the right one.

"What I'd like from you is acknowledgment that your actions harmed me. I want you to hear how your crime impacted—and continues to impact—my life." Her lips twisted in a wry smile. "Every victim wants an apology, a genuine one, and I'm no different." Her smile faded. "To be honest, I'm not holding my breath on that count."

Davis's eyes flickered at that, but quickly reverted to the shuttered watchfulness he'd maintained since Lannis had entered the room.

She hesitated, knowing that few people could understand what she was going to say next. Hopefully, Ms. Connor had done a good job in laying the groundwork. She'd certainly put Lannis through the wringer, discussing the questionnaire she'd finally filled out—in the light of day, at a local coffee shop, in hopes of reducing the chances of a repeat of the nightmare it had initially generated.

"The important part is that we are bound *together* by your crime." She leaned forward and placed her hand on her heart. "Like it or not—I don't, and I'm pretty sure you don't, either—we are in this together, and the only way out for either of us is…together." Lannis searched Davis's eyes, but didn't glimpse understanding in them.

She sighed and leaned back. She'd been prepared for hostility, and she sensed an undercurrent of that, but Davis's lack of response was beginning to rattle her. Lannis caught his gaze. This time the shutters were gone, and she got the full effect of his icy stare.

She straightened in her chair, a frisson of unease climbing her spine. *Oh, yeah. The hostility's there.* She almost forgot what she'd been about to say, but caught herself before it fled her mind. He would not intimidate her with his eyes, his body language, his demeanor.

Lannis shoved her fear aside, gathering her wits and her courage. And refused to cower, refused to back down.

"I can't see my way through this, Robert. I'm as lost as you are, and at least as angry. I did nothing to deserve what you did to me. But I will not go quietly from this room, from your life. We have work to do, and if we can find the way—together—we can both come out of this better people."

Davis let his gaze slide down her body, let it linger on her breasts, then brought it back up to her face.

Lannis's face flooded with heat, and her hands clutched into fists.

"Sure, Ms. Lannis," he said, his voice smooth and urbane.

She couldn't help the shudder that rolled through her at his use of her name. Worse, he saw it, and a moment of gloating crossed his features, swiftly replaced with blandness.

He lifted the corners of his lips in a sardonic smile. "I can…work with you. In fact, there's nothing I'd rather do than work…*together.*"

Panic flashed through Lannis at his not-so-subtle meaning. What had she gotten herself into, and what had she been thinking? This man would never change. A nearly irresistible urge to flee took hold of her legs, and she grasped the edge of the table to counteract it.

Ms. Connor, focused on Lannis, had missed Davis's facial expressions—and therefore the double entendres—but swiveled at his words. She interjected, "Mr. Davis, must I remind you that sarcasm is not acceptable? If you choose to not take this meeting seriously, I will end it." She skewered the man with a look.

No. He will not deprive me of my due. Lannis corralled her panic, subdued it, and lifted her gaze to Davis.

~

"Let me summarize." Robert ticked off the points the annoying little bitch had just made, using his fingertips. "You want to know why. You want an apology. And"—he narrowed his eyes and feigned concern—"you want validation of your suffering." He paused, letting her vulnerability float in the silence.

It took Lannis a moment to process what he'd said, but when the last bit sank in, she shook her head. "No. I don't need validation. My suffering is valid, whether you acknowledge it or not." She shot him a hard look, although Robert didn't feel nearly as unsettled as she probably intended. "Your suffering is valid, too. I'll admit that sometimes it's hard for me to get past my own situation far enough to recognize yours, but that doesn't negate or ameliorate your circumstances."

Well, wasn't that just damned interesting? She'd actually spent time thinking about him. Poor, soft-hearted female, worried about *his* suffering. He almost smiled.

She leaned forward. "What I want, beyond an understandable request for reason and remorse on your part, is to know that pain will not be the sole outcome for the evil you visited upon me."

Yeah, yeah. He didn't dare let Ms. Connor catch on to his real feelings, or she'd jerk him out of this room so fast his head would spin. Carefully, he squelched his response, and Lannis forged on. "I hope one day you'll move beyond remorse to repentance, and make a decision to never rape another woman. Your choices are yours, and the consequences are yours to bear, but that's my wish for you. I hope you can find peace with yourself, your victims, and God."

Anger, hot and unstable, flashed through him. "Leave God out of this." He curled his right hand into a fist, wrestling the unruly emotion under control. Lannis shrank back, granting him a disappointingly hollow sense of satisfaction. Suddenly, he was fed up with it all—of prison, of restorative justice, of trying to please the authorities to earn the right to breathe fresh air.

Did he really have anything left to lose? Or, for that matter, to gain? A black urge to visit his pain on Lannis—the instrument of his being here, no matter how either one of them assigned blame—rose within him, and he gave in to it.

"My only regret is that you didn't keep quiet." He kept his tone calm, conversational, and deadly. "My only remorse is tied to my failure to destroy you at the trial. My wish for me is freedom. My wish for you is unrelenting pain and suffering for the rest of your life."

Lannis flinched at his words, each sentence battering her bravado. Robert derived almost as much pleasure from her response as if he'd punched her with his fist. Blood drained from her face, and her expression, always so open, so readable, told him he'd hit the bull's eye, had succeeded in striking the heart of her vulnerability.

Ms. Connor's expression, on the other hand, was thunderous. "Mr. Davis! Your attitude is diametrically opposed to the concept and practice of restorative justice. I am appalled at your misrepresentation of your intentions." She shook her head in dismay, her eyes wide with shock.

Robert figured she had the right to be outraged. He'd been pretty compliant with her insistence that he enumerate his reasons for going through with this. His heart gave a little flip-flop at her distress, though, which gave him pause. His desire to please her a few weeks ago had stunned him, and now, to deliver a blow to the project she'd poured so much energy into…

He actually felt bad for her.

"I am terminating this meeting." Ms. Connor sent him a blistering glare, and gathered her papers.

Lannis lifted her hand, silently halting Ms. Connor as the social worker stood. "No." Her face had settled into an uncharacteristically stubborn expression. "This is my only opportunity to tell Mr. Davis what he has done to me, the effects of his actions. He doesn't have to give me anything else that I asked for, but I want him to listen to me, at least in this."

"Are you certain?" Ms. Connor's unflappable air deserted her, her voice conveying both shock and anger.

"I appreciate your concern, but this is between him and me. As long as I'm physically safe, which I am"—Lannis gestured at the door, outside which the guard stood—"I'm absolutely positive." Ms. Connor didn't seem convinced, so Lannis added, "If this makes you uncomfortable, you don't need to stay."

Robert was so astonished he leaned forward. She had more moxie than he would have attributed to a woman who hadn't fought him much during the rape. Although, he had to admit she'd exhibited a fair bit of courage during the trial.

Surprise flickered across Ms. Connor's features, and she burst into a full-bodied laugh. "That's my line, girlfriend." She set the papers she'd gathered back on the table, sat, crossed her arms, and said, "Let the games begin."

Lannis turned to face Robert. He quickly masked his grudging admiration for her spirit and lounged back in his chair, which creaked ominously.

"You know, I can terminate this meeting at any time, too, don't you, Ms. Parker?" He raised one hand and quirked an eyebrow. "Oops. I mean, Mrs. Martin."

"Oh, for crying out loud, Robert." Lannis rolled her eyes. "I'll answer to either, and there's no need to get your knickers in a twist over my marriage. You already tried that at the trial, and it didn't help you a bit. I doubt it'll make any difference here, either."

She rested both palms on the table and leaned forward. "Frankly, I don't think you're willing to give up the chance to mess with my mind, so I'd put money on you staying right here." Her expression turned into a dare. "I'm calling your bluff. If you're not man enough to listen to me for a few minutes, go ahead and terminate."

Not man enough? Fury exploded, white-hot against the back of his eyes, and he slammed the flat of his hand against the table. It shuddered under the assault, and Lannis jumped, snatching her hands up. She looked abruptly vulnerable and terrified, and power built within Robert.

"Don't you ever, *ever*, question my manhood." He glared at her, his eyes narrowed. She scooted back in her chair, readying herself to bolt. "You, of all people, should have no reason to question that." His hand curled into a fist again. "I'll stay, I'll listen, I'll let you weep and wail over your lot in life. But don't think it's going to affect anything about me, or our *relationship*." A bit of spittle had gathered at the corners of his lips, and he swiped a forearm across his mouth.

A fine tremor began in her shoulders. It spread to her arms, and she clenched her hands in an attempt to control the shakes. Her lips, pale in her now colorless face, parted. She whispered, almost soundlessly, "Real men don't rape," the words too soft for Ms. Connor to catch.

Shocked into silence, Robert drew back even as Lannis's eyes, deep and troubled, exerted some weird voodoo hold on him. *Real men...* Shame mixed with the rage of a moment ago, and confused, Robert tried to wrest his gaze from hers. Time slowed, until the door banged open and broke the spell. The guard shoved his way into the room and advanced on Robert, one hand on his Taser, the other keying his mike to call for backup.

No longer caring that he'd lose all the privileges he'd earned, Robert placed his hands on the back of his head, ready for the cuffs. He only hoped the guard wouldn't tase him in front of the women.

"No!" Lannis's cry stopped the guard and turned the focus in the room to her.

~

Lannis shot up from her chair and turned to the guard. "Don't."
They were going to haul him away. She could see the dominoes
tumbling, and desperate to halt the process, she cried, "Look at him!
He's still sitting there, even though he's angry. Please." She couldn't
quite wrap her mind around Davis's hate-filled words, but for the
first time, it didn't matter. The man who'd raped her didn't have the
capacity to hurt her any more than he already had. Shock her?
Absolutely. But hurt her? No more.

The officer paused, leveled a sharp look at her. "You sure?"
Without waiting for her response, he addressed the prisoner. "What'll
it be, Davis?"

Robert Davis's expression was, for once, unguarded. He looked
totally stunned. The moment stretched, tension humming until the
intensity wavered.

Davis schooled his features into his usual disdain and leaned
back, hands relaxing, lowering, until they lay flat on the table again.
He shrugged. "You know me. If I wanted to go to solitary, it'd be for
a lot more than smacking a table." A tiny smile lifted the corners of
his lips. "I'll be a good boy."

The guard stood down, releasing his grip on the mike. "I'll stay
inside the room this time," he said, and stepped to the corner nearest
Davis, crossing his arms.

Lannis let out the breath she'd been holding and slid back into
her chair. "Thank you." She gripped the edge of the table and faced
Davis. "Listen to me. You robbed me of my innocence that night.
You stole my right to determine the use of my body, to choose who I
allow to share it. You denied me the right to protect myself. You
shattered my trust in men, in my own judgment, and in God."

A muscle next to his right eye jumped, but otherwise he was
still, so still Lannis would have thought he was immune to her words,
save for the tic.

"The bruises healed. All the physical trauma to my"—she
stopped, strangled by the most accurate words, unable to will them to
pass her lips—"well, you know. It healed, too." Lannis dropped her
gaze, then raised it to drill him.

"But the emotional damage is still there. Just like today, I can't
sit in a room unless I'm close to an exit, and I have to be able to see
everyone. When people get too close, or touch me, my skin crawls
and I literally want to climb out of it. Ms. Connor can attest to that."
She sent a rueful smile at the woman, then fixed her gaze on Davis's

cold blue eyes. "I feel I have to defend myself in the grocery store, parking lots, even in church. I lock my husband out of the house when he runs out to the garage because I am so insecure for my safety.

"You know I fell into promiscuity and abuse of alcohol after you raped me. When I managed to drag myself out of that hellhole, I swung to the opposite end of the spectrum. Isolation. Paralysis. Stuck in a dead-end job, cut off from my family." Lannis paused. "Worst of all, you're in the bedroom with me and Ben. I have flashbacks."

Something shifted in Davis's eyes. He wasn't telegraphing his feelings, but Lannis would lay money on some sense of satisfaction at her struggles. But that was up to him to deal with.

Lannis held his hard look with one of her own. "That's what you have done to me, Robert. That's the burden I carry every moment of my life. You are my worst nightmare, whether I'm awake or asleep." She twisted her lips into a crooked smile, knowing it held no humor. "So you got what you want. I'm sure you think you're happy…but I know you're not, not really, not deep down."

His eyes flickered.

"We need to make peace with each other in order to break this unholy bond. I have found a path to peace through the God who tells me to love my enemies, which I'm trying to do. Here. Now." She leaned forward. "I hope you can find a path that allows you to accept the forgiveness I'm offering, a path that frees you from the shackles of your situation. I don't care what route you take. I just want that for you."

Lannis stood, pushing the chair away from the table with a screech. "If you ever have anything to say to me, Robert, I'll listen. Until then, Godspeed."

She wheeled and strode to the door, not waiting for Ms. Connor. Relief bubbled through her heart, followed by a burst of joy that took her by surprise. She'd done it. She'd faced Robert Davis and had her say.

And she didn't think she read him wrong at the end. His mask of indifference had failed him yet again. His eyes had widened in disbelief, and despair mixed with wary hope had flickered deep within before he'd shuttered them.

Maybe, just maybe, healing for both of them had begun.

Chapter Twenty-Eight

Robert endured a dressing-down from Ms. Connor, who spared neither words nor body language in her twenty-minute rant before she allowed the guard to escort him back to his cell block.

He lent her half an ear, but as upset as she was, she had nothing on him. Emotions swirled unchecked within him, making him feel disturbingly unsettled, to the point of unstable. It became more and more difficult for him to ignore her as she heaped her disappointment on him.

He'd failed. His goal had been to mess with Lannis's mind today, and she'd managed to shake him off like a dog shedding pond water. Oh, he'd had momentary success, but nothing like what he'd planned. What he craved.

Nope. In the end, she'd left *him* rattled and confused. And empty. He shied away from examining that concept too closely.

Anger shot up between bouts of sadness that he'd let Ms. Connor down—where the hell had *that* come from?—and uncomfortable thoughts about his own behavior, which had never concerned him before and shouldn't now. He wanted to call Lannis a goody-two-shoes, a do-gooder, a holier-than-thou thorn in his side. But he couldn't ignore or explain away her genuine quality.

She meant what she said, and it was so far removed from anything he'd ever experienced before, he didn't know how to react.

"Love your enemies"? Yeah, he'd heard that one, even read some of Gandhi and Martin Luther King. But he'd never met anyone who not only meant it, but lived it. Or at least made an authentic attempt at it. And if he understood nothing more about today than this, it was that Lannis Parker Martin truly wanted what was best for him.

Unbelievable.

No one wanted good outcomes for their enemies.

"You may take Mr. Davis back," Ms. Connor said, her voice dripping disgust. She shot him a final dismissive glance.

He'd developed an unhealthy need for Ms. Connor's high esteem, and manipulating her, playing her investment in restorative justice, had dealt it a fatal blow. A pang of sadness sliced through him.

His inability to be what she needed him to be was nothing new. He'd never lived up to any woman's expectations—*except when you rape*, a little voice inside him whispered. Yeah, he acknowledged. *They can't tell me how unimportant I am then.*

He nodded to Ms. Connor, even tried to say, "I'm sorry," but couldn't finish the thought before his throat closed over the words. The guard cuffed him for the return trip, and the opportunity slipped away.

"Good-bye, Mr. Davis. You know how to reach me if you need." Ms. Connor swept out of the room. Probably out of his life, too.

Don't throw me away. Robert slammed the door on the tiny voice before it undid him.

He hadn't done anything to warrant punishment, so the guard disgorged him into the dayroom. Two guys immediately approached him with requests for legal work, but he waved them away. He didn't want to be put in solitary, but he desperately needed some solitude.

That was the trouble with this place. There was no such thing as solitude. He wasn't crazy enough to get put on suicide watch, and he still didn't have the heart for the fight necessary for getting sent to the dungeon—the windowless, sensory-depriving cells used for solitary confinement.

He scrubbed a hand over his face and went to a corner, put his back to it, and turned his mind inward, even as he kept a watchful eye on the activity before him.

He'd ended up exactly where his mother had told him he would. *White trash.* A bottomless, yawning chasm seemed to gape at his feet, and he drew back, leaning hard into the concrete behind him. A frisson of long-forgotten fear raced up his spine, and a memory, long buried, clawed its way into his mind.

Dumpster diving. The first time she'd pitched him into the maw of a sticky, stinking metal monster, he'd screamed in terror. She'd called him white trash so many times that his four-year-old brain thought she was throwing him away. Or maybe he'd only been three. Who knew? His mother hadn't kept stellar records of his upbringing. No baby book for him. She'd gone to the city for his birth certificate when she figured he was finally old enough to get him out of her hair for a few hours a day.

It had taken a few forays into the Dumpster before he discovered it could be a treasure trove. He'd quickly learned to stuff as much food in his mouth as he could before tossing some out to *her*. She'd hog it all if he did, and the unrelenting clutch of hunger in his scrawny belly would go unslaked. He'd learned to lie, telling her he was still digging when, in fact, he'd found a particularly intact bit of meat.

Sometimes she stuck her head in and caught him, but her shrill orders to send the food up held no candle to his hunger. She wouldn't come in after him, and they both knew it. Once he got big enough, he'd go by himself, careful to avoid detection. Cops and passersby took affront at kids stealing from the trash.

Stealing trash. Now there was a concept. Who knew trash was so valuable that taking it was labeled theft. He'd been collared once, sternly instructed to never steal from the trash again, and delivered home to his mother—who'd simpered at the cop and chided him and taught him a valuable lesson.

He could get away with most anything if he delivered what people wanted to hear, and do it with a sincere look on his face.

It was amazing, now that he looked back on it as an adult, he hadn't ended up in foster care or juvie.

School had opened the world to him. He was smart. He picked up on reading and writing like it was a feast for his starved brain. He devoured books, and got moved up in reading groups until he was grade levels ahead of his peers. Robert had begun to understand that there was more to the world than what he'd seen or what he'd experienced.

School was where he got a reprieve from the endless parade of men in and out of his mother's—and therefore, his—life. Most of them ignored him, but some of them resented him, or worse. He'd taken to roaming the streets until they were either asleep or too high to care about "the brat," avoiding a beating for the simple transgression of existing in the wrong space at the wrong time.

He'd been in third grade before he figured out there were stores that sold clothes that hadn't been worn before. He'd hated summertime, weekends, and vacations from school because the Dumpsters became his prime source of food. At least he got a free lunch at school every day. And he took advantage of all the second helpings he could charm the cafeteria ladies into.

He'd vowed to never do drugs. And he'd kept that vow. He drank some alcohol, but sparingly, mostly to fit in with the cultured crowd he had worked so hard to be part of. It was amazing how far plain old courtesy went, and once he'd tumbled onto that, he'd cultivated the trait and milked it for all it was worth. After he'd passed the New Jersey bar, he'd joined a country club, then a church, both for the same reasons. Status symbols, places to network. He'd taken golf lessons, which bored him to death, but the tacit backroom deal making with judges required it.

He'd come home from school one day when he was a senior in high school to find his mother gone from the slum they'd been living in, their meager belongings dumped on the front steps and already picked through. Unless she'd just taken what she wanted and disappeared. He'd never seen her again, and hadn't missed her.

He'd lied his tail off, forged her name on forms, managed to score a place to sleep—inside, most nights, with kids from school. And graduated with honors. Luckily, he'd already secured scholarships and a work-study job, and hit college, intent on achieving the sort of success he'd only read about.

He had.

But the mocking voice in his head said she was right.

He was white trash, and he'd ended up in the human Dumpster.

Robert began to tremble deep inside, and horrified, he realized his hands were shaking.

She'd won—and he didn't know if he meant his mother or Lannis Parker Martin.

Chapter Twenty-Nine

Ben caught the Enforcer's eye across the room, and toasted him with a lift of his beer. Marijuana smoke hung heavy and thick in the air, and Ben tried not to breathe it. It was a futile effort, and he hated the muzzy-headed feeling the secondhand smoke gave him. Not quite high, but not quite full on his game, either. For that reason, he'd nursed his beer for the past forty minutes, declining stronger drinks and the ever-present offers of drugs.

Gang members lounged on couches in the living room of a nondescript house in a nondescript neighborhood, notable only for mind-numbing sameness and lack of hope. Cold weather had driven the drug lord and his minions indoors.

Ben's *one more night* had turned into three weeks, with teasers of information, never enough to call it good, but always enough to keep him coming back. Mike had gotten pretty adamant that it was time to pull out, but even he had to admit Ben was close, damn close.

"BJ." Rolo walked by and slapped Ben on the back. Ben nodded in return, and saluted with the beer bottle again.

Rolo stopped. "You know anything about the shooting a few weeks ago?"

Ben did. Rolo was referring to the homeless guy who called himself Churchill. Ben's informant, murdered on the street, execution style.

"Nope." He took a swig of his beer and set it down on the crooked coffee table. The bottle began to slide, and he halted it with the toe of his boot, waited to see that it stayed put, then crossed his ankle over the other knee. "Too many shootings to know which one you mean."

Rolo narrowed his eyes. "Everybody knows about that one. Where you been that you don't?"

"Out of town. Just got back the day you contacted me." Which had been the day after the shooting, and by rights, a major dealer like BJ should have known about it. But he'd set his course, and had to stick with his story. Ben rubbed an eye that had begun to sting from the smoke. "What about it? Why's it so special?" He blinked up at Rolo.

Rolo looked aghast. "The guy was a cockroach. Talking to the cops. Enforcer had him taken out."

Ben sat up a bit straighter, and his heart thudded in his chest. "Really?" He wished he had his wire on. They had the killer, or at least they knew which cesspool to drag for him. "Anybody know who he gave up?" Ben knew Churchill hadn't given *him* up, or he wouldn't be sitting here.

"Don't know that he ratted on anybody, but Enforcer don't take chances."

Ben relaxed back into his chair. "Good. All's well that ends well, then." He mentally crossed his fingers at the lie, and added it to the list of sins he needed to confess once he was finished with this op.

Rolo fixed him with a sharp gaze. "I'm thinking it's damn odd you didn't hear about it, even if you were out of town."

Ben sighed, acted like he was stifling a yawn to buy himself a few seconds. "Maybe I heard whispers, but somebody gets offed like that, and me being out of town, well…it stands to reason that the chatter might go silent when I walk into a room. Y'all don't trust me, not like if I lived here." He took another swallow of beer. It was warm, and probably tasted at least decent if he'd been into the European style of beer drinking, but he wasn't, and it didn't.

"Where *do* you live?" Rolo looked surprised, like the question had never occurred to him. Which was good. And told Ben no one had followed him, not that he would have missed a tail. He'd been watching.

"Doesn't matter. I'm a businessman, travel a lot, and don't put down roots anywhere."

Rolo seemed to accept his explanation and wandered off. Ben went back to idly surveying the room. Rolo stopped to talk to a group of girls, and several of them glanced at Ben, then back at Rolo. One of them detached herself from the group and approached Ben.

"Rolo says you need some company." She plopped herself onto the sofa next to him and smiled.

"You are a pretty woman." Ben gave her an extensive once-over because it was expected. And ran into a wall he hadn't anticipated. Normally, he'd take some of what she was offering—not all of it, never all of it—to make it look good, to keep his cover. Suddenly, kissing this girl, groping her, even if it was for work, felt wrong, all wrong.

Lannis again.

He sent the girl a lazy smile, took another sip of his beer, and put his arm around her. *Wrong.* Even if it was as innocuous as an arm around his kid sister. His pulse picked up its pace.

He couldn't do this.

Ben glanced at his watch, stood, and said, "Thanks, but I've got a meeting. Didn't realize how late it was." The girl looked at him, in turn surprised, then resigned. She made a dismissive motion at him and scanned the crowd.

He turned to leave, but Rolo intercepted him. "Where you goin' man?"

"Forgot I had a meeting." Ben settled his ball cap on his head.

Rolo grinned at him. "The party's jus' getting started, man." He shoved a cold beer in Ben's hand. "'Sides, Enforcer wants to talk to you 'bout delivery of your order."

The guy was beginning to slur his words and looked a bit loopy. Ben wondered if he'd taken something other than hits off the weed being passed around the room. He shrugged. "Guess I can be a few minutes late."

And maybe he could nail down the location of Enforcer's supply base, the one thing that tied the guy down. He had to have a space adequate for receiving the quantities of bulky marijuana and weapons he was running. The corridor from Chicago to Florida passed through Louisville, and it stood to reason that some of the goods either got on or off here. Enforcer was the biggest dealer in town, at the moment. Thanks to guys like Ben and the Louisville Metro Police, along with gang conflicts, both internal and external, that position was continually shifting.

Ben twisted the cap off the beer and took a sip of the cool liquid. Someone jostled him from behind and he turned, instantly alert—and angry that someone had gotten behind him without his awareness. An inebriated couple staggered past, intent on one of the bedrooms in the back of the house. He raked them with a quick, hard assessment, then satisfied they posed no threat, faced Rolo. "After you."

"Come on, man, you are way too uptight. Have your drink, he'll be with you in a few." Rolo's eyes glittered with a hint of wildness that was hard to read.

Suddenly Ben was sick to death of dealing with druggies. They were unpredictable and crazy. Profound disappointment at his brother's choices dragged at him, and a pang of sorrow knifed through him.

Lannis had issues—and he had to wonder why he'd chosen a woman with substance abuse issues as his wife—but she was different. She worked *hard* to overcome her problem, and she'd succeeded. In spades. She held herself accountable, didn't blame anyone for her bad decisions. Just quietly went about healing herself. What he wished Danny had been capable of doing.

He took a distracted swallow of beer, impatient to get to Enforcer and seal the deal. It was cold and tasted good after the warm one he'd left on the coffee table. Out of frustration, he took another long swig, then set the beer aside and shouldered his way through the crowd toward Enforcer. God, he wished he knew the guy's real name. He felt like he was doing business with a cartoon character.

But Enforcer was anything but cute or innocent. More like a superhero, Ben thought. Street-smart, his muscled bulk enhanced by steroids and cunning enough to maintain his place as a major player, the guy was a formidable opponent. Ben would do well to remember that, which he did. He took the guy seriously, but it was about time for Enforcer to take him seriously.

Halfway across the room, he stumbled. *Odd…didn't see anything.* Rolo appeared on his right, and Ben squinted at him. The guy seemed to waver, like he was viewing him through water, through an enormous fish tank.

Suddenly Rolo didn't look high anymore. The wild glitter of a few moments ago had turned hard, harsh, focused, and cruel.

Adrenaline flooded Ben, along with awareness. *Oh, no.* He'd been had. Set up. Drugged.

When the hell…? And how? Cold fear shot through him and he swung around, striking at Rolo, an instinctive move that should have dropped the guy, a slashing blow to the neck that somehow missed, and he lost his balance, falling heavily into the man.

He commanded his arms to pummel Rolo, commanded his legs to deliver bone-crushing kicks, commanded his body to respond…and nothing happened. Ben sagged against Rolo, who grunted at his dead weight and wrapped his arms around him, capturing Ben's arms at his sides.

Ben panicked, struggled to stand, but Rolo easily contained his efforts and summoned JaJuan with a nod. The kid must have been standing by at the ready, because he was there in a quick couple of strides, and moved without direction from Rolo. The two men lifted him, one on each side. There was no attempt to hide what was going down. They just half dragged, half carried Ben to the door to the basement. A few of the women glanced over and took mild note, but no one made a move to stop them.

Fury consumed him, but it couldn't fuel a counterattack. His body simply wouldn't move. He growled his rage, but it came out as a moan, and worse, he felt drool slide down the side of his jaw. His face, his tongue, his lips felt numb, and fresh panic sliced through his now-fuzzy mind.

He was going to die tonight.

Bastards.

He could have held his own in a fair fight. Give him fists, knives, guns—he could have dealt more bedlam and injury than any of them, even with the numbers stacked against him.

But this… No one could fight this.

Rolo threw open the door and it slammed against the wall, bouncing back so Rolo had to catch it one-handed. They staggered down the stairs, a six-legged, ungainly organism bent on destruction. Rolo just didn't know Ben's focus was on destroying him.

Ben would *not* give up, not ever. But his vision was growing dark around the edges, his strength fading.

His last conscious thought was of Lannis. Agony knifed through him, and he dug deep, called upon his final store of reserves.

He heaved against JaJuan, using his only weapon—his weight. JaJuan, a step below Ben, tottered for a long moment, and let go of Ben to windmill for balance. Unable to slow his own momentum, Rolo slammed into both of them. JaJuan lost his battle to stay upright, and crashed down the stairs.

Dragging Ben and Rolo with him.

Chapter Thirty

LANNIS JOGGED the last few steps to the porch, glad she'd been able to squeeze in a run before dark, which came earlier each day. She stretched, pleasantly tired, but relaxed. Her mind returned to her conversation with Robert Davis a few days ago. She'd been on such a high when she left the prison that she'd sung along with her CDs all the way home. But even joy had to peter out, and the outer expression of it had, about forty miles south of Louisville. It had left her with a quiet glow of contentment that remained with her, and that she longed to share with Ben.

She finally believed what everyone had been telling her. Of course she'd known at an intellectual level, but true acceptance in her heart brought peace. No one could prevent bad things happening; no one could predict or protect from the random crap that visited all lives.

For some reason, her final encounter with Robert had lifted the weight of her memories from her chest, and she actually felt physically buoyant. Maybe this was what the term "walking on air" meant.

She could have made a different choice or two that fateful night five years ago, but what was done was done, and she refused to hold the results of those choices against herself. Other than a naive trust in Robert Davis, that hindsight afforded a much different view. She'd done nothing to deserve what had happened. She'd done nothing more than cross his path.

Victim.

Survivor.

First one, now the other, and now maybe she could add qualifiers to both nouns.

Former victim.

Successful survivor, even flourishing survivor.

Plus, an epiphany of sorts had struck her. She could hardly wait to talk to Ben about it. There was no reason they couldn't adopt. That would help a child already in the world. And with that, her fears faded away. If she could care for an adopted child, she could do just as well with a biological child. Either way, like Maggie said, she'd be a very careful, involved mother, and she'd do everything in her power to keep her child, or—her heart gave a happy skip—children safe. Ben would be such a wonderful daddy. She smiled.

Her cell phone rang, pulling her from her thoughts. She glanced at it before flipping it open. *Mike Ross.* Her heart skipped a beat. *News. Ben!*

"Hi, Mike." Her smile grew wider.

"Hey, Lannis. You home?"

Mike, never one for small talk, sounded a little distracted, or maybe harried.

"Just got here." She felt her happiness begin to slip. "Why?"

"Mind if I stop by? I'm in the neighborhood."

Fear niggled at her. "What's going on?"

"I'll be there in three minutes."

Lannis's fear escalated into full-blown panic. "Damn it, Mike, tell me!" She gripped the phone so hard her fingers hurt. "Is Ben all right?"

"Calm down. I'll be there shortly and we'll talk." He hung up.

Lannis flipped the phone closed, too worried about Ben to call Mike back.

She went into the house, turned on a couple of lights, and saw Mike's car pass through the security gate. It was still light enough for her to spy Maggie seated in the passenger side. Fear clutched her anew, and she went to the front door, threw it open, and waited, arms wrapped around her midriff to protect her from…from what? Two doors slammed and Mike and Maggie approached, Mike's face set, his stride purposeful. Maggie's expression was distressed as she hurried to keep up with her husband.

Lannis felt tears fill her eyes, and she blinked them back. She tried to ask, but the words clogged in her throat.

Mike reached her and grasped her arms, bent until his face was even with hers. "Ben missed his check-in this morning, and I can't raise him."

Strength drained out of Lannis's legs, and she sagged. "No…" Mike caught her before she slid to the floor.

"Come on, Lannis, stand up." He sounded strained, his voice tight. "Let's get inside."

Maggie appeared, and the pity Lannis read in her eyes galvanized her enough to stand and pull away from Mike's grip. She closed her eyes and took a deep, albeit shaky, breath. Opening her eyes, she looked at the other people who loved Ben almost as much as she did.

Almost. "Come in. Tell me everything." Maggie gave her a fierce hug on her way in, and once seated, Lannis leaned forward. "Tell me, Mike."

He rubbed his nose, and Lannis noticed for the first time how exhausted he appeared. Five o'clock shadow, along with bags under his eyes, which were red-rimmed. Lannis's fragile composure wobbled, but she tightened her grip on it, and it held.

"He insisted on going in without a wire off and on the last few weeks. The strategy had been effective, and he thought he'd be able to finish up the loose ends last night."

Lannis's mind reeled. "But…but don't you guys always back up each other? I thought that was standard procedure for safety." Her voice hitched on the last word, and she brought her fist up to her mouth. Panic, along with anger, fluttered in her chest.

Mike hung his head, then lifted it and met her gaze. "Yes, that's standard procedure. But we can suspend it if we feel it's more dangerous to go in wired. In this case, it was safer for him to go without."

Lannis's heart plummeted. She shot up from the chair. "Then he shouldn't have gone in." She pointed an accusatory finger at Mike. "You shouldn't have let him."

Maggie shared a quick, knowing glance with Mike, then looked at Lannis. "Don't blame Mike, honey. It's a mutual decision for the guys."

"Then who do I blame? Who's responsible? Ben?" Lannis laughed, a humorless sound that had more than a tinge of hysteria in it. She struggled to make sense of the situation, as if that might make it easier to accept. Or easier to remedy. Neither of which would be the case.

Maggie stood, reached for Lannis, imploring her with her eyes. "You don't blame anyone, Lannis. It's no one's fault, unless you include the drug dealers, and their gangs."

Lannis held herself stiff in Maggie's embrace, unwilling to relax into the comfort her friend offered, yet unable to jerk herself away from Maggie.

"Besides, Lannis, we only know he missed his check-in, not that anything has happened."

Mike looked up at her, and held his hands out, palms up. "I checked the motel room he was staying at, and his comm equipment was still in place. He's just missing."

Just missing. The words ripped her composure out from under her, and tears flooded her eyes, spilled over, and washed her face. Lannis collapsed into Maggie's arms, sobbing.

"I'm s-sorry," she managed to squeeze out before weeping overtook her entirely.

But Lannis didn't know if she was sorry for angry words at Maggie and Mike, or if she was sorry for Ben and whatever had happened to him, or sorry that she'd finally gotten her act together.

Only to lose him.

Chapter Thirty-One

BEN'S HEAD THROBBED. He bit back a groan, convinced somehow in his mushy-brained state that it was imperative he remain silent. And unmoving. Careful to not tense his muscles and thus give away his wakefulness, he opened his eyes a slit. He kept his breathing deep and slow, and hoped if anyone was nearby, they wouldn't notice the change from unfeigned sleep. Or unconsciousness, as he sluggishly deduced he was not waking from normal slumber.

High, grimy windows reluctantly admitted weak rays of light. He shifted his head slightly to get a better view of a window, and determined the source of illumination to be sunlight, not streetlights. It was impossible to tell what time of day it was, though, just that it was the day side of the clock.

Other than that, no artificial light gave him any clues to his surroundings. He sensed a hard floor beneath him, cold, and now that he concentrated on it, rough. *Concrete?* It smelled moldy, but that wasn't really a news flash. Everything in Louisville smelled like mildew at various times of the year. He dismissed that as irrelevant.

He strained to hear something, anything. A breath, a squeak, a voice. Nothing. Not even a furnace. He realized he was cold, so cold that shivering began to take hold of his limbs. *Not good.* Might give him away. At least he didn't think unconscious people shivered. He didn't know, had never had occasion to think about it.

He flexed his hands, in part to control the involuntary shudders wracking his upper arms, in part to evaluate his ability to move. Relief washed through him when they responded. Deciding his prison—and why had he assumed a state of captivity?—had been left unguarded for the moment, he opened his eyes all the way.

Alone. He turned his head cautiously. No one lurked in the shadows, waited behind him, or peered through the doorway at him. *Thank you, God.* He rolled, pushed himself to his knees, and discovered he needed to take a leak. Desperately. How long had he been out? And more importantly, why?

He staggered upright and ran a quick hand over his head. A bump on the back of his scalp made him wince. Then he nearly moaned from pain at what had to be bruises on his ear and face. He bit back the sound, not knowing yet if he was truly alone. Now that he was more aware, he realized his left eye was swollen, almost swollen shut, and his lip was split. He'd been in a fight…but he didn't remember a fight. He continued a pat down of his own body. He grunted, finding several tender spots on his ribs, and a particularly bad bruise on his leg. He limped toward a stairway leading up, the only exit from what he'd finally determined to be a basement.

Icy fingers of air found their way down the neck of his shirt. Some of the buttons were missing, and Ben drew the shirt together in flimsy protection against the cold. Pain in his hands drew his attention. They were swollen, abraded, and sore from…hell, he didn't know, but it appeared he'd fought back. That conclusion lifted his spirits from desperate to grim.

His head pounded in concert with his heartbeat, and he had sort of a sense of hangover on top of trauma, which didn't make sense. He hadn't drunk enough to get a hangover since college. Ben tried to piece together what had happened, but thinking made the ache intensify. He remembered…

He remembered a party, remembered his impromptu decision to force the issue with the Enforcer. He remembered how he'd suddenly wanted nothing more than to be home, with Lannis, and done with this filthy business. And the last thing he remembered was tangling with Rolo and JaJuan, and falling, maybe pushing.

No sign of Rolo or JaJuan, although now that he was beginning to take note of his surroundings, there were some dark stains on the floor near a chair incongruously positioned in the center of the room.

His hand automatically went for his gun—not there—and he cursed. He reached for the knife he kept at one ankle. Not there, either. Neither was his backup weapon on the other ankle. He patted his pockets with increasing frustration, not that it bothered him that they'd likely robbed him—they had—but that they'd found and stripped him of his weapons.

He gimped around the chair, trying to ignore his sore leg, and crept, step by creaky step up the stairs, placing his feet as close to the edges of the treads as possible to keep squeaks to a minimum. He was becoming more and more convinced he was alone in the house, which suited him fine. He reached the door and gently tried the knob. It turned in his hand, but he stopped before opening it.

He put his ear to the door and held his breath.

Silence, utter and complete. His urgent need for a bathroom clinched his decision, and he slowly opened the door, peering down the dark hall. Recognition dawned, and confirmed he was in the same house, at least. The pain in his thigh helped clear his head, which still felt filled with cotton instead of brain cells.

Finally certain he was alone, Ben found the bathroom and made use of it, groaning in relief. He flushed, then washed his hands and rinsed some of the dried blood from his face. And noticed what he'd missed in his rush to get to the bathroom.

The unmistakable, coppery tang of blood, far more blood than what he'd washed off. And the cloying scent of death. Every cell of his body came alert, and he went very still. His hands itched for a weapon, and a sheen of sweat dampened his hairline, then immediately cooled, sending a chill down his spine.

Logic told him no one was left here as a threat, but his gut tightened anyway. He slid to the next door in the hallway, back to the wall, listening, refusing to take for granted that he was in the clear. He rounded the corner in a swift motion, quartering and clearing the room in a glance.

The room was clear of live bodies, but a glance took in the dead one on the bed.

It was the girl who'd tried to hook up with him at the party. Only now she was nude, on rumpled, bloodied sheets, her legs splayed wide. Her eyes stared at the ceiling in eternal surprise, and a neat little hole decorated her temple on the side Ben could see.

He knew the other side of her head was not as neat, because the ammo had been a hollow-point .38 bullet. He knew this because it had been fired by his gun. Which lay next to her, on the pillow.

His heart stalled.

Had *he* done this?

His heart thudded back into rhythm, hard and fast, and painful. He brought a hand up and pressed his chest to contain the ache. His mind churned, trying to make sense of the scene in front of him. The girl—*Jesus, Lord have mercy*—so young, and so alive a few hours ago.

Only then did he notice her blood had dried somewhat, and in a belated self-assessment, glanced down at his hands, his clothes. No blood that he couldn't account for from his own wounds. He didn't *think* any of the stains on his jeans or shirt belonged to anyone but himself. Relief, too faint to put a dent in his anxiety, fluttered at the edges of his disjointed thoughts, but faded when the logical cop in him asked if he'd just rinsed evidence down the sink. Had he unwittingly washed gun residue from his hands a moment ago?

Rolo had drugged him, he knew that, and time had passed. How much time, he still didn't know. Roofies, or GHB, most likely, either of which would explain his amnesia, but this… Never. He would never have done this.

Not sober, he wouldn't have. But high…

His stomach turned and he wheeled, staggered to the bathroom where he gagged, then retched, heaving bile from his empty stomach until tears squeezed past his eyelids and multiplied, dripping into the filthy, stained porcelain bowl of the toilet.

Finally he quieted, leaned back against the wall, and lifted a trembling hand to his forehead. He had to call for backup, but he couldn't dredge the strength to stand, to face himself in the mirror.

Sweat trickled down the side of his face. Could he have done this?

He didn't *know.*

Chapter Thirty-Two

"LANNIS, HONEY, come over to our house tonight, okay?" Maggie's eyes, compassionate and sympathetic, implored her to acquiesce. And she might have, except for the fear that gripped her, irrational as it perhaps was, that somehow Ben would show up at home and she wouldn't be there. To greet him, to be there for him, to support him if he needed it, which she couldn't really imagine, but he might.

She shook her head *no*, in a brief, tight motion, and wrapped her arms around her middle. "I'll be fine, Maggie." It was a blatant lie and they all knew it, but Maggie searched her eyes for a moment, and then gave her a hug.

"Okay. But you call anytime, you hear?" She grasped Lannis's shoulders and gave her a gentle shake. "No matter what the clock says or how minor you think the issue is."

Lannis's throat closed and she nodded, tears welling up in her eyes again. She blinked them away and walked to the door, opened it. Mike would have left without a special invitation, but Maggie was tenacious enough that she wouldn't, so Lannis made her body language unambiguous. Mike understood and lifted an eyebrow.

"Come on, Maggie." He took her elbow and guided her to the entryway. "It's a school night and the sitter needs to get on home. Lannis *will* call if she needs us." He shot a stern look at Lannis, and an unexpected smile curved her lips.

"Yes." She almost added *sir*, but decided Maggie might misconstrue it as being sarcastic, and didn't. They left and Lannis closed the door, armed the security system, and watched as the couple stopped to embrace before getting in the car. Maggie laid her head on Mike's shoulder for a long moment, and he leaned down to kiss her on the forehead.

The sense of aloneness in the house as they drove off threatened to steal Lannis's breath, and she had a moment's urge to dig her cell phone out of her pocket and call them. *Come back, I'm afraid, and it's so quiet in here it's oppressive.*

She straightened and deliberately turned on the stereo, choosing a CD of quiet, pleasant music for company. It helped, and her heart rate returned to some semblance of normal. She knew she wouldn't sleep tonight, and couldn't function at work without rest. She made that decision quickly, and hit speed dial for the dispatcher.

"Hey, Will, I'm calling in sick." Lannis was thankful her voice didn't waver.

"You got the flu already?" He sounded concerned. "It's pretty early in the season. You got a flu shot, didn't you?"

"Yeah, I got the shot, and no, it's not the flu." Her voice hitched on the last two words, and she swallowed. *Please, please don't let him ask what's wrong*—but of course, he picked up on the emotion in her voice.

"You sound, I dunno, upset. Are you okay?"

Lannis tried to answer, tried to carry off a blasé tone, but her throat closed over the words she didn't want to say. Finally, she managed to blurt, "It's not me, it's Ben."

"Is he in the hospital or something?"

They all knew Ben. He'd stopped to pick her up on occasion, and he'd felt more comfortable at the company picnic shortly after she'd been hired than she had. Lannis's shoulders slumped. "He's…" She couldn't say the word, so settled on, "He missed his check-in and I don't think I'd be worth anything until we hear from him."

"You're kidding!" Will didn't leave her a chance to respond. "Man, that's really bad. I'll juggle the schedule for you, and make sure your shifts are covered for a couple of days."

She'd flown extra for other pilots already, so appreciated that the favors flowed both directions.

"Thanks, Will." She ran a hand through her hair. "I'll call you tomorrow, and hopefully I'll know more." Lannis ended the call, emotionally wrung out from making it, and set the phone on the coffee table.

She supposed she should call Ben's parents—Mike already had—but it felt too much like a death watch, and the prospect made her stomach turn. *Tomorrow.* A sudden yearning for the comfort of her mom's arms struck her. But Millie's stinging rejection still hurt, even after all these months and no responses to Lannis's olive branch offerings. She couldn't tolerate the potential for pain heaped upon an open wound. Not now, not tonight.

That left Lynette. Their repaired relationship was too fresh, too fragile, and Lynette was approaching seven months pregnant by now. The last thing she needed was stress and an interrupted night's sleep.

Lannis sank to the couch and buried her face in her hands. There was nothing she could do, no one to call, no list to create and execute. Everything was in limbo, and everything was out of her control. She snorted. Control was an illusion anyway, but it always made her feel better to *think* she had influence on the outcome of events. And, of course, in many aspects of life, she did have some influence. Maybe it would do her some good to remember those areas.

Like a few days ago, at the prison. Robert Davis might take a step away from the path he'd chosen for his life—or not. She wasn't under any illusion that he would. But he might. And at the Children's Hospital. She provided human contact, love, and affection to otherwise lonely babies. She couldn't discount her influence at work, either. She wasn't the only dedicated professional, but as an equal partner, she contributed to a high-quality, life-saving air ambulance service.

Trying to make a balance sheet of what she could control and what she couldn't didn't solve anything. Without conscious thought, a prayer found its way to her lips, and she whispered, "Dear Lord in heaven, please take care of Ben." Tears pricked at the back of her eyelids, and she rubbed her eyes. "Please…" She couldn't think of anything more to say, so she added, "Amen," and waited, hoping for one of the rare times she felt a gentle response to her prayer. But it didn't come, and she sighed. *Doesn't mean he didn't hear.* She couldn't bear the alternative, that his answer was going to be *no,* so she shoved that thought away.

Lannis lifted her head and stared sightlessly at the kitchen area. No, she had no control over what was going on with Ben, and she'd have to accept that. For now. Meanwhile, she'd do what women had done from time immemorial while waiting for their men.

She stood and headed for the cleaning supplies. Their house would be spotless by the time dawn arrived.

And she realized, with no sense of relief and little joy, that she'd had no craving for alcohol. That was a good thing, a very good thing, but she didn't have the energy to celebrate it. Later. Plus, she couldn't take for granted that the craving would stay dormant. She'd call Althea if she needed to, but for now—she yanked the vacuum out of the closet—her priority was to keep herself busy with productive activities.

Wasn't much, but it might get her through the night.

~

Dawn came and went, the longest night of Lannis's life. By the time the sun peeked over the horizon, she'd vacuumed, dusted, cleaned all the tile and wood floors, finished the laundry, and rearranged most of the cupboards in the house. The last wasn't much of a job, as she and Ben had done that together when she moved in just months ago. None of the rest was very time-consuming, either, because they both valued reasonably orderly surroundings.

Lannis was beginning to experience the almost out-of-body sensation of sleep deprivation, but she still didn't want to succumb. She couldn't stay awake forever, though, and she finally stretched out on the couch, unable to climb into bed without Ben. She'd staved off tears for most of the night, but clutching his pillow instead of his solid, warm body would definitely send her over the edge. If she started crying, she wasn't sure she could stop.

She snagged the afghan and pulled it over her shoulders, checked that the phones were within reach, and rested her head on the throw pillow. There was no use in calling Ben's boss, or even Mike. She could trust that either one of them would contact her as soon as he turned up.

If he turned up.

Lannis slammed the door on that thought and scrunched her eyes closed against it, then snagged the remote and turned the television on, turned the volume way down, but didn't mute it. Anything to keep her from obsessing.

The trill of the landline woke her. She jerked upright, disoriented, and if possible, feeling even more sleep deprived than when she'd dozed off. She grabbed the handset that was ringing and looked for a clock even as she connected. "Hello?" The numbers on the microwave glowed 3:47, and since it was light out, it must be afternoon, she thought. She'd slept far longer than she'd thought, and shouldn't feel this battered.

"Lannis."

It was Mike, and her stomach clenched. "Have you found him?" She slid her legs around and sat all the way up.

"Yes, and he's…" Mike hesitated, not long but enough for Lannis's bullshit meter to spike. "He's okay."

She closed her eyes in relief, sent up a quick prayer of gratitude, and said, "Define *okay*, Mike." She kept her voice controlled, but couldn't camouflage the intensity in her question.

Mike hesitated again, as if he was searching for the right words.

An edge of anger crept into her voice. "Just tell me, Mike."

"He's been roughed up," he said.

Fear of the worst claimed her voice.

Mike hurried to add, "He's at U of L for evaluation."

Her heart lifted. "I'll get down there and pick him up," she began, but Mike spoke over her.

"You can't see him."

The words hung in the air and stole her breath. She sank back onto the couch and gripped the phone with both hands. "Why not?"

She glanced at the television, barely registering the footage of a breaking story in the west end of Louisville. A perky blonde newswoman earnestly addressed the camera, and in the background, Metro Police put a man into a cruiser. Her eyes slid past the screen, her mind engrossed in what Mike had to say.

"There's been a murder, and he's under investigation."

The reporter blocked Lannis's view, but suddenly the man being arrested looked terrifyingly familiar. *Ben?* Ben!

"Even if you come down here, they won't let you in. The soonest will be tomorrow, and that's a big *if* at this point."

Fear coursed through Lannis, and she barely heard the anything past *murder* and *he's under investigation.*

"Maggie's on her way to stay with you, or bring you to our house if you want, but it's real important for you to remember that you are not alone. We'll get this sorted out, but your main job is to stay strong for Ben."

Her hands began to shake, and the phone fell out of her suddenly nerveless fingers. In the swirl of emotions that flooded her, only two thoughts stood out.

Ben would never murder. Never. Kill in self-defense, yes, she could see that, but murder? No.

And how in God's name was she supposed to stay strong for him? He was *her* rock, and she'd just entered uncharted territory.

A half gasp, half sob escaped, and she put her fists up to her mouth to contain it. Indeed, *husband under investigation for murder* was not a subject they'd covered in their marriage preparation class.

The new ticker at the bottom of the screen rolled by: *Suspect taken into custody in murder of as yet unnamed teenage girl, weapon recovered at scene, details at 5…*

A craving for the blessed numbness of alcohol sucker punched her.

Even as she stumbled to her feet, something deep inside went still and silent. Waiting.

Waiting for what? Her thinking was so muddled she couldn't figure out what, but the word *no* welled up from her core, and she whispered it, then repeated it over and over, louder and louder, until it was a near shout.

No. *No.* Lannis wasn't entirely certain what she was rejecting. Alcohol? For certain, but what else? That she couldn't see Ben? She squared her shoulders. Let them try to keep her away from him. Or that she was supposed to stay strong for him?

Well, she had no idea how to go about that, but her first step would be at U of L's emergency room. She snagged her keys and cell phone. And left all the lights on when she strode out of the house.

Chapter Thirty-Three

THE SMALL EXAM TABLE was cold. And hard. The only place Ben's
feet would fit was in the stirrups, which forced his knees apart and up
in the air. A slight breeze from the ventilation system wafted around
his butt and genitals, exposed so the forensics nurse could gather
evidence. Ben gritted his teeth and turned his head so he didn't have
to watch her pluck fifty of his pubic hairs—she was currently on
number thirty-seven—but his gaze collided with Detective Hollis's
instead. He closed his good eye against the guy's cynical leer.

Of all the homicide detectives in the LMPD, figures I'd draw him. Hollis
had led a vocal, heated faction of the police union during last year's
internal affairs hosing. Which, of course, Ben had spearheaded.
Hollis still carried a grudge, believing Ben had set up and shafted
innocent cops. Not true. Ben had nearly lost his life because of those
very cops, who'd been proven to be more crooked than switchbacks
into hidden hollows of the Smoky Mountains.

He flexed his shoulders. There was no bedrail on the
gynecological table to fasten the other end of the handcuffs to, so
Hollis had cuffed his hands together, and the awkward angle of his
arms made his shoulders ache. He didn't know why the detective had
accompanied him into the exam room anyway, other than an attempt
to rattle him. The nurse was specially trained in preserving evidence
and understood the legal requirements for maintaining an unbroken,
well-documented accounting of evidence as well as he or Hollis did,
so that reasoning fell flat, too. Maybe the guy thought Ben would
confide something to the nurse he wouldn't say otherwise.

Not true. He wanted to know, more than Detective Hollis, if
he'd had any involvement in Tawnee's death—he'd only learned her
name a half hour ago. He couldn't live with himself if… He stopped
that train of thought, and brought himself back to the unpleasant
present, only to realize the nurse had asked him something. She and
Hollis waited with expectant expressions on their faces.

"Say what?" He lifted his head and peered at her.

"Tell me exactly what contact you had with the victim, especially
any skin-to-skin or oral contact."

Ben dropped his head back on the table, careful to avoid his
goose egg. "I've told you, told Hollis, told everybody, *I don't*

remember." His temper flared, and he struggled to keep it under control. "Before Rolo drugged me, she came over, sat down, we talked, I put my arm around her shoulder. We were both dressed. My left hand may have grazed her left shoulder—her blouse was sleeveless—but that's it. No other contact."

She switched on some sort of handheld lamp—it glowed like a black light—and turned off the overhead light. Tension flowed out of Ben's arms now that darkness prevented Hollis from ogling his private parts. He wasn't overly modest, but the combination of Hollis's *supervision* and the collection of evidence from his body unnerved him.

The purple light cast a ghostly glow on his skin. "No body fluids," she murmured. "Maybe some skin cells on his bruises." She was talking to Hollis, and Ben bit back his *no kidding* retort. But the grip of fear loosened, letting his breath come a little easier. *Good. A bit of validation for my version of what went down.* Besides, he figured any date rape drug would render him incapable of an erection. Problem was, too much time had elapsed to detect remnants of the chemicals involved in his blood, and if any had remained stable in his urine, which was unlikely, he'd flushed that evidence down the toilet.

This exam would answer the question of sexual contact—which he had no reason to believe had happened. He had no proof, though. The bigger question for him centered around firing the weapon, and they'd already wiped down his hands for gun residue and sent it off.

The overhead light came back on, and he squinted against the sudden light.

Hollis leaned forward, into Ben's field of vision. "How'd they drug you?" The guy's tone, dripping with sarcasm and disbelief, set Ben's teeth on edge.

"I'm careful, never drink anything except bottled beer, always open it myself, never let it out of my sight. But a couple of people bumped me right after I'd opened one Rolo'd handed me. I turned my head to look at them, and I think that's when he slipped it in." He twisted his head to shoot Hollis a glare. "And, yeah, I can't believe I let it happen. But it's the truth."

"Prisons are full of innocent men," Hollis drawled.

A flash of insight cleared Ben's mind. The guy was deliberately trying to provoke him, get him to erupt and say something incriminating. Hell, he'd do the same, if he were the interrogator. He brought his arms up, covered his eyes with a forearm, and braced the other elbow on the edge of the table. "Just do your job, Hollis. Look at everything, from all the angles you can think of."

The nurse touched his penis with cold, gloved hands, and Ben flinched, barely checking his natural reaction to push her away, cover himself. "You might warn a guy," he muttered.

"Hmm?" She looked at him through the *V* of his legs. "Oh. I'm using cotton swabs to collect DNA," she said, and proceeded to drag them across every millimeter of his privates, including some places he didn't expect.

The exam was embarrassing, humiliating even. No wonder rape victims didn't like to report, knowing they'd have to undergo such an intimate exam. Or refuse to cooperate, viewing it as a secondary violation. Hell, *he* felt violated, especially with Hollis getting some sort of sick satisfaction from watching Ben's powerlessness in the situation.

But this was the only way to prove—to himself as well as the police—what he'd done or not done last night. So he'd endure and even welcome the intrusion.

She pulled the large paper napkin that was supposed to be a sheet over Ben, and said, "Done. Here are some scrubs. You can dress now." She'd already bagged and tagged everything he'd been wearing. He sat, wincing at the bruises on his ribs, and took the blue cotton clothing.

The nurse turned her attention to her documentation. Ben managed the pants without much difficulty, although it took some creative manipulation to get the belt tied. Without being asked, Hollis stepped forward and undid one side of the cuffs so he could pull the shirt on but reattached it as soon as both arms came through.

A disturbance in the hallway, not at all unusual for this particular ER, moved closer. One voice rose above the others, and Ben's head snapped up.

"I want to see him! Let me *go!*"

Aw, shit! Lannis. A tsunami of emotions flooded Ben. For a heartbeat, his voice froze up. He took a step toward the door, and Hollis blocked his way.

"Don't even think it, Martin," he growled.

Ben stopped. He didn't have much to bargain with, but if the guy had a bit of heart, he might let Ben at least speak with Lannis. "Come on, man. Let me—"

Hollis grabbed the front of Ben's shirt and shoved him against the wall. The metal tray used to keep the nurse's equipment at hand clattered, and she grabbed the sealed evidence kit so it wouldn't bounce to the floor. Her face paled, and she made a valiant effort to minimize the fear in her eyes.

Ben sucked in a breath to keep from groaning. Hollis's arms were grinding into his bruised rib cage, and the pain made him light-headed.

"You are not exempt from the rules." Hollis's face was only an inch from Ben's, and the onions the guy had had for lunch caused Ben's stomach to start a slow roll.

Ben nodded, his mouth going dry. Dear God in heaven, he didn't want Lannis to see him like this, battered and restrained. More than that, he longed to hold her, to reassure both of them that everything would work out, to find respite in the simple comfort of her presence. But if she didn't back off, they'd arrest *her*. "Lannis, darlin'," he called out, pitching his voice to override the noise on the other side of the door.

The scuffling sounds went silent.

"Ben?"

The hope in her voice nearly undid him, but Hollis's grip deepened. The last thing he needed was to piss the guy off more than he already had. He clenched his jaw, controlled his unruly emotions, then lifted his head. "I'm okay. I'm not allowed to see you right now." His voice broke on the last word.

"Mike said you're hurt." Her tone was flat, but he could hear the fear humming beneath the words.

"Not badly, Lannis. Just bumps and bruises."

Hollis said, "Get rid of her."

"She's not a dog, Detective," Ben said. The words popped out without thought, probably an unwise move on his part, but he wouldn't let this guy talk about Lannis so disparagingly.

"Um, can I leave?" The nurse had retreated to the corner farthest from Ben and Hollis, and couldn't reach the door unless they moved. He glanced at her, and realized she was trembling.

He flicked his gaze to Hollis, and said, "Stand down, Hollis. I'm not a threat or a flight risk. You've scared the nurse, and none of this is necessary." He waited a beat, and added, "Sir."

"Ben?" Lannis raised her voice, a note of frustration and maybe a hint of temper in it.

Hollis glanced at the nurse, then released Ben and stepped back. "Ma'am. Sorry to alarm you." He inclined his head at her. "Please. You are free to go."

She squeezed past them and opened the door, slipped through, and tugged it closed behind her.

But it was open long enough for Ben to catch a glimpse of Lannis. A security guard had hold of her by the elbow, preventing her from storming the door, a look of sheer determination on her face.

She saw him, too, and her eyes lit up.

Smart woman that she was, she didn't waste time on anything but the essential.

I love you, she mouthed, as the security guard jerked her out of his line of vision.

Ben let Hollis muscle in front of him. Tension drained from his body, and with it, his strength. The cumulative stress and pain of the day sapped whatever reserves he had left, and his vision began to go fuzzy at the edges. His knees gave out, and he began a slow slide down the wall.

Just before everything went gray, he heard Hollis shout, "Hey, I need help in here!"

~

"THE ORDERLY SHOULDN'T have let you in," the security guard said, and pulled Lannis away from Ben's room. She let the guy lead her back the way she'd come earlier. She steeled herself for the repeat trip through the chaos of the main ER.

She was glad Mike had warned her, but even so, her heart skipped at Ben's eye, swollen shut, and his split lip. Bruised or not, the weight of anxiety at Ben's condition lifted at the sight of him standing, under his own power, and looking so normal otherwise. Even the silver glint of handcuffs on his wrists couldn't dilute her elation at seeing him for the first time in several weeks.

"Hey, I need help in here!"

The muffled shout came from behind her, and Lannis twisted to see where it came from. There was only one door down that hall, and it was the one she'd just left. The security guard dropped her arm and sprinted toward the voice. Lannis raced after him.

"Ben!" she called. The guard beat her by only a stride, and threw the door open. Ben lay slumped on the floor, half sitting against the wall, with a man in a suit leaning over him. The guy had a two-fisted hold on Ben's shirt.

Dread erupted into panic, and she elbowed her way past the guard, who was radioing for medical assistance. "What happened? What did you do to him?" Lannis shot a glance at the guy, but quickly refocused on Ben.

She crouched, felt for his carotid pulse—steady, but faster and weaker than it should be—and pulled him the rest of the way down to the floor, cradling his head in her lap. She stretched, reaching for the stool at the foot of the exam table, and pulled it toward Ben. It screeched across the linoleum floor, then thumped softly when she let go of it. "Grab his legs and elevate them on this," she said, not caring who responded. The suited guy reacted quickly, doing as she'd instructed, though his face darkened at what he clearly perceived as her interference.

The security guard grabbed her by the upper arm and tugged none too gently. "You are not authorized in here, young lady."

Lannis yanked away from his grip, and clutched Ben's shoulder. "You're not helping him! If you can't do that, I will!"

The guy in the suit spoke up. "Let her be, Drake." He stuck his arm out to restrain the security guard.

Drake shot a half-confused, half-miffed glance at Suit Guy. "It's your call, Detective."

The pieces fell into place for Lannis. Suit Guy was a cop, a detective. Her anxiety got the best of her. "Did you hurt him, Detective?" Her voice rose. "Did you hit him?"

The man's jaw tightened. "No. He passed out."

Footsteps thundered down the hall, and medical personnel filled the tiny room. Without fanfare or much effort, they took Ben from her, placed him on a board, then lifted him to a wheeled gurney. They hooked him up to a cardiac monitor, and someone said, "Normal sinus rhythm," and another called out his blood pressure. "Ninety-eight over fifty-four, pulse is one twelve."

Lannis relinquished her position immediately, relieved that experts had arrived to care for Ben now. She stood, and realized her hands were shaking. She clenched them into fists in a bid to control the trembling.

The emergency staff rolled the stretcher bearing her husband down the hall and disappeared as quickly as they'd come. Drake went with them.

"Was he faking it?" The detective's tone commanded Lannis's attention, and she snapped her gaze to his.

"What do *you* think?" She lifted a hand and pointed at him. "He *passed out* on your watch, in your care, and while you were alone with him." She leaned in and narrowed her eyes, poking his chest with each accusation. "I think you need to worry more about your culpability than whether or not he was faking it."

The detective's eyebrows rose. "You honestly think I—"

"You can't fake low blood pressure or a weak pulse, mister." Lannis barely refrained from calling him a jerk, like she wanted to. She spun on her heel and started down the hall to find Ben.

"Mrs. Martin." The words cracked through the air.

Lannis stopped, fought her frustration into submission, and turned. She crossed her arms and stared down Detective Suit Guy. She tapped a toe impatiently.

"I've seen some masterful fakes in the ER," he said dryly.

Lannis's temper threatened to spill over, and some of her attitude slipped out in her tone of voice. "And you are…?"

He hadn't moved a muscle since getting out of the way of the ER staff, and his stillness might have intimidated Lannis if she hadn't been so angry. In fact, she was certain he did it on purpose, for that very reason.

"Detective John Hollis." He finally moved, pulling his badge out for her to inspect. "Louisville Metro Police."

She flicked her gaze down, but didn't approach him to read it. She looked back at his eyes, so dark they looked black from a distance. "Can't really say I'm pleased to meet you, Detective," she muttered.

He stowed the badge with a practiced flip of his wrist. "When is the last time you spoke with Ben?"

"I don't have to talk to you, and you are *not* going to trick me into saying something you can twist around and use against him." She spun and took off down the corridor, her heart thudding in her chest, her pulse pounding in her ears. If she didn't remove herself from this guy's presence, she'd just make things worse for Ben.

She spotted one of the nurses who'd responded to help Ben, and she angled toward the room the nurse had just left, dodging several staff on the way. Beeping from monitors and soft, but insistent dings from alarms filled the air, along with a man's voice— not Ben's—yelling that he'd been kidnapped by aliens. No one lifted an eyebrow in response to any of the noise, and Lannis followed suit and ignored it. She slipped into the room.

A doctor leaned over Ben, listening, prodding, and saying, "…CT of his head and abdomen, rule out internal bleeding." Another nurse finished taping on an IV and turned it on. When she let go, Ben's hand flopped down on the bed, and Lannis's heart sank.

"Is—is he going to be okay?" Her throat tightened up and she could barely get the words out. She flattened herself against the wall, staying clear of their work area.

The doctor slipped his stethoscope around his neck and said, "Yeah, I think he just fainted, but we have to make sure nothing else is going on. I don't see any signs of bleeding." He flashed a look at her. "We'll know in about forty-five minutes." He returned his attention to the nurse. "Go ahead with the ammonia, see if it brings him around."

The nurse picked up a tiny vial and snapped it open just beneath Ben's nostrils. An acrid smell drifted Lannis's direction, and she wrinkled her nose. Ben twitched, then turned his head away and moaned. Lannis couldn't hold herself back, and rushed to the side of the bed the doctor had just vacated. She grabbed his free hand— which wasn't very free after all. Somewhere in the hustle of the transfer, the handcuffs had been removed, but not completely. They now encircled just one wrist, the one she was holding, and attached to the frame of the bed. Tears filled her eyes, but she blinked them back.

"Ben, I'm here, honey." She squeezed his hand. His uninjured eye fluttered open and his gaze landed on her. A slight smile lifted the corners of his lips.

"Darlin'." His voice was a shadow of its normal timbre and strength. He gripped her hand. "God, I've missed you."

Lannis hiccupped, a strangled sound of relief and joy. "Me, too, Ben," she whispered. A tear trickled down her cheek, and she swiped at it.

An automated blood pressure cuff inflated and Ben closed his eyes, relaxing his grip on her. "You won't be allowed to stay. In fact, I'm surprised they let you in at all."

She rested her forehead on his arm. "They tried to stop me."

"When it's time, go. I'll be fine."

"Well, isn't this a heartwarming reunion." Hollis's voice, already maddeningly familiar, came from the doorway, and Lannis jerked her head up to glare at him.

"What do you want?" she said, tightening her hold on Ben's hand. Then she remembered the reason she'd been so upset with Hollis, and turned. "Did he hit you, Ben?"

He opened his eye and raised an eyebrow. "What?"

She shot another *drop dead* look at Hollis. "Did Detective Hollis hit you? Is that why you *passed out* after I left?"

Hollis had the nerve to look amused.

Ben slanted a glance at him. "No, Lannis." He shifted his gaze back to her. "I haven't had anything to eat or drink for a day and a half. I just went wonky for a minute, that's all."

Hollis had been leaning against the doorjamb, and pushed himself up. "Thanks, Martin. I appreciate your vote of confidence." The words dripped with sarcasm. He didn't wait for Ben to respond, and walked into the room. "Ma'am, I do have to ask you to go to the waiting room now."

Lannis hesitated. He added, with a spark of interest, "Or I can arrest you for obstruction."

"Oh, for crying out loud." Ben shot Hollis a tired glance, then returned his gaze to her. "Go. You wouldn't like it."

Lannis caught the look that passed between the two men, a silent message not meant for her to intercept, and reluctantly stood. She leaned over the bed and kissed the only spot on Ben's face that wasn't bruised or raw, just above his right eyebrow. "I'll call Joel for you, honey." She resolved to track down the lawyer at home, if need be.

He nodded and patted her awkwardly on the shoulder with his free hand. "Don't worry. I'm safe, nothing's hurt that won't heal, and this will all work out."

A technician entered the already crowded room. "Benjamin Martin? I'll take you for your CT now." The young woman checked Ben's wristband for his name, and maneuvered the stretcher toward the door, then out into the busy ER.

"Hey, Lannis? Would you call my folks, let them know what's going on?" His request floated back.

"Yes—" Lannis watched as he rounded the corner and disappeared from sight. She sagged, exhausted from the roller coaster of emotions over the last day.

Hollis spoke from behind her, and she didn't even have the energy to flinch, though an internal shudder rippled down her spine. "Once he's medically cleared, he'll be held for questioning. If we have just cause, the judge will rule on whether to release him on bail, or remand him until trial." He paused, then added with poorly concealed gloating, "You'd be best off calling that lawyer if you want a real reunion, unless you'd prefer conjugal rights in prison."

Lannis stiffened and pivoted. "You are a sick man, Detective." She raked him with a scathing look. "And a bully." With a flash of insight, she knew her next words were true, far more than they would have been in the days before her visit with Robert Davis in prison. "I have faced far more dangerous men than you." She left the words *and survived* unsaid.

His eyebrows lifted in surprise.

"If being Ben's, and by extension, my adversary is more important to you than uncovering the truth, then so be it." She shrugged. "Now, if you'll excuse me…" Lannis shouldered past him, only to be stopped by his hand, heavy on her arm and far too near her breast for comfort.

Her breathing hitched, but she forced her lungs to expand, to draw in the air she needed, then deliberately dropped her gaze to his fingers. A long moment passed, long enough for her to think, *Hail Mary, full of grace… Dear Lord, I need some help here.*

Hollis dropped his hand. "I pride myself on being a good detective, Mrs. Martin. Unbiased, tenacious, maybe even tough. But I get the job done, and done well. If your husband is innocent of murder, I will prove it. If he's guilty…" He let the sentence trail off.

Lannis looked back up at him, her lips tight and teeth clenched. It took a moment for the tension to ebb enough that she could speak. "I—we will deal with that if and when the time comes, Detective."

She gave him a curt nod, and strode into the bedlam of the ER, letting it cover the trembling of her lips, the tears that had leaped into her eyes.

And took a page from Ben's playbook. *Never let 'em see you sweat.* In this case, don't show Hollis her fear. A goal suddenly difficult to attain, thanks to tremors that now originated deep in her core reverberated outward and threatened to take her to her knees.

What if…? She slammed her mind on the thought, and replaced it with, *Stay strong for Ben.*

And prayed for the grace to be capable of carrying off that impossible task.

Chapter Thirty-Four

"DAVIS." The guard caught Robert's eye and jerked his chin. "Over here." Robert sighed and stood, not needing to make excuses to the men clustered around him.

"Hey, Law, that's too bad, man." Murmured condolences filled the air as he rose. It never boded well to gain the attention of the guards, even if a guy hadn't done anything to warrant it. The men sent him knowing looks, and a spurt of helpless anger flared at their implied pity. But the emotion was as pointless as it was impotent, and he let it die.

"You're wanted in Admin."

Robert didn't even wonder why. Nothing mattered anymore. Lannis Martin's visit had sucked all the fight out of him. He went through the motions of being the cell-block lawyer, but his heart wasn't in it anymore, never had been for his clients, and now not even for himself.

He couldn't sleep at night, trying to dissect her motivation for forgiving him, her apparent interest in his well-being. Her victim statement hadn't fazed him; he'd intended for her to suffer. True, he hadn't given much thought to the aftermath, but he hadn't had any empathy for any of his victims, and found it surprising that she expected him to care.

But she'd shaken him with her insistence that *he* mattered to *her*. He couldn't wrap his mind around that concept. It was as foreign as someone speaking a Chinese dialect and expecting him to understand and respond appropriately.

The escort brought him to a room in the same area where his meetings with Ms. Connor had taken place, where he'd met with Lannis. As instructed, he entered and sat. Emotionless, he waited.

The door opened a few minutes later, and he lifted his gaze. Ms. Connor bustled in, full of color and life and purpose. He stared at her in bemused silence.

He never imagined Ms. Connor would request his presence again, so her summons and presence made his eyebrows rise. A flicker of curiosity sparked deep within him.

"Mr. Davis." She sent him a stern look, and her tone was steely.

She obviously hadn't forgiven him. Tension eased within Robert. *This* he knew how to deal with.

"Mrs. Martin spoke at some length with me the other day." Ms. Connor peered at him with disapproval in her eyes. "Against my professional judgment, I'm going to honor her request and recommend you for placement in a special program our institution implemented a few years ago."

Curiosity deepened into intrigue. Poor Ms. Connor, having to compromise her values over him. He would have smiled if he'd had the energy.

"We are considering eight inmates, but only have slots for six." She paused and skewered him with her gaze. "I am personally and professionally very disappointed in your response to the opportunity offered you through restorative justice. That aside, Mrs. Martin made a strong case for your rehabilitation. As one of your victims, her support carries a lot of weight. You meet all the criteria for this program—except that you've not had a very long history of nonviolence within these walls—but Warden Mitchell has instructed me to include you over the other possible candidates."

Robert straightened. Warden Mitchell had instructed her…? Coming to the attention of the warden was even worse than being singled out by the guards. Everything about this meeting was unexpected, and a frisson of unease climbed his spine. The cell block was a known quantity. It sucked and he hated it, but he knew what to expect. This was beginning to sound like change, and he wasn't at all sure he wanted it. Especially if Ms. Lannis Parker Martin thought it would be a good idea for him.

"If you don't mind, Ms. Connor, may I ask what this program involves?" Robert shifted in his chair, growing more wary by the second.

"Certainly." She peered at him over the rims of her glasses. "We match abused or abandoned dogs with inmates. You will live in a private cell, in an area segregated from the general population, along with your five compatriots. You will be taught how to care for and train your animal for use as either a drug- or bomb-sniffing dog, or as a service animal."

Private cell? Only six inmates? Robert's interest was piqued. There had to be a catch. Besides the fact that he was indifferent to animals, had never had a pet, and in fact, harbored a hidden fear of big dogs. He assumed the animals would be kenneled except for when they got them out for training, and that was fine with him. This might be a cushy deal, or as cushy as possible while in prison. It beat the hell out of making license plates, or working in the laundry or the kitchen. And he hadn't earned the privilege of any of those jobs yet.

"You and the dog assigned to you will be inseparable. It will sleep with you—" Ms. Connor droned on, but Robert quit processing her words. He broke into her litany of rules and regulations.

"Are you serious?" He leaned forward. "I have to live with a *dog*? Who dreamed up this cockamamie scheme?" Once started, his mouth kept spouting words without the benefit of his brain's filter for appropriateness. "And why do you keep picking on me for your experiments, Ms. Connor? What did I do to warrant special attention?"

His words fell like boulders into a still mountain lake. Ms. Connor simply regarded him in silence. After a long moment, she said, "You are not the center of anyone's universe, Mr. Davis. Several inmates were targeted for this project. And it was primarily Mrs. Martin's influence that involved you in either the effort toward restorative justice or now this, the canine program." She lifted a well-manicured hand and held one finger aloft. "You may decline this opportunity, and live out the rest of your sentence in this institution as an average Joe, getting very little out of your experience because you've chosen to put nothing into it." She raised a second finger. "Or you can choose to try to better yourself, to challenge your beliefs about yourself, and to pay back to the community in some way for the damage you have caused in your victims' lives."

The idea of *getting something out of this experience* sent a flicker of amusement through him. So far he'd gotten tased, solitary confinement, and sleep deprivation. He hadn't—and still didn't— expect any more than that from prison.

And he didn't know about *bettering himself*, because he figured being an attorney pretty much covered the bases on that score, at least educationally. And he'd belonged to one of the most exclusive country clubs in New Jersey. He didn't figure anyone could get much *better* than that.

But his breath caught at the next part of her statement, the part about challenging his beliefs about himself. He'd never told anyone about his mother, about running away from the white trash label all his life, about his horror of ending up here after all, like this was his destiny, where he belonged, no matter how hard he tried to escape it. How did she know this about him? Had she read his mind?

Every cell in him rebelled at the *pay back to the community* part. He didn't owe anyone. Not the community, not his victims, nobody.

"The choice is yours, Mr. Davis. I have done my job, presenting the option to you. If you want my advice—"

He didn't.

"—you'll take advantage of this opportunity." She sent him a tight, wry smile. "You never know what you might learn about yourself, about life." She closed the folder. "What have you decided?"

Robert hedged, and he wasn't sure why, because in spite of the perks this program offered, he couldn't wrap his mind around the concept, or rather, the concept in relation to himself. "Can I think on it?"

She softened, just enough that something deep inside him brightened.

"No, Mr. Davis. There are other inmates who deserve a chance at this program if you decline."

"So the deadline is right now," he said flatly.

"Yes, it is." She waited, serene and unruffled.

He felt sweat form on his upper lip. Why did he feel the need to please this woman? He shied away from the thought as soon as it formed, appalled that it even existed.

In the end, the lure of privacy trumped the ignominy of living with a dog.

"All right, Ms. Connor. I accept." Robert wondered what he'd just gotten himself into, what new twist this direction would add to his life.

A flicker of surprise crossed her face, quickly masked with her trademark efficiency. "Well, then, Mr. Davis. You'll be transferred tomorrow." She stood, nodded her head, and moved toward the door. She hesitated, then turned to look back at him. "Good luck. I hope you find success, for your sake, and for Mrs. Martin's."

Chapter Thirty-Five

"Ben!" Lannis pushed away from the car where she'd been waiting with poorly disguised impatience and launched herself into his arms. He looked more exhausted than she felt, his bloodshot eyes rimmed with reddened, gritty-looking lids. He folded her into his embrace, his body solid and warm beneath her hands. And *real*. Much better than the memories she'd nurtured during the long weeks of his absence. She drank in the unique scent and sense of him, and felt the tension of the past twenty-four hours drain away.

He rested a cheek on her head, then—far too soon for her liking—straightened and set her away. His eyes warmed, but his lips stayed in a tight, flat line.

She motioned to the car. "Do you want to drive, or should I?" His gaze flicked to the restored Mustang, but he didn't answer, and his expression went shuttered. A moment passed in silence, and Lannis realized he wasn't going to speak. That was so out of character for him that a niggle of unease wormed its way under her skin. She took his arm and drew him away from the building that housed the DEA office. He didn't resist, but he didn't seem overly eager to accompany her, either.

His lack of enthusiasm contributed to a growing sense of withdrawal, as if nonparticipation could influence the direction his life had taken.

A flurry of emotions clamored for Lannis's attention, a sudden spurt of insecurity leading the pack. Flustered, she said, "I didn't know if you wanted to grab something on the way home—to eat, I mean—or if you'd rather have steaks on the barbeque, plus, I made beef stew, so there are lots of choices…" Her voice trailed off. She was babbling and sounded like an idiot. She stopped and faced him, now that they'd put half a dozen paces between them and the door. She could see Mike talking with Herm behind the glassed entrance.

"Ben, honey, you've been through a lot. I won't pretend to understand how you feel." She ran a hand through her hair. "But don't shut me out." She gazed into his eyes, willing him to let down his guard. Of course, she had no idea how he'd respond if he did. She steeled herself for an outburst, or even tears.

His expression grew even grimmer, and he finally spoke. "You drive. Stew's fine." He shrugged his duffel onto his shoulder and strode past her to the car, tossed his bag in, and settled himself in the passenger seat.

Tears pricked at the back of her eyelids, and Lannis blinked them into submission, angry at their appearance and nonplussed at Ben's actions. He'd never pushed her away before. Her heart sank, and the insecurity she'd felt a few moments ago rushed in like a tsunami. She tensed all her muscles, battling the unruly emotion. *No.* A feeling wasn't always the basis for truth, and she rejected it as unfounded. Besides, it took two people to make a relationship, and she wouldn't sit by, letting him define *them* without her input. She lifted her head and squared her shoulders.

They made the drive in silence, which continued until she'd parked in the garage.

"I'm going to take a shower." Ben vaulted out of the car before the garage door made it closed. Lannis followed more slowly, stopping at the duffel he'd dropped in the laundry room. She sorted his clothes and tossed a load in the washer, added soap, and hit the buttons to begin the cycle, glad for the anchor of normalcy. The shower went on at the other end of the house, and she left the laundry room for the kitchen.

The aroma of beef stew filled the house. Setting the table and adding salad and rolls completed the dinner preparations. Almost as an afterthought, she lit a pillar candle and placed it in the center, pleased at the cozy, welcoming tableau.

The shower went off, and she sat to wait for Ben.

She waited for nearly ten minutes before deciding she'd given him the space he seemed to need. She rose, walked down the hall, and realized no light shone from the crack of the door.

"Ben?" She pushed the door open, the lingering humidity and clean scent from his shower wafting across her skin. Light from the hallway spilled across the bed, illuminating Ben's prone form, facedown on top of the comforter. He'd pulled on a pair of boxer shorts, but was otherwise bare. "Honey, are you all right?"

He didn't move, and a soft snuffle was her answer. A rush of compassion filled her, and she chose to focus on that rather than the quick, sharp stab of disappointment at missing out on the homey reunion she'd hoped for.

She eased out of the room and returned to the kitchen. It took only moments to blow out the candle and store the stew in the fridge. She shut down the house as she made her way back to the bedroom. It was early, but she hadn't slept well for two nights, and neither had Ben. Her heart rose at the prospect of sleeping next to him, and in spite of the exhaustion that plagued both of them, different parts of her anatomy quickened as well.

Lannis slipped into the bedroom and softly closed the door. Three minutes in the bathroom, another thirty seconds to shed her clothes and pull a fresh nightgown over her head, and she was ready. She turned the bathroom light off and approached the bed. She slowed, feeling shy after the time apart, and a bit unsure of her reception given Ben's actions on the way home.

Her mind flashed to the last time they'd been in bed together, and her courage took a nosedive. They'd fought, and his call-out left their dispute unresolved. Over a month to let the argument fester, to let attitudes that made sense at the time solidify, even develop a life of their own.

But she'd worked through her fear of bringing a child into the world by facing Davis, and the prospect of pregnancy now filled her with a more normal sense of trepidation rather than dread—none of which Ben knew.

They needed to talk—about a lot of things—and the mess that embroiled Ben topped the list. In the meantime, both of them needed the solace and comfort that only they could bring to the other. Emboldened by the thought, she lifted the covers.

"Ben, honey, come to bed." She put her hand on his shoulder and he flinched, then went still, his breathing no longer deep and even. She pulled her hand away. "You're cold. You fell asleep on top of the covers. Come in and get warm."

His muscles tensed, and the mattress dipped as he rolled to a sitting position, his back to her. Lannis reached across the expanse between them and ran her hand across the cool skin of his torso. He stood, breaking the connection, and leaving her nothing to do but drop her hand to her side. He turned, his face shadowed, and hesitated, then spoke.

"I'll sleep on the futon."

Lannis's stomach plummeted. "Why?" She heard the plaintive tone in her voice, and it laid bare the stab of abandonment she felt at his words.

"I—" He scrubbed a hand across his face, exhaustion and frustration clear in the abrupt motion. He raised his gaze to meet hers, his eyes too dark for her to read. "I can't." He took a tight breath. "Until I know what I did in that house, I can't sleep with you."

She blinked. Now that he'd verbalized it, she could understand. Actually, it was easier to deal with than silence, and a bit of relief trickled in to salve the pain of rejection, because he wasn't rejecting *her*. She chose her words carefully. "I hear you saying you can't live with yourself, and you want to protect me. I appreciate that"—she shrugged—"but I think this is really about you forgiving yourself." She leaned forward. "I love you unconditionally, Ben. As unconditionally as one person can love another. So it doesn't matter to me what happened, *especially* since you were drugged."

Lannis stood and walked around the end of the bed. Ben didn't move, but tension rolled off him in waves, and increased the closer she got to him. "Please don't shut me out." She held her hand out to him. And waited.

The moment stretched, the silence interrupted only when the furnace kicked on. Her arm grew heavy, but not as heavy as her heart as the seconds ticked by without a response from him.

He finally shook his head and stepped away. "I'm sorry." His voice held regret, and that, combined with the misery beneath it, softened the sting of his answer. But not much.

Lannis tried to ignore the disappointment that rolled through her, and cleared her throat in attempt to keep her voice from wobbling. She dropped her arm to her side and said, "All right. I'll respect your decision, Ben." Her lips began to tremble and she clamped them together for a moment before she could speak. "You know where to find me. When you're ready."

Ben gave her a curt nod, picked up his pillow, and padded down the hallway without a backward glance.

Though he couldn't have seen the tears that dampened her cheeks in the dark, Lannis couldn't understand how he didn't hear the anguish of her heart as he disappeared from her sight.

Chapter Thirty-Six

*M*ANGY CUR could not have described the dog any more succinctly. It was a *she*, and dull yellow fur hung in clumps from her shoulders and hips. Her snout was pointy, her ears were pointy, and her nose a shiny black coin that matched one of her eyes.

Yep, he had that correct. *One* of her eyes.

The other was a pale robin's-egg blue.

He'd drawn the ugliest mongrel of the bunch. Part Australian shepherd, part golden retriever, with a healthy dose of indeterminate mutt thrown in.

Just his luck. There were two German shepherds to be trained for K-9 units, a beagle for a search-and-rescue team, an Irish setter for an autistic kid with epilepsy, and a full-sized poodle destined for a psychiatric hospital. All handsome dogs. And all assigned, one by one, to the other inmates.

She was supposed to be "rehabilitated." He caught a whiff of Ms. Connor's influence in the matching of this particular animal with him. If he succeeded at his task, the dog would move on to be trained for bomb-sniffing.

Robert Davis regarded his mutt warily. She returned the sentiment, cowering about three feet away from him, just out of kicking range. Her unmatched gaze disconcerted him, even more than the fact that he was now closer to an animal than he'd ever been in his life. He wiped a damp palm on his pants leg, trying to do it surreptitiously, so the handler, or trainer, or whatever his proper title was, wouldn't notice his nervousness.

"How many of you have had pets?" The guy, tall and lanky, in his forties and already bald as a cue ball, stepped back to survey the class.

Robert glanced around. No one raised their hand, but someone muttered, "If rats count…" A wry grin split his face. He could identify with that, and he spoke. "Yeah, me, too." A murmur of agreement rippled through the group, and some of the tension eased.

"I've been on the receiving end of a K-9 takedown," one guy volunteered. He pulled his sleeve up to show a nasty-looking scar on his forearm.

"And you're *here?*" Robert was shocked into speaking to the inmate, who nodded.

"I want to do something good with my life, or what's left of it. You know, redeem myself a little bit, even though I can't undo what got me incarcerated."

Robert looked away. Quickly. *Figures.* He'd gotten stuck in this program with a bunch of do-gooders with *positive attitudes.* He could just see Ms. Connor smirking in her office at the big, fat joke she'd pulled on ol' Davis, hoping some of that attitude would wear off on him and turn him around.

He didn't think so, and he made a raspberry sound. His dog flinched at the noise, and belly crawled away from him.

Cripes. This wasn't going to work. Dog was scared of him, he was scared of the dog…

"—so you need to be the alpha in your relationship. This doesn't mean you dominate or intimidate. Far from it. You need to establish a trust relationship with the animal, which is why from this moment on, each pair is inseparable. You won't even take a leak without your dog, and conversely, you are responsible for scooping and disposing of your animal's waste."

Robert's head began to ache. He opened his mouth to say he'd reconsidered—he had; he hadn't banked on signing up for doggy sewer duty—but the handler kept on talking.

"—and one of your first tasks will be to name your partner."

He felt like he'd taken a roundhouse kick to the solar plexus. *Name* this sorry excuse for a mutt? He'd never been responsible for another living organism's needs, and he'd never *named* anyone or anything.

In fact, his victims populated their special corner of his mind as nameless entities devoid of personality, humanity, or value. Pretty much like this dog. He glanced down at her again. She curled her lip and snarled at him.

He bared his teeth.

Without warning, she lunged at him and snapped her jaws—filled with nasty-looking, sharp teeth—a hairbreadth from his leg.

Robert recoiled in alarm, tripped over something—he didn't see what—and went down hard. He grunted and rolled instinctively into a crouch, arms up to protect his face, ready to defend his life with all the martial art skills at his disposal. Adrenaline, along with naked fear, raced through him. He didn't know how to defend himself from an animal. Just other men.

She growled at him, a canine Godzilla, her upper lip twitching in barely restrained threat, and Robert's heart thudded painfully.

The instructor stepped between them, making a quick *stay still* motion with one hand, and simultaneously crooning to the dog. "Hush, hush, you're all right," he said to her, and in the same calming tone, directed his words at Robert. "Davis, settle down. She's more afraid of you than you are of her." He flicked a glance toward him, then back to the dog. "Dogs always meet aggression with aggression. In order to change her behavior, you need to change yours."

The words, at odds with the tone in which the instructor delivered them, struck Robert to the core. Especially the ones about him being afraid of her. Shame swept through him, and his face heated. He stood, slowly, and swiped at the nervous sweat that had formed on his upper lip. He could feel his pulse still hammering his veins from the terror of the dog's attack, and his palms were damp.

"I want out." Robert blurted the words without intending them, and felt his face go from heated to flaming. He was doing the one thing he'd focused all his energy on avoiding since his arrest.

Showing fear.

And it rolled through him, loosing an avalanche of emotions, a cacophony of unruly feelings too intense and frightening to process or control.

To his horror, he realized his hands were shaking, and he could smell the stench of his own fear.

He took a step back, then another, battling an urge to turn and flee. *And then what?* He was in prison. There was no place to run *to.* And running could get him shot. Killed.

The idea hung tantalizingly in his mind.

Maybe he'd be better off dead.

His victims thought so. And he could see their point. Which, in itself alarmed him. Not so much that his victims would be happy, or at least relieved, if he were dead, but that he had the insight to recognize it.

All his victims except Lannis Parker Martin.

"I want out," he said again, his voice rising.

He covered his ears with his hands, a vain attempt to silence the Pandora's box of accusations swirling through his mind.

Throwaway child. White trash. You don't deserve to eat, to be safe, to live, to succeed. You don't matter. You don't matter. You don't matter.

His future flashed before him. An eternity of bleak mornings followed by soul-killing monotony within these walls. And nothing— *nothing*—to anticipate once he got out.

Robert clenched his teeth and dug deep for a kernel of hope, any scrap of redeeming value as a lifeline. Of all the things he'd thought could anchor him, give him courage to go on—his accomplishments, his career, his money—no, it wasn't any of those things that surfaced for him to hold on to.

Rather, it was Lannis's face, Lannis's words. Words of forgiveness, of encouragement. Foreign concepts, confusing and contrary to the hardscrabble, fight-for-everything-he-wanted approach he knew so well. Robert rejected the memory, but couldn't make it disappear.

"I hope you can accept forgiveness, find a path that frees you from your shackles. I don't care what route you take. I just want that for you."

Whether it was Lannis's sentiments or his own reserves, scraped up from the murky depths of his subconscious, his capacity for self-preservation kicked in. No running. No dying, either via suicide or death by cop. If he decided to end his life, he didn't need to goad the SWAT team or guards into firing on him. The whirlwind of emotions ebbed, the edges softening, blurring enough that he could drag in a lungful of air. He exhaled, and dropped his hands to his sides.

And said it again, a whisper this time. "I want out."

The instructor, one hand patting the trembling dog at his feet, glanced at Robert. Instead of the disdain or anger he'd expected, the guy's eyes held compassion. "Sorry." He didn't sound sorry at all. He sounded…chipper.

Great. A Boy Scout.

"You're in the program, and you stay. The same way the dogs do. You will work through your issues together." He sent Robert a lopsided smile. "So come over here and make friends."

Robert shook his head. No way. He wasn't going to touch that animal. "She already tried to bite me."

"Because *you* showed aggression." The instructor spoke slowly, with exaggerated patience.

Robert's heart had finally settled back into his chest, but accelerated at the prospect of touching the dog.

"Come on." The handler beckoned him, still speaking in that overly calm voice. "Be calm and nonthreatening. Hold the back of your hand to her nose, don't make any sudden moves, let her take the next step."

Robert licked his lips, which had gone dry, and forced his legs to close the space between him and the dog. He crouched, following the lead of the trainer, and gathered his courage. He flexed his hand behind his back, then relaxed it and extended it the way he'd been told.

The dog looked wary, but tipped her head in a tentative, delicate motion that brought her nose close to his hand.

Robert began to sweat, but held his hand steady.

"Notice her body language," the handler said softly. "She's not baring her teeth or growling."

The trainer was right. Her body language was cautious, and more defensive than aggressive.

She stretched forward a tad, and her nose brushed the back of his hand.

He couldn't help it. Her nose was cold, and surprised, he flinched.

"It's okay, that's an accepting nudge she's giving you. Steady," the instructor murmured.

Robert took a breath and stayed still. She'd retreated when he flinched, but inched forward again. She sniffed, which tickled the hairs on the back of his hand, then licked him.

Startled at the sight of her long pink tongue and the unexpected sensation on his skin, he jerked away, only to find the handler's hand firm on his arm.

"Settle down. She's trying to make friends with you." He urged Robert to approach the dog again. "Let her. Then I'll teach you how to pet her."

Wary, but unwillingly intrigued, he reached for her, and she licked him again. Knowing what to expect helped, and Robert didn't cringe this time. She licked him again, and he marveled at how smooth her tongue was. Like he'd ever thought about a dog's tongue before. His breath whooshed out on a relieved exhale, and he smiled.

"It feels…I don't know, weird." He glanced at the instructor, who grinned and winked.

"Probably does, the first time." The guy reached around the dog's head and scratched behind her ear. She immediately forgot about Robert, leaned into the scratching, and closed her eyes in what could only be described as bliss.

Robert tried the other ear, feeling the coarse yet soft fur, the definition of her skull and the stiff, wrinkled base of her ear beneath his fingertips. She leaned into him, and he felt a spurt of satisfaction. He'd done it. He'd touched this dog. And the competitive part of him reveled in the fact that he'd won a bit of her attention away from the trainer.

"Okay, gentlemen." The handler stood. "Let's go over the basics of caring for your animal."

Robert had been so caught up in the experience that he'd forgotten the other inmates. He glanced at them, but stayed crouched with his dog, loathe to relinquish his achievement, and feeling no compunction to move. If he were honest with himself, he'd admit to actually liking the sensations of fur, warmth, and her unexpected movements against his hands. He'd never experienced anything like this before. She shifted and lay down, resting her snout on her front legs. She released a contented sigh and leaned against Robert's thigh.

An unfamiliar feeling snaked through him. He paused, trying to identify it. Part anxiety at the unknown, part thrill, part…contentment? The anxiety made sense. So did the thrill. He'd thought of this assignment as just that. An assignment. Something he had to do to please Ms. Connor, a motivation that still made him uneasy. But maybe it was going to be like learning to fly.

An adventure.

His dog stood, and he let go of her with a reluctance that surprised him. She wandered over to the grassy area behind Wilkinson—the trainer had finally introduced himself—and squatted.

Robert watched with horrified fascination as she deposited a smelly pile of steaming poop. Finished, she did a stiff-legged thing with her hind feet and scattered a few bits of dormant grass on top of it, then wandered back over to him and sat.

He hung his head, then girded himself and followed Wilkinson's instructions. Get a way-too-thin clear plastic glove and a small paper bag. Don the glove.

He balked at the next step, which was to approach the now cooling mess, but aware of not only Wilkinson's gaze, but also that of the other five inmates, he resolutely walked toward it. The only way to save face at this point was…to pick up dog shit.

It took three tries, with him gagging harder each time until throwing up would have been a relief, before he managed to do the deed and drop the entire disgusting glob into the bag.

He sealed it and took it to the lidded receptacle, then washed his hands. He took a lungful of fresh air to clean out his sinuses, and wondered again what he'd agreed to. And why.

Robert took another look at his new partner, who thumped her tail lazily on the concrete and opened her mouth, letting her tongue loll out.

He could have sworn she was laughing at him, but it was a pure laughter, not derisive, demeaning, dehumanizing scorn. Her ears perked up at his gaze.

"—so tomorrow morning after breakfast, we'll meet here again, and you can introduce us to your companion by name." Wilkinson indicated a stack of supplies. "Get yourselves settled, and get to know your buddy."

Robert got in line for the collars, leashes, and doggie beds. He'd seen them advertised in high-end in-flight catalogs on airlines, but flipped right past them. These beds were nothing more than soft, well-worn, ready-for-Goodwill blankets. He snagged his share for…

He glanced at her again.

What should have been a trivial assignment suddenly loomed as a truly weighty task, and he wondered, in a spurt of uncharacteristic insecurity, if he was up to it.

What *was* he going to name her?

~

GODZILLA WHINED. It was a pathetic sound, from the corner where Robert had arranged blankets for her bed, and after about the fourteenth time, it grated on his nerves.

"Shut up," he muttered, and drew an arm over his head in a vain attempt to block out the sound. His euphoria over a private cell—complete with control over the lighting, a first since he'd been arrested back in April—had evaporated a dozen whimpers ago.

She'd started as soon as he flipped the switch and darkness had fallen. Now, her claws made odd scratching sounds on the concrete floor in concert with her obviously distressed cries. Uneasy, he got up and turned the light back on to see what she was doing. Her whines stopped abruptly as light flooded the small room, and she sat, offering a single tentative thump of her tail. She'd rearranged his neat doggy bed into a messy wad. And her eyes, the mismatched gaze becoming more tolerable to him, now had a ring of alarmed white around each iris. Which lent a grisly, horrifying aspect to her appearance, unnerving him yet again.

His fingers fumbled on the switch, but he got the light off quickly so he wouldn't have to look at the dog.

Not much chance of him sleeping, not with *that* in the corner. He began to sweat.

She whimpered again, then escalated to a continuous string of keening cries that sounded like it could turn into full-blown howls, and he hastily turned the light back on.

Silence. Blessed silence. Godzilla began to sit, then stood again, nearly vibrating with anxiety.

Robert sighed. "Okay, I won't turn the light off." He flopped on his bed, turned his back to her, and covered his eyes with his forearm. At least it was easier to block out the light than to mitigate the irritating, high-pitched whining.

He closed his eyes, determined to get some rest in spite of the new surroundings, which had him as unsettled as Godzilla apparently was. A few minutes passed, and he congratulated himself on figuring out how to keep her quiet. He rolled over and faced the wall.

Something hard and sharp poked him in the back. Robert jerked upright, spinning into a combat stance without thinking, adrenaline flooding his system.

Godzilla leaped away from his bedside and thudded into the opposite wall, then cowered with bared teeth in a soundless snarl.

His breath came in short bursts. She'd poked at him with her front paw. He now realized the hard, sharp thing had been her claw. The revelation helped clear his mind, and he flashed back on Wilkinson's words. *Aggression for aggression...*

He softened his stance, slowed his breathing. "It's okay, dog. You're okay." The words didn't matter, and he felt foolish for repeating himself, but forced an approximation of the tone Wilkinson had used. Sweat beaded on his lip, but he let it be, not wanting to move abruptly and scare Godzilla into biting him.

After a few moments of his crooning nonsense, Godzilla relaxed her lip. Heartened, Robert hunkered down and held out his hand, the same way the trainer had shown him earlier. She gazed up at him, still frightened, if he understood the white that showed around her mismatched eyes. He repressed a shudder. If he ever got to sleep tonight, he'd have nightmares.

In small degrees, she dropped her defensive posture and eased forward to sniff his hand.

"Good dog, good dog," he murmured. She allowed him to scratch behind her ear, and released a sigh that sounded as world-weary as he felt. "Yeah, I know. It all sucks, doesn't it."

She leaned into his touch and closed her eyes. Robert stood, careful to not alarm her again, and switched off the light.

Godzilla whimpered, and, suspicious at the timing, he turned it back on.

She stopped and looked up at him with soulful eyes.

Off. The whining started.

On. It stopped.

"For crying out loud—" He snapped his mouth closed, glad no one had heard him talking to her like she could understand, and in a pun, no less. That was exactly what she was doing. Crying out loud. He rolled his eyes.

His opportunity to sleep in a dark room, by himself and without fearing for his life, was slipping through his fingers. He gritted his teeth in frustration. There had to be a way. If she'd only do what he told her…

"Lie down, dog." Robert pointed at the corner and the untidy heap of ragged blankets.

She swung her head and looked at them, then returned her gaze to him and crept forward to nudge his hand with her nose.

"What?" He looked down at her in consternation. She clearly wanted *him*, wanted to be near him. In fact, she appeared to want his touch, as unfathomable as it seemed to Robert.

Maybe if he moved her bed over next to his and hung his hand over the edge… He grabbed the doggie bed and dropped it on the floor within arm's reach of his, and pointed at it.

She poked and scratched at it, circled, then lay down, and looked at him expectantly.

He turned the light off.

She whined, and he stepped over her and lowered himself onto his bed, then touched her head. She bumped his hand with her snout, and licked him, but didn't stop crying. Instead, she skulked closer and upward, as if he might not notice what she was doing that way, until her head nestled near his hip.

A frisson of fear shivered through Robert, and she went motionless. He reminded himself she'd never bitten him, so he ignored his anxiety, now damn curious to see how far she'd go.

All the way, it turned out. She wormed and wiggled all the way into his bed, until she warmed him from shoulder to hip. She settled her head on his shoulder and heaved a contented exhale, her breath tickling across his neck.

Astounded, it was Robert's turn to lie motionless. He didn't know whether to be terrified that her teeth were mere inches from his carotid arteries and his face—or to be flattered at her attention.

In the end it didn't matter. He fell asleep before he had time to mull it over enough to come to a conclusion, never mind act on it.

He woke to the scrabble of Godzilla's claws on his chest as she lurched out of bed—his bed—in response to the wake-up buzzer. She fled to the corner, trembling, and danced in what looked like universal language for *I gotta go*. Robert had to go, too, but alarm at the prospect of having to clean up dog piss galvanized him into action, in spite of the cobwebs clouding his brain.

"Hey," he shouted, and banged on the door. "Dog needs out!" He heard a guard making his way down the hallway, too far away and far too slowly for Robert's peace of mind. "Can you speed it up?"

"Save your breath, Davis." The guy didn't seem to change his pace as he opened cell after cell, ever so methodically. "I'll get there when I get there."

He glanced at Godzilla, who started to crouch right in the middle of the room. "No!" He lunged toward her, having no idea what he could do to stop her, and she shot him a terror-filled glance.

And peed on the floor.

Robert stopped short. He scrubbed a hand over his face. Sighed. Glared at Godzilla, who'd finished and retired to the corner with a guilty expression on her face.

A guilty expression? On her face?

He didn't know that animals could have feelings, or an ability to express them. Part of him said she deserved to be kicked out the door—which would probably be the only way to get himself kicked out of the program. But another smaller, yet vocal part of him felt a sense of kinship with her helpless anticipation of violence.

If it had been him, as a kid, he would have gotten a beating for far less than what she'd just done. Kicking her *felt* like the right thing to do. As an outlet for frustration, it worked. But yesterday he'd learned a new way to deal with a threat, namely Godzilla, and he'd already put new skills into practice. Successfully. So maybe he could do something different for her than what he'd received as a youngster.

Wilkinson had challenged him to change his behavior. Robert knew Ms. Connor harbored that hope. He shoved the specter of his victims away and buried them in his psyche so he wouldn't have to deal with them right now, too.

Nope. Just him and Godzilla, and right here, right now. "Yeah, we'd better figure out a better way to start the day, huh, girl?" He cast his gaze about for supplies to clean up the spreading liquid on the floor. Not enough toilet paper, no paper towels. Only his bedding, the dog's bedding, or his towel. Revulsion at soiling his sheets had him reaching for her pile of rags, but they were all quilted and he didn't trust that he could clean them adequately, or that they would dry well.

The puddle crept toward his bare feet and made his decision for him. Guard was still three cells away, with inspection first on the agenda. He picked up his towel, eyed its relative cleanliness, and sighed again. Godzilla relaxed at his amiable tone, and sniffed as he mopped up her mess. By the time the guard opened his cell, the floor was clean enough that he could stand to walk on it, and he was in the midst of hand washing the terrycloth.

With a start like that to the day, the rest of it would be a piece of cake.

He hung his towel to dry and washed his hands. And glanced at Godzilla.

She cocked her head to one side and opened her mouth in a grin, her tongue lolling out in happy abandon.

Then again, he'd learned a lot since yesterday, and one of the big lessons was that life with a dog wasn't quite as predictable as he'd somehow expected.

He regarded her through narrowed eyes.

Yep. She was female, and a dog, and therefore doubly unpredictable. The day *could* get worse.

Inexplicably, the prospect lightened his mood.

~

"The first order of business is introducing your dogs to us." Wilkinson had already shepherded the group through the morning routine of caring for the animals. Food, water, grooming, a brief walk. "Davis, what have you decided to name your companion?"

Robert's mind went blank. He'd forgotten about the assignment overnight, what with the whining and lights and adjustments in sleeping arrangements. "Uh…" He'd defaulted to thinking of her as Godzilla, but suspected that name wouldn't garner him any points. A flash of inspiration hit. "Uh, Zilla." Then a bit more strongly, "Zilla."

Wilkinson's eyebrows rose. "Zilla? How'd you settle on that?"

Robert shifted his weight to his other foot. "Well, uh…" He lit on the most likely explanation he thought might fly. "It's sort of a play on 'Priscilla,' an old girlfriend's name." The lie flowed off his tongue with the smoothness of an aged red wine.

The trainer nodded, still looking a bit nonplussed, but accepting of Robert's reasoning. He moved on to the next man, and Robert released a soft sigh of relief. He tuned out the rest of the naming ceremony, too tired and too tense to feign interest.

This whole experience was hard. The perks came with a cost, and sleeplessness when he'd expected the exact opposite topped the list. Wilkinson said something and the other inmates moved, jolting

Robert back into the present. He turned to the guy next to him, the one who sported dog-bite scars on his forearm.

"Hey, man, I'm sorry. What'd he say?" He felt like he'd been the object of a cue stick every step of this journey, and he was getting tired of being clueless.

"No problem." The wiry black dude with white hair gestured to the one-acre yard attached to the canine training unit. "We each get an hour a day to exercise the dogs. You're first today." He made a *go on* motion, and added, "You don't want to waste your time, man."

Robert dipped his head in understanding, even though he had no idea what he was supposed to do, and muttered, "Thanks."

He tugged on Zilla's leash and headed for the yard. He could get in a good four or five miles around the perimeter, and maybe she'd sleep tonight if she got tired enough. Halfway through his first lap, Wilkinson appeared and waved him down.

"How about some Frisbee, or tug of war?" He made the suggestion with a sense of command concealed in the guise of nonchalance.

Robert slowed, then stopped. "Uh…"

"Here, let me show you." The trainer picked up a tennis ball and said, "Let her off the leash."

Robert unsnapped Zilla's leash, then stood and shoved his hands in his pockets.

Wilkinson patted his thigh. "Wanna play, Zilla?" He threw the ball and Zilla's entire body vibrated.

Rather than race after it like Robert had seen dogs do in parks, she sent him a beseeching gaze. Asking his permission? Astonished, he nodded and said, "Go ahead." Feeling silly, he added, "Fetch," for lack of what might be an appropriate doggie command.

She took off like a shot, her whole being focused on the ball. She tumbled when she got to it, but righted herself quickly and snatched the ball. Wilkinson had walked toward Robert, and Zilla trotted back, the ball between her jaws. "Good dog," Wilkinson said, and crouched, clapping his hands together. She dropped it at his feet, then darted out and back several times, a clear invitation for him to throw again.

The trainer stood and handed the slobber-covered ball to Robert. "Here. You try it."

He hesitated, but accepted the ball and gave it a halfhearted toss. Zilla repeated her frenzied chase and capture, then trotted back to him, pride shining in her mismatched eyes. Robert took the ball, now even slimier, and lobbed it double the distance. As she tore off in pursuit, he turned to Wilkinson. "What's the point of this? Just to get them tired out?" Which had been his plan, but this method seemed to have no point—and even less benefit for him.

Wilkinson looked surprised. "Oh, no. This program is hard work for them, and they need the break. The exercise provides an appropriate outlet for excess energy and frustration, which aids in staying focused during training sessions." He clapped Robert on the shoulder. "Plus, it's a great bonding activity for the two of you."

Robert snorted. "She bonded with me just fine last night. Climbed right up in my bed."

Wilkinson laughed, then sobered. "You must have a magic touch, then. I had my doubts as to her capability to let anyone get close."

Zilla trotted up and presented her trophy to Robert again, adoration shining in her eyes. He grimaced as he picked it up, and threw it hard this time, nearly to the fence. He wiped his hand on his pants leg as she raced after it.

"And it's a good release for you, too." Wilkinson kept his eyes on Zilla.

"What do you mean?" The only release Robert needed was the one that would set him on the outside of these walls. And, he thought belatedly, sex. But that paled to his yearning for freedom.

"Play." Wilkinson turned to regard Robert. "You know—no pressure, no agenda, no goal. Just hang out."

A cynical laugh escaped Robert before he could silence it. Hell, he didn't know how to play. Every activity he'd done in his life had been for the purpose of survival or maneuvering to attain a position of power. He derived pleasure from many of those endeavors, but not one of them embodied the goals Wilkinson had just listed.

"Seems pretty boring to me," he finally said.

The trainer's gaze held his. "Sometimes it is. But you'd be amazed at what happens to your mind when you indulge in play. Give it a try."

Zilla had returned, and Robert stooped to take the ball from her—and to hide his insecurity. Wilkinson chose that moment to go back inside, leaving him with his thoughts. Which were disconcertingly uninspired.

Robert had mastered a lot of skills in his life, but he wasn't the least bit convinced that *play* could prove useful in any sense. Worse, a small voice inside jeered at him. *You're going to fail at this, too! You can't even* play! Anger boiled up from deep inside, a cloud of undefined, unfocused rage. He broke into a jog, then accelerated into a flat-out run, no longer caring what Zilla wanted to do, or attempting what Wilkinson had not-so-subtly challenged him to do.

It took a few moments for him to notice, but suddenly he realized Zilla was next to him, loping at his side, her tongue flopping. He glanced back and saw she'd abandoned the ball in the middle of the yard, in order to join him.

She'd joined him on her own. Of her own free will.

She'd chosen him.

Robert raised his gaze to the sky, not seeing the low gray clouds for the moisture that had formed in his eyes. His breathing hitched, and he blew out forcefully.

Zilla faltered at the noise, but regained her stride quickly, surging forward to stay with him.

Zilla had chosen him.

He swallowed past a lump in his throat and punched up his pace, arms pumping, feet pounding, trying to outrun something he couldn't name, couldn't define.

Zilla dug in and kept up.

Chapter Thirty-Seven

January

Bᴇɴ sʜᴜᴛ ᴅᴏᴡɴ the chain saw and swiped the sweat from his brow. Silence echoed as the roar of the saw ceased, and scents of newly cut wood mingled with heated oil and gasoline exhaust. His hand came away from his forehead tinged with red. He'd felt the sting from a piece of bark that had ricocheted from a particularly stubborn branch, but didn't think it had drawn blood. *Guess I was wrong.* He rubbed it off on his work jeans, which were full of rips that allowed cold air to wend its way past his knees now that he'd stopped moving.

The bleak winter landscape echoed the starkness of his soul, and he welcomed the cold as a distraction. On second thought, maybe it would serve him better as a penance. Bare trees towered over him in silent accusation at his inability to lift himself out of his funk through the recent holiday season.

He'd tried. Lannis had bought a miniscule tree and decorated it with a string of blinking lights and some gingham ribbons. It hadn't broken the stranglehold of depression that dogged him.

For Christmas, she'd bought him a season pass for the local minor league baseball team. It was a thoughtful gift, and he appreciated it. Ben hoped he'd be a free man and able to enjoy it come spring. On his part, he'd dredged up the energy to go online and buy her a gift certificate for the aviation supply company she favored. It was an unimaginative and far from intimate gift. Lannis had expressed delight anyway, and he'd felt even worse about their first Christmas as a married couple.

His name floated through the trees, a question and summons rolled into the extended, one-syllable word. Lannis's voice. He sighed, and his lips tightened. She was home. He slid his safety glasses up to rest on his head. Perspiration trickled down his forehead, coalesced on his eyebrows, and hung there, suspended.

"Over here," he called. The sound bounced around the three acres of heavily wooded land where he'd been working off frustration, guilt, and a burgeoning sense of fear. He almost couldn't admit to himself that he'd chosen the chore because he might lose the privilege of living and working as he pleased.

Almost. But as hard as he tried, he couldn't escape the reality that had him running scared. A bead of sweat dropped on his cheek, and he absently wiped it away.

He didn't want to think about it.

He didn't want to acknowledge that his life's work, atoning for Danny's mistakes, had landed him squarely in the same place: a special hell reserved for drug addicts. Maybe Ben hadn't made the same choices Danny had, but not knowing how culpable he was for Tawnee's murder shamed him in the same way Danny's choices had.

He'd rather know. As awful as the knowledge might be, it would end the agony of uncertainty.

The investigation had ground to a halt, waiting for lab results to come in, and that fed his anxiety. He had a healthy appreciation for his lawyer's insistence on independent corroboration—or rebuttal—of the state's overworked and understaffed facilities. But no matter who did the analysis, DNA and other forensic testing took time. Besides, once he'd given his statement to Hollis, there was quite simply no one else to interview. The entire gang had gone to ground like the savvy street rats they were.

Lannis appeared, her forest-green winter coat flashing between dormant gray tree trunks as she traversed the path. She caught sight of him and her face lit up. She waved, and Ben felt like a heel as he waved back.

She was the other reason he'd hiked out here. He wanted her so badly he ached. He put his hand over his heart and pressed against his ribs. Who would have known heartache was real, not just poetic license? He was pretty sure it wasn't a heart attack. He didn't exhibit any other symptoms, and his last physical was clean. Besides, the ache only came when she was near, or in the middle of the night when the rest of his body longed for her, too.

But until the questions around his involvement or non-involvement in Tawnee's death were resolved—

She'd reached him and smiled up at him, a ray of sunshine in a long stretch of days that hadn't seen a glimmer of the sun. She rose up on her tiptoes to kiss him, resting her hands on his biceps. At the last moment, he turned his head so her lips brushed his jawline, not his mouth, and he looked past her, unwilling to torture himself with the pain in her eyes.

She stepped back and dropped her hands to her sides. "You're hurt." Her tone was flat.

He shot a glance at her, then swung his gaze back to the deep woods beyond. She'd schooled her features into a carefully neutral expression, but he recognized the ploy for what it was. "It's nothing." He leaned over and hoisted the saw, then kicked the last few pieces of debris to the side. "I'm done for the day." When she didn't move, he nudged her, expecting her to turn and trudge back to the house, but she held steady.

Surprised, he looked at her, and this time her gaze captured his. Her eyes sparked with anger, the bland expression of a moment ago replaced by one of pure mutiny. He stepped back.

"No, Ben." It was her turn to tighten her lips. "Do *not* shut me out again." She stomped her foot, a small, abrupt motion totally at odds with the roundhouse kick he knew she was capable of delivering.

"I'm not shutting you out." His words sounded hollow and false to his own ears, and he knew she wasn't fooled.

She erupted. "You might be done for the day, but I'm done for now. I've been patient and…and…*solicitous*—"

She had been. He'd begun feeling like he was living with Mother Teresa, all understanding and forgiveness, and perversely, it had made him feel all the more the ass, even less deserving of her love.

"—and just damn respectful of your feelings, but I'm done." She wheeled and marched off.

Ben stood rooted to the spot as her words sank in. "Wait," he called, and hitched the tools so he could jog without dropping them. She didn't slow, and he called again, "Lannis, wait up." Instead, she broke into a run. He dropped the chain saw and sprinted after her.

He caught her in short order and grabbed her shoulder, swung her around to face him—and his heart plummeted to his feet. Tears washed her now-reddened cheeks, and she brought up an arm to dash them away. She lifted her chin and glared at him with all the defiance that had captured his heart the first time they'd met. This time he knew how much emotion she hid beneath her show of bravado, though, and another layer of guilt joined the rest.

Her lips trembled, but she shoved his arm away and said, "All the time I was working through *my* problems, you were there for me, Ben, right there at my side. And I was *working*. You're not." A hiccup suspiciously similar to a sob stopped her, but she swallowed and kept on. "You're having a great big pity party for yourself, and no one else is invited."

Was that what she really thought? Ben's hackles rose, and he started to deny her accusation, but she didn't give him the chance.

"You can't have it both ways, Ben. It's a two-way street. We're *married*. That means that when you have rough times, I've got your

back. It doesn't mean you're the only one who gets to be strong."
This time she let him see all the way to her soul, hiding nothing in the
depths of her eyes.

Beneath the anger, he could see pain and disappointment. *God,
the pain…* That was that last thing he wanted, the one thing he'd been
trying to protect her from. And the disappointment—well, that was
the one thing he'd been trying to protect *himself* from. He'd failed on
both counts.

Lannis kept talking, heedless of the toll on his psyche. "I'm
standing by you, Ben, encouraging you to talk about your fears, but
you won't talk. I've taken your lead, let you have the damn space you
think you need, but you're just running away. Sleeping alone. Lying to
your parents." She took a shuddering breath. "The most important
things I learned were honesty and trust. And I learned them from
you." She raked him with her gaze. "Seems you need a remedial
course."

She pivoted and marched away, her breath little white clouds
puffing out and dissipating as she walked through them.

Ben lifted a hand to stop her, but let it sag back to his side.

He didn't know how to do this any better. He knew what he
expected from Mike. His partner had met him at the gym for an
extended sparring bout yesterday, had offered him an opportunity to
beat the crap out of something more tangible than Detective Hollis's
allegations.

He knew how to protect his parents and his sister, Mindy, from
a rerun of Danny's soul-killing last days, at least until Hollis came up
with concrete evidence and charged him. Simple. Pretend it was no
big deal, nothing to lose sleep over. Keep his distance, stay busy. He
knew how to be strong, how to lead, how to survive.

But he didn't know how to *be* with Lannis.

Hell, right now, he didn't even know how to keep breathing.
The farther she walked away from him, the tighter his lungs got. He
sucked in a giant breath just to prove he could, then abandoned the
tools and followed her.

It hurt to admit it, but she was right. He'd shut her out and
failed to take his own damn good advice. *You're not alone. You'll be okay
as long as you don't isolate yourself. Be honest. Trust me, trust in God.*

The crack of the door slamming in the dusk ahead sounded like
a gunshot, and he winced, then picked up his pace.

He scraped his boots against the wire brush built into the
concrete outside the back entrance, but didn't spend much time on
getting them clean, and pushed his way into the house.

"Lannis," he called. She didn't answer. He felt raw, vulnerable, and not a little confused. It made him angry. Anger was good. It beat feeling like a failure any day, so he grabbed on to it and gave voice to it. "Lannis." This time he shouted the word, and stormed through the mud room.

A quick glance proved she wasn't in the kitchen, although he saw she'd pulled fresh vegetables out to begin cooking dinner. One more thing he could have done to make her day easier, since he was on mandated leave. He turned down the hallway, noting the light spilling from the bedroom.

Three more steps brought him to the door…and nearly brought him to his knees. She'd dragged her suitcase out of the closet and was pitching clothes into it, unfolded and without much deliberation.

"What are you doing?" It was a lame question on his part, as it was pretty obvious what she was doing.

She didn't slow, or look at him. "Packing."

Fear blossomed in his gut and spread up his back, down his arms, stealing his breath. Ben tamped it down, or tried, anyway. He swallowed, then inhaled. He didn't think he could keep the panic out of his voice, but he couldn't stay silent. "Where are you going?" It came out more casually than he expected, and gave him enough courage to lean against the door frame.

She shook her head, then shrugged one shoulder. "I don't know." She lifted her gaze to his, and the ache in his heart turned into a twisting, sharp pain. "It's tearing me apart, the wall you've built. If you can't let me share the burden, if the only way you can cope is to push me away, then I need to take care of myself, remove myself from a toxic situation."

She flipped the suitcase closed, zipped it, and picked it up. She sent him a pointed look. "Excuse me, please."

"Don't…" He straightened, suddenly feeling naked and exposed.

Pain crossed her features, but she shook her head again and stopped the trembling of her lips by flattening them into a determined line. She stepped toward him, and he had a wild impulse to rip the suitcase out of her hands, throw it in the corner, stop her, stop her somehow, stop her any way he could—

"No. Don't go." His voice was guttural, and he blocked the doorway.

"Ben, don't do this." Lannis's voice shook just a little, and she tensed, drawing in on herself the way she did when—

Aw, shit! When she felt threatened, when her rape memories got stirred up. Ben felt the blood drain from his face and he stepped back. Put his hands out, palms up.

Her hands were trembling and she shoved them in her pockets to camouflage it, but she looked him dead in the eye. "You need help, Ben. Talk to somebody. A priest, a psychiatrist, whatever. I don't care. Just get the help you need."

His anger flared. "I don't need a shrink."

She stood her ground, silent and—*damn it*—strong in spite of her fear, waiting. Blood rushed back into his face as he recognized the truth in her assessment.

He moved aside.

Let her pass, which she did without touching him.

And put his fist through a wall as the taillights of her Prius flickered through the trees and diminished to nothingness.

~

LANNIS PULLED OFF the interstate into a rest area and coasted to a stop in a parking slot, but didn't shut down her car. Half a dozen vehicles clustered near the building, including a couple of semis, and she purposely waited until she'd accounted for all the drivers before she decided to get out. The well-lit space should have made her feel secure, but walking away from Ben had left her so shaken that her old habits had surged to the fore again.

It didn't help that he'd frightened her, though she knew it had been unintentional. She drew a deep, shuddering breath, turned the car off, and opened the door. She stood, glancing around, her senses on high alert. No threat, she thought, and gave herself a mental kick. *Guess I'll never get over that part.*

A slight smile softened the muscles of her face as she forgave herself the sentiment. She couldn't control the feeling, but she didn't have to act on it. A second inspection of the lot revealed a whole lot of "normal," and Lannis secured the car and strode to the restrooms. A chilly breeze lifted her hair and raised goose bumps on her arms, so she picked up her pace.

After leaving the house, leaving Ben, she'd driven aimlessly for a couple of hours. She rejected the idea of a motel outright, not able to countenance the impersonal isolation. She'd considered calling Maggie, but didn't want to admit she and Ben were at odds. It offended Lannis's deep-seated sense of privacy—although if Ben decided to open up to Mike, that would be a good thing.

She entered the restroom and splashed her face, welcoming the icy water. It soothed her gritty eyes, exhausted from alternately crying and trying to hold the tears back. She sighed, trying to keep from obsessing over Ben, and over whether she'd made a mistake by leaving. Or over where she belonged at the moment, which qualified as a big, fat oxymoron, as her entire problem was that she didn't belong anywhere right now. And yet…

Somehow she'd gravitated to the road home. I-71 toward Cincinnati, then points beyond. Her childhood home, Mom, Lynette, and all the comfort family could generate—even if Millie continued to maintain her silence.

Her lips firmed with resolve. *That* particular issue had just come to a head, and Lannis hadn't even seen it coming. Lannis could bear temporary discomfort in her relationship with Ben or with her mother, but both of them… She'd let Millie take the lead since the trial, while keeping the lines of communication open. However, tonight her patience had come to an abrupt end. As she left the house, she'd detoured into the den to grab her flight bag, and snagged her copy of the court transcript. She'd had no firm plan at the time, but stuffed it in her flight bag anyway.

Her subconscious must have percolated as she drove—hence the familiar rest area—and about ten minutes ago had burbled up a fully realized course of action. The time had come to confront her mother. And restore the frayed mother-daughter bond. She hoped, anyway.

Lannis stopped at the vending machine for a soda and peanuts, then strode to her car, checked the backseat to make sure no one lurked in the darkness there, and slid into the driver's seat. She merged into traffic and pulled out her cell phone. A glance told her she hadn't missed a call from Ben, which she knew. She didn't allow the edge of disappointment to distract her. She suspected there would be plenty more disappointment in her near future, but she was banking on the "good coming out of bad" school of thought. The other outcome didn't bear contemplating.

So she didn't. She hit speed dial, waited for a response, and said, "Hi, Mom. I'm coming home for a visit."

~

It was well after midnight when she parked in the driveway she'd ridden her tricycle on as a child. A familiar pang of loss shimmered through her. *Ah, Daddy, why'd you have to die so young?* Tears stung the backs of her eyelids, and she blinked them away. The engine ticked softly as it cooled. A fortifying breath later, Lannis stretched and grabbed her overnight bag. Millie had left the porch light on, and it cast a pale glow over the bare branches of the forsythia hedge. Frost sparkled on the brick walkway as she climbed out and latched the car door softly.

"Lannie?"

She swung around, startled, and saw Millie framed in the doorway, clutching the top of a green plush robe to her throat.

"I thought you'd be asleep." She hefted her bag. "Don't you work in the morning?" Millie's normal routine would have her rising a mere four hours from now.

Her mother pushed the storm door open a bit farther as Lannis approached. "I have some comp time coming and I decided to use it, so I'm free. Besides, I couldn't sleep, knowing you were on the road."

Lannis stomped her feet on the welcome mat, her breath soft puffs of white in the chilly air. She stepped inside, warmth enveloping her as Millie closed the door. She dropped her bag, ready to shed her coat, when Millie surprised her a second time by wrapping her arms around Lannis. She stiffened in the unexpected embrace for a heartbeat, then returned it. Tension deep within her eased as Lannis melted into her mother's arms.

I missed you, Mom—and I've needed this so badly for so long. Her heart swelled with emotion as Millie patted her shoulders and hugged her close.

"Something's wrong between you and Ben," Millie murmured, "for you to show up on such short notice."

Lannis's breathing hitched. When she could speak, the words came out in a strangled rush. "No—well, yes, sort of…" She took a deep breath and disentangled herself from the embrace. She hadn't anticipated talking about this until morning, at least, and scrambled for a way to explain without sullying Ben's image in Millie's estimation.

Finally she shrugged. "It's a rough patch, but we'll be fine." Her voice wobbled just a little on the last word, and Millie searched her eyes for a moment.

"You're tired." Millie turned and headed up the stairs. "Get some rest and we'll talk in the morning." She paused in front of the room that had been Lannis's and grasped her hand, squeezed it. "Sweet dreams."

Lannis's throat tightened and she nodded, too overcome with emotion and fatigue to speak. She closed the door, and memories of her childhood flooded her. Along with memories of the night Ben had pulled her out of a nightmare—was it just a year ago?—when she'd reestablished connections with her family.

Sweet dreams. A choked laugh made its way past her lips. The most she hoped for was that nightmares didn't haunt her tonight. She felt too drained, too alone, too vulnerable to deal with one if it chose to roar into her psyche, and she suddenly missed Ben with an ache that had her pressing her fist to her breastbone. Lannis took a deep breath, and the ache eased.

She sent a silent prayer for him heavenward, then dropped her arm to her side and pulled her sleepwear from the bag. She changed quickly, hung her clothes over the back of the chair, and collapsed into bed.

~

A phone rang, insistent but muted, and dragged Lannis from a deep sleep. She heard the soft murmur of a woman's voice down the hall and scrubbed at her eyes, confused. *Who's here?* She reached for Ben but encountered a wall instead, and the sharp pain in her knuckles drove her the rest of the way into consciousness. "Ouch," she muttered, and shook her hand.

Recognition clicked into place. *Not home.* Yes, home. Just her other one. She propped up on an elbow to peer at the clock, which wasn't digital so she couldn't read it. The woman's voice—*Mom*—rose, then went silent, and Lannis gave up on wondering what time it was.

Still dark, and she was still tired. Didn't much matter what the numbers on the dial said. She threw the covers back and padded down the hall. "Is everything okay?" She rapped softly on the door. "Who called?"

The door swung open, flooding the hall with light. "It's Lynnie! She's gone into labor!" Millie pivoted and almost ran to the closet. "I told Rich we'd meet up with them at the hospital."

Lannis, left briefly speechless, found her voice. "But…she's not due for another—"

"Five weeks." Millie tossed slacks and a blouse out of the closet, and Lannis snagged them out of the air by reflex.

Lannis's breath caught. She didn't know much about preemies except for the really sick ones she helped transport. Most of those were in the twenty- to thirty-week gestational range. "Does Lynnie have risk factors?"

Millie reappeared from the closet, straightening her bra straps with businesslike efficiency. "No." She flashed a glance at Lannis. "Do you want to come with me?"

"Of course!" Lannis handed Millie's clothes to her. "I'll be ready in a couple of minutes." Heart in her throat, Lannis returned to her room and jerked her jeans up, shoved arms into her shirt, feet into sneakers, and tore down the stairs, beating Millie by seconds.

They threw themselves into Lannis's car and made the drive in tense silence. Millie's anxiety showed in her posture, as if she could make the Prius go faster by leaning forward. Lannis glanced at her once or twice, grateful she had the task of driving to keep her focused.

Rich met them in the waiting area of the labor and delivery suites, granting Millie a quick hug and Lannis an indecipherable look. He addressed his mother-in-law. "She's dilated to four, and if they can stop labor, she'll be on bed rest. The baby's fine, no distress."

Lannis spoke up. "Where's Carly?"

He slanted his gaze at her and grimaced. "Neighbors. We just put this plan in place a few days ago. Thought we had time."

"Mr. Foley?" A nurse stood at the door to the closed-off unit. "You can come on back."

Rich said, "I'll keep you updated, and tell Lynnie you're both here. She'll appreciate the support." He strode through the doors, which closed softly on their hydraulic mechanism, the electronic lock falling into place with a *snick*.

Lannis let her breath whoosh out. At least Rich hadn't been overtly hostile. Maybe Ben's intervention had borne fruit. Of course, Rich had taken his lack of job security by the horns and found a new one with a much better outlook—at least that's what Lynette had said in an e-mail shortly after her unplanned trip to Louisville. And he'd kept up with the counseling Ben had badgered him into.

Now, if Ben would only take his own advice...

"You want some coffee, Mom?" The thought of coffee made her own stomach heave in rebellion, but it looked like they would be here for a bit, and she needed something to keep her occupied. She glanced at Millie, then did a double take.

Distress deepened worry lines into creases on her mother's face, dark circles beneath Millie's eyes making her look as though she'd been battered.

"Oh, Mom." Lannis pulled her into her arms. Millie let her head drop onto Lannis's shoulder. They stood, linked for a moment while Millie fought to regain her composure, then straightened.

"They'll be okay," Lannis said, though she knew she couldn't predict or promise the outcome. But it seemed the right thing to say at the moment, a thread of hope for both of them to latch on to.

Millie dipped her head in agreement and said, "I worry so much about Lynnie." She shot a glance at Lannis. "You've always been the strong one, able to handle everything life throws at you, but Lynnie…she doesn't have the steel in her spine to weather rough times."

I've always been the strong *one?* Lannis blinked. "Not hardly."

She clamped her lips together before she said something she'd regret. Millie's expression sharpened, and Lannis hastened to add, "Lynnie's way stronger than you think." She knew Lynette hadn't told Millie about the problem with Rich, and she wasn't about to betray her sister's confidence. The couple needed time and space to work through their problems, and Millie's awareness would only muddy the waters.

Her lips lifted in a humorless smile. "Besides, in high winds, flexible trees bend instead of break."

Millie considered that, then brushed tears from her cheeks and sniffed. "Thank you, Lannie. I'm not used to leaning on anyone. Not since your Dad…"

"I know," Lannis murmured. "Me, too." She sent her mom a wry smile. "Guess we have that in common, don't we?"

Millie managed a laugh. "Yes, that along with our stubbornness."

Lannis's smile died. *Stubbornness that drove us apart for no apparent reason.* Everyone has a reason for what they do, a small voice deep within insisted. Startled, Lannis stepped back and considered Millie.

"Mom——" She almost put words to the thought, then hesitated. This was an emotional, intense moment, and neither of them had had enough sleep. Asking could backfire, and in a big way, but then again, maybe the only way to repair their relationship was to approach when the walls were down.

Millie looked at her expectantly, and Lannis, for better or worse, made her decision. "Is there a reason that you were so upset over the trial?"

Millie's expression clouded over. Lannis plowed on, fearful she'd close up and refuse to speak. "I just have to think there was more to it than thinking I had morning-after regrets, or intentionally set someone up in order to harm them. That's not the person you raised me to be." Even though she tried, she couldn't keep the twinge of hurt from her voice.

Her mother tightened her lips until they went white, her expression shuttered. Pain showed in her eyes. And pieces of a puzzle slid into place, with methodical, unhurried rhythm, revealing a truth far different from what Lannis ever imagined. *Of course.* It wasn't about her at all. It was about someone else, someone Millie loved. Someone…falsely accused?

Compassion blossomed in Lannis's heart. "That's what it is, isn't it?" she said, grasping her mother's shoulders in a tender embrace. "Who, Mom? Was it Dad?" Her heart sank at the thought of her gentle, loving father enduring that kind of attack. She couldn't believe that of him, and her mind shied away from the concept even as it formed.

Millie's eyes filled with tears, and she brought both hands up to cover her mouth. She shook her head, and Lannis said, "No, it wasn't Dad? Or *no*, I'm totally off base?" But Lannis knew beyond a shadow of a doubt that she'd figured it out. "Who?"

"E-Ed." The name tore from Millie's throat and her expression turned horrified, as though she hadn't meant for it to escape.

Lannis rocked back on her heels. "Uncle *Ed?*" She couldn't believe that of her mother's brother any more than she could believe it about her dad. "Oh God, no!"

Millie's tears welled up and overflowed, and she nodded. "Y-yes, when he was in college. It nearly ruined him, and it *did* ruin his reputation." Her voice turned bitter. "The tart moved on after her charges were proven false, but the damage was done. That's why he moved to California. For a new start where no one knew him." She skewered Lannis with her gaze. "She was like a black widow spider, searching out young men to accuse and drag through the sewer—and extort money from, legally, in civil law suits once the criminal investigations fell through."

Lannis's breath sounded harsh to her ears, and she choked out, "Did he pay her off?"

Millie's eyes glinted. "No, he refused, pushed back, came up with enough evidence in his favor to exonerate himself. Used up his college fund to finance a private investigator and the lawyer." She lifted her chin. "Eventually, they collected enough evidence to take *her* to trial." Millie shook her head. "But she batted her eyes and wiggled her hips at the men in the jury…and they acquitted her."

"Oh, Mom." Lannis sighed. "I'm so sorry. That's awful." She opened her arms in silent invitation to Millie. "It's a sticky wicket, no matter how it goes down. But that's not what happened with me."

She paused, then offered, "If you ever want to read it, I have the transcript."

After a long moment, Millie accepted Lannis's embrace but said nothing.

And Lannis let her pain go, relieved to understand the roots of her mother's silence over the past several months.

How true, the old adage of not judging someone until you'd walked a mile in their shoes.

Lannis's heart broke for Uncle Ed, but she was glad she and Millie were back on a path toward each other. She sighed. Leaving Ben to seek his own healing had netted Lannis healing with her mother, and hopefully with Rich. She sent another quick prayer heavenward for Lynette and the baby.

But how long until Ben found himself again?

Her arms tightened around Millie, who returned the hug, unaware of Lannis's inner turmoil.

The door to the delivery room swished open and she and Millie sprang apart, both turning to the door. Rich stood silhouetted in the square of soft light. "They can't stop the labor. The baby's on its way."

Chapter Thirty-Eight

Bᴇɴ ʜᴀᴅ ʟɪᴠᴇᴅ in this house for twelve years, most of them alone. He'd never felt lonely, though, until tonight. After the divorce, he'd felt only relief at Deb's absence. During the intervening years, the house had been a refuge from work, but nothing more. Comfortable enough in his own skin, he'd come and gone with no sense of incompleteness or loss.

But since Lannis had driven away, the sense of loss staggered him as surely as a solid hit to his solar plexus would have. *Where did she go?* It rattled him that he didn't have a clue. Well, that wasn't entirely true, but the list was as short as it was nebulous. Mike and Maggie's? He hoped she'd gone there, but he doubted it. She was far too private, wouldn't want to deal with the inevitable questions. Home to Millie, or Lynette and Rich? Maybe, but those were hard relationships for her right now, too. Or a hotel? His heart broke anew at the thought. He'd had enough of that himself during the weeks he'd been undercover, and identified with the sense of disconnect a hotel could foster. His jaw tightened. He didn't want that for her.

He wanted to get in his car and follow her. If she'd listen, he'd tell her he'd get his act together, that he'd talk to someone…tomorrow. He wanted her home, here, with him. Now. But he felt too volatile and couldn't risk being with her until he'd taken some steps to protect her from his temper. He ducked his head, wishing he could avoid the obvious. *Guess I'm no better than Rich.* He shook the thought off before it veered into raping and murdering while under the influence of illegal drugs.

Besides, chasing after her would be futile, and he knew it. He cringed at her assessment, but hell, she was right. Pushing her away had seemed like a good plan at the time, but it had backfired. He prowled the empty rooms, wearing a path of impatient footsteps as rage at his helplessness grew. Too dark to finish the chain-sawing job, too late to call Mike—not that Ben could come up with words to express his terror at the gaping hole in his future—and he had no patience for his current shop project. In fact, he felt more like throwing the pieces against the wall, but it had taken him three months to track down the parts from a classic car dealer in California.

He snorted, and took small consolation in the fact that he'd retained enough sanity to make that decision. His knuckles ached from his lapse in control after Lannis left, and he massaged them gingerly, wincing when he touched a particularly tender spot. He supposed he should be glad he hadn't broken a bone, but the reality was that the pain kept him grounded.

Abruptly, the house seemed too limiting, so he grabbed his coat, heading for the garage. He didn't have a plan or a destination, just his car and cell phone, and until he could tolerate the silence of the house, he'd take the coward's way out.

By three a.m., he'd discovered the streets of Louisville offered no respite from the sense of imprisonment, a silent but damning confirmation that the problem resided entirely within him. No surprise there. He'd flipped his cell phone open and selected Lannis's number so many times he'd lost track, his thumb hovering over the SEND button, then flipping it closed without completing the call. He'd pulled over three times and started to text her, but he didn't have words either way. He shoved a hand through his hair, then parked downtown and struck out for the Second Street Bridge. The bridge had a pedestrian walkway, and spanned the Ohio River not far from where the crooked cops had ordered his body to be disposed of a year and a half ago.

The night he met Lannis. The night she'd saved his life, both unwillingly and unwittingly. He hadn't intended to come here, but maybe it was fitting. If he couldn't escape his failures, perhaps the memories would clear his mind. Cold wind bit the exposed skin of his face and tugged at his ball cap. He clamped a hand on its bill and settled it more firmly on his head.

Patches of black ice slowed him as he hiked up the incline, and wind eddied, buffeting him from all directions. He finally gave up on his ball cap and tucked it into a pocket. When he reached the middle of the span, he stopped and faced upriver, the wind bringing tears to his eyes and whipping his hair to and fro. Stars twinkled above, and the reflection of the city's lights glittered in the ebony river.

He sucked in a deep breath and grasped the railing with his bare hands. No traffic rumbled across the bridge at this time of night, and for a moment, he entertained the illusion that he was the only person left in an abandoned city and all his troubles had been stripped away in the wind. A siren wailed in the distance, shattering the illusion.

A homeless guy headed up the bridge on the other side of the roadway. Ben's senses sharpened and he eyed the shabbily dressed man, assessing him out of habit. A little unsteady on his pins and probably armed with a small knife, but too involved in a conversation with unseen companions to focus much on reality. Ben dismissed him as a potential threat and relaxed. Even so, he kept track of the guy's progress without conscious thought.

He sighed. His failure to correctly assess his adversaries had landed him in both of his bad situations—and Lannis ended up tangled in the fallout both times. With that depressing realization, Ben turned slightly in order to keep a better eye on the dude, who had nearly reached the center of the bridge also, but on the downriver side.

Once the DNA evidence came back—hell, he couldn't get his mind around anything beyond that, but he forced himself, anyway. If the DNA cleared him from involvement in Tawnee's death, maybe it was time for him to hang up his undercover job. He didn't know of anyone who'd had this much bad luck and survived, much less kept at it. He didn't like the desk job side of his work, but he did want to live long enough to have a family with Lannis.

Which brought him full circle. Back to her.

She'd distracted him on this op, and he could lay none of it at her feet. Undemanding, unquestioning, strong, independent when she needed to be. In his face when she needed to be. Ben squirmed a little at last evening's confrontation. She was right on so many levels. He couldn't ask for a better life partner, and it was past time he stopped automatically trying to control everything about their relationship. He'd had to at first, to save both of them, and later, he'd stepped back while she did the hard work of recovery.

But he hadn't realized how thoroughly he'd slipped back into a role of managing her emotions in order to keep his in line. He tried to tell himself his motives were pure, but the notion rang hollow. She didn't need protecting, and the only person who'd benefited had been him.

Something about the homeless guy caught his attention, and Ben straightened. He'd slung one leg up to the railing and was struggling to get the rest of his body up. Was he…? Yes, the idiot was climbing the railing. "Hey!" Ben shouted, and charged across the empty traffic lanes. "Hey, what are you doing?"

The man paid him as much mind as he had up until now, which was none at all, and continued his struggle. He'd managed to get one arm around the rail and had only to shift his center of gravity in order to succeed in vaulting himself into the river. Horrified, Ben wondered if he could cover the four or five yards between them in time. The only thing in his favor was the guy's inebriated state, and Ben used it to his advantage. He shouted again. "Stop! Police!"

Ben launched from a couple of yards away and tackled him, grabbing the guy's coat with one hand and wrapping his arm around his waist with the other. At the last moment he shifted his trajectory to send his momentum downward, on the solid side of the railing.

The impact drove his breath away, and he hoped it did the same to the other man. For a moment Ben thought he'd broken the guy's grip on the rail, but he was stronger than he looked and hauled both of them higher on the rail.

Ben caught a dizzying glimpse of a hundred and fifty feet of nothing, with inky water beyond. *Jesus…* Everything about his life became crystal clear in that moment.

Lannis's role as equal in their relationship. She'd grown far beyond needing his mentorship.

His need to control versus trusting God the way he professed he did.

Perhaps most important, Ben had foisted the burden of Danny's failures and his own potential involvement in Tawnee's death upon himself. No one else, including God, expected him to carry those responsibilities on his own shoulders.

Adrenaline shot through his system and he let his weight sag back onto the safe side, then let go of the guy's coat to deliver a lightning-fast jab to his head. That did the trick. The man's grip weakened, then broke. They crashed to the concrete deck and rolled. Ben made sure he came up on top and panted, "Hey, take it easy, buddy—let's think about this for a minute, okay?"

The guy was much younger than Ben had assumed, close to his age, and maybe not so homeless. His well-worn desert camouflage jacket offered little protection from the wind, but wasn't military surplus. The name tape read HOWARD, rank CAPTAIN, US ARMY. The guy stared up at Ben with eyes that were astonishingly aware, and full of enough anguish to drive any man to insanity.

"Let me go—I need to die, I need to stop hurting Anna," he gasped. "She'll be better off when I'm gone."

Maybe Ben had made an erroneous conclusion when he'd assumed the guy was conferring with nonexistent companions on his way up the bridge. Maybe he'd just been thinking out loud. "No, she won't. Captain Howard. Sir." Ben panted with the exertion of trying to contain the man, and his muscles tensed, now knowing he was grappling with a trained soldier. "You need to hang on, keep trying. Don't give up." Ben had seen enough at the soup kitchen where he volunteered to know every man there had a story. Addiction, substance abuse, mental illness, PTSD, all driven by pain no different than Ben's.

Story or not, Ben wasn't about to let his guard down. A good plan, because Howard lunged upward with an attempt at a head butt. Ben deflected it and rolled, twisting the guy's arm up behind him in a lightning move perfected in hours of training and street fights. He yanked his belt from its loops and secured Captain Howard's hands behind him. Sweating, Ben finally sat up enough to dig his cell phone out, keeping his knee squarely in Howard's back. Speed dial got him Louisville Metro Police.

"Second Street Bridge, I got a jumper in custody." By the time the call ended, the flashing lights of a patrol unit turned up the street. When the officer arrived, Ben was more than ready to relinquish responsibility for the guy. The cop got out of his car and spared only a glance for the trussed-up veteran before turning his attention on Ben.

"Aren't you—"

To his mortification, his picture had been liberally splashed over the local news channels, as well as the paper. A spurt of irritation mixed with embarrassment shot through Ben, and his answer was curt. "Yeah."

The cop shrugged. "Hope it turns out well for you." He looked down at Howard, and addressed him. "Buddy, you're lucky this guy happened to be here."

"No, I'm not," Howard ground out.

"You'll probably think differently after you sleep it off. Besides, nothing's so bad you can't get through it. Just ask your knight in shining armor."

Ben rolled his eyes and edged away, eager to be gone before the inevitable reporter showed up. He didn't need any more publicity.

It wasn't until he'd returned to his car that he realized everything he'd said to the guy was advice he needed to take for himself. *Hang on. Keep trying. Don't give up.* And that a whole string of events had placed him on the bridge at that critical moment—notably the stinking mess with Tawnee.

In a backhanded way, maybe he'd just done penance for his real—or perceived—guilt over her death. A life lost, a life saved.

He took a deep breath and knew where he needed to go next. Saint Martin's was open all night, and a priest came in at six a.m. to hear confessions. As he slid into his car, his cell phone trilled. He dug it out, glanced at it, and his heart lifted. *Lannis.*

He flipped it open. "Darlin'," he said, his heart full and every emotion he'd felt over the past eight hours in his voice.

"Ben?"

"Yeah." He infused as much warmth as he could muster into the word.

"I'm at the hospital in Dover. Lynnie's having her baby early." She hesitated, then said, "I know you're not supposed to leave the state, but do you think you can get permission and come?"

He smiled for the first time in weeks. "I'll be there. You can count on me." He fired up the Mustang. "And, Lannis? I'm going to get the help you want me to get." He couldn't promise anything, but for the first time in a couple of months he believed what he said next. "We're going to be okay. No matter what happens."

Chapter Thirty-Nine

THE GUNSHOT RANG OUT, a sharp *crack* in the cold air, and even expecting it, knowing it was a blank, Robert flinched. Zilla surged against the leash, jerking his arms with an astonishing display of strength for a sixty-pound animal. He'd tensed his arm muscles in anticipation, but his shoulders smarted, and a brief thought about rotator cuff injury flitted through his mind. Wrestling her back to his side took all his strength and the thought slid right on out of his consciousness.

"Heel, Zilla," he commanded in a voice that belied his churning anxiety. If she didn't master gun training, she'd wash out of the police dog portion of the program, which narrowed her options. Considerably.

An icy shiver of fear crawled up his spine. He'd never failed at anything before—unless he counted the trial that put him here, but he viewed that as a cruel trick, not a failure. But he couldn't call the current situation anything except a dangerously uncomfortable flirtation with that concept.

Only it was more than a concept. It was a reality that had consequences. He knew where he would go if he failed Zilla. Back to the general population. The prospect filled him with dread, especially now that he'd had a taste of humane treatment.

Speaking of which, what would happen to *her*? He shuddered, his mind picturing what happened to unwanted dogs. He didn't want that for her, didn't want her to be discarded, put down because he hadn't tried hard enough.

Problem was, he was trying.

He shook off the chill of fear and crouched next to Zilla, now that she'd calmed herself enough to stand at his side. Trembling from nose to tail, but standing. "Good girl." He reassured her with a pat on the head and she leaned into his palm, a soft whimper escaping as she did. She shifted her head and gazed into his eyes with her mismatched pair. Funny, but the oddness didn't bother him anymore. "It's okay, Zilla. We'll try again. The noise won't hurt you." His effort was futile, and so far, fruitless, and he really had to wonder if he was wasting his breath, trying to rationalize with an animal. But she was so intuitive, he sometimes forgot she couldn't understand abstract concepts.

Wilkinson ambled over, and Robert gave Zilla a final pat, then stood. He kept his expression neutral, though his heart began to thud in uneasy anticipation of Wilkinson's appraisal of both his and Zilla's performance.

"What do you think?" Wilkinson gave Zilla a scratch behind her ear.

"Me?" Robert looked around in case someone else had approached and the trainer wasn't talking to him.

The guy's lips twitched, like he was trying not to smile. "Yes, you."

"Uh…" He'd be damned if he would verbalize the laundry list of shortcomings they'd both exhibited in the past few days. He rolled his shoulders and decided to go with the obvious. "She doesn't seem to be getting any better with the guns."

"What do you suggest?" Wilkinson glanced at him, then shifted to study the tree line beyond the wall, his manner relaxed and unhurried.

Was the trainer toying with him? He'd always been up front and seemed trustworthy, but Robert expected ulterior motives and therefore searched for them. There was nothing more effective in a power play than to appear harmless, then go for the kill when the prey had dropped its guard. He would know.

And if Zilla was out of the program, so was he. He glanced at the foreboding wall of the main prison. The fear he'd suppressed a few minutes ago breached his tenuous control. He tightened his grip on Zilla's leash and tugged her closer to him. "D-don't kick her out—I'll keep working with her. Extra. At night." Once started, he couldn't seem to stop the fire hose of words. "We'll get through this. Can you give her an extension? Or an exemption, or…whatever?" He swallowed his pride and added, "Please."

Wilkinson swung his gaze back, and Robert was stunned to see surprise written all over the man's face.

"We're not going to kick her out, Davis." He grinned, still loose limbed and amiable. "You, however…"

What was likely meant as a good-natured taunt struck Robert to the core. He covered his confusion by bending to adjust Zilla's collar.

Apparently unaware of the specter of expulsion lurking in Robert's eyes, Wilkinson continued. "Nah, we'll just find a different avenue of service for her. Not all dogs can handle police work."

Robert's breath eased out, and he closed his eyes for a moment. *Reprieve...*

"Service dog for epilepsy alert or the blind, companion for people with psychiatric issues, a nursing home dog." Wilkinson's voice drifted over his shoulders, and Robert finally regained his composure.

"You've been together for what, almost two months now? What's your recommendation?"

Robert straightened. No one had asked his recommendation for something that mattered since before his arrest last April. He'd viewed his work with other inmates and their legal woes as a diversion. A hobby. He hadn't missed it a bit since he'd been reassigned here, with Zilla. This question mattered. A lot.

Because Zilla mattered.

Wilkinson paused for a moment, then prodded. "What are her strengths?"

The focus of Robert's thoughts shifted from failure to potential, like a prism had splintered ordinary light into a rainbow of unexpected possibilities. "Well," he said, caution still overriding hope, "she responds to my moods without me saying anything, and she's smart." He glanced at Wilkinson to gauge his response, and saw the other man was nodding and weighing his words. Robert couldn't help adding, "Real smart. I've watched the other dogs struggle with learning some of the commands, or impulse control in maintaining their focus, but Zilla doesn't have any problems with that. But she is fearful of loud noises, and she's scared of the dark."

"I'm not surprised." Wilkinson looked down at her. "She was treated pretty badly, mostly by a big man." He glanced at Robert, a rueful expression on his face. "That's why I doubted whether she'd be able to overcome her history and develop a bond. You've done a good job."

Robert felt his face heat. This man's opinion meant as much to him as graduating from college or law school, or passing the New Jersey bar exam, or getting his pilot license had.

He'd never earned the words "good job" for an accomplishment that benefited someone other than himself.

"Thank you," he managed. Wilkinson wasn't going to kick either one of them out. The tightness in his gut unfurled at the realization.

"I'll contact some of the other service dog organizations and see if we can't find her a good fit." Wilkinson glanced around and focused on another animal and inmate pair. "Hey, Manuel, paciencia, hombre. Esta es la escuela por el perrón, y es muy difícil." *Manuel, patience, man. This is school for the dog, and is very difficult.* He trotted toward them, all semblance of loose-limbed relaxation gone.

The fizz of goodwill stayed with Robert for the rest of the afternoon, and he even entered his cell with a modicum of anticipation, although he had no idea what he might be anticipating. Zilla ate with enthusiasm, then padded over to him for the evening grooming ritual. The routine had turned into an oasis of calm for both of them, and he settled into brushing her coat, now glossy and smooth. As usual, she leaned into him, an expression of pure doggy bliss in her eyes.

Robert allowed his mind to go blank, something he didn't think he'd ever done before getting this cell, with Zilla. He sure as hell hadn't had the luxury growing up, always on alert for danger. Once he'd conquered danger, it seemed he manufactured it, like his life couldn't be complete without it.

Hence, the adrenaline rush of defending criminals in court, the chess game of getting away with murder, at least vicariously. And the not-so-vicarious thrill of exerting his power through rape.

His thoughts drifted to his legal woes. The statute of limitations on the Illinois case had run out, but the victim was pursuing a civil case. He'd probably lose, because she didn't have to prove her allegation beyond a reasonable doubt in civil court. However, Robert was now officially bankrupt, so she wouldn't collect. He thought it was stupid to spend money on a lawsuit; if he were her lawyer, he'd advise against it. What was the point? But maybe it was worth it to her to get his guilt in writing.

Pennsylvania, on the other hand, hung like an anvil over his head. If convicted there, the best he could hope for was that his incarceration in Kentucky would count toward their penalty.

No matter what happened, he'd be in prison for a long time. Looking that far into the future—heck, just looking ahead for the next seven and half years made him want to puke. The only way to survive it all was to stick with the present moment.

Which brought him back to the task at hand. He found a burr buried deep in the fur of Zilla's armpit, and wondered how he'd missed it. It was tightly caught in the soft hair, and he began working at it. She yelped and he slowed down, taking more care to be gentle. "Sorry, girl." It occurred to him that he'd never touched another living being so much, nor had he cared how they might feel.

Well, that ought to make Ms. Connor happy. He was becoming downright insightful about his behavior and motivations. He snorted and Zilla jerked away, then let loose a half yowl, half snarl. Her sharp teeth snapped at his arm, a deliberate miss on her part.

Robert quickly dropped his hand, ready to abandon the effort to remove the burr if he needed to, and opened his mouth to soothe her—but a series of muffled, sharp retorts drew his attention and he swiveled toward his window. Zilla crouched and belly crawled under his bed, now whimpering.

He stood and did a pull-up on the ledge of the window, knowing the narrow pane was frosted, but trying to see through it anyway. A siren broke the quiet of the evening, and the loudspeaker crackled to life in the hallway.

"Lockdown procedures are now in place." The electronic bolt slid tight with a *snick*, barely audible over the racket of the siren and loudspeaker. "Report to the access door when ordered for inmate count."

Zilla began to howl, along with all the other dogs in the unit. Robert wanted to cover his own ears against the din, too, but he wanted to see what was going on more. He craned his neck and saw a reddish-orange glow flickering in the main prison. The perimeter lights, always on, seemed to be doubly bright, and the *pop-pop* of what he now recognized as gunfire continued in uneven bursts.

His heart began to race, and he dropped lightly to the floor at the same time a guard slammed the square face-level access door open. "Davis," the guy barked. "Over here. Now."

Robert took the three steps necessary and positioned himself at the center of the barred opening. "What's going on?"

The guard slammed the panel closed without answering, and Robert's heart thudded into triple-time. It sounded like a riot in the main prison, and it looked like a fire.

Fear caught him, closed his throat as surely as a pair of hands strangling him. His haven, if they didn't open the door, would be a death chamber—and while he knew some of his victims would celebrate his fiery demise, he sure as hell didn't want to go that way.

"Hey," he shouted. "Hey, it's a fire! Let me out!" He beat his fists on the metal, which didn't even rattle and probably bruised his hands, but terror blocked all sensation. He could hear other inmates shouting and pleading, but the cacophony of the siren, now joined by the wail of fire engines from the outside, drowned out the individual words.

He whirled, panic filling him. His gaze raked the room. There was no way out, except through the electronically locked door, and now another thought chilled him. What if the electronic system failed? He threw himself at the metal, battering it with his shoulder, his howls of pain mixing with Zilla's howls of fear until he couldn't tell them apart.

After the third attempt, he clutched his shoulder and crumpled halfway to the floor. The lights flickered and went out. He could smell smoke now, and he couldn't tell if it was his imagination or real, but he thought the air felt hotter. A bead of sweat trickled down the side of his face, and then suddenly, unexpectedly, the locking mechanism clicked open. He scrambled to his feet and shoved at the door, his heart in his throat.

It swung open and revealed an eerie scene, dim emergency lights wavering as smoke wafted through the hall.

"That way!" A guard gestured with his gun, his face half-hidden in the crook of his arm. Robert staggered out and ran down the hallway, instinct screaming at him to get to safety.

Zilla!

The primal drive to survive carried him forward another step or two, but…

Zilla! Scared of the dark, scared of loud noises. He skidded to a stop, already knowing what he'd only allowed himself to suspect. She wasn't at his side. She was probably still under his bed.

She needed him.

Guards, inmates, and dogs surged past him, a river intent on escaping the flames, the smoke.

He cursed his decision, but wheeled and fought his way through the crowd. One of the guards grabbed him and tried to turn him, but he flung the guy away.

"Come on! Get out!" The guard shouted at him, then waved his weapon. "I'll shoot!"

Robert ignored him and sprinted back toward his cell. But the smoke had thickened and he couldn't tell which doorway was his.

He coughed, then coughed again. Lifted his head and rasped, "Zilla! Zilla!"

And dove into the smoky inferno.

~

SIRENS SPLIT THE NIGHT, and Robert clutched a terrified Zilla closer to his chest. Her struggles tested his ability to contain her without squeezing out what little air she had left in her lungs. Or his. He coughed, an extended, wheezing exhale that left him near collapse.

He must have made a wrong turn somewhere. The darkness was confounding, with surreal orange flickers along the ceiling that he made sure to keep behind him. The crazed wind created by the fire howled around him, swirling smoke into eddies and angry, roiling clouds when reflections from the flames illuminated the cell block enough for him see anything. He thudded into a wall and followed it, using his feet to guide him.

Zilla paused her frantic scrabbling to escape, and her head lolled to the side. Robert muttered, "Hang in there, hold on, girl." He added, "We're almost out," even though he was losing hope. He crouched, trying to stay below the layer of smoke. The unit wasn't that big and the ceilings were high, the only saving grace in the situation. But he'd been staggering around far longer than necessary to get out. Somehow he'd missed the hallway to the yard. His arms trembled and panic began to build in his core.

Drop the dog and save yourself. The thought came out of nowhere, and he stumbled.

Six weeks ago he would have. Without hesitation.

But not now. Abandoning Zilla wasn't possible, not anymore. The thought didn't even tempt him. He owed her… Well, he wasn't too clear on what he owed her, but he knew truth when it hit him in the face. He just knew to the marrow of his bones that he owed her. If he—if *they* got out of this alive, he'd chew on the concept for a while, but for now, he lowered his head and redoubled his determination to survive. *With* Zilla.

Or die trying.

He didn't want to die.

Even if his life had turned out to be a sorry excuse of an existence, he wanted to live. And he carried the reason in his arms. The one living being who accepted him for who he was, not the mess he'd made of things nor the glittery success he'd achieved. But she didn't just accept him. She loved him.

In that moment, Robert understood the concept of laying down one's life for a friend. Making a sacrifice of self for another's benefit.

Like Lannis Parker Martin. Damn it, he didn't have time to think about her! Except that she'd put aside her very natural desire for revenge and traded it in lieu of his welfare.

Not unlike his refusal to leave Zilla in the conflagration. For the first time, he understood Lannis. He did precious little for the dog, just saw to her daily needs, which anyone could do, and she showered him with unconditional—and unearned—devotion in return. Pretty lopsided relationship. Even he could see that.

So maybe he understood what he owed the dog better than he realized.

An opportunity to be human.

The emergency siren of the prison shut off, leaving his ears ringing in the relative silence. Which wasn't silent at all. The fire's hot wind still buffeted him and he could hear shouts from outside, which would point to safety if they didn't echo and shimmer in the air, like the smoke.

He blanked out all thought, gritted his teeth, and called upon the physical reserves he knew he had. At least, he hoped he did. Years of martial arts training had taught him his mind would crumble before his body did, and if ever he needed to remember that lesson, this was the time.

Zilla quit struggling entirely, then went limp in his arms. Her dead weight—*no, not dead, no, please no!*—dragged him down, slowed him, threatened his grip. Panic, tamped down earlier, now exploded. "No—no—no—" His breath rasped in and out, the single syllable in sync with the pounding of his footfalls. He needed help! And he needed it now.

"Please, please God, let her be okay." He gasped out the words. Maybe Lannis's God would come through if he asked. He didn't deserve a miracle, and if his victims had anything to say about it, he wouldn't get one. For Zilla's sake, though, he'd ask.

Tears filled his eyes, bathing them with watery relief, then spilling over to course down his blistered cheeks. Nearly blind with terror and pain, it took him a moment to realize the darkness ahead was less dense, and that a shadowy rectangle was barely visible.

A spurt of hope gave strength to his limbs, and he staggered toward the shape. The closer he got, the lighter the rectangle became, finally revealing the main door to the yard. He burst through it, inhaling crisp, cold air with the greed of a dying man, and maybe he was.

The air felt like shards of glass entering his lungs, and he gasped, then tried to avoid the pain by *not* breathing. It didn't work. His body overrode his mind and sucked in another breath, then another, the searing agony of it causing his vision to narrow, then waver. He made it two more steps before his legs gave out. He pitched forward onto his knees, clutching the motionless dog in his arms.

Shouts that sounded a million miles away pricked at his awareness, and he slumped to the ground as everything went dark.

"Zilla," he whispered. With a supreme effort, he tugged her inert mass closer to him.

~

Robert woke to a chaotic scene that could have come straight from the fires of hell, and for a long moment he wondered if that was where he'd ended up. Smoke billowed against a night sky filled with crystalline stars sparkling on velvet blackness. Something covered his face, and abruptly terrified of smothering, he reached to bat it away.

"No, buddy, leave it there. It's oxygen." A guy leaned into his field of vision, and Robert recognized the uniform of an EMT.

Now that he'd said so, Robert felt the flow of air—*oxygen*—into his nostrils, and tension ebbed from his muscles.

Until he remembered Zilla.

He ripped the mask from his face and surged upward. "Zilla— my dog—" He twisted to the side and cast his glance in a frantic arc, searching for her.

The EMT lunged backward, out of his reach, then grabbed his shoulders and pushed Robert back. Another set of hands came from behind and overpowered him. He bucked at them, trying to battle his way to Zilla, his chest heaving with his efforts. "Where is she? Let me go!"

Somehow he managed to break free, and what he saw chilled his blood.

A small heap of fur twenty feet distant, just outside the door he'd exited.

Robert dragged himself upright and wove his way to her on trembling legs that threatened to give way beneath him. "Zilla…" He'd never thought a heart could actually break, but he could feel his cracking open. It hurt worse than his charred lungs. A sob ripped from his throat and he fell to his knees next to her. The EMTs followed him, but gave him a wide berth. A small, rational part of his brain noted the absence of a guard, and gratitude filled him that he'd been granted the opportunity to mourn her.

His hand shook as he reached out to stroke her lifeless body. Robert bowed his head, paying no heed to the tears that dripped from his eyes, or the sobs he couldn't control, or the EMTs who stood to the side witnessing his private grief. His fingers dug into her fur.

Her ribs rose and fell, her heartbeat a rapid tattoo beneath his hand. He jerked his head up to look at her. "Zilla?" The tip of her tail lifted, then dropped, not a rousing thump of welcome, but indisputable evidence of life.

"Zilla!" He half rose and turned to the EMTs. "She's alive! Come help her! She needs the oxygen more than I do!" The two men stood rooted, clearly taken aback at both his request and his manner, so he took matters into his own hands. He scooped Zilla into his arms and lurched to the triage area where they'd been treating him. He laid her gently on the ground and grabbed the oxygen mask he'd discarded and held it to her nose. She made a small effort to turn her head away, but he crooned to her and followed her snout with the mask.

Too exhausted to resist, she allowed the mask, and moments later another mask got placed on his face. This time Robert accepted it and sank down on the grass next to her. One of the EMTs took his arm and expertly started an IV. Robert paid him no attention, the prick of the needle inconsequential to everything else that had happened over the past hour.

The only thing that mattered was Zilla, whose breathing seemed less labored to his untrained eye. A sense of calm acceptance came over him, at once so foreign and so familiar as to be instantly recognizable. He might even go as far as to call it peace.

His breath shuddered out, and along with it, tension eased. It had been so much a part of his makeup that he wasn't sure who he was without it.

Maybe this was what Lannis talked about.

Robert was far from stupid. Nor did he have a problem with giving credit where credit was due. He fingered Zilla's soft ear and whispered, "Thanks…God."

It should have felt weird to say it, but it didn't.

He didn't know what tomorrow would bring, except for the big changes obvious in the prison. But as long as they let him and Zilla stay together in the program, he didn't care. He succumbed to the fatigue that was dragging his eyelids earthward, and lay down next to Zilla.

She wriggled closer and sighed.

Cold air, hard ground, sirens, a fire—none of it made a difference to Robert, and he fell asleep, his arm around Zilla, his heart closer to a sense of peace than he'd ever experienced before in his life.

Chapter Forty

February

"HI, HONEY." A draft of cold air eddied around Lannis's ankles as Ben's greeting resonated from the garage. The door thumped closed behind him, and Lannis turned from the stove to smile at him. "I'm home."

"How'd it go today?" She thought she could tell by the life in his voice, but she wanted to hear it firsthand.

"Great. Herm's disappointed, but he understands. And he's already got a word in for me for the state police job." He shed his jacket and hung it on the hook next to the door. "It sounds like a kick. Rappelling out of helicopters to cut down marijuana plots in the Appalachians." He grinned, his face lighting up at the prospect.

"Wonderful," Lannis said dryly. Right up Ben's alley. Physical, outdoors, still catching drug dealers but on a different level. He and Mike would stay tight, but the friendship would evolve into something less intense. She knew, from hours of pillow talk in their darkened bedroom, that Ben relished the opportunity to be part of a team. Now eager to leave the solitary and dangerous life of undercover work, he anticipated the same sort of bond he'd built with his military buddies.

She shook her head, just a slight movement, but he caught it. He set the mail down on the counter and swept her up in his arms.

"I know. Why would I jump out of a perfectly good airplane—or in this case, helicopter?" He nuzzled her neck. "Right?"

A delicious shiver of pleasure curled through her nerve endings. "Yeah." The word came out breathless. "I'm sort of partial to staying inside them, as long as they're in one piece."

"I have some news." His voice sobered.

A niggle of worry wound its way in at his tone. "More than a sea change in your career?" Lannis tried to keep her voice light, and leaned back so she could see his face. His eyes sparkled, and his almost-dimple had deepened, so she relaxed.

"Joel called."

Her heart skipped at the lawyer's name. "The DNA?" They hadn't expected the results until next week, but maybe…

"I'm cleared." He couldn't hold back a smile. "No gun residue, no blood other than my own, no DNA matches. It was a frame, a setup." His eyes clouded. "Poor Tawnee, though. They gang raped her before they killed her. The only positive that came out of it is DNA matches for every one of the bastards." He paused, then added with a note of steely satisfaction, "Including the Enforcer. The drug lord I was trying to nail."

She inhaled, a quick intake of breath that hung suspended for a heartbeat. "They got an ID for him?"

"Sure did." He pulled Lannis closer and propped his chin on the top of her head. "He needs to be taken off the streets. They're out serving warrants on all of them now."

She wrapped her arms around his waist and rested her head on his chest. A weight lifted from her heart. "So it's over."

"Yep. Except for the court appearances, but I'm looking forward to those."

"Did Detective Hollis say anything?"

Ben snorted. "Are you kidding? Hell, no." He set Lannis away and met her gaze. "I don't expect any kind of acknowledgment from him." He shrugged. "He was just doing his job. No hard feelings."

Lannis knew what it cost Ben to say that, and even more important, to mean it. He'd made remarkable progress with a counselor over the past month. He'd regained his ability to let certain relationships alone—like Detective Hollis—and tempered his sense of responsibility for others. Like Danny.

"I got an e-mail from Lynnie today." She tipped her head toward the office.

"Yeah?" Ben reached around Lannis to snag a roll from the bread basket, and bit into it. "How's Jason doing?" He chewed as he spoke, and leaned against the counter.

"Cute. Growing. Normal for a preemie his age. Going home in a couple of days." Lannis's pulse kicked up, and she glanced away for an instant, a thrill racing through her veins as she gathered courage to speak the next few words.

She thought back to their conversation a few weeks ago about her visit with Robert Davis in prison. Not the details. Ben, though he understood the philosophy behind her reasons for making the trip, didn't want the details. Nor did Lannis need to divulge them. Instead, she'd focused on the epiphanies that had come to her during the drive home. Their subsequent discussions regarding adoption versus pregnancy had been academic, but that aspect was about to change.

She looked back at Ben and took in the sight of him, strong and tall, and so handsome he stole her breath. Her gaze traveled from his booted feet, up legs encased in jeans that hugged muscled thighs, to his button-down shirt open at the throat. She enjoyed the view for a moment, then captured his gaze. Or maybe he captured hers.

She felt dizzy, like she was balanced on the precipice of a cliff, ready to step off into an unknown space—but it wasn't scary. Rather, it was exhilarating. A new adventure.

"I was thinking…" she said.

Ben inclined his head toward her and slowly came alert, searching her face for a clue to what she was up to. He set the uneaten portion of the roll on the counter. "You were thinking…" he said, with a *go on* motion of his hand.

Lannis couldn't contain a smile, but held on to it so it didn't blossom into a full-fledged grin. She lifted her chin. "I was thinking that it's time for us to make a cute little baby, too."

Ben went still, so still that she could see his pulse speeding up to match hers. His eyes darkened and his nostrils flared. "Are you sure, darlin'?" He remained motionless, but she watched his knuckles go pale as he gripped the counter.

She stepped forward, feeling bold and female and every bit the seductress. "Yes," she said as she placed her palms flat on his chest. "I am." She lifted up on her toes and sought his mouth. He obliged, slanting for better access and crushing her to his torso in a heated kiss that *did* steal her breath.

When he finally tore himself away, Lannis felt wanton and disheveled, and found she'd reached up to thread her hands in the thick texture of his hair. "What are you waiting for?" she murmured.

His eyes were hooded and black with desire, and she could feel the evidence against her abdomen. "You're fertile. Now." His voice was guttural. "I need to hear it, Lannis. No mistakes. No second thoughts tomorrow, or two weeks from now."

She thought she was beyond blushing with him, but telltale heat climbed her neck and flooded her cheeks. They'd been following a natural family planning regime, and he knew her body's cycles as well as she did. Perhaps even better, as he bore the brunt of the restraint required to make it work.

"Yes," she breathed. Then louder, "Yes, Ben. I'm ready." Joy bubbled from deep inside as the shackles of fear that had bound her for so long fell away. In case he didn't get it, she added, "I want to have your baby."

He didn't need more confirmation, and swept her up into his arms. She squeaked and snaked her arms around his neck. He paused to turn the stove burner off, then strode toward the bedroom.

~

Full darkness had fallen by the time Lannis drifted back to the kitchen. Her skin felt unusually soft and silky, still ultrasensitive from Ben's lovemaking, and her legs were just recovering enough starch for her to walk. She brushed her hair out of her face and turned the stove on again. Thankfully, dinner was a simple vegetable soup and could handle sitting out for as long as they'd been otherwise occupied. Her face heated again at exactly how they'd occupied themselves.

If they hadn't made a baby, she'd be surprised. The real surprise, though, was how peaceful she felt at the prospect. She set the table with efficient movements, then glanced at the mail. With nothing left to do but wait, she picked it up and idly went through it.

One envelope was addressed to her, a computer-generated sticker, and she automatically glanced at the return address, mildly curious. Her breathing hitched, and she felt the pleasant lethargy of the past few minutes slip away.

The prison. It was light, a regular-sized envelope, with no clue as to its sender. She sank into a chair, wishing she'd worn more than a worn sleep shirt—braless, of course—and pajama pants. She debated for a moment. Should she open it now, or wait for Ben to wake? The soup began to simmer, releasing the soft aroma of herbs and broth into the air.

Lannis firmed her lips and sat straighter. Whether it was the confidence that Ben was just down the hall or the comfort of the homemade soup, or her own growth, the grace of faith… Whatever the source, she felt certain she could handle the contents, and with a decisive movement, picked up a knife and slit the envelope open.

A single-page letter slipped partway out, and she plucked it the rest of the way, shaking it open and laying it flat. She caught a glimpse of handwriting and closed her eyes, took a breath, sent up a prayer for… For what? Strength? Courage? Maybe just presence, and that's what she got. Calm infused her, and her spirit stilled.

Lannis opened her eyes and dropped her gaze to the paper. Her eyes widened, and she jerked her hand away in a reflex she couldn't control, then scanned the page, reading more quickly the farther down she got. Her heart thudded and adrenaline shot through her system, making her hands tremble.

The letter was short. By the time she'd read it, tears filled her eyes and slid unheeded down her cheeks, dripping onto the table. Emotion, overwhelming and too complex to analyze, built from her core, burbled up and spilled over. She stuffed her fist into her mouth to contain a sob, then reconsidered and called, "Ben!" Her voice came out thready and weak, and she knew he wouldn't hear her. She gulped in a lungful of air, put some backbone into it. "Ben!"

"Coming." He appeared in the hallway, hopping on one foot as he stuck the other into a pair of sweatpants. He glanced at her and his expression hardened. "What's wrong?" He yanked the pants up and strode to the kitchen.

Lannis motioned at the letter, and he snatched it up, scanned it. If possible, his face hardened even more, then an eyebrow rose, and by the end, the other one matched its mate. He whistled, a low, soft sound.

"Why don't you read it out loud?" His tone gentled, and he held the page out to her.

She shook her head. "C-can't," she whispered, and fresh tears washed her cheeks.

He sat, knee to knee, and took her hand. "Then I'll read it for you. Might make it more real." He squeezed her hand and began. "Dear Mrs. Lannis Parker Martin…"

> *I want to apologize for the pain I've caused you. If I could take back the events of that night, I would, but I can't. I am sorry I brutalized you and forced sex upon you. I apologize for using you to meet my twisted needs. I am sorry you have struggled to deal with my abuse and the aftereffects. I have no excuse, and take full responsibility for my actions.*
>
> *If I can provide restitution, say the word. I am willing to do anything within my power. I don't have a lot of options from prison, but will do what I am able.*
>
> *I hesitate to mention this, because this letter is about you, not me, but I thought you might be interested to know that I've begun seeing the chaplain here.*

"…signed, Sincerely, Robert Davis." Ben placed the page on the table and grasped Lannis's other hand in his. "It's over for you, too, Lannis."

She launched herself into his arms and gave herself up to the sobs she could no longer hold in. The storm subsided after several minutes and she sagged against him. Ben ran his hand up and down her back in a soothing, familiar rhythm. Somehow she'd ended up on his lap, and she rested her head on his shoulder.

"I didn't think this day would ever come." She sniffed, and scrubbed a hand across her nose. "It's like a curtain has gone up on my world, and the sun is shining."

Ben's voice rumbled through his chest. "You did good, Lannis." He dropped a kiss on her forehead. "I'm proud of you." He hesitated, then added, "I gotta say, I thought you were nuts, but I'm glad you followed your conscience."

She wiped her eyes, and smiled up at him. "A new day, a new chapter... And I'm so glad I get to spend it with you."

"Me, too, darlin'. Me, too."

Her heart soared, full of joy for the promise of the future.

Epilogue

May

Sun sparkled on newly green grass, and puffy white clouds scampered across the sky. A warm breeze lifted Lannis's hair, and she absently smoothed it out of her face. She'd finally had to resort to maternity clothes, most of which she'd borrowed from Lynette. Today's outfit was a pale yellow blouse and matching slacks topped with a lace jacket.

She shifted in her folding chair and leaned in to talk to Ben. "Do you think they'll start on time? It's a long drive home," she said, pitching her voice low.

He glanced at his watch. "I'd bet my life on it."

He fidgeted, so unusual for him that Lannis furrowed her brow. She abruptly realized why he'd feel uncomfortable, and she relaxed. "You're okay," she whispered. "They'll let you out." He shot an annoyed look at her and she winked.

"I know." He frowned, then let the corner of his mouth quirk upward. "But I don't have to like being here."

Music from a boom box, amplified into an ancient sound system, sent strains of the graduation march into the air. The breeze whipped bits of it away, creating an odd, stuttering effect. A column of men approached the grassy area in front of the seating, walking with dignity at odds with their attire.

Lannis's breath caught. She'd prepared for this moment for months, thought she was ready, but couldn't control the old instinct of self-preservation. Ben slid a hand over to her lap, palm open and facing up. Grateful for his awareness, she slipped hers into his and gripped him.

The men stopped, turned as a unit, and quietly ordered their companions to sit.

Robert Davis was third in line, the tallest man, and the only Caucasian. His expression held a wealth of emotion, as did that of the other five inmates. She could read pride, self-consciousness, and beneath it, a wave of sadness in his. He sought her out of the small gathering of observers and sent her a brief, courtly nod.

Zilla, his dog, sat happily at his side, her tongue lolling out, a wide canine grin on her face. The dog's mismatched eyes gave her a quizzical, almost goofy look. Lannis leaned closer to Ben so she could peer over the shoulder of the person ahead of her for a better view. Zilla's short, thick fur—an almost indeterminate shade of yellow-brown—shone, a testament to Davis's attention, as it didn't appear to be a type of coat prone to shininess.

The warden stepped to a microphone and began to speak. "The men you see here have been afforded a unique opportunity within these walls. They earned the privilege of preparing these dogs for further training in such areas as police K-9 units, bomb or drug sniffing, search and rescue, aid for persons hampered by any number of disabilities, pet therapy, and more. I am pleased to report a one-hundred-percent success rate for this class, only the second class in our history to attain that goal."

A smattering of applause greeted this statement, and Lannis felt a spurt of pride that her advocacy for Davis had borne fruit. In an obviously well-practiced drill, each man introduced his dog and conducted a demonstration of skills. Zilla's devotion to Davis showed in her eagerness to please him, as she quivered in anticipation of each task, and sent adoring glances at him when he praised her performance. Delight filled Lannis's heart as she watched them work together, and a smile blossomed on her face as she clapped for Davis, for Zilla. She felt an almost irrepressible urge to leap up and shout *bravo*, and then she realized what that meant.

It meant she was cheering for the man who'd raped her.

The concept was so bizarre a moment of dizziness assailed her, and her smile faded. *But that's the whole point of forgiveness, of reconciliation, of restorative justice, isn't it?* Yes, she thought. *Yes, it is.*

Joy, both quiet and exuberant burbled up from deep within, and she turned to Ben, her smile returning. "I love you," she whispered, and squeezed his hand. He glanced at her, surprise in his eyes, and mouthed, "I love you, too."

Ms. Connor, tall and regal in a deep purple suit that only she and a few other people on the planet could pull off, took the microphone. "The culmination of the ceremony today is the presentation of dogs to the acquiring agencies." She turned to the inmates. "Each of you has accomplished a great deal over the past months. Not only have you achieved success in training these animals, you have done it in the face of great adversity. The fire in January wreaked havoc on the entire facility, but your group maintained a focus and discipline that is unmatched in our history. You not only helped rebuild your own unit, but took the initiative to research methods of assisting the dogs through what amounts to canine post-traumatic stress disorder." She paused and looked at each man, individually. "I am proud of you."

Moisture pricked the back of Lannis's eyelids and she wiped at them surreptitiously, but the inmates didn't harbor a need to conceal their emotions. Tears tracked down the cheeks of several of the men, and they stood even straighter in their prison jumpsuits.

Ms. Connor turned and briskly began the transfer. A state police officer collected a German shepherd for training as a drug dog, and a second shepherd went to the Jefferson County Sheriff's Department with an eye toward airport security at Louisville's Standiford Field. A beagle went to a tri-county search-and-rescue unit near the Appalachian Trail. The other two dogs went to companion or aid societies, and each group drifted off to accomplish greetings and instructions.

Finally, only Robert Davis and Zilla remained.

Lannis tightened her grip on Ben, and then Ms. Connor said, "In a highly unusual move, the final dog has been assigned to a private family. The trainer and the inmate felt this was the best option for Zilla." Her gaze homed in on Lannis. "Mr. and Mrs. Ben Martin, please come forward to meet the newest member of your family."

Lannis stood, and with Ben's hand on the small of her back, made her way to Robert Davis. Her mouth went dry, and she couldn't remember what she'd planned to say. Ben reached around her and put his hand out, giving her a moment to compose herself.

Davis hesitated a beat, then grasped Ben's hand and gave it a businesslike pump. "You'll take good care of her?"

"Yes, I'll take good care of both of them." Ben sounded a bit testy, like he'd just taken a bite out of a lemon.

Davis grimaced. "Touché." His expression smoothed and he flicked a glance at Lannis's midsection. "I see congratulations are in order." He bent down and ruffled Zilla's fur. "Your family will grow in more ways than one, then. I'm happy for you." He sounded genuine in spite of his somber mien.

"Thank you." Lannis crouched and put the back of her hand near Zilla's head, and waited. The dog sniffed, delicately at first, her breath tickling the hairs on Lannis's arm. Then she lapped out with her tongue and licked. Lannis grinned. "You are a sweetheart, aren't you?"

She stood, hesitated, then said, "I'm still puzzled that you chose to give her to us. Why?" She looked up at him, leaning back into Ben as she did. She'd almost forgotten how tall Davis was. A good three inches taller than Ben.

He shrugged and looked away, at the walls of the prison yard, or maybe the trees beyond. "Giving back." He fell silent, but Lannis sensed he had more to say. He finally turned his gaze to her. "And for her. Even though she graduated from the program, she's fragile. She needs stability and no expectations other than to be part of a family." His eyes clouded, and he cleared his throat. "Zilla means more to me than any person or being on this earth. I hurt you more than anyone has, before or since. It balances out, in a weird way, I suppose. It's an atonement, even though the gift of her life, from me to you, will never make up for what I did."

Lannis's throat tightened, swallowing suddenly impossible. She blinked new tears away and lifted her chin, the sun on her face and breeze in her hair reminding her of the freedom she had in walking away from this place in an hour. "I—I understand," she managed.

In a move she hadn't anticipated and didn't stop to think over, she stretched her arm out, offered him her hand. It hung suspended for a long moment, and then Robert Davis took it gently between both of his. His eyes clouded, then filled, and they stood, connected and too full of emotion to speak. His face contorted, and he broke the connection and stepped back.

He sank to his knees next to Zilla and buried his face in her ruff. He drew her close and held her. Time seemed to slow. His shoulders shook, and Lannis heard a soft sob, quickly controlled, and muffled by the dog's fur.

Lannis had succeeded in holding back tears until now, but she lost the battle and they trickled down her cheeks, chilling her face as they evaporated in the wind.

Ben settled his arm around her shoulders and pulled her close.

At long last Davis lifted his head, and without turning around, said in a low voice, "I don't have any right to ask this, but would you send me a picture of her once in a while?"

Still overcome, Lannis managed a nod, and Ben voiced her agreement, with a gruff, "Yes, we will. Just make sure we know where to find you." Even he sounded affected by the poignancy of the moment.

Davis nodded, then stood, patted Zilla one more time, and handed the leash to Lannis. He took a deep breath and said, "God go with you." He pivoted and walked away, his spine straight, his gait measured.

Zilla quivered, uneasy at his departure, and whined. But she obeyed the "stay" command he'd given. Lannis stooped to comfort the dog, who looked alternately from her to Ben, questions in her intelligent eyes.

"It's okay, sweetie," Lannis murmured. "We're all going to be okay." Zilla stopped whimpering and shoved her snout into Lannis's hand, insisting on the comfort of her touch.

She stood, and Ben took her hand.

"Let's go home, darlin'," he said.

Lannis smiled up at him, and glanced down at Zilla. She placed a hand on her abdomen, as the baby fluttered little butterfly kicks that were barely perceptible, but real nonetheless.

"Yes, Ben. Let's go home."

Acknowledgments

With apologies to the core purpose of Restorative Justice: None of my research has uncovered anyone less committed, at least initially, to the process than the character of Robert Davis in this book. My portrayal of his attitude is entirely fictional.

Detectives Shugart and Lampe of Louisville Metro Police Department, for answering my questions and especially for arranging the tour of Louisville Metro Corrections.

With apologies to Louisville Metro Corrections, I acknowledge that errors in the release of inmates is exceedingly rare, and that my use of such an event is entirely fictional.

I owe much to my writing community, especially Louisville Romance Writers and critique partners Caroline Fyffe and Sandy Loyd.

Thanks to my awesome and exacting editor, Pam Berehulke of Bulletproof Editing. I am indebted for your help in making this work the best it could be!

Thanks to my talented cover artist, Marion Sipe of Dreamspring Design, who transforms concepts into art.

On a personal level, gratitude (and more) to:
My family, for your love and support.
My husband, for everything.

On Writing This Book

The seeds of this story were sown as I watched South Africa come to grips with the abolishment of apartheid. Nelson Mandela's Truth and Reconciliation Commission sparked my imagination. The process of acknowledging harm caused and offering reparation allowed the first steps for healing of a rift that seemed impossible to breach.

Years later, I happened upon a documentary on television about Restorative Justice. It followed four victims and/or their families and the perpetrators of the horrific crimes that bound them together. In each case, the perpetrators expressed remorse for what they'd done, accepted society's punishment, and desired to offer whatever reparation they could. And in each case, the victims and their families found themselves stuck, unable to get past their grief and anger in order to heal. With the guidance of social workers, these two groups met with each other. Amazing transformations took place, even in the most heinous cases.

Then there was the piece on public radio that included an interview of a woman whose husband had been killed during a home invasion, and her daughter raped. She took the extraordinary step of reaching out to the perpetrators in prison. Some of the men responded, took ownership of the harm they had caused, and turned their lives around. She became involved in championing the process of Restorative Justice.

The common denominator in all these stories was the recognition—on the parts of the victims or their families—that bitterness and unforgiveness had no effect on the perpetrators, and in fact, caused *them* more pain. Healing for both sides came as each recognized the other's humanity, along with the damage that violence causes to the dignity of both victims and perpetrators.

Restorative Justice aims to restore that dignity.

If you are interested in learning more about Restorative Justice, these websites are a good start:

http://www.pfi.org/cjr/
http://www.restorativejustice.org/
http://www.rjlou.org

And here's a great article and Facebook page that address the positive outcomes of a program where abused or neglected dogs are paired with inmates—another imagination sparker for me!

http://parade.condenast.com/259321/michelechollow/second-chances-for-dogs-and-inmates/

https://www.facebook.com/MissouriPuppiesforParole